Praise for Carl Hiaasen

'His eye for the absurd lends his storytelling a hilarious momentum' *Sunday Times*

'Hiaasen is fast emerging as our most nimble satirist . . . sharp but never slick, humane but never sentimental' *Newsweek*

'Hiaasen is a one-man force of nature' *Vanity Fair*

'[Hiaasen] makes a formidable challenge to Elmore Leonard as the most vibrant chronicler of everyday life in Florida' *Daily Telegraph*

'Hiaasen brings classic farce to the modern thriller. There is little humour darker than his, and little funnier' *Evening Standard*

'Tight, stylish writing, deliciously wry touches . . . Hiaasen is also seriously funny, and highly recommended' *Irish Times*

'Hiaasen is terrific; it is quite a feat to be madly, appallingly, bitingly funny and at the same time thrilling enough to bring one up with a jolt' *Observer*

'Hiaasen is the funniest writer of crime fiction around . . . The surreal heaps on the farcical to produce the thriller with the highest laugh-out-loud score for many months. Since Hiaasen's last book, to be exact' *The Times*

TOURIST SEASON

Carl Hiaasen was born and raised in Florida. His other novels are *Double Whammy, Skin Tight, Native Tongue, Strip Tease, Stormy Weather, Lucky You* and *Sick Puppy,* which together have been translated into twenty languages. Since 1979 he has worked at the *Miami Herald* as a magazine writer, investigative reporter and metropolitan columnist.

His latest novel is called *Basket Case.*

ALSO BY CARL HIAASEN

Double Whammy
Skin Tight
Native Tongue
Strip Tease
Stormy Weather
Lucky You
Sick Puppy
Basket Case

Carl Hiaasen Omnibus
(comprising: *Tourist Season, Double Whammy,
Skin Tight*)

AND WITH BILL MONTALBANO

Powder Burn
Trap Line
A Death in China

CARL HIAASEN

TOURIST SEASON

PAN BOOKS

First published in the USA in 1986 by G. P. Putnam's Sons, Inc., New York

First published in Great Britain 1987 by Macdonald & Co. Ltd

This edition published 1992 by Pan Books
an imprint of Pan Macmillan Ltd
Pan Macmillan, 20 New Wharf Road, London N1 9RR
Basingstoke and Oxford
Associated companies throughout the world
www.panmacmillan.com

ISBN 0 330 32236 2

21 23 25 27 29 28 26 24 22 20

A CIP catalogue record for this book is available from
the British Library.

Phototypeset by Intype London Ltd
Printed by Mackays of Chatham PLC, Chatham, Kent

For my son Scott

ONE

On the morning of December 1, a man named Theodore Bellamy went swimming in the Atlantic Ocean off South Florida. Bellamy was a poor swimmer, but he was a good real-estate man and a loyal Shriner.

The Shriners thought so much of Theodore Bellamy that they had paid his plane fare all the way from Evanston, Illinois, to Miami Beach, where a big Shriner convention was being staged. Bellamy and his wife, Nell, made it a second honeymoon, and got a nice double room at the Holiday Inn. The view was nothing to write home about; a big green dumpster was all they could see from the window, but the Bellamys didn't complain. They were determined to love Florida.

On the night of November 30, the Shriners had arranged a little parade down Collins Avenue. Theodore Bellamy put on his mauve fez and his silver riding jacket, and drove his chrome-spangled Harley Davidson (all the important Evanston Shriners had preshipped their bikes on a flatbed) up and down Collins in snazzy circles and figure eights, honking the horns and flashing the lights. Afterwards Bellamy and his pals got bombed and sneaked out to the Place Pigalle to watch a 325-pound woman do a strip-tease. Bellamy was so snockered he didn't even blink at the ten-dollar cover.

Nell Bellamy went to bed early. When her husband lurched in at 4:07 in the morning, she said nothing. She may have even smiled just a little, to herself.

The alarm clock went off like a Redstone rocket at eight sharp. We're going swimming, Nell announced. Theodore was suffering through the please-God-I'll-never-do-it-again phase of his hangover when his wife hauled him out of bed. Next thing he knew, he was wearing his plaid swim trunks, standing on the beach, Nell nudging him toward the surf, saying you first, Teddy, tell me if it's warm enough.

The water was plenty warm, but it was also full of Portuguese men-of-war, poisonous floating jellyfish that pucker on the surface like bright blue balloons. Theodore Bellamy quickly became entangled in the burning tentacles of such a creature. He thrashed out of the ocean, his fish-white belly streaked with welts, the man-of-war clinging to his bare shoulder. He was crying. His fez was soaked.

At first Nell Bellamy was embarrassed, but then she realized that this was not Mango Daiquiri Pain, this was the real thing. She led her husband to a Disney World beach towel, and there she cradled him until two lifeguards ran up with a first-aid kit.

Later, Nell would remember that these were not your average-looking bleached-out lifeguards. One was black and the other didn't seem to speak English, but what the heck, this was Miami. She had come here resolved not to be surprised at anything, and this was the demeanor she maintained while the men knelt over her fallen husband. Besides, they were wearing authentic lifeguard T-shirts, weren't they?

After ten minutes of ministrations and Vaseline, the

lifeguards informed Nell Bellamy that they would have to transport her husband to a first-aid station. They said he needed medicine to counteract the man-of-war's venom. Nell wanted to go along, but they persuaded her to wait, and assured her it was nothing serious. Theodore said don't be silly, work on your tan, I'll be okay now.

And off they went, Theodore all pale-legged and stripe-bellied, a lifeguard at each side, marching down the beach.

That was 8:44 A.M.

Nell Bellamy never saw her husband again.

At ten sharp she went searching for the lifeguards, with no success, and after walking a gritty two-mile stretch of beach, she called the police. A patrolman came to the Holiday Inn and took a missing-persons report. Nell mentioned Theodore's hangover and what a lousy swimmer he was. The cop told Mrs. Bellamy that her husband had probably tried to go back in the water and had gotten into trouble in the rough surf. When Mrs. Bellamy described the two lifeguards, the policeman gave her a very odd look.

The case of Theodore Bellamy was not given top priority at the Miami Beach police department, where the officers had more catastrophic things to worry about than a drunken Shriner missing in the ocean.

The police instead were consumed with establishing the whereabouts of B. D. "Sparky" Harper, one of the most important persons in all Florida; Harper, who had failed to show up at his office for the first time in twenty-one years. Every available detective was out shaking the palm trees, hunting for Sparky.

When it became clear that the police were too

preoccupied to launch a manhunt for her husband, Nell Bellamy mobilized the Shriners. They invaded the beach in packs, some on foot, others on motorcycle, a few in tiny red motorcars that had a tendency to get stuck in the sand. The Shriners wore grim, purposeful looks; Teddy Bellamy was one of their own.

The Shriners were thorough, and they got results. Nell cried when she heard the news.

They had found Theodore's fez on the beach, at water's edge.

Nell thought: So he really drowned, the big nut.

Later the Shriners gathered at Lummus Park for an impromptu prayer service. Someone laid a wreath on the handlebars of Bellamy's customized Harley.

Nobody could have dreamed what actually happened to Theodore Bellamy. But this was just the beginning.

They found Sparky Harper later that same day, a bright and cloudless afternoon.

A cool breeze kicked up a light chop on the Pines Canal, where the suitcase floated, half-submerged, invisible to the teenager on water skis. He was skimming along at forty knots when he rammed the luggage and launched into a spectacular triple somersault.

His friends wheeled the boat to pick him up and offer congratulations. Then they doubled back for the suitcase. It took all three of them to haul it aboard; they figured it had to be stuffed with money or dope.

The water skier got a screwdriver from a toolbox and chiseled at the locks on the suitcase. "Let's see what's inside!" he said eagerly.

And there, folded up like Charlie McCarthy, was B. D. "Sparky" Harper.

"A dead midget!" the boat driver gasped.

"That's no midget," the water skier said. "That's a real person."

"Oh God, we gotta call the cops. Come on, help me shut this damn thing."

But with Sparky Harper swelling, the suitcase wouldn't close, and the latches were broken anyway, so all the way back to the marina the three of them sat on the luggage to keep the dead midget inside.

Two Dade County detectives drove out to Virginia Key to get the apple-red Samsonite Royal Tourister. They took a statement from the water skier, put the suitcase in the trunk of their unmarked Plymouth, and headed back downtown.

One of the cops, a blocky redhead, walked into the medical examiner's office carrying the Samsonite as if nothing were wrong. "Is this the Pan Am terminal?" he deadpanned to the first secretary he saw.

The suitcase was taken to the morgue and placed on a shiny steel autopsy table. Dr. Joe Allen, the chief medical examiner, recognized Sparky Harper instantly.

"The first thing we've got to do," said Dr. Allen, putting on some rubber gloves, "is get him out of there."

Whoever had murdered the president of the Greater Miami Chamber of Commerce had gone to considerable trouble to pack him into the red Samsonite. Sparky was only five-foot-five, but he weighed nearly one hundred ninety pounds, most of it in the midriff. To have squeezed him into a suitcase, even a deluxe-sized suitcase, was a feat that drew admiring comments from the coroner's seasoned staff. One of the clerks used up two rolls of film documenting the extrication.

Finally the corpse was removed and unfolded, more or less, onto the table. It was then that some of the amazement dissolved: Harper's legs were missing below the kneecaps. That's how the killer had fit him into the suitcase.

One of the cops whispered, "Look at those clothes, Doc."

It *was* odd. Sparky Harper had died wearing a brightly flowered print shirt and baggy Bermuda-style shorts. Sporty black wraparound sunglasses concealed his dilated pupils. He looked just like any old tourist from Milwaukee.

The autopsy took two hours and twenty minutes. Inside Sparky Harper, Dr. Allen found two gallstones, forty-seven grams of partially digested stone crabs, and thirteen ounces of Pouilly Fuissé. But the coroner found no bullets, no stab wounds, no signs of trauma besides the amputations, which were crude but not necessarily fatal.

"He must have bled to death," the redheaded cop surmised.

"Don't think so," Dr. Allen said.

"Bet he drowned," said the other cop.

"No, sir," said Dr. Allen, who was probing into the lungs by now. Dr. Allen wasn't crazy about people gawking over his shoulder while he worked. It made him feel like he was performing onstage, a magician pulling little purple treasures out of a dark hole. He didn't mind having medical students as observers because they were always so solemn during an autopsy.

Cops were something else; one dumb joke after another. Dr. Allen had never figured out why cops get so silly in a morgue.

"What's that greasy stuff all over his skin?" asked the redheaded detective.

"Essence of Stiff," said the other cop.

"Smells like coconuts," said the redhead. "I'm serious, Doc, take a whiff."

"No, thank you," Dr. Allen said curtly.

"I don't smell anything," said the assistant coroner, "except the deceased."

"It's coconut, definitely," said the other cop, sniffing. "Maybe he drowned in piña colada."

Nobody could have guessed what actually had killed Sparky Harper. It was supple and green and exactly five and one-quarter inches long. Dr. Allen found it lodged in the trachea. At first he thought it was a large chunk of food, but it wasn't.

It was a toy rubber alligator. It had cost seventy-nine cents at a tourist shop along the Tamiami Trail. The price tag was still glued to its corrugated tail.

B. D. "Sparky" Harper, the president of the most powerful chamber of commerce in all Florida, had choked to death on a rubber alligator. Well, well, thought Dr. Allen as he dangled the prize for his protégés to see, here's one for my slide show at next month's convention.

TWO

News of B. D. Harper's death appeared on the front page of the Miami *Sun* with a retouched photograph that made Harper look like a flatulent Gene Hackman. Details of the crime were meager, but this much was known:

Harper had last been seen on the night of November 30, driving away from Joe's Stone Crab restaurant on South Miami Beach. He had told friends he was going to the Fontainebleau Hilton for drinks with some convention organizers from the International Elks.

Harper had not been wearing a Jimmy Buffett shirt and Bermuda shorts, but in fact had been dressed in a powder-blue double-knit suit purchased at J. C. Penney's.

He had not appeared drunk.

He had not worn black wraparound sunglasses.

He had not been lugging a red Samsonite.

He had not displayed a toy rubber alligator all evening.

In the newspaper story a chief detective was quoted as saying, "This one's a real whodunit," which is what the detective was told to say whenever a reporter called.

In this instance the reporter was Ricky Bloodworth.

Bloodworth wore that pale, obsessive look of

ambition so familiar to big-city newsrooms. He was short and bony, with curly black hair and a squirrel-like face frequently speckled with late-blooming acne. He was frenetic to a fault, dashing from phone to type-writer to copy desk in a blur—yet he was different from most of his colleagues. Ricky Bloodworth wanted to be much more than just a reporter, he wanted to be an authentic *character*. He tried, at various times, panama hats, silken vests, a black eye-patch, saddle shoes, a Vandyke—nobody ever noticed. He even experimented with Turkish cigarettes (thinking it debonair) and wound up on a respirator at Mercy Hospital. Even those who disliked Bloodworth, and they were many, felt sorry for him; the poor guy wanted a quirk in the worst way. But, stylistically, the best he could do was to drum pencils and suck down incredible amounts of 7-Up. It wasn't much, but it made him feel like he was contributing something to the newsroom's energy bank.

Ricky Bloodworth thought he'd done a respectable job on the first Sparky Harper story (given the deadlines), but now, on the morning of December 2, he was ready to roll. Harper's ex-wives had to be found and interviewed, his co-workers had to be quizzed, and an array of semi-bereaved civic leaders stood ready to offer their thoughts on the heinous crime.

But Dr. Allen came first. Ricky Bloodworth knew the phone number of the coroner's office by heart; memorizing it was one of the first things he'd done after joining the paper.

When Dr. Allen got on the line, Bloodworth asked, "What's your theory, Doc?"

"Somebody tied up Sparky and made him swallow a rubber alligator," the coroner said.

"Cause of death?"

"Asphyxiation."

"How do you know he didn't swallow it on purpose?"

"Did he cut off his own legs, too?"

"You never know," Bloodworth said. "Maybe it started out as some kinky sex thing. Or maybe it was voodoo, all these Haitians we got now. Or *santería*."

"Sparky was a Baptist, and the police are calling it a homicide."

"They've been wrong before."

Ricky Bloodworth was not one of Dr. Allen's favorite newspaper reporters. Dr. Allen regarded him as charmless and arrogant. There had been times, when the prospect of a front-page story loomed, that Dr. Allen could have sworn he saw flecks of foam on Bloodworth's lips.

Now the coroner listened to Bloodworth's typing on the end of the phone line, and wondered how badly his quotes were being mangled.

"Ricky," he said impatiently. "The victim's wrists showed ligature marks—"

"Any ten-year-old can tie himself up."

"And stuff himself in a suitcase?"

The typing got faster.

"The victim was already deceased when he was placed in the suitcase," Dr. Allen said. "Is there anything else?"

"What about the oil? One of the cops said the body was coated with oil."

"Not oil," Dr. Allen said. "A combination of benzophenone, stearic acids, and lanolin."

"What's that?"

"Suntan lotion," the coroner said. "With coconut butter."

Ricky Bloodworth was hammering away on his video terminal when he sensed a presence behind him. He turned slightly, and caught sight of Skip Wiley's bobbing face. Even with a two-day stubble it was a striking visage: long, brown, and rugged-looking; a genetic marvel, every feature plagiarized from disparate ancestors. The cheekbones were high and sculptured, the nose pencil-straight but rather long and flat, the mouth upturned with little commas on each cheek, and the eyes disarming—small and keen, the color of strong coffee; full of mirth and something else. Skip Wiley was thirty-seven years old but he had the eyes of an old gypsy.

It made Bloodworth abnormally edgy and insecure when Skip Wiley read over his shoulder. Wiley wrote a daily column for the *Sun* and probably was the best-known journalist in Miami. Undeniably he was a gifted writer, but around the newsroom he was regarded as a strange and unpredictable character. Wiley's behavior had lately become so odd that younger reporters who once sought his counsel were now fearful of his ravings, and they avoided him.

"Coconut butter?" Wiley said gleefully. "And no legs!"

"Skip, please."

Wiley rolled up a chair. "I think you should lead with the coconut butter."

Bloodworth felt his hands go damp.

Wiley said, "This is awful, Ricky: 'Friends and

11

colleagues of B. D. Harper expressed grief and outrage Tuesday . . .' Jesus Christ, who cares? Give them coconut oil!"

"It's a second-day lead, Skip—"

"Here we go again, Mr. Journalism School." Wiley was gnawing his lower lip, a habit manifested only when he composed a news story. "You got some good details in here. The red Royal Tourister. The black Ray-Bans. That's good, Ricky. Why don't you toss out the rest of this shit and move the juicy stuff up top? Do your readers a favor, for once. Don't make 'em go on a scavenger hunt for the goodies."

Bloodworth was getting queasy. He wanted to defend himself, but it was lunacy to argue with Wiley.

"Maybe later, Skip. Right now I'm jammed up for the first edition."

Wiley jabbed a pencil at the video screen, which displayed Bloodworth's story in luminous green text. "*Brutal?* That's not the adjective you want. When I think of brutal I think of chain saws, ice picks, ax handles. Not rubber alligators. No, that's *mysterious*, wouldn't you say?"

"How about *bizarre?*"

"A bit overworked these days, but not bad. When's the last time you used *bizarre?*"

"I don't recall, Skip."

"Try last week, in that story about the Jacuzzi killing in Hialeah. Remember? So it's too early to use *bizarre* again. I think *mysterious* is the ticket."

"Whatever you say, Skip."

Wiley was boggling, when he wanted to be.

"What's your theory, Ricky?"

"Some sex thing, I guess. Sparky rents himself a bimbo, dresses up in this goofy outfit—"

"Perhaps a little S-and-M?"

"Yeah. Things go too far, he gags on the rubber alligator, the girl panics and calls for help. The muscle arrives, hacks up Sparky, crams the torso into the suitcase, and heaves it into Biscayne Bay. The goons grab the girl and take off in Sparky's car."

Wiley eyed him. "So you don't believe it's murder?"

"Accidental homicide. That's my prediction." Bloodworth was starting to relax. Wiley was rocking the chair, a look of amusement on his face. Bloodworth noticed that Wiley's long choppy mane was starting to show gray among the blond.

Bloodworth said, a little more confidently, "I think Harper's death was a freak accident. I think the girl will come forward before too long, and that'll be the end of it."

Wiley chuckled. "Well, it's a damn good yarn." He stood up and pinched Ricky's shoulder affectionately. "But I don't have to tell *you* how to hit the hype button, do I?"

For the first edition, Ricky Bloodworth moved the paragraph about the coconut oil higher in the story, and changed the word *brutal* to *mysterious* in the lead.

The rest of the afternoon Bloodworth spent on the phone, gathering mawkish quotes about Sparky Harper, who seemed venerated by everyone except his former wives. As for blood relatives, the best Bloodworth could scrounge up was a grown son, a lawyer in Marco Island, who said of his father:

"He was a dreamer, and he honestly meant well."

Not exactly a tearjerker, but Bloodworth stuck it in the story anyway.

After finishing, he reread the piece once more. It had a nice flow, he thought, and the tone graduated smoothly: shock first, then outrage and, finally, sorrow.

It's good, a page-one contender, Bloodworth told himself as he walked down to the Coke machine.

While he was away, Skip Wiley crept up and snatched the printout of the story off his desk. He was pretending to mark it up with a blue pencil when Bloodworth came back.

"What now, Skip?"

"Your lead's no good."

"Come on, I *told* you—"

"Hey, Ace, it's not a second-day story anymore. Something broke while you were diddling around. *News*, they call it. Check with the police desk, you'll see."

"What are you talking about?"

Wiley grinned as he tossed the pages into Ricky Bloodworth's lap. "The cops caught the guy," he said. "Ten minutes ago."

THREE

Brian Keyes slouched on a worn bench in the lobby of the Dade County jail, waiting to see the creep the cops just caught. Keyes looked at his wristwatch and muttered. Twenty minutes. Twenty goddamn minutes since he'd given his name to the dull-eyed sergeant behind the bullet-proof glass.

Keyes had run into this problem before; it had something to do with the way he looked. Although he stood five-ten, a respectable height, he somehow failed to exude the authority so necessary for survival in rough bars, alleys, police stations, jails, and McDonald's drive-throughs. Keyes was adolescently slender, with blue eyes and a smooth face. He looked younger than his thirty-two years, which, in his line of work, was no particular asset. An ex-girlfriend once said, on her way out the door, that he reminded her of a guy who'd just jumped the wall of a Jesuit seminary. To disguise his boyishness, Brian Keyes had today chosen a brown suit with a finely striped Cardin tie. He was clean-shaven and his straight brown hair was neatly combed. Still, he had a feeling that his overall appearance was inadequate—not slick enough to be a lawyer, not frazzled enough to be a social worker, and not old enough to be a private investigator. Which he actually was.

So the turtle-eyed sergeant ignored him.

Keyes was surrounded by misery. On his left, a rotund Latin woman wailed into an embroidered handkerchief and nibbled on a rosary. "*Pobrecito*, he's in yail again."

On the other side, an anemic-looking teenager with yellow teeth carved an obscenity into the bench with a Phillips screwdriver. Keyes studied him neutrally until the kid looked up and snapped, "My brother's in for agg assault!"

"You must be very proud," Keyes said.

This place never changed. The hum and clang of the electronic doors were enough to split your skull, but the mayhem in the lobby was worse, worse even than the cell blocks. The lobby was crawling with bitter, bewildered souls, each on the sad trail of a loser. Girlfriends, ex-wives, mothers, brothers, bondsmen, lawyers, pimps, parole officers.

And me, Keyes thought. The public defender's office had tried to make the case sound interesting, but Keyes figured it had to be a lost cause. There'd be some publicity, which he didn't need, and decent money, which he did. This was a big-time case, all right. Some nut hacks up the president of the Chamber of Commerce and dumps him in the bay—just what South Florida needed, another grisly murder. Keyes wondered if the dismemberment fad would ever pass.

From the governor on down, everybody had wanted this one solved fast. And the cops had come through.

"Mr. Keyes!" The sergeant's voice echoed from a cheap speaker in the ceiling.

Keyes signed the log, clipped on a plastic visitor's badge, and walked through three sets of noisy iron gates. A trusty accompanied him into an elevator that smelled like an NFL locker room. The elevator stopped on the fifth floor.

Ernesto Cabal, alias Little Ernie, alias No-Way José, was sitting disconsolately on the crapper when the trusty opened the cell for Brian Keyes.

Ernesto held out a limp, moist hand. Keyes sat down on a wooden folding chair.

"You speak English?"

"Sure," Ernesto said. "I been here sixteen years. By *here* I mean here, dees country." He pulled up his pants, flushed the john, and stretched out on a steel cot. "They say I kill dees man Harper."

"That's what they say."

"I dint."

Ernesto was a small fellow, sinewy and tough-looking, except for the eyes. A lot of cons had rabbit eyes, but not this one, Keyes thought. Ernesto's brown eyes were large and wet. Scared puppy eyes.

Keyes opened his briefcase.

"You a lawyer, Mr. Keyes?"

"Nope. I'm an investigator. I was hired by your lawyers to help you."

"Yeah?"

"That's right."

"You're a very young guy to be an investigator," Ernesto said. "How old? Dirty, dirty-one?"

"Good guess."

Ernesto sat up. "You any good?"

"No, I'm totally incompetent. A complete moron. Now I've got a question for you, *chico*. Did you do it?"

"I tole you. No."

"Fine." Keyes opened a manila file and scanned a pink tissue copy of the arrest report.

Ernesto leaned over for a peak. "I know what that is, man."

"Good, then explain it."

"See, I was driving dees car and the policeman, he pull me over on a routine traffic stop . . ."

Oh boy, Keyes thought, *routine traffic stop*. This guy's been here before.

" . . . and told me I'm driving a stolen be-hickle. And the next thin I know I'm in jail and dey got me charged with first-degree murder and robbery and everythin else."

Keyes asked, "How did you come to be driving a 1984 Oldsmobile Delta 88?"

"I bought it."

"I see. Ernesto, what do you do for a living?"

"I sell fruit."

"Oh."

"Maybe you see me at rush hour. On LeJeune Road. I sell fresh fruits in bags."

Somewhere down the cell block another prisoner started to bang on the bars and scream that his TV was broken.

Keyes said, "Ernesto, how much does your very best bag of fruit sell for? Top-of-the-line?"

"Mangoes or cassavas?"

"Whatever. The best."

"Maybe one dollar . . . oh, I see what you getting at. Okay, yeah, that's right, I doan make much money. But I got some great buy on this Oldsmobile. You can't believe it."

"Probably not."

"I got it from a black guy."

"For?"

"Two hundred bucks."

Ernesto seemed to sense he was losing ground. "Some buy. I dint believe it either."

Keyes shrugged. "I didn't say I didn't believe you. Now, according to the police, you were arrested on Collins Avenue on Miami Beach. You ran a series of red lights."

"It was tree in the morning. No one was out."

"Where did you meet the man who sold you the car?"

"Right dare on Collins. Two nights before I got busted. I met him a few blocks from the Fountain-blow. Dare's a city parking lot where I hang."

"The one where you do all your B-and-E's?"

"Shit, you just like the policeman."

"I need to know everything, Ernesto, otherwise I can't help. Okay, so you're hanging out, breaking into cars and ripping off Blaupunkts, whatever, and up drives this black guy in a new Olds and says, 'Hey, Ernie, wanna buy this baby for two bills?' That about it?"

"Yeah, 'cept he dint know my name."

Keyes said, "I don't suppose you asked the gentleman where he got the car?"

Ernesto laughed—a muskrat mouth, full of small yellow teeth—and shook his head no.

"Don't suppose you asked his name, either?"

"No, man."

"And I don't suppose you'd recognize him if you ever saw him again?"

Ernesto leaned forward and rubbed his chin intently. A great gesture, Keyes thought. Cagney in *White Heat.*

"I see dis guy somewhere before," Ernesto said. "I doan know where, but I know the face. Big guy. Big black guy. Gold chain, Carrera frames, nice-looking guy. Arms like this, like a foking boa constripper. Yeah, I'd know him if I saw him again. Sure."

Keyes said, "You had a remote suspicion that the car was hot, didn't you?"

Ernesto nodded sheepishly.

"Why didn't you unload it?"

"I was going to, man. Another day or two it'd be gone bye-bye. But it was such a great car . . . aw, you wouldn't know about thins like that, man. You prolly got a Rolls-Royce or somethin. I never had a nice car like that. I wanted to cruise around for a while, that's all. I woulda fenced it eventually."

Keyes put the file back in the briefcase. He took out a recent photograph of B. D. Harper.

"Ever seen this man, Ernesto?"

"No." The puppy eyes didn't even flicker.

"Ever killed anybody?"

"On purpose?"

"On purpose, by accident, any way."

"No, sir!" Ernesto said crisply. "Once I shot a guy in the balls. Want to know why?"

"No thanks. I read all about it on your rap sheet. A personal dispute, I believe."

"That is right."

Keyes rose to leave and called for a guard. Then he thought of something else. "Ernesto," he said, "do you believe in black magic?"

The little Cuban grinned. "*Santería*? Sure. I doan go to those thins, but it be stupid to say I do not believe. My uncle was a *santero*, a priest. One time he brought a skull and some pennies to my mother's house. He killed a chicken in the backyard—with his teeth he killed dis chicken—and then dipped the pennies in its blood. Two days later the landlord dropped dead." Ernesto Cabal made a chopping motion with his hand. "Juss like that."

"You know what I'm getting at, don't you?"

"Yes, Mr. Keyes. I never heard of no *santero* using suntan oil for anythin . . ."

Keyes started to laugh. "Okay, Ernesto. I'll be in touch."

"Don't you forget about me, Mr. Keyes. Dis is a bad place for an innocent man."

Brian Keyes left the jail and walked around the corner to Metro-Dade police headquarters, another bad place for an innocent man. He shared the elevator with a tall female patrol officer who did a wonderful job of pretending not to notice him. She got off on the second floor. Keyes went all the way up to Homicide.

Al García greeted him with a grin and a soft punch on the shoulder. "Coffee?"

"Please," Keyes said. García was much friendlier since Keyes had left the newspaper. In the old days he was like a sphinx; now he'd start yakking and never shut up. Keyes thought it might be different this time around.

"How's business?" García asked.

"Not great, Al."

"Takes time. You only been at it—what?—two years. And there's plenty of competition in this town."

No fooling, Keyes thought. He had arrived in Miami

in 1979 from a small newspaper in suburban Baltimore. There was nothing original about why he'd left for Florida—a better job, no snow, plenty of sunshine. On his first day at the Miami *Sun*, Keyes had been assigned the desk next to Skip Wiley—the newsroom equivalent of Parris Island. Keyes covered cops for a while, then courts, then local politics. His reporting had been solid, his writing workmanlike but undistinguished. The editors never questioned his ability, only his stomach.

There were two stories commonly told about Brian Keyes at the Miami *Sun*. The first happened a year after his arrival, when a fully loaded 727 fireballed down in Florida Bay. Keyes had rented an outboard and sped to the scene, and he'd filed a superb story, full of gripping detail. But they'd damn near had to hospitalize him afterward: for six months Keyes kept hallucinating that burned arms and legs were reaching out from under his bedroom furniture.

The second anecdote was the most well-known. Even Al García knew about Callie Davenport. She was a four-year-old girl who'd been kidnapped from nursery school by a deranged sprinkler repairman. The lunatic had thrown her into a truck, driven out to the Glades, and murdered her. After some deer hunters found the body, Cab Mulcahy, the managing editor, had told Brian Keyes to go interview Callie Davenport's grief-stricken parents. Keyes had written a real heartbreaker, too, just like the old man wanted. But that same night he'd marched into Mulcahy's office and quit. When Keyes rushed out of the newsroom, everyone could see he'd been crying. "That young man," Skip Wiley had said, watching him go, "is too easily horrified to be a great journalist."

Besides Keyes himself, Skip Wiley was the only person in the world who knew the real reason for the tears. But he wasn't telling.

A few months later Keyes got his private investigator's license, and his newspaper friends were amused. They wondered how the hell he was going to hold together, working for a bunch of sleazoid lawyers and bail bondsmen. Brian Keyes wondered too, and wound up avoiding the rough cases. The cases that really paid.

"Still doing divorces?" Al García asked.

"Here and there." Keyes hated to admit it, but that's what covered the rent: he'd gotten damn good at staking out nooner motels with his three-hundred-millimeter Nikon. That was another reason for Al García's affability. Last year he had hired Brian Keyes to get the goods on his new son-in-law. García despised the kid, and was on the verge of outright murdering him when he called Keyes for help. Keyes had done a hell of a job, too. Tracked the little stud to a VD clinic in Homestead. García's daughter wasn't thrilled by the news, but Al was. The divorce went through in four weeks, a new Dade County record.

Now Brian Keyes had a friend for life.

García poured the coffee. "So you got a biggie, Brian."

"Tell me about it."

"It's a touchy one. Can't say much, especially now that you're lined up with the other side."

"Did you work the Harper case?"

"Hell, *everybody* up here worked that case."

Keyes tried to sip the coffee and nearly boiled his upper lip.

"Hey," García said, "that piece-of-shit rag newspaper

you used to work for finally printed something intelligent this morning. You see it?"

"My paper was in a puddle."

"Ha! You should have read it anyway. Wiley, the asshole that writes that column. I hate that guy normally—I really can't stand him. But today he did okay."

Keyes didn't want to talk about Skip Wiley.

"He wrote about this case," García went on. "About that little scuzzball we arrested."

"I'll be sure to get a copy," Keyes said.

"I mean, it wasn't a hundred percent right, there was a few things he screwed up, but overall he did an okay job. I clipped it out and taped it on the refrigerator. I want my boy to read it when he gets home from school. Let him see what his old man does for a living."

"I'm sure he'll get a charge out of it, Al. Tell me about Ernesto Cabal."

"Dirtbag burglar."

"Was he on your list of suspects?"

García said, "What do you mean?"

"I mean, you've got thirty detectives working on this murder, right? You must have had a list of suspects."

"Not on this one."

"So what we're talking about is blind luck. Some Beach cop nails the guy for running a traffic light and, bingo, there's Mr. Sparky Harper's missing automobile."

"Luck was only part of it," García said sourly.

Keyes said, "You caught Cabal in the victim's car, but what else?"

"What else do we need?"

"A witness or two might be nice."

"Patience, Brian. We're working on it."

"And a motive?"

García held up his hands. "Robbery, of course."

"Come on, Al, this wasn't a knife in the ribs. It was the ritual murder of a prominent citizen. How did Harper get into those silly clothes? Who smeared suntan oil all over him? Who stuffed a goddamn toy alligator down his throat? Who sawed his legs off? Are you telling me that some two-bit auto burglar concocted this whole thing?"

"People do crazy things for a new Oldsmobile."

"You're hopeless," Keyes said.

"Don't tell me you believe Cabal's story? Brian, you got to get this liberal-crusader shit out of your system. I thought two years away from that newspaper would cure you."

"You've got to admit, it's a very weird case. You guys checked out the car, right?"

"It was clean, except for Cabal's prints."

Keyes took out a legal pad and started jotting notes. "What about the suitcase?"

"No prints. Its model number matches a batch sent to Jordan Marsh about a year ago, but we can't be sure. Could've just as easily come from Macy's."

Keyes said, "Any sign of the missing legs?"

"Nope."

"Did you trace that terrific Hawaiian wardrobe?"

"Ugh-ugh." García made a zipper motion across his lips.

"Oh, you got something, uh? A store, perhaps. Maybe even a salesman who remembers something odd about this particular customer—"

"Brian, back off. This is a very touchy case. If the chief even suspected I was talking to you, I'd be shaking out parking meters for the rest of my life. I think we'd better call it quits for today."

Keyes put the legal pad back in his briefcase. "I'm sorry, Al. I appreciate what you're doing." Keyes was telling the truth. García didn't owe him a damn thing.

"Normally I wouldn't mind, Brian, it's just that this one is Hal's case. He's the lead detective. Went out to the scene and all. I don't want to screw it up for him."

"I understand. What's he got you doing?"

García rolled his eyes. "Checking out dead-enders. Take a look at this." He slid a sheet of paper across the desk.

It was a typed letter. Keyes scanned it quickly. He started to read it again, when García snatched it away.

"Crazy, huh? It came in today's mail."

Keyes asked for a Xerox copy.

"No way, Brian. The PD's office would cream over something like this. And it's crap, take my word for it. It's going right into the old circular file as soon as I make a couple routine calls to the feds."

"Read it out loud," Keyes said.

"I'll deny I ever even saw it," García said.

"Okay, Al, you got my word. Read it, please."

García slipped on a pair of tinted glasses and read from the letter:

Dear Miami Chamber of Commerce:

Welcome to the Revolution.

Mr. B. D. Harper's death was a milestone. It may have seemed an atrocity to you; to us, it was poetry. Contrary to what you'd like to believe, this was not the act of a sick person, but the raging of a powerful new underclass.

Mr. Harper's death was not a painful one, but it was unusual, and we trust that it got your attention. Soon we start playing for keeps. Wait for number three!

>*El Fuego,*
>*Commandante, Las Nòches de Diciembre*

Al García removed his reading glasses and said, "Not half-bad, really. For a flake."

"Not at all," Keyes agreed. "What do you make of that *number-three* business? Who was victim number two?"

"There wasn't any, not that I know of."

"So who are the Nights of December?" Keyes asked.

"A figment of some nut's imagination. 'The Fire,' he calls himself. *El Fuego* my ass. I'll check with the Bureau, just in case, but J. Edgar himself wouldn't have taken this one seriously. Still, I might ask around with the guys on the antiterrorism squad."

"And then?" Keyes asked.

"A slam dunk," García said. "Right into the wastebasket."

FOUR

Cab Mulcahy poured the coffee. Skip Wiley drank.

"The beard is new, isn't it?"

"I need it," Wiley said, "for an assignment."

"Oh. And what would that be?"

"That would be confidential," Wiley said, slurping.

Cab Mulcahy was a patient man, especially for a managing editor. He had been in newspapers his entire adult life and almost nothing could provoke him. Whenever the worst kind of madness gripped the newsroom, Mulcahy would emerge to take charge, instantly imposing a rational and temperate mood. He was a thoughtful man in a profession not famous for thoughtfulness. Cab Mulcahy was also astute. He loved Skip Wiley, but distrusted him whole-heartedly.

"Cream?" Mulcahy offered.

"No thanks." Wiley rubbed his temples briskly. He knew that the effect of this was to distort his face grotesquely, like pulling putty. He watched Mulcahy watching him.

"You missed the deadline yesterday, Skip."

"I was helping Bloodworth with his story. The kid's hopeless, Cab. Did you like my column?"

Mulcahy said, "I think we ought to talk about it."

"Fine," Wiley said. "Talk."

"How much do you really know about the Harper case?"

"I've got my sources."

Mulcahy smiled paternally. Wiley's column was on his desk. It lay there like a bird dropping, the first thing to await Mulcahy when he arrived at the office. He had read it three times.

"My concern," Mulcahy began, "Is that you managed to convict Mr. Cabal in this morning's newspaper, without benefit of a trial. You have, for lack of a better word, *reconstructed* the murder of B. D. Harper in your usual slick, readable way—"

"Thank you, Cab."

"—without any apparent regard for the facts. This business about sexual torture, where did that come from?"

Wiley said, "Can't tell you."

"Skip, let me read this out loud: 'Harper was tied up, spread-eagle, and subjected to vicious and unspeakable homosexual assaults for no less than five hours.' Now, before you start whining, you ought to know that I took the liberty of calling the medical examiner. The autopsy showed absolutely no signs of sodomy."

"Aw, it's the imagery that's important, Cab. The utter humiliation of this gentle man. Sodomized or not, can you deny that he was horribly humiliated by this crime?"

"Your concern for the late Mr. Harper's dignity is touching," Mulcahy said. He turned his attention to a stack of newspaper clippings on another corner of his desk. Wordlessly he riffled through them. Wiley knew what they were: more columns.

"Here we go," Mulcahy said, holding up one. "On

the subject of B. D. 'Sparky' Harper, this is what you wrote a mere three months ago: 'If there has ever been a more myopic, insensitive, and avaricious cretin to lead our Chamber of Commerce, I can't recall him. Sparky Harper takes the cake—and anything else that isn't nailed down. He is the Sultan of Shills, the perfect mouthpiece for the hungry-eyed developers, hoteliers, bankers, and lawyers who have made South Florida what it is today: Newark with palm trees.' "

"I remember that column, Cab. You made me apologize to the New Jersey Tourist Bureau."

Mulcahy leaned back and gave Skip Wiley a very hard look.

Wiley squirmed. "I suppose you want to know why I crucified Harper a few months ago and made a hero out of him today. It's simple, Cab. Literary license. You wouldn't understand."

"I've read a book or two. Try me."

"I did it to dramatize the crime problem," Wiley said. "The Harper murder symbolizes the unspeakable mayhem in our streets. Don't you see? To make people care, I needed to bring Sparky Harper and his killer to life. Don't look at me like that, Cab. You think I'm a hypocrite? Sure, Harper was a fat little jerk. But if I put that in the paper, no one would care about the murder. I wanted to give 'em goose bumps, Cab."

"Like the old days," Mulcahy said with a sigh.

"What's that supposed to mean? I get more goddamned letters than I ever did. People read the hell out of my column. You should see the mail."

"That's the trouble, Skip. I *do* see the mail. People are starting to hate you, I mean *really* hate you. Not just the usual fruitcakes, either."

Not true, Wiley said to himself. The people who counted were on his side.

"So you've been taking some heat, eh?"

Mulcahy looked away, out the window toward the bay.

"A few ad cancellations, perhaps? Like maybe the Richmond Department Store account—"

"Skip, that's one of about forty things on my list. It isn't funny anymore. You're fucking up on a regular basis. You miss deadlines, you libel people, you invent ludicrous facts and put them in the paper. I've got a lawyer downstairs who does nothing but fight off litigation against your column. We've had to print seven retractions in the last four months—that's a new record, by the way. No other managing editor in the history of this newspaper can make that claim."

Wiley was starting to feel a little sorry for Mulcahy, whom he had known for many years. Cab had been the city editor when Wiley had come to work at the *Sun*. They had been drinking buddies once, and used to go bass fishing together out in the Everglades.

It was a shame the old boy didn't understand what had to be done, Wiley thought. It was a shame the newspaper business had gotten such a frozen grip on his soul.

"The public defender's office called me this morning," Mulcahy continued. "Mr. Cabal's lawyer didn't appreciate your description of his client as 'yellow-bellied vermin culled from the stinkpot of Castro's jails for discharge at Mariel's harbor of shame.' The Hispanic Anti-Defamation League sent a telegram voicing similar objections. The League also notes that Señor Cabal is *not* a Mariel refugee. He arrived in this country from Havana with his family in 1966. His older brother later received a Purple Heart in Vietnam."

"Perhaps I got a little carried away," Wiley said.

"Hell, Skip." Mulcahy's voice was tired and edged with sadness. "I think we have a big problem. And I think we're going to have to do something. Soon."

This was a conversation they had been having more often, so often that Wiley had stopped taking it seriously. He got more mail than any other writer, and the publisher counted mail as subscribers, and subscribers as money. Wiley knew they wouldn't lay a glove on him. He knew he was a star in the same way he knew he was tall and brown-eyed; it was just something else he could see in the mirror every morning, plain as day. He didn't even notice it anymore. The only time it counted was when he got into trouble. Like now.

"You aren't going to threaten to fire me again, are you?"

"Yes," Mulcahy said.

"I suppose you want me to apologize to somebody."

Mulcahy handed Wiley a list.

"I'll get right on it—"

"Sit down, Skip. I'm not finished." Mulcahy stood up, brandishing the stack of columns. "You know what makes me sad? You're such a damn good writer, too good to be turning out shit like this. Something's happened the last few months. You've been slipping away. I think you're sick."

Wiley winced. "Sick?"

Mulcahy was a slim man, gray and graceful. Before becoming an editor, he had had a distinguished career as a foreign correspondent: he had covered two wars and a half-dozen coups, and had even been shot at three times. Wiley had always been envious of this; in all his years as a journalist he had never once been shot at. He had never dodged a real bullet. But Cab Mulcahy had, and he had written poetically about the experience. Wiley admired him, and it hurt to have the old boy talk like this.

"I took all your columns from the last four months," Mulcahy said, "and I gave them to Dr. Courtney, the psychiatrist."

"Jesus! He's a wacko, Cab. The guy has a thing for animals. I've heard this from seven or eight sources. Ducks and geese, stuff like that. The paper ought to get rid of him before there's some kind of scandal—"

Mulcahy waved his hands, a signal for Wiley to shut up.

"Dr. Courtney read all these columns and he says he can chart your illness, starting since September."

Wiley clenched his teeth so tightly his fillings nearly cracked. "There's nothing wrong with me, Cab."

"I want you to see a doctor."

"Not Courtney, please."

"The *Sun* will pay for it."

Well, it *ought* to, Wiley thought. If I'm nuts, it's this place that's to blame.

"I also want you to go to an internist. Courtney says the mental degeneration has occurred so rapidly that it could be pathological. A tumor or something."

"A guy who screws barnyard animals says that *I'm* pathological."

Mulcahy said, "He's paid for his opinions."

"He hates the column," Wiley said. "Always has." He pointed at the stack of clippings. "I know what's in there, Cab. The one I did six weeks ago about shrinks.

33

Courtney's still mad about that. He's trying to get back at me."

Mulcahy said, "He didn't mention it, although it was a particularly vile piece of writing. 'Greedy, soul-sucking charlatans'—isn't that what you said about psychiatrists?"

"Something like that."

"If I'd been here that morning, I'd have yanked that column," Mulcahy said evenly.

"Ha!"

"Skip, this is the deal. Go see the doctors and you can keep your column, at least until we find out what the hell is wrong. In the meantime, every word you write goes through me personally. Nothing that comes out of your terminal, not even a fucking obituary, gets into this newspaper without me seeing it first."

Wiley seemed stunned. He shrank into the chair.

"Jeez, Cab, why don't you just cut off my balls and get it over with?"

Mulcahy walked him to the door. "Don't write about the Harper case anymore, Skip," he said, not gently. "Dr. Courtney is expecting you tomorrow morning. Ten sharp."

Brian Keyes read Skip Wiley's column as soon as he got back to the office. He laughed out loud, in spite of himself. He had become amazed—there was no other word for it—at how much Wiley could get away with.

Keyes wondered if Ernesto Cabal had seen the newspaper. He hoped not. Wiley's column would absolutely ruin the young man's day.

Assuming Ernesto was innocent—and Keyes was

leaning in that direction—the next step was figuring out who would have wanted B. D. Harper dead. It was a most unusual murder, and robbery seemed an unlikely motive. Dumping the body in a suitcase was like the Mob, Keyes thought, but the Mob didn't have much of a sense of humor; the Mob wouldn't have dressed Sparky up in such godawful tacky clothes, or stuffed a rubber alligator down his throat.

Finding a solid suspect besides Ernesto Cabal wasn't going to be easy. B. D. Harper had not risen to the pinnacle of his trade by making enemies. His mission, in fact, had been quite the opposite: to make as many friends as possible and offend no one. Harper had been good at this. He positively excreted congeniality.

Sparky had lived and breathed tourism. His singular goal had been to lure as many people to South Florida to spend as much money as was humanly possible in four days and three nights. He lay awake nights scheming new ways to draw people to the tropical bosom of Miami.

As a reporter, Brian Keyes had come to know B. D. Harper fairly well. There was nothing not to like; there simply was nothing much at all. He was an innocuous, rotund little man who was jolliest when Florida was crawling with snowbirds. For years Harper had run his own successful public-relations firm, staging predictable dumb stunts like putting a snow machine on the beach in January, or mailing a ripe Florida orange to every human being in Prudhoe Bay, Alaska. This was in the boom days of Miami and, in a way, Sparky Harper had been a proud pioneer of the shameless, witless boosterism that made Florida grow.

In later years, as head of the Chamber of Commerce,

Harper's principal task was to compose a snazzy new bumper sticker every year:

"Miami—Too Hot to Handle!"

"Florida is . . . Paradise Found!"

"Miami Melts in Your Mouth!"

Brian Keyes's personal favorite was "The Most Exciting City in America," which Sparky propitiously introduced one month after Miami's worst race riot.

Harper shrewdly had peddled his lame slogans by affixing them to color posters of large-breasted women sunbathing on the beach, sprawling on the bows of sailboats, or dangling from a hang-glider—whatever Sparky could arrange. The women were always very beautiful because the Chamber of Commerce could afford to hire the top models.

The annual unveiling of the new tourism poster made Sparky Harper neither controversial nor unpopular. As far as anyone could tell, it was the only tangible thing he did all year to earn his forty-two-thousand-dollar salary.

As for the murder, Keyes thought of the usual cheap possibilities: a jealous husband, an impatient loan shark, a jilted girlfriend, a jilted boyfriend. Nothing seemed to fit. Sparky was a divorced man with a French poodle named Bambi. When he dated at all, he dated widows or hookers. He had been known to get bombed on occasion, but he never made an ass of himself in public. And he wasn't a gambler, so it was unlikely that the Mafia was into him.

Keyes guessed that whoever killed Harper might not have known him personally, but probably knew who he was. With garish methodology the killer had seemed to be making a very strong statement, which is why

Keyes couldn't dismiss the "Nights of December" letter, nutsy as it was.

Keyes decided that he needed the autopsy report. He drove to the medical examiner's office and asked for a copy. Dr. Joe Allen wasn't in, so Keyes decided to wait. As he sat in a tiled room that smelled sweetly of formalin, he started to read Allen's report line-by-line. Halfway through, his curiosity got the best of him and he unsheathed the color slides. One by one Keyes held them up to the light.

The more he studied the gruesome photographs, the more Keyes was convinced that Ernesto Cabal was telling the truth: he'd had nothing to do with B. D. Harper's murder. It was beyond Ernesto's stunted imagination to have conceived something like this.

"Don't smudge up my slides!" Dr. Joe Allen stood at the doorway, laden with files.

"'Mornin', Doc."

"Well, Brian. I hear you've hit the big time." Joe Allen had always liked Brian Keyes. Keyes had been a solid reporter and it was a damn shame he'd given it up to become a P.I. Joe Allen wasn't crazy about private investigators.

"This was no robbery, Joe."

"I don't know what it was," Dr. Allen said, "except that it was definitely death by asphyxiation."

"Have you ever heard of a B-and-E artist to show such flair?" Keyes asked.

"It seems the police are of that opinion."

"I'm asking for yours, Joe."

Dr. Joe Allen had autopsied 3,712 murder victims during his long career as the Dade County coroner, so he had seen more indescribable carnage than perhaps any other human being in the whole United States. Throughout the years Joe Allen had charted South Florida's progress by what lay dead on his steel tables, and he was long past the point of ever being shocked or nauseated. He performed meticulous surgery, kept precise files, took flawless photographs, and compiled priceless morbidity data which earned him a national reputation. For example, it was Dr. Allen who had determined that Greater Miami had more mutilation-homicides per capita than any other American city, a fact he attributed to the terrific climate. In warm weather, Allen noted, there were no outdoor elements to deter a lunatic from spending six, seven, eight hours hacking away on a victim; try that in Buffalo and you'd freeze your ass off. After Dr. Allen had presented his findings to a big pathologists' convention, several other Sun Belt coroners had conducted their own studies and confirmed what became known as the Allen Mutilation Theorem.

Throughout the years a few spectacular cases stood out vividly in Dr. Allen's recollections, but the rest were just toe tags. Brian Keyes hoped Sparky Harper might be different.

The coroner put on his glasses and held up two of the more sickening slides, as if to refresh his memory. "Brian," he said, "I don't think they've got the right man in jail."

"So how do I get him out?"

"Give them a better suspect."

"Swell, Joe. Anyone in particular?"

"In my opinion, Mr. Harper was the victim of a ritual slaying. I'd say that several persons were involved. I would also say that neither robbery nor sexual assault was the motive. I wouldn't rule out the possibility of an occult ceremony, possibly even human sacrifice. On the other hand, the body showed no common signs of torture—no cigarette burns, welts, or bruise patterns. But you can't ignore what happened to the legs."

Keyes asked, "What *did* happen to the legs?"

"The legs were removed after death occurred, probably so the body could be concealed in the suitcase. But it's the way the legs were removed that's so interesting."

Keyes said, "Joe, are you doing this just to make me sick?"

"The legs weren't just hacked off with an ax, which is the most efficient way," said Dr. Allen, pausing to choose his words. "It appears from the wounds that Sparky's legs might have been removed by a large animal. They might actually have been . . . twisted off."

"God! By what, wild dogs?"

Dr. Allen shook his head somberly. "Judging from the bite pattern, it was no dog. It was something much bigger. Don't ask me what, Brian, because I just don't know."

"Joe, you always brighten my day."

"Happy hunting, my friend."

FIVE

Brian Keyes's office was on the sixth floor of a dreary downtown bank building off SW Second Avenue, near the Miami River. The consulate of El Salvador was located down the hall, so most of the other tenants lived in perpetual fear of a terrorist attack and behaved accordingly. They all had chipped in to hire extra security guards for the lobby, but the security men had turned out to be professional burglars who one night looted the entire building of all IBM office machinery.

Brian Keyes was not affected by this crime because the only typewriter in his office was an old Olivetti portable, a leftover from his days of covering politics for the Miami *Sun*. The other items of potential value were an antique desk lamp and a telephone tape recorder, but the lamp was broken and the tape recorder was made in Korea so the burglars wanted no part of either.

The highlight of the office was a fifty-gallon salt-water aquarium, a going-away present from his friends at the newspaper. Keyes had erected it in the foyer, where a secretary ordinarily might have sat, and filled it with whiskered catfish that sucked the algae off the glass.

Except for the aquarium, the place was just as

cramped, ratty, and depressing as Keyes had feared it would be. He was rarely there. Even when he had nothing to do, he'd find an excuse to leave the bank building and stroll around downtown. He had an answering service, and an electronic beeper that fit onto his belt. The beeper didn't make Keyes feel particularly important; every shyster lawyer, dope dealer, and undercover agent in Dade County wore one. It was mandatory.

On the morning of December 5, Keyes was down at Bayfront Park, munching a sandwich and watching the tugboats, when the beeper on his belt went off loudly enough to wake a derelict two benches away.

Keyes found a pay phone and called his service. Al García was trying to reach him. It was important. Keyes phoned Homicide.

"Meet me on the beach," García said. "The Flamingo Isles, near Sixty-eighth and Collins. Look for the cop cars out front."

The Flamingo Isles was not a classic Miami Beach motel. There was nothing charming about the color (silt) or the architecture (Early Texaco). At this motel there were no striped canvas awnings, no wizened retirees chirping in the lobby, no lawn chairs lined up on the front porch, no front porch whatsoever. Basically the Flamingo Isles was a dive for pimps, chicken hawks, and hookers. Rooms cost ten dollars an hour, fifteen with porno cassettes. It was rumored that some of the vestibules were equipped with hidden movie cameras to secretly record the sexual antics of Florida tourists. It was not a good place for an innocent man, but Keyes was hopeful that this was where Sparky Harper had spent his final earthly moments. If so, it meant that

Harper had likely died in some bizarre sexual accident and not at the larcenous hands of Ernesto Cabal.

Keyes goosed his little MG convertible across the causeway and made it to the motel in eighteen minutes flat. Al García already was interviewing a Jamaican maid in the lobby. He kept hollering for an interpreter and the maid kept insisting in perfect English that she spoke perfect English, but García wouldn't believe her. He finally enlisted a black Miami Beach detective to take the maid's statement, and went upstairs, Keyes in tow. They entered room 223.

"Here you have it," García said.

A pile of men's clothing lay in the middle of the floor: blue silk socks, turned inside-out; an undershirt; a pair of soiled Jockey shorts; and a powder-blue double-knit suit with a J. C. Penney label. The legs of the suit had been sheared off below the knees. Lying beneath the clothes was a pair of highly polished black Florsheims.

The room showed no signs of a mortal struggle. There was a half-finished bottle of Seagram's and a couple cans of soda on the dresser. On the nightstand, next to the Magic Fingers machine, sat three plastic bottles of Coppertone tanning butter with coconut oil. A fingerprint man studiously dusted the containers; he was crouched on his haunches, oblivious of everything.

With a long pair of tweezers, García picked a plastic bag off the floor. The red-and-white lettering on the bag said: "Everglades Novelties."

"This," García intoned, "was used to transport the instrument of death."

"The toy alligator?"

García nodded.

"So this is where it happened."

"The murder? No, we don't think so."

Suddenly a big redheaded cop barged out of the bathroom. It was Harold Keefe, the lead detective.

"Who're you?" he asked Keyes.

"A friend of Al's." Keyes looked at García. García had an *oh shit!* look in his eyes.

"Don't touch anything," Keefe growled on his way out the door. "Al, don't let him touch anything, got it?"

García checked the bathroom to make sure no other detectives were sneaking around. He didn't say another word until the fingerprint man packed up his kit and left.

"Christ! I didn't know that bastard was in the john!"

"Relax, Al. He doesn't know who I am."

García started stuffing B. D. Harper's clothing in a clear plastic evidence bag. "Check out the stains on the floor," he told Keyes.

Two streaks of dried blood made a wavering trail from the bedroom to the bathroom. It was not very much blood, certainly less than one would have expected.

"The lab guys are on their way," García said, "so I'm gonna give it to you once. Then I want you to get out of here before I get in trouble."

"Whatever you say, Al."

"On the night of November 30, two men rented this room for one week. They paid cash in advance, three hundred and sixty bucks."

"What'd they look like?"

"One was described as a muscular black male in a tight yellow pullover," García said, "and the other was a young Latin male wearing blue jeans."

Keyes grimaced. "I suppose you showed Cabal's mug shot to the desk clerk."

"Yeah, and she's seventy-five percent sure it was him."

"Seventy-five won't cut it in court, Al."

"Don't worry, she'll be one hundred percent positive by the time this goes to trial."

"Anyone see them with B. D. Harper?"

"We got a couple faggots in room 225 who saw the Latin male enter this room about eleven P.M. with a chubby Anglo matching Harper's description. They heard some loud voices, and then the door slammed. The fairies peeked out just in time to see Harper being led down the stairs by the black dude and the little Cuban. Oh yeah, and the Cuban is carrying a red Samsonite."

"So they took Harper someplace, killed him, cut his legs off, stuffed him in the suitcase, and—"

"Brought him back here," García said. "This is where the weird shit happens. These blood smears come from dragging the corpse into the bathroom. That's where they dress him up in that stupid flowered shirt and smear the Coppertone all over and stuff him in the suitcase."

"Don't forget the sunglasses," Keyes said.

"Right. Then they drive out to Key Biscayne and heave him into the bay."

"Why all the trouble?"

García said, "Beats the hell out of me. Anyway, the black guy and the Cuban haven't been back since early on the morning of December 1. The maid just opened the room today. She saw the blood on the floor and called the Beach police."

"Well, this is great news, Al."

"I'm not finished. Remember I told you I had a line on those goofy clothes? Well, I got a sales clerk at a joint down the street who says she sold them to a skinny little Cuban guy on November 29."

"Ernesto?"

"She's eighty percent sure. The creep was wearing a floppy hat, so she's not absolutely certain."

"Give her time," Keyes said glumly. Things were looking bleak for Señor Cabal. Keyes wondered if he'd been wrong about the little guy. Maybe he wasn't just a crummy car burglar trying to get by.

García knotted the top of the evidence bag and scanned the room to make sure he hadn't missed anything. "Time for you to hit the road," he told Keyes. "And remember, I don't know your fucking name."

"Right, Al."

Keyes was in the parking lot, strolling toward the MG, when he heard García call from a balcony.

"Hey, Brian, you wanna *really* help your client?"

"You bet."

"It's easy," García shouted. "Find the black guy."

Keyes arrived at the county jail just as Mitch Klein was leaving. Klein was a scruffy young lawyer with the public defender's office who apparently had drawn the short straw when they farmed out Ernesto Cabal's case. As he walked out of the jail, his shirt damp and his tie loose, Klein did not look like a happy man. He looked like a man who couldn't wait to get into private practice.

Klein greeted Keyes with a lugubrious nod and said, "What's the bad news for the day?"

"They found a motel room on the beach with Harper's clothes and some blood on the floor. Little Cuban guy rented it the night before Harper vanished."

"Beautiful," Klein grumbled.

"The good news is, a big black guy was working with the Cuban. He matches the description of the character Ernesto says sold him the Oldsmobile. Maybe I can find him."

Klein rolled his eyes and made a lewd pumping motion with his right hand. "I think Ernesto is full of shit," he said.

Wonderful, Keyes thought, the guy's own lawyer is dumping on him.

When Keyes entered the cell, he noticed that Ernesto lay stark naked on the cot. Ernesto blinked at Keyes like a gecko lizard stunned by the sunlight.

"Dey took my close."

"Why?"

"'Fraid I'm gonna hang myself."

"Are you?"

"Not now."

"Glad to hear it."

Ernesto rolled over on his stomach, exposing stringy white buttocks. Two prisoners in another cell hooted in appreciation. Ernesto ignored them.

"That man Klein wants me to cop a plea. Says he's trying to save my life. He says dey strap my ass in a lektric chair if diss case go to jury. You thin' he's right?"

Keyes said, "I'm no lawyer."

"Too bad. That Klein, he's got nice shoes. You could use some nice shoes, no?"

Keyes told Cabal about the Flamingo Isles motel. The Cuban sat up excitedly when he heard the part about the black man and B. D. Harper.

"Was the black guy wearing Carrera frames?"

"I don't know."

"I'll bet it's the same dude who sold me that goddamn car."

"I'll try to find him, Ernesto."

"Hey, you tell Klein?"

"Yes."

"What's he say?"

"He said it sounded very promising."

"I seen the black guy before." Ernesto stood up and started pacing the cell. Keyes found his nakedness a little disconcerting. Mainly it was the tattoo: a commendable likeness of Fidel Castro's face, stenciled deftly on the tip of Ernesto's most private appendage.

"Think hard, Ernesto. Where did you see the black guy? On the beach? In a bar? At Sunday school?"

"Sone-thin like dat." Ernesto clasped his hands behind his back and stared through the bars of the cell. "I'm gone thin about it."

Keyes decided it was time to break the bad news. He told Ernesto about the desk clerk at the Flamingo Isles and the saleswoman at the clothing store, about how they had looked at his mug shot and were almost positive that he was the one.

"Dumb bitches," Ernesto said stoically.

Keyes said, "A skinny Cuban rented that motel room, and a skinny Cuban bought those loud clothes for B. D. Harper."

"Not *diss* skinny Cuban."

Ernesto sat down on the cot and, mercifully, crossed his legs.

"Do you want me to get your clothes back?"

"Thas all right, man."

"Where do I start looking for the friendly car salesman?"

"Pauly's Bar. Juss ask round. Big black guy with glasses. Not many of dose on the Beach, man."

"Did he have an accent?"

Ernesto giggled. "He's *black*, man. 'Course he had an accent."

"Jamaican? Haitian? American?"

"He's no Jamaican, and he's no street nigger. Diss boy been to school." Ernesto was very sure of himself. "Diss man, he's slick."

Keyes told Ernesto to think on it some more. He'd need all the help he could get. Especially at Pauly's Bar.

SIX

Dr. Remond Courtney didn't blink. He merely said: "I'm not sure I heard you right, Mr. Wiley."

"Oh, sorry." Skip Wiley got up and ambled across the office. He leaned over and positioned his large face two inches from the doctor's nose. "I said," Wiley shouted, as if Courtney were deaf, "is it really true that you have sex with mallard ducks?"

"No," Courtney replied, lips whitening.

"Mergansers, then?"

"No."

"Ah, so it's geese. No need to be ashamed."

"Mr. Wiley, sit down, please. I think we're avoiding the subject, aren't we?"

"And, what subject would that be, Dr. Goosefucker? May I call you that? Do you mind?"

Courtney looked down at the notebook in his lap, as if referring to something important. Actually the page was blank. "Why," he said to Skip Wiley, "all this hostility?"

"Because we're wasting each other's time. There's nothing wrong with me and you know it. But you had to be an asshole and tell my boss I've got a pathological brain tumor—so here I am, about to do something truly pathological." Wiley smiled and grabbed Dr. Courtney by the shoulders.

The psychiatrist struggled to maintain an air of superiority (as if this were just some childish prank) while trying to squirm from Wiley's grasp. But Wiley was a strong man and he easily lifted Courtney off the couch.

"I never said you had a tumor, Skip."

Dr. Remond Courtney was remarkably calm, but he'd had plenty of practice. He was by trade a professional witness, a courthouse shrink-for-hire. He was impressive in trial—cool, self-assured, unshakable on the stand. Lawyers loved Dr. Courtney and they paid him a fortune to sit in the witness box and say their clients were crazy as loons. It was laughably easy work, and Courtney was conveniently flexible in his doctrines; one day he might be a disciple of Skinner and, the next, a follower of Freud. It all depended on the case (and who was paying his fee). Dr. Courtney had become so successful as an expert witness that he was able to drop most of his private patients and limit his psychiatric practice to three or four lucrative corporate and government contracts. Dr. Courtney had hoped this would minimize his exposure to dangerous over-the-transom South Florida fruitcakes, but he'd learned otherwise. By the time a big company got around to referring one of its employees to a psychiatrist, the screaming meemies had already set in and the patient often was receiving radio beams from Venus. The worst thing you could do in such a case, Remond Courtney believed, was lose your professional composure. Once a patient knew he could rattle you, you were finished as an analyst. Domination required composure, Dr. Courtney liked to say.

"Skip, I can assure you I never said anything about a brain tumor."

"Oh, it's *Skip* now, is it? Did you learn that at shrink school, Dr. Goosefucker? Whenever a patient becomes unruly, call him by his first name."

"Would you prefer 'Mr. Wiley' instead?"

"I would prefer not to be here," Wiley said, guiding Dr. Courtney toward the window of his office. Below, fifteen floors down, was Biscayne Boulevard. Courtney didn't need to be reminded of the precise distance (he'd had a patient jump once), but Skip Wiley reminded him anyway. He reminded Dr. Courtney by hanging him by his Italian-made heels.

"What do you see, doctor?"

"My life," the upside-down psychiatrist said, "passing before my eyes."

"That's just a Metro bus."

"A bus, you're right. Lots of people walking. Some taxicabs. Lots of things, Mr. Wiley." The doctor's voice was brittle and high. He was using his arms to fend himself off the side of the building, and doing a pretty good job. After a few seconds Courtney's paisley ascot fluttered from his neck and drifted down to earth like a wounded butterfly. Skip Wiley thought he heard the doctor whimper.

"You okay down there?"

"Not really," Courtney called up to him. "Mr. Wiley, your time's almost up."

Wiley dragged Courtney up through the window.

"Your ankles sweat, you know that?"

"I'm not surprised," the doctor said.

"So you're sticking with this idea that I'm crazy? That's what you're going to tell Mulcahy?"

Courtney brushed himself off. The palms of his hands were red and abraded, and this seemed to bother him. He straightened his blazer. "You're very lucky I didn't lose one of my contact lenses," he told Wiley.

"You're lucky you didn't lose your goddamn life." Plainly unsatisfied, Wiley sat down at the doctor's desk. Courtney reclaimed his spot on the couch, a brand-new spiral notebook on his lap.

"In my opinion, it started with the hurricane column," the psychiatrist said.

"Come on, doc, that was a terrific piece."

"It was uncommonly vicious and graphic. 'What South Florida needs most is a killer hurricane . . .' All that stuff about screaming winds and crumpled condominiums. My mother saw that . . . that trash," the doctor said with agitation, "and the next day she put her place on the market. The poor woman's scared to death. An ocean view with a nine-point-eight-mortgage—assumable!—and still she's scared out of her mind. Wants to move to bloody Tucson. All because of you!"

"Really?" Skip Wiley seemed pleased.

"What kind of drugs," Dr. Courtney started to ask him, "provoke this kind of lunacy?"

But Skip Wiley was already on his way out the door, a honey-maned blur.

Cab Mulcahy strolled into the newsroom shortly after five. He was a composed, distinguished-looking presence among the young neurotics who put out the daily newspaper, and several of them traded glances that said: *Wonder what brings the old man out?*

Mulcahy was looking for Wiley. Actually, he was looking for Wiley's column. Mulcahy harbored a fear that Wiley would devise a way to sneak the damn thing into print in defiance of their agreement.

The city editor said he hadn't seen Wiley all day, and reported that no column had arrived by messenger, telephone, or teletype. The city editor also pointed out that, without a column, he was staring at a big sixteen-inch hole on the front page, with deadlines fast approaching.

"Ricky Bloodworth's offered to do the column if Wiley doesn't show up," the city editor said.

"Has he now?"

"He worked up a couple pieces in his spare time. I saw 'em this morning, Cab, and they're not bad. A little purple, maybe, but interesting."

"No way," Mulcahy said. "Tell him thanks just the same."

The city editor looked dejected; Mulcahy knew that he had been yearning to rid himself of the Wiley Problem for a long time. The city editor did not get on well with Skip Wiley. It was a bad relationship that only got worse after Wiley let it slip that he was making five thousand dollars a year more than the city editor, not including stock options. *Stock options!* The city editor had gone home that night and kicked the shit out of his cocker spaniel.

"Did you call Wiley's house?" Mulcahy asked.

"Jenna hasn't seen him since he left for the doctor's this morning. She said he seemed fine and dandy."

"That's what she said?"

"*Ver-batim,*" the city editor said. "Fine and dandy."

Mulcahy phoned Dr. Remond Courtney and told him that Skip Wiley hadn't showed up for work.

"Oh?" Dr. Courtney did not seem surprised, but it was hard to tell. Courtney was an expert at masking his reactions by saying things like *Oh* and *I see* and *Why don't you tell me about it.*

"I was wondering," Mulcahy said impatiently, "how things went today?"

"How things went?"

"With you and Mr. Wiley. You had an appointment, remember?"

More silence; then: "He became abusive."

"Became abusive? He's *always* abusive."

"Physically abusive," Courtney said. He was trying to remain clinical so Mulcahy wouldn't suspect how scared he'd been. "I believe he threatened my life."

"What did you do?"

"I talked him out of it, of course. I think we were doing much better by the end of the hour."

"Glad to hear it," Mulcahy said, thinking: Wiley's right, this guy is useless. "Tell me, did Skip say where he was going after his visit?"

"No. He left in a hurry. It had been a strenuous session for both of us."

Mulcahy said, "So what's the verdict?"

"Verdict?"

"What the hell is wrong with him?"

"Stress, fatigue, anxiety, paranoia. It's all job-related. I suggest you give him a year off."

"I can't do that, doctor. He's a very popular writer and the newspaper needs him."

"Suit yourself. He's a nut case."

A nut case who sells newspapers, Mulcahy thought ruefully. Next he tried Jenna.

"I still haven't seen him, Cab. I'm getting a little worried, too. I've got a spinach pie in the oven."

Jenna had the most delicious voice of any woman Cab Mulcahy had ever met; pure gossamer. Even *spinach pie* came out like *Let's do it!* The day Skip Wiley moved in with Jenna was the day Cab Mulcahy decided there was no God.

"Does he usually call?" Mulcahy asked.

"He doesn't do anything in a usual way, you know that, Cab." A silky laugh.

Mulcahy sighed. In a way it was his fault. Hadn't he introduced them to each other, Jenna and Skip, one night at the Royal Palm Club?

Jenna said, "Skip makes contact two or three times a day, in various ways. Today—nothing, after noon."

"What did he say," Mulcahy ventured, "when he . . . made contact?"

"Not much. Hold on, I gotta turn down the stove. . . Okay, let me try to remember . . . I know! He said he was on his way to get a new muffler for the car, and he also said he murdered the psychiatrist. Is that part true?"

"Of course not," Mulcahy said.

"I'm glad. He's got such a crummy temper."

"Jenna, did Skip mention when he might be making contact again?"

"No, he never does. He likes to surprise me, says it keeps the romance fresh. Sometimes I wonder if he's just testing me. Trust is a two-way street, y'know."

"But he comes home for dinner?"

"Almost always," Jenna said.

"If he comes home tonight," Mulcahy said, by now eager to escape the conversation, "please have him call the newsroom. It's important."

"I'm getting worried, Cab," Jenna said again. "This spinach is starting to clot."

What an actress, Mulcahy thought, she's just terrific. When Skip Wiley first seduced Jenna, he'd thought he was getting himself a gorgeous blond melon-breasted bimbo. That's how he had described her to Mulcahy, who knew better. He had warned Wiley, too, warned him to proceed with extreme caution. Mulcahy had seen Jenna in action once before; she was magnetic and purposeful far beyond Skip Wiley's ragged powers of comprehension. But Wiley hadn't listened to Mulcahy's warning, and chased Jenna shamelessly until she'd let herself get caught.

Mulcahy's speculation about Wiley's weirdness included the possibility that Jenna was the key.

Mulcahy swept the clutter from the desk into his briefcase, put on his jacket, and threaded his way through the newsroom toward the elevators.

"Cab, just a second." It was the city editor, looking febrile.

"If Wiley doesn't show, run a feature story in his slot," Mulcahy instructed, still walking. "A parade story, something mild like that. And at the bottom run a small box in italics. Say Wiley's out sick. Say the column will resume shortly."

The city editor didn't skulk off the way Mulcahy expected him to. Mulcahy stopped short of the elevators and asked, "What's the matter?"

"The highway patrol just called," the city editor said uneasily. "They found Wiley's car, the old Pontiac."

"Where?"

"In the middle of Interstate 95. At rush hour."

"No Wiley?"

The city editor shook his head grimly. "Engine was running, and Clapton was blasting on the tape deck. The car was just sitting there empty in traffic. They're towing it to Miami police headquarters. I've sent Bloodworth over to see what he can find out. Want me to call you later at home?"

"Sure," said Cab Mulcahy, more puzzled than before.

"About the column, Cab . . ."

"Yeah?"

"Sure you won't give Ricky a shot?"

Mulcahy rarely frowned or raised his voice, but he was on the verge of doing both. "You got a parade story for tomorrow? Don't tell me you don't. There's *always* a parade in this goddamn town."

"Yes, Cab. However, it was a very small parade today."

"I don't care."

"Belize Nationalism Day?"

"Perfect. Go with it. Run a nice big picture, too."

"But, Cab . . ."

"And call Jenna. Right away."

The screen door on Pauly's Bar was humming with flies. Inside there were six barstools, a gutted pinball machine, a boar's head, and a life-size cutout of Victoria Principal, a bourbon stain on her right breast. The bar itself was made of cheap pine and appeared to be recently repaired, bristling with fresh nails and splinters.

Behind the bar was a long horizontal mirror, its fissures secured with brown hurricane tape.

At first glance Pauly's was not a raucous joint, but a careful person could sense an ominous lethargy.

Brian Keyes decided to be the perfect customer. He slipped the lumpy-faced bartender a twenty-dollar bill and discreetly assured him that no, he wasn't a cop, he was just trying to buy some information.

The bartender, who wore a mesh tank top and a shiny mail-order toupee, turned out to be somewhat helpful; after all, twenty dollars was a banner night at Pauly's. Keyes knew from looking around the place that the man he hunted would be remembered here, and he was right.

"Don't get many big niggers in here," the bartender remarked, secreting the money in a pocket. "Then again, they all look big at night." The bartender laughed, and so did a greasy wino two stools down. Keyes smiled and said ha-ha, pretty funny, but this one you'd remember especially because of the fancy black sunglasses.

The bartender and the greasy wino exchanged looks, their grins getting bigger and dirtier. "Viceroy!" the bartender said, "Viceroy Wilson."

"The football player?"

"Sure."

"I don't believe it!" Keyes said.

"Well, take a look here," and then the bartender tossed an official NFL football at Brian Keyes, knocking over his Budweiser. Viceroy Wilson, former star fullback for the Miami Dolphins, had autographed the ball with a magnificent flourish, in red ink right under the stitch.

"He's a regular," the bartender boasted.

"No!"

"He sure is!"

"Well, I really need to talk to him."

"He don't give autographs to just anybody."

"I don't want an autograph."

"Then why you asking for him? He's not a man that likes to be asked for."

"It's personal," Keyes said. "Very important."

"I'll bet," croaked the wino. Keyes ignored him. He had a feeling these guys were full of shit anyway. Keyes was an avid football fan and, looking around, he wasn't able to picture the great Viceroy Wilson—bad hands, bankrupt and all—rubbing elbows with a bunch of pukes at Pauly's. Viceroy Wilson didn't belong in a rathole dive on South Beach; Viceroy Wilson belonged in Canton, Ohio, at the Football Hall of Fame.

"I'll get him for you," the wino volunteered, oozing off the barstool.

"Hey, what if he don't want to be got?" the bartender said. "Viceroy's a very private man."

"Twenty bucks," the wino said. Keyes handed it to him and ordered another beer. Twenty dollars apparently was now the going rate for everything at Pauly's. The wino shuffled out the door.

"Kiss your money good-bye," the bartender said reproachfully.

"Relax," Keyes told him, knowing it would only have the opposite effect. People in bars don't like to be told to relax.

"I'm beginning to think you're a narc!" the bartender said loudly. He calmed down when Keyes laid another twenty bucks on the bar next to the beer glass.

Forty minutes later the screen door wheezed open

and stayed that way for several moments. A cool salty breeze tickled Keyes's neck. He longed to turn around but instead just sipped on the beer, pretending that the 235-pound black man (Carrera sunglasses dangling on his chest) who loomed in the tavern mirror wasn't really glaring at him as if he were the proverbial turd in the punch bowl.

"I don't think I know you," Viceroy Wilson growled.

Brian Keyes was in the process of spinning around on the barstool, about to say something extremely witty, when a black fist the approximate size and consistency of a cinderblock slammed into the base of his neck.

At that instant Keyes's brain became a kaleidoscope, and he would later be able to recall only a few jagged pieces of consciousness.

The sound of the screen door slamming.

The taste of the sidewalk.

The cough of an automobile's ignition.

He remembered opening one eye with the dreadful thought that he was about to be run over.

And he remembered a glimpse of a vanity license tag—"GATOR 2"—as the car peeled rubber.

But Keyes didn't remember shutting his eyes and going nighty-night on the cool concrete.

"Hello?"

Brian Keyes stared up at the round, friendly-looking face of a middle-aged woman.

"Are you injured?" she asked.

"I think my spine is broken." Keyes was lying outside Pauly's Bar. The pavement smelled like stale beer and urine. Unseen shards of an ancient wine bottle dug into his shoulder blades. It was eleven o'clock and the street was very dark.

"My name is Nell Bellamy."

"I'm Brian Keyes."

"Should I call an ambulance, Mr. Keyes?"

Keyes shook his head no.

"These are my friends Burt and James," Nell Bellamy said. Two men wearing mauve fez hats bent over and peered at Brian Keyes. They were Shriners.

"What are *you* doing here?" one of them asked benignly.

"I got beat up," Keyes replied, still flat on his back. "I'll be fine in a month or two." He ran a hand over his ribs, feeling through the shirt for fractures. "What are *you* doing here?" he asked the Shriners.

"Looking for her husband."

"Theodore Bellamy," Nell said. "He disappeared last Saturday."

"Give me a hand, please," Keyes said. The Shriners helped him to his feet. They were big, ruddy fellows; they propped him up until the vertigo went away. From inside Pauly's Bar came the sounds of breaking glass and loud shouting in Spanish.

"Let's take a walk," Keyes said.

"But I wanted to ask around in there," Nell said, nodding toward the bar, "to see if anybody has seen Teddy."

"Bad idea," Keyes grunted.

"He's right, Nell," one of the Shriners advised.

So they set off down Washington Avenue. They were a queer ensemble, even by South Beach standards. Keyes walked tentatively, like a well-dressed lush, while Nell handed out fliers with Teddy's picture. The Shriners ran interference through knots of shirtless refugees who milled outside the droopy boarding houses and peeling motels. The refugees flashed predatory smiles and made wisecracks in Spanish, but the Shriners were imperturbable.

Nell Bellamy asked Keyes what had happened inside the bar, so he told her about Viceroy Wilson.

"We saw a black fellow speeding away," Nell said.

"In a Cadillac," Burt volunteered.

"Burt sells Cadillacs," Nell said to Keyes. "So he ought to know."

The four of them had reached the southern point of Miami Beach, near Joe's Stone Crab, and they were alone on foot. This part of South Beach wasn't exactly the Boardwalk, and at night it was generally deserted except for serious drunks, ax murderers, and illegal aliens.

With Nell leading the way, the entourage strolled toward the ocean front.

Burt remarked that he once had seen the Dolphins play the Chicago Bears in an exhibition game, and that Walter Payton had made Viceroy Wilson look like a flatfooted old man.

"That was in '75," the Shriner added.

"By then his knees were shot," Keyes said halfheartedly. He didn't feel much like defending any creep who'd sucker-punch him in a place like Pauly's. In all his years as a reporter he had never been slugged. Not once. He had been chased and stoned and menaced in a variety of ways, but never really punched. A punch was quite a personal thing.

"You should file charges," Nell suggested.

Keyes felt silly. Here was this stout little woman

searching godforsaken neighborhoods in the dead of night for her missing husband, while Keyes just moped along feeling sorry for himself over a lousy bump on the neck.

He asked Nell Bellamy about Theodore. She mustered herself and told, for the sixteenth time, all about the convention, the venomous jellyfish, the unorthodox lifeguards, and what the cops were saying must have happened to her husband.

"We don't believe them," Burt said. "Teddy didn't drown."

"Why not?"

"Where's the body?" Burt said, swinging a beefy arm toward the ocean. "There's been an easterly wind for days. The body should have floated up by now."

Nell sat on a seawall and crossed her legs. She wore blue slacks and a modest red blouse, not too vivid. Biting her lip, she stared out at the soapy froth of the surf, visible even on a moonless midnight.

The loyal Shriners shifted uncomfortably, conscious of her grief. For the sake of distraction Burt said, "Mr. Keyes, what'd you say you do for a living?"

Keyes didn't want to tell them. He knew exactly what would happen if he did: he'd have a missing-persons case he really didn't want.

"I work for some lawyers in town," he said ambiguously.

"Research?" Nell asked.

"Sort of."

"Do you know many people? Important people, I mean. Policemen, judges, people like that?"

Here we go, Keyes thought. "A few," he said. "Not

many. I'm probably not the most popular person in Dade County."

But that didn't stop her.

"How much do you charge the lawyers?" Nell asked in a businesslike tone.

"It depends. Two-fifty, three hundred a day. Same as most private investigators." No sense ducking it now. If the fee didn't scare her off, nothing would.

Nell got up from the seawall and daintily brushed off the seat of her pants. Excusing herself, she took the Shriners aside. Keyes watched them huddle in the penumbra of a streetlight: a chubby, pleasant-faced woman who belonged at a church bake sale, and on each side, a tall husky Midwesterner in a purple fez. Nell seemed to do most of the talking.

Keyes ached all over, but his head was the worst. He checked his pants pocket; miraculously, his wallet was still there. Just thinking about the three-mile hike back to the MG exhausted him.

After a few moments Nell approached again. She was holding a folded piece of paper.

"Do you take private cases?"

"Did I mention that my fee doesn't include expenses?"

Not even a flicker. "Are you available to take a private case?"

"But, Mrs. Bellamy, you just met me—"

"Please, Mr. Keyes. I don't know a soul down here, but I like you and I think I can trust you. My instincts usually are very sound. Most of all, I need someone with . . ."

"Balls," Burt said helpfully.

"You marched into that awful tavern like a trooper," Nell said. "That's the kind of fellow we need."

The decent thing to do was to say no. Keyes couldn't take this nice woman's money, feeding her false hope until poor Teddy finally washed up dead on the beach. Could be weeks, depending on the tides and the wind. It would have been thievery, and Keyes couldn't do it.

"I'm sorry, but I can't help."

"I know what you're thinking, but maybe this'll change your mind." Nell handed him the folded paper. "Someone left this in my mailbox at the hotel," she explained, "the morning my husband disappeared."

"Read it," said the Shriner named James, breaking his silence.

Keyes moved under the streetlight and unfolded the letter. It had been neatly typed, triple-spaced. Keyes read it twice. He still couldn't believe what it said:

Dear Mrs. Tourist:

Welcome to the Revolution. Sorry to disturb your vacation, but we've had to make an example of your husband. Go back North and tell your friends what a dangerous place is Miami.

El Fuego,
Comandante, Las Noches de Diciembre

SEVEN

Brian Keyes delivered a photocopy of the new *El Fuego* letter to Homicide the next morning. Afterward he went to the office to feed the tropicals and check his messages. The Shriners had called from the county morgue to report that no one matching Theodore Bellamy's description had turned up in the night inventory of Dade County corpses. There was another call-me message from Mitch Klein, the public defender. Keyes decided not to phone back until he knew more about the letter.

At noon Keyes returned to police headquarters. "Let's go eat," Al García said, taking him by the arm. García didn't think it was a swell idea to be seen around the office with a private investigator. They rode to lunch in the detective's unmarked Dodge, WQBA blaring Spanish on the radio. García was nonchalantly dodging deranged motorists on Seventh Street, in the heart of Little Havana, when he stubbed out his cigarette and finally mentioned the letter.

"Same typewriter as the first one," he said.

Keyes wasn't surprised.

"The Beach police think it's a crackpot," García added in a noncommittal way.

"What do you think, Al?"

"I think it's too hinky for a crackpot. I think to myself, how would this *Fuego* know about Bellamy so soon? Almost before the cops! And I think, where's the connection between this Bellamy guy and B. D. Harper? They didn't even know each other, yet after each one comes these death letters. Too hinky, like I said."

"So you're ready to spring Cabal?"

García laughed, pounding on the steering wheel. "You're hilarious, Brian."

"But Ernesto didn't kill Harper and he damn sure didn't snatch this drunk Shriner."

"How do you know?"

"Because," Keyes said, "the guy's a burglar, not a psychopath."

"Know what I think, brother? I think Ernesto is *El Fuego*."

"Give me a break, Al."

"Let me finish." García pulled the Dodge into a shopping center and parked near a Cuban café. He rolled down the window and toyed with another cigarette. "I think your little scuzzball client is *El Fuego*, but I also think he didn't dream up this scheme all by his lonesome. I agree with you: Cabal ain't exactly a master criminal, he's a fuckin' burglar, and not very good at that. This whole thing sounds like a bad extortion scam, and our pal Ernesto, he don't have the brains to extort a blow-job from a legless whore. So he had help. Who? you're asking me. Don't know for sure, but I'll bet it's this mysterious superhuman black dude Cabal's been crying about . . ."

Keyes related his encounter with Viceroy Wilson at Pauly's Bar.

"You deserve a good whack on the head for showing

your shiny angel-food face in that snakepit," the detective said. "You wanna file A-and-B on the sonofabitch?"

"Just find him, Al."

"Yes sir, Mr. Taxpayer, I'll get right on it."

"This might help." Keyes handed García a scribbled note that said "GATOR 2." "It's the tag on the Caddy that Wilson was driving."

"Hey, you do good work. This'll be easy," García said. "Come on, let's get a sandwich and some coffee."

Both of them ordered a hot Cuban mix and ate in the car, wax paper spread across their laps.

"Al," Keyes said, savoring the tangy sandwich, "what do you make of the name of this group? *Las Noches de Diciembre*—the Nights of December, right?"

García shrugged. "Usually Cuban groups name themselves after some great date in their history, but the only thing I know happened in December is Castro came to power—nothing they'd want to celebrate. 'Course, there is another possibility."

"What's that?"

García paused for another enormous bite. Somehow he was still able to speak. "They something planned for *this* December. As in, right now. And if what we've seen already is any indication"—he glanced over at Keyes—"it's gonna be a treat."

Daniel "Viceroy" Wilson stood six feet, two inches tall and weighed 237½ pounds. He usually wore his hair in a short Afro, or sometimes plaited, but he always kept enough of a gritty beard to make him look about half as mean as he really was.

One of the things Wilson fervently wished this

afternoon, skulking in the parking lot of the world-famous Miami Seaquarium, was that he could own this fine Cadillac he was driving. It didn't seem right that it belonged to the Indian, who didn't appreciate it, didn't even use the goddamn tape deck. One time Wilson had left a Herbie Hancock cassette on the front seat, and the Indian had thrown it out the window with a bunch of Juicy Fruit wrappers and bingo tickets onto I-95. At that moment Wilson had contemplated killing the Indian, but when it came to Seminoles, one had to be careful. There was a wealth of mystical shit to be considered: eagle feathers, panther gonads, and so on. Wilson was much more fearful of Indian magic than of jail, so he let the Herbie Hancock episode slide. Besides, for the first time in years, Wilson had something to look forward to. He didn't want to spoil it by pissing off the Indian.

Still, he'd have loved to own the Caddy.

Life had not been kind to Viceroy Wilson since he was cut from the Miami Dolphins during the preseason of 1978, a month before his own Cadillac Seville had been repossessed. Since then Wilson had been through three wives, two humiliating bankruptcies, a heroin addiction, and one near-fatal shooting. Yet somehow he had managed to maintain his formidable physique in such a way that he could still bring silence to a crowded restaurant just by walking in the door. Wilson's fissured face looked every day of his thirty-six years, yet his body remained virtually unchanged from his glory days as a star fullback: taut, streamlined calves; a teenager's spare hips; and a broad, rippling wedge of a chest. Wilson's strength was in his upper body, always had been; his shoulders had been his best weapons inside the twenty-yard line.

As a rule, Viceroy Wilson didn't go around clobbering strangers in stinky taverns. He believed in the eternal low profile. He was not homesick for the Orange Bowl locker room, nor did he especially miss getting mobbed for his autograph. A free case of Colt .45 was the only reason he'd signed that football in Pauly's Bar. Generally Viceroy Wilson believed that the less he was recognized in public, the better. Part of this attitude was personal preference (autographs being a bitter reminder of the Super Bowl years), and part of it was a necessary adjustment in order to lead a successful life of crime.

Exactly why he'd sucker-punched the skinny white guy in Pauly's, Wilson wasn't sure. Something—a street instinct, maybe—told him not to let the dude get a good look at his face. Something about the back of his head said trouble. Thick brown hair, shiny, straight, razor-cut. Sculptured around the collar. Yeah, *that* was it. Cops got haircuts like that. Wilson was sure this man wasn't a cop, which made him even more of a useless jive asshole. Who else would get a haircut like that? It really annoyed Viceroy Wilson just to think about it, and he was glad he'd smacked the guy and put an end to his curiosity. Now was no time to have razor-cut strangers nosing around, asking coplike questions.

Viceroy Wilson did not think of himself as a common criminal. Since leaving the National Football League (after eight bone-battering seasons, seventy-three touchdowns, and 7,889 yards rushing), Wilson had become a dedicated anarchist. He had come to believe that all crimes were perfectly acceptable against rich people, although the term "rich" was admittedly subjective, and varied from one night to the next.

Wilson himself was no longer rich, having been neatly cleaned out by sports agents, orthopedic surgeons, ex-wives, ex-lawyers, accountants, mortgage companies, real-estate swindlers, and an assortment of scag peddlers from Coconut Grove to Liberty City. With a shift in economic fortunes Wilson had been forced to quit shooting heroin, so he'd turned to reading in his spare time. He spent hours upon hours in the old public library at Bayfront Park, amid the snoring winos and bag ladies, and it was there Wilson decided that America sucked, especially white America. It was there that Viceroy Wilson had decided to become a radical.

He soon realized two things: first, that he was ten years too late to find a home in any sort of national radical movement and, second, there were no English-speaking radicals in all of South Florida anyway.

So for years Viceroy Wilson had quietly burgled apartments and scammed dope and boosted cars, all the while nurturing romantic hopes of one day inflicting some serious shit on the white establishment that had mangled his knees and ruined his life. Wilson remained proud of the fact that he'd never robbed a liquor store, or stolen an eight-year-old Chrysler, or snatched a purse bulging with food stamps. Politically, he was careful about picking his victims.

Then *El Fuego* came along and Viceroy Wilson felt redeemed.

He didn't know what the name *El Fuego* actually meant, but it sure sounded bad, and as long as it didn't translate into something like "The Fart," Wilson could live with it. They shared the name anyway, all of them.

They were a team. More of a team than the goddamn Dolphins ever were.

It was four-thirty by the digital clock on the Cadillac's dash, and the last porpoise show had ended at the Seaquarium. Tourists were starting to trickle out in a splash of godawful colors.

Viceroy Wilson adjusted his Carrera sunglasses, lit up a joint, jacked up the a/c, and mellowed out behind the Caddy's blue-tinted windows. He imagined himself an invisible, lethal presence. This was fun. He liked the dirty work. "Thirty-one Z-right," he called it. That had been his jersey on the Dolphins: number thirty-one. And "thirty-one Z-right" was head-down-over-right-guard, the big ball-buster. Five, six, seven nasty yards every time. Viceroy Wilson had absolutely loved it.

"Pick a pale one." Those were his orders today. "Pale and comely." Now what the fuck did *that* mean? Pale was pale.

Wilson studied the tourists as they strolled by, scouting the parking lot for their precious rental cars. The boss was right: it was a bountiful crop. In no time Wilson selected a redhead, tall and creamy-skinned, with lots of cinnamon-colored freckles. Her hair was thick and permed up to bounce, and she wore a crimson halter over silky blue jogging shorts. Minneapolis, Wilson guessed, maybe Quebec. A real alien. Best of all, her husband-boyfriend-whatever was only about five-two, a hundred-ten pounds, tops. He stood there shielding his eyes from the afternoon sun, squinting pathetically as he searched for the maroon Granada or whatever it was they'd be driving.

Viceroy Wilson polished off the joint and slid out of

the Cadillac. That old familiar growl was building in his throat.

Thirty-one Z-right!

Brian Keyes felt uncomfortable whenever he ventured back to the newsroom. In a way, he missed the chaos and the adrenalized camaraderie; then again, what did he expect? Him and his one-man office with a tank full of algae-sucking catfish.

Whenever Keyes revisited the *Sun*, old friends flagged him down, briefed him on the latest atrocities against truth and justice, and offered to get together at the club for a drink. Keyes was grateful for their friendliness, but it made him feel odd. He was something of a stranger now, no longer entrusted with Serious Information, the currency of big-city journalism. Nonetheless, he was glad when they waved and said hello.

This time Ricky Bloodworth was the first to corner him.

"Tell me about Ernesto Cabal," he said breathlessly. "I'm doing a big weekender on the Harper case."

"Can't help you, Rick. I'm sorry, but he's a client."

Bloodworth's voice climbed to a whine. "You're talking like a lawyer now, not like the Brian I used to know."

Keyes shrugged. Bloodworth was irrepressibly annoying.

"At least tell me if you think he's guilty. Surely you can do that, cantcha?"

"I think he's innocent," Keyes said.

"Right," Bloodworth said with an exaggerated wink. "Sure, Brian." He scooted back to his desk.

Keyes figured the cops hadn't told Bloodworth about the *El Fuego* letters, which was just fine. Bloodworth would have gone nuts with that stuff, and then so would the city. Nothing like a little panic to muck up an investigation.

Cab Mulcahy was waiting in his office. Slate-colored suit, crisp white shirt, navy tie. Same civilized handshake, same crinkly smile. And there was the coffeepot steaming on the corner of the desk. Same place it had been the night Brian Keyes had walked in with his resignation.

"It was good of you to come on short notice. Mind if I close the door?"

"Not at all, Cab." Keyes had been surprised to get the message on his beeper; he'd been wondering about it all afternoon. A new job offer—that was his best guess. But why would the *Sun* want him back? The place was crawling with raw talent, kids who were plenty tough enough.

"Cab, are you going to ask me to come back to work?"

Mulcahy smiled kindly and shifted in his chair. "To be honest, Brian, I hadn't thought about it. But if you're interested, I'm sure we can—"

"No. No, I'm not." Keyes wondered why he didn't feel more relieved. "I was just curious."

"I called you," Mulcahy said, "because I want to hire you as a private investigator. We have a very sensitive case. You're the only one who can handle it."

Keyes was well-versed in the rudimentary techniques of bullshitting that the *Sun* taught all its top editors. The phrase "You're the only one who can do it" generally translated to "No one else will touch it." But this time Mulcahy did not appear to be shoveling anything. He appeared to be genuinely upset.

"Brian, Skip Wiley has disappeared."

Keyes did not move a muscle. He just looked at Mulcahy; a look of disappointment, if not betrayal. Cab Mulcahy had been afraid this might happen. He had dreaded it, but there was no other way.

"I'm sorry, Brian. I'd never ask unless we were desperate."

"Disappeared?"

"Vanished. They found his car yesterday in the middle of 1–95. He didn't show up at home last night."

Home. Keyes chuckled: Come on, Cab, just say it, I'm not going to break down in tears. Wiley didn't show up at *Jenna's* last night. God, the old man was funny sometimes, Keyes thought. Trying to spare me a little pain. It was two years ago that Jenna had dumped him for Wiley—Wiley, of all people! Why couldn't it have been an artist, or a concert musician, or some anorexic-looking poet from the Grove? Anyone but Skip Wiley—and right in the bitter worst of the Callie Davenport business. What a couple: Jenna, who adored Godunov and Bergman; and Wiley, who once launched a write-in campaign to get Marilyn Chambers an Oscar.

"Did you call the cops?" Keyes asked.

Mulcahy shook his head and reached for the coffee. "We decided not to. I've pretty much ruled out foul play." He told Keyes about Wiley's eccentric behavior, and about his visit to the psychiatrist the day before.

"So you think he's hiding out?"

"I do. So does Dr. Courtney."

Remond Courtney's opinions didn't carry much weight with Brian Keyes, who knew something of the doctor's meager talent. In the aftermath of the terrible 727 crash, when Keyes was being fingered by imaginary severed limbs, Dr. Courtney had advised him, by way of therapy, to get a job as an air-traffic controller.

"Forget that idiot shrink," Keyes said. "What about Jenna? What does she think?"

Mulcahy said, "She's pretty worried. She thinks Skip might do something crazy."

"Would that surprise you, Cab? Wiley may be talented, prolific, tough as hell—all the things you people put a premium on—but he's also a card-carrying flake. He could be anywhere. Vegas, Nassau, Juarez, who knows? Why don't you just wait a few days? He'll get so miserable not seeing his byline in the paper that he'll rush right back with a stack of fresh columns."

"I don't think so," Mulcahy said. "I hope you're right but I just don't think so. I need him back now, here— where we can keep an eye on him."

So that's it, Keyes thought. Mulcahy was worried less about Wiley's well-being than about all the trouble a man like that could create. Wiley presented an explosive public relations problem for the Miami *Sun*; no newspaper can afford to have its star columnist turn up as the proverbial sniper in the schoolyard.

And in Skip Wiley's case, another factor loomed large: he had an enormous public following. If his column didn't appear for a few days running, lots of readers would stop buying the *Sun*. If the days turned into weeks, the attrition would show up in the next ABC audits. And if that happened, Cab Mulcahy would have to answer to the highest possible authority; good journalism is fine, but circulation is sacred. No wonder Mulcahy was nervous.

"You know him better than any of us," Mulcahy said. "You sat next to him in the newsroom for three years. You recognize his moods, how he thinks, *if* he thinks . . ."

"I haven't seen him since I left the paper."

Mulcahy leaned forward. "He hasn't changed that much, Brian. True, his behavior is a bit more extreme, and his writing is certainly more irresponsible, but he's still the same Skip Wiley."

"Cab, you're talking to the worst possible person. You ought to know that: I can't take this case. I'm not ready to deal with him." Keyes stood up to leave. "Why, Cab? Why would you do this to me?"

"Because Jenna asked for you."

Keyes sat down hard. His heart was skipping along nicely now. All he could think was: Cab better not be lying.

"I told her I didn't think it was fair," Mulcahy said with a sigh. "But she's very worried about him. She said it would be a great favor if I asked you to look into it, and not some stranger."

Keyes knew it wouldn't do any good to lecture himself about Jenna, and it was pointless to act like he was going to waltz out of Mulcahy's office and forget the whole thing. The old man was right—it wasn't fair.

Mulcahy was careful not to go on too much about Jenna. "Please, Brian, will you try to find Wiley? We'll pay you five hundred a day, plus expenses."

"Jesus, you guys are really scared of what he might do!"

Mulcahy nodded glumly. "He's got a considerable

temper, as you know. Watching him these last few months has been unsettling, to say the least. I'm sure you read the infamous hurricane column, or maybe some of the others. 'Rats as Big as Bulldogs Stalk Condo.' 'Snakes Infest Bathroom Plumbing at Posh Resort.' 'Mystery Disease Sweeps Shuffleboard Tourney.' Wiley was very shrewd about it. One day he'd write a rousing Good Samaritan column, then a funny man-on-the-street piece, then a tearjerker about some little kid with cancer . . . and then he'd quietly slip in one of those gems. He became single-minded about it. He became . . . perverse." The editor lowered his voice. "I think this disappearance is part of a plan. I think he intends to embarrass the newspaper in some extraordinary way."

"You don't think he's playing games just to get a raise?"

Mulcahy shook his head firmly.

"What about the possibility that something really happened? Maybe Skip got kidnapped."

"Maybe that's what he wants us to think," Mulcahy said, "but I don't buy it, Brian. No, if I know Wiley, he's out there,"—Mulcahy waved a manicured hand toward the bay window—"biding his time, enjoying the hell out of this. And I want him found."

"Suppose I do," Keyes said.

"Call me immediately. Don't do a thing. I'm not asking you to confront him, I'd never do that. Just find him, tell me where he is. Leave the rest up to us."

"You and Jenna?"

"He listens to her," Mulcahy said apologetically.

"He worships her," Keyes said. "It's not the same thing."

"You'll take the case?"

Keyes didn't answer right away, but he knew what he'd say. Of course he'd take the case. Part of it was the money, part of it was Jenna, and part of it was that goddamn brilliant Wiley. A long time ago it would have been pure fun, tracking down an old comrade lost on a binge. But that was before Jenna. Fun was now out of the question.

Keyes told himself: This will be a test, that's all. To see how thick is the scar.

"Let's wait twenty-four hours, Cab. In the meantime, why don't you run one of Ricky Bloodworth's columns in Skip's slot tomorrow? Run the kid's picture, too. If that doesn't make Wiley surface, then maybe you're right. Maybe it's something serious this time."

"Brian, I don't know about Bloodworth . . ."

"I understand he's chomping at the bit. So publish one of his masterpieces. And if that doesn't bring Wiley charging back to the newsroom tomorrow, I'll take the case."

"It's a deal. And you can start first thing."

"We'll see," Keyes said. "Believe it or not, Cab, I've got other clients with worse problems than yours."

"What could be worse than a maniac like Wiley?"

"For starters, there's a very nice lady whose husband vanished in broad daylight on Miami Beach, and there's also a not-so-nice Cuban burglar in the county jail looking at Murder One."

"Not anymore." It was Bloodworth himself, inserting his rodent face through a crack in the door.

"This is a private conference!" Mulcahy barked.

"Wait a second. Ricky, what is it?"

"I thought you ought to know, Brian. Just got word from the police desk." Bloodworth waved a notebook momentously. "Ernesto Cabal killed himself about an hour ago."

EIGHT

Viceroy Wilson came into the room wearing tight red Jockey shorts and nothing else. This vision would have provoked cries of glee or terror from most women, but Renee LeVoux was speechless. Viceroy Wilson had stuffed a towel in her mouth before lashing her to the bed the night before.

Renee was mystified and afraid. She didn't know who this was, or where she was, or what was about to happen. She was sure of only one thing: her vacation was in shambles.

In the parking lot at the Miami Seaquarium, she had barely seen the inky specter that had swept her into the car and promised to kill her if she so much as twitched her honky lips.

The trunk of the automobile had been cramped and uncomfortable, but it had a new-car smell, which Renee thought was a good sign. She had shut her eyes and tried not to cry aloud. All she could hear was Wilson Pickett singing "Wait Till the Midnight Hour," which her captor had played over and over on the tape deck, full blast.

Although it had seemed like eternity, Renee LeVoux actually spent only twenty-seven minutes in the trunk of the Cadillac. Viceroy Wilson had driven straight from the Seaquarium to a cheap motor inn on the Tamiami Trail. There he'd popped the trunk and lifted Renee LeVoux over one shoulder like a sack of tangelos.

Inside the room, he'd wordlessly removed her halter and jogging shorts, gagged her, and tied her to the bed. He'd noticed that she was trembling, so he'd tossed a thin blanket across her, as if she were a horse.

Renee had slept fitfully, straining against the ropes, certain that she would awake any moment to be violated by the biggest black man she'd ever seen.

But nothing had happened. Aside from intermittently checking the knots at Renee's wrists and ankles, Viceroy Wilson had paid almost no attention to his beautiful captive. Instead he'd watched Mary Tyler Moore on television, skimmed the *New Republic*, and done one hundred push-ups, Marine-style.

The next morning, when she heard him turn on the shower, Renee began to cry again. Viceroy Wilson poked his glistening head out the bathroom door and glared. He put a finger to his lips. Renee nodded meekly and became quiet.

Viceroy Wilson had no interest in pale white girls with strawberry hair. During his time in the NFL he had known an astounding variety of women with an equally astounding range of sexual appetites. It had gotten boring toward the end, and dangerous. When Wilson had reinjured his right knee before the crucial Pittsburgh Steelers game in 1977, the Miami Dolphins had put out a press release saying it had happened in a practice scrimmage—when in fact Viceroy's knee had hyperextended on a water bed beneath two limber sisters who worked in a foundry on the Allegheny.

Later, when he became a revolutionary, Viceroy

Wilson made a vow not to mix sex and sedition. He wanted to be remembered as a very professional terrorist.

He attached no symbolism to the red Jockey shorts.

"What're you lookin' at?" he asked Renee LeVoux as he toweled off.

From the bed his prisoner just stared in fright.

Moments later a key rattled in the door and another man slipped into the motel room. Viceroy Wilson greeted him with a grunt and a nod of the head. Renee was struck by the difference in the two figures and thought it odd that they could be partners. Wilson's companion was a wiry Latin-looking man who spoke sibilantly and moved catlike about the room. Craning her neck from the bed, Renee could see the two of them conferring in the kitchenette. Soon she smelled coffee and bacon, and her stomach began to make noises. Viceroy Wilson approached the bed and removed the gag from her mouth.

"If you scream, you're dead."

"I won't, I promise."

"Your name is Renee?"

She nodded; obviously they had her purse. "You can have all the money in my wallet," she offered.

"We don't want your money." Viceroy Wilson slid one hand under her head and lifted it slightly off the pillow; with the other he held a cup of coffee to her lips. She slurped at it timorously.

"Thank you."

"What's your boyfriend's name?"

Wilson put the coffee cup down. Renee LeVoux noticed that he had a pencil and a piece of paper.

"Why do you want to know?" she asked.

"We're going to write him a letter. Tell him you're okay."

"Oh no!"

"Oh yes."

Now there were two faces hovering over her, one black and indifferent, one thin and fierce. The thin man was sneering. He tore the blanket away and saw that Renee was dressed only in her panties.

"Don't hurt me!" Renee cried.

The thin man brandished a shiny knife.

"Oh please no," Renee cried.

The black man ferociously seized the thin man by the wrist and twisted his arm. The thin man yelped and the knife fell into the bedding.

"Hay-zoose, don't ever try that shit again," Viceroy Wilson said. He was thinking to himself: This is the problem when you work with Cuban lunatics. They can't go five minutes without pulling a pistol or a blade. They couldn't help it—it was something in their DNA molecules.

"Renee, my name is Mr. Wilson. This here is Mr. Bernal."

Renee said, "How do you do?"

Wilson sighed. "We need the name of your boyfriend, and we need it now."

"I'm not telling. I don't want you to hurt him."

"Girl, we don't want to hurt him. We want to let him know what happened to you."

Puzzled, Renee asked, "What *did* happen to me?"

"You've been kidnapped by a group of dangerous radicals."

"God! But I'm nobody."

"That's true," said Jesús Bernal, fishing through the bed for his blade.

"Why me? I'm just a tourist."

"Did you enjoy the porpoise show?" Bernal asked.

Renee nodded apprehensively. "Yes, very much. And the trained whale."

"Shamu," Bernal said. "That's the whale's name."

This guy was sickening, Wilson thought. He might even be worth killing someday.

"Did you ride the monorail?" Bernal went on mockingly. He wore a mean smile.

"No, David wanted to see the shark moat instead."

Now we're getting somewhere, Wilson muttered. "David who?"

"I won't tell you!"

Wilson slipped one hand around Renee's freckled neck. It felt soft and cool. He gave a sharp, tennis-ball squeeze; that was plenty.

"David Richaud," Renee said, starting to sob. "R-i-c-h-a-u-d."

Viceroy Wilson carefully wrote down the name. "And where are you staying?"

"At the Royal Sonesta."

"Thank you, Renee, my sweet," said Jesús Bernal, bobbing at the foot of the bed.

"Shut up and type," said Wilson, shoving the paper at his companion. Bernal bounced over to the kitchen table and sat down at a portable electric typewriter.

Viceroy Wilson turned to his victim and said, "Do you believe that fuckhead went to Dartmouth?"

Jesús Bernal may have come to the cause with impressive credentials, but he was not highly regarded by Viceroy Wilson. Jesús Bernal had once held the title of defense minister for a rabid anti-Castro terrorist group called the Seventh of July Movement. The group was named for the day in 1972 when its founders had launched a costly and ill-fated attack on a Cuban gunboat off the Isle of Pines. In later years an acrimonious dispute had arisen over the name of the group, with some members claiming that the Isle of Pines attack had actually occurred on the *sixth* of July, and demanding that the group should be renamed. A compromise was reached and eventually the terrorists became known as the First Weekend in July Movement.

Throughout the late 1970s this organization took credit for a large number of bombings, shootings, and assassination attempts in Miami and New York. According to the Indian, Bernal was named defense minister chiefly because of his Ivy League typing skills. As Viceroy Wilson knew, one of the most vital roles in any terrorist group was the composing of letters to take credit for the violence. The letters had to be ominous, oblique, and neatly typed. Jesús Bernal was very good in this assignment.

He had been recruited to *Las Noches de Diciembre* after a bitter falling-out with his comrades in the First Weekend in July Movement. Actually Bernal had been purged from the group, but he never talked about why, and Viceroy Wilson had been warned not to ask. He tolerated Bernal, but he had no instinctive fear whatsoever of the Cuban. And he was getting awful damn tired of this macho switchblade bullshit.

"We're moving out soon," Wilson told Renee LeVoux. He balled up the towel and started to stuff it back in her mouth.

"Wait," she whispered. "Why did you tell me your names?"

Wilson shrugged.

"You're going to kill me, aren't you?"

"Not if you can swim," Wilson said, inserting the gag. "And I mean fast."

Renee's eyes widened and she tried to scream. The more she tried, the redder she got, and all that came out was a throaty feline noise that filled the tawdry motel room. She tossed back and forth on the bed, fighting the ropes, trying to spit out the gag, until Viceroy Wilson finally said "Dammit!" and whacked her once in the jaw, knocking her cold.

Meanwhile, preoccupied at the Smith-Corona, the man writing for *El Fuego* began to type:

Dear Mssr. Richaud:
Welcome to the Revolution!

Four items of special interest to Brian Keyes appeared in the Miami *Sun* of December 6.

One was a lengthy front-page story about the jailhouse suicide of Ernesto Cabal, accused killer of B. D. "Sparky" Harper. One hour before the tragic incident, Cabal had complained of stomach pains and been transported to the infirmary, where he drank a half-pint of Pepto-Bismol and declared that he was cured. While confined to the clinic, however, Ernesto apparently had pilfered a long coil of intravenous tubing, which he smuggled back to his cell. No one checked on him for hours, until they found him cold and dead at dinnertime. Using the I.V. tube as a noose, Cabal had managed to hang himself, naked as usual, from a water pipe. The duty sergeant remarked to the *Sun* that it was difficult to make a really good noose out of plastic tubing, but somehow Cabal had done it. When asked why none of the other inmates on the cell block had alerted the guards to Ernesto's thrashings, the sergeant had explained that the little Cuban "was not all that popular."

The second item to catch Keyes's attention (he was reading on a musty sofa next to the aquarium in his office, where he had spent the night) was the inaugural column of Ricky Bloodworth. The headline announced: "Miami Rests Easier as Harper Mystery Ends." The column was a fulsome tribute to all the brilliant police work that had landed Ernesto Cabal in jail and driven him to his death. "He knew the evidence was over-whelming and he knew his freedom was over," Bloodworth wrote, "so he strangled himself to death. He was nude, alone, and guilty as sin." Then came a quote from the big redheaded detective, Hal, who said that the Harper case was closed, as far as he was concerned. "This is one of those rare times when justice triumphs," Hal beamed.

Keyes noticed that there was no quote from Al García. And there was no mention of the *El Fuego* letters.

The third article of interest was not very long, and not prominently displayed. The story appeared on page 3-B, at the bottom, beneath a small headline: "Police Seek Missing Woman." The article reported that one Renee LeVoux, twenty-four years old, a visitor from Montreal, had been abducted from the parking lot of the world-famous Miami Seaquarium shortly before five P.M. the previous day. Incredibly, there were no witnesses to the crime. Miss LeVoux's male companion, whom police declined to identify, had been knocked unconscious by a single blow to the back of the neck, and was of no help. Anyone with information about Miss LeVoux's whereabouts was encouraged to call a Crime Stoppers phone number.

Brian Keyes made a mental note to find out more about that one.

Finally he spotted the one news item that he'd actually been looking for. Mercifully it was buried on 5-B, next to the advertisements for motorized wheelchairs.

The headline said: "County Lawyer Stabbed in Mêlée." Splendid, Keyes thought ruefully, it made the final edition after all. Keyes wondered if the *Sun* had gotten the story right, and forced himself to read:

An attorney for the Dade County public defender's office was assaulted Wednesday night at the Royal Palm Club.

Mitchell P. Klein, 26, was standing at the bar when he was suddenly attacked by another patron, police said. The assailant pulled Klein's hair, ripped at his clothes, and tried to choke him, according to witnesses. As Klein attempted to break away, his attacker threw him to the floor and stabbed him in the tongue with a salad fork, police said.

The suspect, described as a well-dressed white male in his early thirties, escaped before police arrived. Witnesses said the man did not appear to be intoxicated. Klein was taken to Flagler Memorial Hospital, where he was treated for minor injuries and released early this morning. Due to oral surgery, he was unavailable for comment.

Careless reporting, Keyes grumbled, as usual.

For one thing, it hadn't been a salad fork, but one of those dainty silver jobs designed for shrimp cocktails and lobster. Second, he and Mitch Klein hadn't been standing at the bar; they were sitting in a booth.

Still, it *had* been a reckless gesture, something Skip Wiley himself might have tried. Keyes wondered what had gotten into him. Was he finally losing his grip? Assaulting an officer of the court in a nightclub, for God's sake, in front of a hundred witnesses. He couldn't believe he'd done it, but then he couldn't believe what Klein had said as they were talking about Ernesto's suicide.

"The only reason you're upset," Klein had said, "is that the case is over, and so's your payday."

This, after Keyes had told him all about the *Fuego* letters, all about Viceroy Wilson, all about Dr. Joe Allen's opinion that Ernesto Cabal was the wrong man. After all this—and four martinis—Mitch Klein still had the loathsome audacity to say:

"Brian, don't tell me you really gave a shit about that little greaseball."

That was the moment when Keyes had reached across the table, seized Klein by his damp curly hair, and deftly speared the lawyer's tongue with the cocktail fork. No choking. No ripping of clothes. No grappling on the floor. There was, however, a good bit of fresh blood, the sight of which surely contributed to the later embellishments of eyewitnesses.

Keyes had gotten up and left Mitch Klein blathering in the booth, the silver fork dangling from his tongue, blood puddling in the oysters Bienville.

And that had been the end of it.

Now, the next morning, Keyes was certain the cops would arrive any minute with a warrant.

Actually it turned out to be Al García, all by himself. He knocked twice and barged in.

"What a pit!" he said, looking around.

"Why, thank you, Al."

García sullenly peered into the murky fish tank.

"Don't smear up the glass," Keyes said.

"Those are the ugliest guppies I ever saw," García said.

"They're catfish," Keyes said. "They eat up the slime."

"Well, they're doing a helluva job. It looks like somebody pissed in this aquarium."

"Anything's possible," Keyes muttered. He lay on the sofa, the newspaper spread across his chest. García picked it up and pointed to the article about Mitch Klein.

"Did you do this, Brian?"

"I got mad. Klein went to see Ernesto yesterday and told him the case was locked. Told him he didn't have a chance. Told him to plead guilty or they were going to charbroil him. Ernesto wanted to fight the charges but Klein told him to quit while he was ahead. Ernesto was going nuts in jail, all the queers chasing him. He had that incredible tattoo on his joint. The one I told you about."

"Fidel Castro."

"Yeah," Keyes said. "Well, some maniac tried to bite it off one night in the shower. Thought if he chomped off Ernesto's dick, it would kill the real Fidel in Havana. Witchcraft, he said. Somehow Ernesto got away from the guy, but he was scared out of his mind. He said he'd do anything to get out of jail. So when Klein told him he'd better plan on twenty-five to life, I guess Ernesto figured he was better off dead."

"But Brian—"

"Why didn't that cocksucker Klein talk to me before he went over to the jail? That case wasn't locked, no way. You know I'm right, Al."

"All I know," the detective said, "is that we'll never know. You gotta calm down, brother."

Keyes closed his eyes. "Maybe I'm just mad at myself. I should have told Klein about *El Fuego* as soon as I saw the second letter. But how was I to know the sonofabitch was in such a hurry to dump the case? Whoever heard of pleading your man five days after the goddamn crime?"

"He thought it was a loser," García said. "He was just trying to expedite things."

Keyes sat up angrily, looking ragged.

"Expedite things, huh? Well, he expedited his client right into the morgue."

García shrugged. "You hungry?"

"I thought you were here to arrest me."

"Naw. Klein's making noises about pressing charges. Assault with a deadly cocktail fork, something like that. Fortunately for you, nobody at the state attorney's office likes the little prick, so he's having trouble getting a warrant. He'd probably forget all about it if you'd pay his hospital bill. Can't be much—what's six little sutures on the tongue?"

Keyes smiled for the first time. "I suppose it's the least I could do."

"Make him an offer," García advised. "If you're lucky, you might not even have to say you're sorry."

"What about the Harper case?"

"You read the paper. It's closed, man. Nothing I can do."

"But what about Bellamy and the other *Fuego* letter?"

"Talk to Missing Persons," García said dryly, "and they'll call it a probable accidental drowning. And they'll say, 'What letter?'"

The detective lumbered around the office, poking at books and files, flipping through notebooks, taking up time. Keyes could tell that something was bugging him.

"For what it's worth," García said finally, "I agree with you. There's more to the Harper murder than the late great Ernesto Cabal. I bitched and moaned about keeping the case open, but I got outvoted."

"What're they afraid of?"

"It's the start of the the season," García said. "Snow-birds on the wing, tourist dollars, my friend. What's everyone so afraid of? Empty hotel rooms, that's what. A gang of homicidal kidnappers is not exactly a PR man's dream, is it? The boys at the Chamber of Commerce would rather drink Drano than read *El Fuego* headlines. Not now, Brian, not during the season."

"So that leaves me the Lone Ranger," said Keyes.

"I'll do what I can," García said, "quietly."

"Great. Can you get the state to pay my fee?"

The detective laughed. "No, Kemosabe, but I got you a present. An honest-to-God clue. Remember the tag on the Cadillac at Pauly's Bar?"

"Sure," Keyes said. "GATOR 2."

"Well, guess who it comes back to."

"The legendary Viceroy Wilson!"

"Nope. The Seminole Nation of Florida, Incorporated."

"Swell," Keyes said, flopping back on the couch. "That's some swell clue, Tonto."

Cab Mulcahy arrived at work early, canceled two appointments, and asked his secretary to please hold all calls, except one. For the next three hours Mulcahy sat in his office and eyed the telephone. He loosened his necktie and pretended to work on some correspondence, but finally he just closed the drapes (to shield himself from the rest of the newsroom) and sat down in a corner chair. Through the window, Biscayne Bay was radiant with a sailboat regatta; Hobies skimmed and sliced fierce circles, leaping each other's wakes, orange and lemon sails snapping in the warm morning breeze. It was a gorgeous race under an infinite blue sky, but Cab Mulcahy paid no attention. It was one of the darkest days of his career. Ricky Bloodworth's column had turned out just as half-baked, unfocused, and banal as Mulcahy knew it would be. Yet he had thrown away twenty-two years of integrity and printed it anyway.

Why?

To flush Skip Wiley from his hideout.

It had seemed like a good plan. No sense blaming Keyes.

But what had Mulcahy done? He'd unleashed a monster, that's what. He glanced again at the phone. Where the hell was Wiley? How could he sit still while a jerk like Bloodworth came after his job?

Mulcahy pondered one plausible explanation: Skip Wiley was dead. That alone would account for this silence. Perhaps a robber had snatched him from his car on the expressway and killed him. It was not a pleasant scenario, but it certainly answered the big question. Mulcahy figured that death was the only thing that would slow Wiley down on a day like today. The more Cab Mulcahy thought about this possibility, the more he was ashamed of his ambivalence.

He could hear the phone ringing every few minutes outside the door, at his secretary's desk. Readers, he thought, furious readers. How could he tell them, yes, he agreed, Bloodworth's writing was disgraceful. Yes, it's a bloody travesty. Yes, he's a congenital twit and we've got no business publishing crap like that.

Much as he wanted to, Mulcahy could never say all that, because journalism was not the issue here.

There was a firm, well-rehearsed knock on the door. Before Mulcahy could get up, Ricky Bloodworth stuck his head in the room.

"I hate it when you do that," Mulcahy said.

"Sorry." Bloodworth handed him a stack of columns. "Thought you might want to take a gander at these."

"Fine. Go away now."

"Sure, Mr. Mulcahy. Are you feeling okay?"

"A little tired, that's all. Please shut the door behind you."

"Any one of those could run tomorrow," Bloodworth said. "They're sort of timeless."

"I'll keep that in mind."

Mulcahy sagged behind his desk and scanned the columns. With each sentence he grew queasier. Bloodworth had generously penciled his own headline ideas at the top of each piece:

"Abortion: What's the Big Deal?"

"Capital Punishment: Is the Chair Tough Enough?"

"Vietnam: Time to Try Again?"

Mulcahy was aghast. He buzzed his secretary.

"Seventy-seven calls about today's column," she reported. "Only three persons seemed to like it, and one of them thought it was satire."

"Has anyone phoned," Mulcahy asked, "who remotely *sounded* like Mr. Wiley?"

"I'm afraid not."

Mulcahy's stomach was on fire; the coffee was going down like brake fluid. He opened the curtains and balefully scouted the newsroom. Ricky Bloodworth was back at his desk, earnestly interviewing two husky men in red fez hats. Mulcahy felt on the verge of panic.

"Get me Brian Keyes," he told his secretary. Enough was enough—he'd given Keyes his lousy twenty-four hours. Now it was time to find Skip Wiley, dead or alive.

NINE

"How's the fish?" Jenna said.

"Very good," said Brian Keyes.

"It's a grouper. The man at the market promised it was fresh. How's the lemon sauce?"

"Very good," Keyes said.

"It's a little runny."

"It's fine, Jenna."

She lowered her eyes and gave a shy smile that brought back a million memories. A smile designed to pulverize your heart. For diversion, Keyes took a fork and studiously cut the fish into identical bite-size squares.

"I liked your hair better when it was shaggy," Jenna said. "Now you look like an insurance man."

"I'm in court so much these days. Gotta look straight and reliable up on the witness stand."

Keyes wondered how much small talk would be necessary to finesse the awkward questions: Where've you been? What've you been up to? Did you get our Christmas card? He was no good at small talk, and neither was Jenna. Jenna liked to get right to the juicy stuff.

"Are you seeing anybody?"

"Not right now," Keyes said.

"I heard you were dating a lady lawyer. Sheila some-thing-or-other."

"She moved," Keyes said, "to Jacksonville. Got on with a good firm. We're still friendly." Surely, he thought, Jenna could see how uncomfortable this was.

"So you're living alone," she said, not unkindly.

"Most nights, yeah."

"You could call, just to say hi."

"Skip doesn't like it," Keyes said.

"He wouldn't mind," Jenna said, "every now and then."

But in fact, when Jenna had first dumped him for Skip Wiley, Brian Keyes had phoned every night for three weeks, lovesick and miserable. Finally Wiley had started answering Jenna's telephone and singing "When You Walk Through a Storm." Immediately Keyes had quit calling.

"You look like you've lost about eight pounds," Jenna remarked, studying him across the table.

"Nine," Keyes said, impressed. "You look very good." The understatement of the century.

She had come straight from her jazz exercise class, which she taught four times a week. She was wearing a lavender Danskin, pink knit leg warmers, and white sneakers. Her blond hair was bobbed up, and she wore tiny gold earrings that caught the light each time she turned her head. Keyes noticed a fresh hint of lipstick, and the taste of an elusive perfume. As if all that weren't enough, she had a terrific new tan, which fascinated Keyes because Jenna was not a beach person.

"It's been a while since you've been here," she said, pouring white wine.

"You've really done some work on the place."

"Damage, you mean. It's Skip, mostly."

Keyes pointed to a cluster of pockmarks high on the living-room wall, beneath a stuffed largemouth bass. "Are those bullet holes?"

"Now, don't get all worried."

Keyes got up for a closer look. "Looks like a .38."

"He got mad one night watching the TV news. The governor was talking about growth, how growth was so essential. The governor was saying how one thousand new people move to Florida every day. Skip's opinion about that was considerably different than the governor's. Skip didn't think the governor should have been quite so happy."

"Why did he shoot the wall?" Keyes asked.

"Because he couldn't bring himself to shoot the TV—it's a brand-new Trinitron," Jenna said. "I forgot you don't like spinach."

"It's fine. Jenna, why is there a coffin in your living room?"

"I know, I know. I hate it, too. Skip says it makes a good cocktail table. He bought it at the flea market. He keeps his newspaper clippings inside there."

"That's a bit odd, don't you think?" Keyes said.

"At the very least he should get it refinished."

Keyes ate faster. This was more traumatic than he had feared. Meeting in her house—the place she shared with Wiley—had not been Keyes's idea. Jenna had insisted. She had wanted to be here, she said, in case Skip called.

If Jenna seemed genuinely worried about her lover's whereabouts, Keyes was not. His heart was with the Ernesto Cabal case—what was left of it—and tracking

Skip Wiley was just a sporting way to pass some time, pay some bills . . . and see Jenna again.

Keyes had a simple theory about Wiley's disappearance. He figured Skip had orchestrated the whole thing to gouge a fatter salary out of the Miami *Sun*. Wiley's usual strategy, when he wanted more money, was to arrange for friends at the *Washington Post* and the *New York Times* to call up with phony or wildly inflated job offers. Then he'd charge into Cab Mulcahy's office and threaten to defect. Mulcahy quit falling for the Fantastic Job Offer ruse about two years ago, so Keyes figured Wiley was merely trying out a new scheme.

Keyes also now realized that the idea of publishing a Ricky Bloodworth column might have backfired, and that Wiley was holed up somewhere, howling with glee over Mulcahy's torment. Keyes now believed—though he dared not tell Mulcahy—that Wiley might wait weeks before emerging. He might wait until his readers began rioting.

And Keyes also believed that Jenna might be in on it.

"Did you love me, Brian?"

"Yes." He started to gag. He hoped it was just a fish bone going down the wrong way. Jenna came around the table and patted him on the back.

"Deep breaths," she said soothingly. "Don't eat so fast."

"Why," Keyes rasped, "did you ask me that question?"

"Skip says you were madly in love with me."

"I told you that myself," Keyes said, "about thirty thousand times."

"I remember, Brian."

God, there's the smile.

"How about now?" Jenna asked. "Still feel the same way?"

Oh no, you don't. Keyes shifted into a tough-guy mode. "This is business, Jenna. Let's talk about Skip. Where do you think he could be?"

"I don't know."

"Oh really."

"Brian! This isn't funny. I think he's in trouble. I think somebody's got him."

"Why?"

"Because he's a good target," Jenna said. She started clearing the table. "You sit still, I'll do this. Let's see, you take your coffee black . . ."

"Cream and sugar," Keyes said painfully. "But I think I'll wait."

"Okay. As I was saying, Skip's a very well-known person, a genuine celebrity. That makes him a perfect target for kidnappers. Look at Patty Hearst."

"Or Frank Sinatra, Jr.," Keyes said.

"Exactly."

"You ever read *The Ransom of Red Chief*?"

"Sure," Jenna said. "What are you getting at?"

"Nothing."

Every so often Keyes's attention was drawn to the coffin, which dominated Jenna's otherwise-cozy living room. The coffin was plain and vanilla-colored, made of smooth Dade County pine. A pauper's coffin. Jenna had done a valiant job of trying to disguise it as normal furniture. She had placed cocktail coasters neatly on each corner of the lid, and in the center she had stationed a blue Ming vase with fresh-cut sunflowers. For more camouflage she had added a thick stack of magazines, with *Town and Country* on top. Despite all this, there was no mistaking the coffin for anything else. Keyes wondered morbidly if he ought to peek inside, just to make sure Wiley wasn't there.

"There's been no ransom demand, has there?" he asked Jenna.

"Not yet. Let's sit on the couch." Jenna put a James Taylor album on the stereo and went into the bedroom. When she came out, her hair was down and she was barefoot.

"If Skip wasn't kidnapped," she said, "then maybe Cab's right. Maybe he just went crazy and wandered off." She curled up on the couch. "I wish I had a fireplace."

"It's seventy-four degrees outside," Keyes said.

"What happened to my young romantic?"

Keyes smiled bashfully; God, she never let up. He fought to keep a proper tone to his voice. "Is there a possibility . . . have you two been getting along?"

"Better than ever," Jenna said. "We made love the afternoon he left. Twice!"

"Oh."

"Right there, where you're sitting."

"Sorry I asked."

Keyes kept waiting for Jenna to say: *I know how hard it was for you to take this case.* But she never did, and gave no sign of comprehending his distress.

"You've got to find him, Brian. I don't want to get the police involved, and I *don't* want a lot of publicity. It could ruin his career."

Or cinch it, Keyes mused. He asked, "Do you think he's gone insane?"

"I'm not sure I'd know the difference." Jenna took off her earrings and laid them on the coffin. Elegantly she poured herself another glass of wine. Keyes sipped cautiously. The Chablis gave a dangerous urgency to his loneliness.

Jenna said, "Lately Skip's been wilder than usual. He wakes up ranting and goes to bed ranting. You know, the usual stuff: toxic waste, oil spills, the California condor, the Biscayne Aquifer. Armageddon in general. About a week ago a man came to the door selling time-shares in Key Largo, and Skip attacked him with a marlin gaff."

Keyes asked, "Does he get incoherent?"

Jenna laughed softly. "Never. He's a very cogent person, even when he's violent. He always makes perfect sense."

"Well, if he's been kidnapped—which I doubt—all we can do is wait for a ransom demand. But if he's off somewhere in a frenzy, we've got to find him before he really hurts someone. Jenna, I need some ideas. Where the hell could he be?"

"The wilderness," she said wistfully, gazing at her imaginary fireplace. "That's where to start."

"You mean the Everglades."

"Where else? What other wilderness is there? The rest is all gone."

Jenna was vice-secretary of the local Sierra Club, so Keyes knew it wouldn't take much to launch her off on a big speech. He had to be careful. "Jenna, the Everglades are three times bigger than Rhode Island," he said. "I'll need a few more clues."

"Oh, I don't know," she said. The wine was almost gone. She went to the refrigerator and opened another bottle.

Remembering Jenna drunk, Keyes thought: This could be promising.

"I've got an idea," Jenna said as she filled their glasses. "Here, hold this." Quickly she cleared the top of the coffin, uprooting the vase, collecting the coasters, sweeping the magazines to the carpet. Then she unfastened the clasps and opened the lid. She'd been telling the truth: the coffin was full of newspaper clippings.

Jenna dropped to her knees, the wineglass poised in her left hand. Methodically she began to explore Skip Wiley's unusual personal library. "A few months back," she said, "he did a column about a place near the dike."

Keyes knelt next to her and joined the search. Concentration was impossible, Jenna looking the way she did, smelling so warm and familiar.

"He used to go fishing at this place," she was saying, "when he was a boy. Not long ago he discovered that they'd built a huge development right there, next to the old dike on the edge of the Glades. A retirement community, they called it. Stocked with three thousand geezers from Jersey. Skip was livid."

"I remember the column," Keyes said. " 'Varicose Village.' "

"Right! That'd be a good place to start. Maybe he's camping out. Planning something big."

"Oh boy," Keyes said.

Somehow Jenna located the column amid the random litter of Wiley's coffin. She slid over to show it to Keyes and practically nestled in his lap. He was not certain if she was doing this out of pity, or just to tease. He wanted to give her the benefit of the doubt. He also wanted to take her in his arms and make her forget all about Skip Wiley.

"The name of the place," Jenna said, all wine-woozy, "is Otter Creek Village. Three miles off State Road 84, it says here. Near the old bombing range."

"I can find it."

"He grew up not far from there," Jenna said. "And his family had a cabin out at Sawgrass."

"Okay, I'll look around out there tomorrow."

"Thank you, Brian," Jenna said. She kissed him lightly on the lips and snuggled against his shoulder. Keyes slipped his right arm around her; it was a brotherly little hug, not a very good one. He wished he weren't so damn nervous. Still, he was thrilled to be there, alone with Jenna and no crazy Wiley, just old JT singing "Fire and Rain" on the stereo. Keyes loved the scent of Jenna's neck, and the sweet narcotic sound of her breathing. He could have stayed that way for hours, hopelessly consumed by her presence, clutching her like a bedtime doll. With Keyes, nothing had changed; as for Jenna, it was hard to tell.

"Brian?"

"Yes, Jenna."

"I'm getting sleepy." She looked up from his chest. "I think I'd better go to bed."

She uncurled like a cat, stretching the lavender leotard in a dozen breathtaking ways. She closed the coffin, yawned, and said, "Well."

Keyes waited, clinging to hope.

But then she said: "It's time for you to go home and get some rest."

"Good idea," Keyes said with a brave smile.

He drove off in a pinprickly sweat—euphoric, suicidal, utterly confused. All over again, he thought. God help me.

TEN

Overnight the weather cooled, and a fresh north wind brought an early whisper of winter.

Brian Keyes awoke at dawn, surprised by the dry chill. He slipped into blue jeans, foraged for a sweater, and went outside to crank up the car. The old MG was a marvelous summertime sportster, but on cold mornings the engine balked. Keyes let it warm for a full ten minutes. He used the time as unwisely as possible, reliving the dinner with Jenna and devising romantic strategy.

From Miami he took the turnpike north to Road 84, a clamorous truck route that runs cross-state from Fort Lauderdale. Despite the gray gauze in the sky and the whipping wind, the highway was clogged with boxy Winnebagos, custom vans, and station wagons dragging metallic-purple bass boats—the usual weekend lemmings.

Over the years civilization doggedly had followed Road 84 toward the lip of the Everglades. Heading west, Keyes could chart the march of the chain saws and bulldozers. What once had been misty pastureland and pine barrens were now golden-age trailer parks; medieval cypress stands had been replaced by 7-Elevens and coin laundries. And spreading like a spore across the mottled landscape was every developer's wet dream, the condominium cluster.

Later as he walked along the dike, hands in his pockets, Keyes marveled at the contrast: to the western horizon, nothing but sawgrass and hammock and silent swamp; to the east, diesel cranes and cinderblock husks and high-rises. Not a hundred yards stood between the backhoes and the last of South Florida's wilderness. It had been a while since Keyes had driven this far west, and he was startled by what he saw. No wonder Skip Wiley had been so pissed off.

Keyes was nearly two miles from where he'd parked the car when he came to the Otter Creek condominium. He smiled, remembering Wiley's snide column. "Talk about false advertising. There's no creek, and there's damn sure no otters—no live ones, anyway."

Otter Creek Village consisted of three cheerless buildings set end-to-end at mild angles. Each warren stood five stories high and was painted white with canary-yellow trim. Every apartment featured a tiny balcony that overlooked a notably unscenic parking lot. From the dike Keyes could see a solid acre of shuffleboard courts, crisp formations of aluminum lounge chairs, and a vast ulcer-shaped swimming pool. In the center of the complex, surrounded by a twenty-foot chain-link fence, was an asphalt tennis court with faded lines and no net. The entire recreation area was outfitted with striped table umbrellas, sprouting like festive mushrooms from the concrete.

But Otter Creek was quiet today. No one floundered in the pool, and the shuffleboard courts lay deserted; the cold weather had driven the retirees inside.

Keyes finally spotted one old gentleman, bundled in fluorescent rain gear, walking a hyperactive terrier along the banks of a murky manmade canal. "Great fishing in your own backyard!" is what the Otter Creek brochure promised. Keyes didn't know much about fishing, but he had grave doubts about any creature that could procreate in such fetid water.

On the other side of the dike, in the Glades, the wind sent ripples through the dense sawgrass. Keyes broke out the binoculars and scanned the marsh. Somewhere out there, not far, stood the Wiley family cabin. Jenna had said you could find it with a good pair of field glasses, so Keyes had brought the Nikons.

Before long he spotted a row of snowy egrets, hunched along a tall fence; except it wasn't a fence, but a rooftop, an angular anomaly among the bush cattails and the scrub. Keyes trotted down the dike for a better look. The closer he got, the more the cabin showed above the swamp. The walls were made of plywood, the roof of corrugated tin. There was a crooked porch, a faded outhouse, and torn screens fluttering in the windows.

Keyes was most impressed by the fact that Wiley's cabin had been built on cypress stilts, smack in the middle of wetlands. There was no way to get there by foot.

He hiked along the dike until he drew even with the cabin; from the roof the egrets eyed him warily, flaring their nape feathers. Keyes guessed he was still a hundred yards away, with nothing but dark water and lily pads between him and the shack. He trained the Nikons and searched for signs of habitation.

The place looked empty and disused. A rusted

padlock hung on the door, and the rails of the porch were plastered with petrified bird droppings. There was no boat anywhere, no smoke from the flue, no trace of a human being.

Except for the boots.

Brian Keyes knelt on the gravel of the dike and fiddled with the focus dial on the binoculars.

They were boots, all right. Brown cowboy boots, brand-new ones, judging from the shine off the toes. The boots lay on a plank beneath the warped door of the outhouse, and from their pristine condition (absent of bird speckles) it was apparent they hadn't been there very long.

Keyes knew what he had to do now: he had to find a sensible way to get out to Wiley's cabin. Swimming was out of the question. He had not quit the newspaper business to go frolic in the muck with water moccasins, not even for five hundred bucks a day.

So Brian Keyes went looking for a boat.

"Sit down, García."

Al García settled in a chair. Harold Keefe, the big redheaded detective, cleared his throat, as if he'd been practicing for this. He picked up a copy of the Miami *Sun* and waved it in front of García's face. "You wanna explain this!"

"Explain what, Hal?"

"This quotation here from Metro-Dade detective Alberto García. *The case is still under investigation: I can't comment.* You wanna explain that!"

García said, "No comment is what I'm supposed to

say. That's department policy. It's right there on the fucking bulletin board."

Hal rolled up the newspaper and slammed it on the desk, as if killing a cockroach. "Not for *this* case it's not policy. This case is closed, remember?"

García ground his teeth and tried not to say something he'd regret. "Hal, this guy Bloodworth calls me out of the blue last night, okay? Says he's talked to these two guys, these Shriners, who tell him about their missing pal, Mr. Bellamy. You 'member Bellamy, don't you?"

Hal just scowled and waved his hand.

"Anyway," García said, "this hump Bloodworth says he heard there's some connection between Bellamy and Sparky Harper. Extortion letters is what he heard. Says he's writing a story on Bellamy's disappearance."

"Oh, and that he did." Hal fingered the newspaper. "Ran Mr. Bellamy's picture, offered a five-thousand-dollar reward for any information, et cetera. Nothing wrong with that, García. But you didn't have to say what you said, especially the way you said it."

"All I said was no comment."

"And where'd you learn how to do that, the Meyer Lansky School of Public Relations? You made it sound like we're hiding something." Hal rose to his feet. "Why couldn't you just say the case is closed? Say we caught the killer and he tragically took his own life in jail. That's the last chapter of the Sparky Harper case. Period."

"Then what about Bellamy?" García asked.

Hal's face was redder than García had ever seen it, and basketball-sized sweat marks showed under the arms of his blue polyester shirt. Obviously Hal had been having a crummy day.

"Bellamy was a drunk. Fell in the ocean and drowned," Hal said. "Forget about fucking Bellamy."

"Then what about the *Fuego* letter?"

Hal folded his hands, a contrived gesture of civility. Harold Keefe was not a man who looked natural with folded hands. He said, "I'm glad you mentioned the letters. We've determined that they're a hoax."

García raised his eyebrows, but didn't say a word. He sensed that Hal was building up to something memorable.

"We showed the *Fuego* letters to Dr. Remond Courtney, the famous psychiatrist. He says the letters are phony, and the boys in the lab agree. Didn't surprise me at all, since there's been no ransom demands, no bodies . . ."

"'Cept for Harper," García mumbled.

"Forget fucking Harper! I'm talking about Bellamy and the other one."

"What other one?"

"Here. Turned up this morning." Hal passed a Xerox copy across the desk.

The letter was identical to the others. "Who's Mssr. Richaud?" García asked, trying not to sound too interested.

"David Richaud is the male friend of one Renee LeVoux." Hal pronounced it lay-vox. "Miss LeVoux disappeared three days ago from the parking lot of the Seaquarium. Richaud filed a missing-persons report. Yesterday this letter was delivered to his hotel on Key Biscayne."

"What's the guy's story?" asked García.

"He says the lady was kidnapped. Claims the perpetrator whacked him on the head and knocked him out."

"You don't sound like you believe him."

Hal laughed caustically. "This one's got 'domestic' written all over it. They had a fight, she grabs a cab and heads south with the vacation money. Richaud gets furious and figures the best way to find her is to get the cops involved. Pretty obvious, I'd say."

"Hmmm," said Al García.

"Which brings us to the letters." Hal opened a drawer and pulled out a file. García knew that now was a good time to start worrying.

"Had a little talk with the chief this morning," Hal said. Al García looked unimpressed; Hal was always having little talks with the chief.

He said, "The chief seems to think these letters are being generated from within the police department."

García snorted. "He thinks *El Fuego* is a cop?"

"The chief," Hal said sternly, "is quite serious. He ordered me to start an internal investigation. He thinks someone around here is writing these phony letters in order to keep the Sparky Harper case alive."

"Why?"

Hal shrugged disingenuously. "Ambition, spite, maybe even professional jealousy. Who knows? In any case, the chief's theory makes perfect sense. Whoever's sending these crazy letters obviously is getting the names out of Missing Persons."

Enough is enough, García thought. "Hal," he said, "you're full of shit. And so's the chief."

Hal's face turned the color of grape juice.

"Somebody's snatching tourists," García said, "and

all you guys want to do is cover up. I got a better idea: why don't we just go out and catch the goddamn kidnappers? Come on, Hal, it'll be fun. Just like the old days, back when you were a cop and not a two-bit office politician."

Ominously Hal opened the file. Inside was a pink memorandum, nothing else. "Detective García," he said, "as of today you're on limited duty. It's indefinite, until our investigation is completed. I.A.D. wants to talk to you, so you might think about getting a lawyer."

"Beautiful," García muttered.

Hal slapped the file shut. "You'll be working the late shift," he said, "at the motor pool."

"Oh-oh, the combat zone."

"It's not so bad . . . oh, by the way, there'll be some officers coming by your house later. Just to look around."

"Hal, they'll be wasting their time. I don't own a typewriter."

"Just the same, try to cooperate."

"But, Hal—"

"You may go now," said Harold Keefe, in his best high-school principal's voice, "and try to stay out of trouble until this is over. Don't talk to any more reporters . . . or private eyes, for that matter."

García leaned over and loudly planted his knuckles on the desk. "Hal," he said, "you're too dumb to see it, but this whole thing's gonna blow up in your fat Irish face."

Brian Keyes drove west at a furious speed, slowing at every intersection, scouting each tacky shopping plaza.

Finally he spotted a peeling sign that said "Canoe Rentals" and screeched off the highway.

The name of the place was Mel's Bait and Tackle, and Mel himself was very busy dipping live shiners from the bait well. He told Keyes to take a seat near the soda machine and he'd get around to him in a little bit. Keyes politely mentioned that he was in a slight hurry, but he might as well have told it to the stuffed buck on the wall.

After fifteen minutes or so, Mel finally turned around, holstered his dip net, and asked Keyes what exactly he could do for him.

"I'd like to rent a canoe."

"I'll need a deposit," said Mel, eyeing him. "And I'll need to know how'n hail you gonna get that canoe on toppa yore car."

Mel had a point. The canoe was four feet longer than the MG.

"I'll need to borrow some rope."

"No sir, you'll be need'n to *buy* some."

"I see," Keyes said. "And the boat racks?"

"Those I'll rent ya."

By the time the negotiations ended, Keyes was out thirty-seven dollars and his American Express card, which Mel confiscated as a security deposit.

Keyes made a courageous solo attempt to tie the aluminum canoe on the MG, but the boat flopped off the roof and landed with a crash on the macadam. The noise brought Mel shuffling out of the tackle shop, cursing heatedly. He was an older fellow—late fifties, paunchy, tired-looking—but he proved to be one strong sonofabitch when it came to canoes. He told Keyes to go sit inside and read some magazines, and in five minutes the job was neatly done.

"Lemme ask you sumpthin', if you don't mind," Mel said. "I don't see no fishing rods and I don't see no shotguns and I don't see no bow and arrow. So just where 'n hail you goin' with this canoe, and what you gonna do when you get there?"

Keyes plucked the binocular case from the car and held it up for Mel to see. "I'm a birdwatcher," he said brightly.

Mel nodded, but he looked skeptical. "Well," he said after a pause, "good luck with your snipes or wood-peckers or whatever the hail yore after. But don't put no more scratches on my damn boat!"

The canoe was lashed so tightly to the MG that the ropes sang on the highway. Back on the dike, Keyes had a hell of a time unraveling Mel's knots. Finally he was able to drag the canoe off the MG and slide it down the bank into the water. He climbed in tentatively, the oar tucked under one arm. He lowered himself to his knees and gingerly rocked the canoe, testing its stability. It seemed steady.

Keyes centered himself and began to paddle down the dike canal toward Wiley's cabin.

It was an adventurous feeling, gliding so low and alone through the Everglades. Keyes was swept away by the lushness of the scenery, a welcome distraction from his anxiety. He was no great outdoorsman but his discomfort was born of unfamiliarity, not fear. Keyes had been raised in the relentlessly civilized environs of Washington, D.C., and the only wild animals he'd ever confronted were the brazen gray squirrels of Rock Creek Park. Except for one miserable summer at a snotty boys' camp in northern Virginia, Keyes had spent almost no time out of the city. Since moving to Florida he'd heard the hoary tales of panthers, poisonous snakes, and killer alligators, and though he dismissed most of it as cracker mythology, Keyes did not savor the idea of a chance encounter. Wiley, if indeed he was out here, would be beast enough.

Keyes found a steady rhythm for the oar, and his confidence grew with each stroke. Even against the wind he made good time down the canal. By now it was an hour past noon and the gray clouds had dissipated; the sun quickly burned off the last of the morning's chill. The wetlands stirred under the heat. The cicadas and grasshoppers brassily came to life in the sawgrass, and once an old mossback terrapin clambered off the dike like a rolling helmet, plopping into the water three feet from the canoe. High overhead Keyes spotted a line of turkey vultures gliding in the thermals, scouting for carrion.

Somehow the dike sealed the Glades from the clamor of suburban Broward County; though Keyes was only a solid four-iron away from civilization, he could neither see it nor hear it. He felt himself distant, and growing tranquil.

After more than an hour he located the cabin. Keyes paddled faster, the bow of the canoe swishing through the ragged grass and pickerel weed. At fifty yards he slowed and let the canoe glide while he raised the binoculars one last time.

The western boots still lay beneath the outhouse, and the cabin still looked empty.

Brian Keyes didn't notice that the snowy egrets had flown away.

As he tied up to a rotted piling, a green chameleon scampered off the porch to munch a palmetto bug in the shadows. Keyes climbed lightly from the canoe, but the planks still shuddered under his weight. He took each step as if walking on ice, thinking: There's no way Skip Wiley could be hiding here, not the way he bangs around.

Keyes tested the padlock with a hard yank, and the rusty hasp gave way with a snap. He opened the cabin door with the toe of his sneaker and peered inside.

It looked like a dungeon for Boy Scouts.

Spiderwebs streeled from the ceiling, and a crisp snake-skin fluttered from the pine beam where it had long ago been shed. A shaky card table, once used for dining, buckled under unopened tins of Spam and sausage, the labels faded and curled. In the rear of the cabin was a bunk bed with two plastic air mattresses, each flattened and stained by mildew. In a corner two sleeping bags were rolled up tight, flecked with papery dead moths. A stack of heat-puckered magazines lay nearby; the most recent was a *Playboy* from December 1978.

In the kitchen area he found a sixty-gallon Igloo cooler; inside was a six-pack of flat Budweisers and three plastic jugs of drinking water. Keyes was about to open one of the jugs when he noticed a sediment of dubious origin suspended near the bottom. The water, he decided without tasting, had also been there a very long time.

The cabin was no larger than fifteen by thirty feet, but Keyes found plenty of crannies to explore. He was actually enjoying himself, poking through drawers and dusty cupboards, looking for signs of Wiley. He felt a little like an archaeologist over a new dig.

What finally persuaded him to retreat was the killer leaf.

Keyes had been using a whippy length of cane to clear out the spider nests, and he flicked it casually at a wrinkled gray-veined leaf beneath the card table. Suddenly the leaf sprang off the floor and, teeth bared, whistled past Keyes's ear. He stumbled out the door, shouting and brandishing the cane stick impotently. The angry bat followed him, diving in tight arcs, breaking off the attack only when hit by sunlight.

Keyes was not sure where the creature went, but he warily scanned the stratosphere from a protective crouch. He decided the bat was welcome to the solitude of the cabin; he'd wait outside for Skip Wiley or whoever owned those cowboy boots.

The afternoon passed slowly through the binoculars. Keyes didn't lay eyes on another human being, and he found himself living up to his lie, watching the birds of the Everglades: cormorants, ospreys, grackles, red-shouldered hawks, even a pair of roseate spoonbills. Finding the birds was an amusing challenge but, once spotted, they did not exactly put on a breathtaking show. The fact was, most of the birds seemed to be watching *him*.

Keyes finally was forced to avail himself of the outhouse—an act of sheer courage—and he stopped on the way out to study the mysterious cowboy boots. They were Tony Lamas, size eleven, with no name inside. Keyes was careful not to move them.

As the sun dropped and a lemon twilight settled on the shack, Keyes knew it was decision time. Once darkness came, there was no getting out of the Glades without a beacon. He'd have to spend the night with no food, no water and, most critically, no bug repellent. December wasn't a prime mosquito season, but a horsefly had already extracted a chunk of Keyes's ankle to remind him that billions of other starving insects were waiting their turns.

And then there was Mel, who had warned him to have the canoe back at dusk, or else. Keyes imagined all the random damage that a man like Mel could do with his American Express card, and decided to call it a day.

He fitted the binoculars into the case and climbed into the canoe. He slipped the half-hitch over the piling and pushed off with both hands. As the canoe skimmed away from the cabin, Keyes rose to his knees and reached for the oar.

But the oar was gone.

It *couldn't* be. But it was.

Fore and aft, the bottom of the canoe was empty.

Keyes carefully turned around so he could see the cabin—it couldn't be more than twenty yards away. He needed to get back there, to get his feet on something solid. Then he'd try to figure out what the hell was going on.

He inched to the prow and found a comfortable position. With both hands Keyes began to paddle vigorously, fracturing the calm of the pond. Yet the canoe scarcely moved.

The boat was nestled firmly in a patch of hyacinth weeds. The fat green bulbs and fibrous stems clung to the hull and made it impossible to get up a head of steam. Keyes desperately needed something to hack the boat free.

The uneasiness in his gut started to feel a little like panic. He feared that he was being watched; that whoever owned the western boots had stolen the oar from the canoe, and that whoever had stolen the oar didn't want him to go.

"Skip!" Keyes shouted. "Skip, are you there?"

But the marsh swallowed his voice, and only the shrill cicadas replied.

Keyes decided it was vital not to abandon the canoe. He regarded himself a competent swimmer, but realized that this was not Lake Louise at scenic Camp Trailblazer—this was serious swamp. With no buddy system, unless you counted eels.

Keyes couldn't be sure how deep the tea-colored water was, but he knew the weeds would make swimming treacherous. He was scared of getting tangled underwater, or sucked down by the muck. True, it was only twenty yards to the cabin, but it was a nasty goddamn twenty yards.

He leaned across the bow and began ripping up the hyacinths and tossing them aside in sodden stringy slumps. Painstakingly Keyes labored to clear a channel for the stymied canoe, but night came too quickly. He tried again to paddle by hand; this time the canoe moved six, seven, maybe eight feet before the knotted lilies seized it.

Brian Keyes was stuck. Robbed of detail, the cabin became a blocky shape in the darkness; to the east, the dike formed a perfectly linear horizon. Keyes sat back on his heels, his hands dripping water down the gunwales. His face was damp, and gnats were starting to buzz in his ears and eyes. He wasn't thinking about Mel anymore. He was thinking that this could be the worst night of his life.

Overhead, nighthawks sliced the sky, gulping bugs, and a big owl hooted twice from a faraway oak. The wind was dead now, so Keyes could hear every secret rustling in the swamp, though he could see almost nothing. After an hour he stopped trying to see at all, and just imagined—imagined that the sharp splash near the dike was only a heron spearing a minnow; imagined that the creaking plank was just a wood rat exploring the empty cabin; imagined that the piercing wail that seemed to float forever across the Glades was only a bobcat ending a hunt.

Keyes lay down in the canoe and propped his head on the leather binocular case. Even the sky was blank, held starless by the high clouds. With some effort he managed to close his eyes and tune out the traffic of the wilderness.

He thought of Jenna and felt stupid: she'd done it to him again, with one lousy dinner. He was marooned out here because he'd listened to her, and because he'd enjoyed the improbable notion that she needed him. He should have known there'd be trouble; with Jenna, you could bank on it. Keyes imagined her at that moment, puttering around the kitchen making dinner, or doing those damn Jane Fonda leg-lifts on the living-room rug. If she were worried at all, it was about Skip Wiley, not him.

Wiley. Stealing the oar from the canoe was the sort of stunt Wiley would pull, Keyes thought. But why didn't I hear anything? Where could he be hiding? And what was he waiting for? For Christ's sake, the joke was over.

Keyes sat up slowly in the canoe, suddenly aware that the crickets and the nighthawks had fallen silent. The Everglades had become perfectly still.

Something was wrong.

Keyes knew, from watching Tarzan movies as a kid, that whenever the jungle became quiet, something terrible was about to happen. The cannibals were about to attack or the elephants were about to stampede or a leopard was about to get dinner—any of which seemed preferable to one of Skip Wiley's surprise visits. Keyes wished like hell that he'd brought the cane bough with him on board the canoe.

A shadow materialized on the porch of Wiley's cabin.

It was a man's form, erect but motionless. In the emptiness of the night Keyes could hear the man breathing. He also heard the frantic hammering of his own heart.

"Wiley?"

The figure didn't move. Featureless, it appeared to face him with folded arms.

"Skip, get me outta here, dammit." Keyes forced a laugh, brittle with fear. With bloodless knuckles he clutched the gunwales of the canoe. "Skip?"

The shadow on the porch stepped back until it filled the frame of the cabin door. Muscles knotting, Keyes peered at the mute figure. He felt a cool drop of sweat trickle down his spine, and he shuddered. He was ready to dive from the canoe at the first glint of a gun.

"Look, I don't know who you are, but I don't mean any harm," Keyes said.

Nothing from the specter.

"Please, wave your hand if you can hear me," Keyes implored.

To his astonishment, the pensive shadow raised its right hand and waved. Keyes smiled inwardly, thinking: At last, progress!—not realizing that the man's gesture was not a wave at all, but a signal.

Idiotically Keyes raised his own right hand in amiable reciprocation. He remained so transfixed by the figure at the cabin that he didn't see what he should have seen: a dark brown hand, bare and smooth, rising from the water and alighting on the starboard side of the canoe, precisely where his own hand had been.

When Keyes finally was distracted from the silent watcher, it was not by other sights or sounds, but by a paralyzing centrifugal sensation.

The canoe was spinning out from under him.

He was in the air.

He was in the water.

He was blinded, and he was choking.

He was swallowed into the throat of the swamp.

ELEVEN

"**Wake up, Jungle** Boy!"

Brian Keyes blinked the sting from his eyes and started coughing up swamp water.

"Not even a civil hello. How do you like that?"

"Hello, Skip," Keyes said, between hacks.

They were in a clearing, deep in a cypress hammock. Smoke hung sweetly in the night air and a fire crackled, shooting sparks into the canopy. Hands bound, Keyes sat on bare ground against the trunk of a dwarf cypress. A cool breeze announced that he'd been stripped to his underwear. A tendril of wet hydrilla weed clung to his forehead.

"Cut me loose, Skip."

Wiley grinned, his huge elastic face full of good humor.

"What do you think of the beard, Brian?"

"Very nice. Cut me loose, you asshole."

Chuckling, Wiley ambled back to the campfire. Keyes saw that he wasn't alone; other figures moved quietly on the fringe of the clearing, conversing in low tones. Soon Wiley returned carrying a coffee mug.

"Hot tea," he declared. "All natural herbs. Here, it'll put lead in your pencil."

Keyes shook his head. "No thanks."

"So how're things in the private-eye business?"

"A little strange, at the moment."

Wiley was barefoot. He wore pleated khaki trousers and a cream-colored smock with two red horizontal stripes (pseudo-African, Keyes guessed). His rebellious hair had been raked straight back, giving a blond helmet effect, and the new beard bristled thick and reddish. Keyes had to admit that Skip Wiley was still a man of considerable presence.

"I guess you want an explanation."

"Naw," said Keyes. "This happens all the time."

"You're deep in the Everglades," Wiley said. "This is my camp. I'm hiding out."

"And doing the worst Kurtz I ever saw."

"Let's wait for history to make that judgment. And stop that funny business with your hands. That's not rope, it's oiled sawgrass. You keep trying to get loose and it'll cut through the veins of your wrist. Bleed to death in nine minutes flat."

Keyes craned a glance over his shoulder and saw that Wiley was telling the truth. He stopped struggling.

"Where are my clothes?"

"We've got 'em hung by the fire, drying out."

"We?"

"*Las Noches de Diciembre.* The Nights of December."

"Oh, Skip, no," Keyes said dispiritedly. It had not occurred to him that Wiley was mixed up with the kidnappings, yet it made perfect sense. Wiley had never been predictable, except in his passion for extremes. The symbolism of Bellamy and Harper was so obvious that Keyes felt dim and stupid.

"Don't look so bummed out," Wiley said. "Now's a

good time to meet the rest of the guys." He clapped his enormous hands. Three figures emerged from the shadows and assembled behind him. Keyes looked up to their faces, backlighted by the fire.

"Brian, I'd like you to meet the group. The big fellow here is Viceroy Wilson—you may have heard of him."

Keyes said, "I think we met at Pauly's Bar."

"Yeah," Wilson said, "my fist met your head."

"And this," Wiley said cheerfully, "is Jesús Bernal."

Bernal was a jittery little Latin in a stringy undershirt. Keyes immediately noticed a strong resemblance in stature and complexion to Ernesto Cabal; no wonder Al García's witnesses had been eighty percent sure.

Jesús Bernal shot Keyes a contemptuous glance before slipping into the shadows. Wilson followed in a sullen gait.

"Viceroy hates you 'cause you look like a cop, and Jesús is just a little shy," Wiley explained. He threw his arm around the third man. "But here's the guy who made all this possible. Tom Tigertail. Tommy, say hi to Mr. Keyes."

Tommy Tigertail leaned forward to study the half-naked prisoner. Tommy was a handsome young Seminole: late twenties, medium height, lean but showing plenty of muscle. He had longish black hair and a classic Creek face, with high cheekbones and Oriental eyes. He wore jeans but no shirt, just a towel slung around his neck.

"You're not hurt," he said to Keyes.

"Naw, a little queasy is all."

"You put up a strong fight," Tommy said. "Swallowed half the pond."

"You were the one under the canoe?"

Wiley piped, "Tommy's one helluva swimmer!"

Expressionless, Tommy walked back to the fire to join the others.

"That young man," Wiley whispered proudly, "is worth five million dollars. Can you believe it? He made it all on Indian bingo. Got four bingo halls in South Florida—see, gambling's legal on the reservations. Perfectly legal. You can't put a casino on Miami Beach but you could open one smack in the middle of the Big Cypress. It's goddamn brilliant irony, isn't it, Brian? Little old blue-hair paleskins from all over creation come to bet Seminole bingo and the Indians make a killing. Ha! Bury my heart at Chase Manhattan! Tommy's the business manager so the tribe cuts him in for the biggest chunk. Already he's put away five fucking million dollars!"

"So what's he doing out here instead of the Galt Ocean Mile?"

Wiley looked disappointed at the remark. "Tommy's out here," he said, "because he *believes* in me. He believes in what we're doing."

"And what is that, Skip?"

"Well, in Tommy's case, we're launching the Fourth Great Seminole War. In the case of my little Cuban friend, we are advancing the cause of international right-wing terrorism. And as far as Mr. Viceroy Wilson is concerned, we are kicking the living shit out of whitey." Wiley bent over and dropped to a whisper again. "See, Brian, each of these guys has his own particular constituency. My job, as I see it, is to make them feel equally important. It's a delicate balance, believe me. These are not the most stable human beings in the world, but they've got loads of energy. It's damned inspiring."

Keyes said, "What about you, Skip? What's your constituency?"

"Come on!" Wiley's brow furrowed. "You don't *know*?"

Somewhere in the brush an animal scampered, emitting a high-pitched trill, Keyes glanced toward the darkness apprehensively.

"Relax," Wiley said. "Just a raccoon. My constituency, Brian. Along with the eagles, the opossums, the otters, the snakes, even the buzzards. All of this belongs to them, and more. Every goddamn acre, from here west to Miami Beach and north to the big lake, belongs to them. It got stolen away, and what we're going to do . . ." Wiley made a fist and shook it. " . . . is get it back."

Keyes thought: A cross between Dr. Dolittle and Che Guevara. Wait'll I tell Cab Mulcahy.

"Don't give me that you-poor-sick-boy look," Wiley said. "I'm just fine, couldn't be better. You're the one who's got a problem, Brian. A big goddamn problem, I might add. Before this is over you're gonna wish you were back at the *Sun*, covering the bozos in the mayor's race."

Keyes said, "I'll take some of that tea now."

He was trying to slow Wiley down, keep him from getting too wound up. Keyes remembered what Wiley could be like on one of his fast burns, all reckless fury.

Wiley held the hot mug to Keyes's lips and let him sip.

"Brian," he said giddily. "We're gonna empty out this entire state. Give it back to Tom and his folks. Give it back to the bloody raccoons. Imagine: all the condos, the cheesy hotels, the trailer parks, the motor courts, the town houses, fucking Disney World—a ghost town, old pal. All the morons who thundered into Florida the past thirty years and made such a mess are gonna thunder right out again ... the ones who don't die in the stampede."

Skip Wiley's brown eyes were steady and intense; he was perfectly serious. Brian Keyes wondered if he was face to face with raw insanity.

"How are you going to accomplish this miracle?" he asked.

"Publicity, old pal. *Bad* publicity." Wiley cackled. "It's my specialty, remember? We're going to take all the postcard puffery and jam it in reverse. The swaying palms, the murmuring surf, the tropical sun—from now on, Transylvania South."

A postcard to end all postcards, Keyes thought.

"When I say bad publicity," Wiley went on, "search the extreme limits of your imagination. Think back to some of the planet's great disasters—the bubonic plague, Pompeii, Hiroshima. Imagine being tourism director for the city of Hiroshima in 1946! What would you do, Brian? Or think modern times: try to sell timeshares in West Beirut! Christ, that's a tall order, but it's nothing compared to what it's going to be like down here when we're finished, me and the guys. By the time we're through, old pal, Marge and Fred and the kids will vacation in the fucking Arctic *tundra* before they'll set foot on Miami Beach."

Wiley was pacing before the fire, his voice booming through the copse. Viceroy Wilson sat impassively on a tree stump, Kleenexing the lenses of his sunglasses. Jesús

Bernal swatted at gnats and moved herky-jerky in the firelight, tossing his knife at a tree. Tommy Tigertail was out there somewhere, but Brian Keyes couldn't see him.

"Did you kill Sparky Harper?" Keyes asked Skip Wiley.

"Ho-ho-ho."

The suntan oil, the rubber alligator, the tacky Hawaiian shirt. Keyes thought: Who else but Wiley?

"And Ted Bellamy, the Shriner?"

"I'm afraid he's dead," Wiley said, tossing a stick in the fire.

"What about the girl at the Seaquarium?" Keyes asked.

"Brian, settle down. We're simply trying to establish credibility. Nobody took us seriously after the Harper episode. Jesús, *amigo*, get my briefcase."

"My God, Skip, you're talking about *murder*! Three innocent people—four, if you count Ernesto Cabal. You set him up, didn't you?"

"It was Viceroy's idea, to get rid of the car," Wiley acknowledged. "He was your client, I know, and I'm sorry he killed himself. By the way, did you really stab his lawyer in the tongue with a shrimp fork? That was wonderful, Brian, I was so goddamn proud when I heard about it. Made me think you must've learned something, all that time sitting next to me. For what it's worth, we had planned to spring little Ernesto when the time was right."

"*Es verdad*," Jesús said, delivering the briefcase.

"Speak English, you shmuck," Wiley snapped. He turned to Keyes, complaining: "The man was born in

Trenton and still he's doing Desi Arnaz. Drives me nuts."

Jesús Bernal slouched away, pouting. Wiley opened the briefcase and said, "Might as well get the preliminaries out of the way. Pay attention, Brian." Wiley held up a pair of plaid swim trunks. "Theodore Bellamy," he said.

"I believe you," said Keyes.

Next Wiley produced a crimson halter top. "Renee What's-her-face, the Canadian girl."

Keyes nodded blankly.

With both hands Wiley dangled a man's silver necklace with a gaudy octagonal charm. "Sparky Harper was wearing this," Wiley said, studying it in the firelight. "It says 'Sunshine State Booster of the Year, 1977.' Got his name engraved on the back. Be sure to point that out."

Wiley dropped the articles into the briefcase and snapped it shut. "You'll take this back to Miami, please."

Keyes felt relieved. He'd been contemplating the possibility of dying out here in the swamp and not liking the idea at all, dead in his underwear and covered with bug bites.

"Saw Bloodworth's column," Wiley said. "What a hack."

"He's not in your league, that's for sure."

"He's a dim-witted gerbil who can't write his name. *Strangled to death* is redundant, doesn't he know that?" Wiley fumed. "If it'd been you, you would have put it together two days ago. You'd have connected everything—Harper, Bellamy, Renee. Hell, you would have printed our letters."

"And you would have loved it," Keyes said.

Wiley wasn't listening. "Brian, I know you've still got good police sources. What do you hear?"

Viceroy Wilson edged a little closer. He was always interested in cop news.

"Metro homicide closed the Harper case when Ernesto died," Keyes said. "As for the other two, a big zero. Missing persons, that's all."

"Damn!" Wiley exploded. "Those silly shitheads have got murderous terrorists on the loose and they don't even know it! See what I mean about credibility, Brian? What do we have to do? Tell me, Viceroy, you're the historian. Did the SLA have this problem?"

"Naw, they had Patty Hearst," Wilson replied laconically. "Got plenty of ink. Maybe we can brainwash us some famous white bitch."

"*Sí*," said Jesús Bernal, digging his knife from a gumbo-limbo tree. "Pia Zadora!"

Wiley sat cross-legged in front of Keyes. "See what I'm up against," he muttered.

"Skip—or is it *El Fuego* now?"

"Skip is fine."

"Okay, what do you want from me?"

"We need a witness," Wiley said momentously. "Someone impeccable. Someone who can go back to Miami and attest that we are legitimate, that we're deadly serious. Brian, we want *recognition*. We want the police and the press and the politicians and the tourist board to take us seriously."

"In other words, you want your names in the paper?"

"The Nights of December? Yes. Mine? No. Not until the time comes." Wiley leaned closer. "If you go back and tell the cops about me, it would complicate our plans. Jeopardize everything. Now, should you decide to play Boy Scout and spill the beans, fine. But if you do, Brian, you'll deeply regret it. All hell will break loose, and what's happened so far—the kidnappings, Sparky Harper, the rest—is gonna seem like *Mister Rogers' Neighborhood*. You understand what I'm saying? If I should pick up the *Sun* tomorrow and see my face, then me and my comrades shift into overdrive. Moderation goes out the window. And then I'm afraid some folks you and I both know, and care about, are going to wind up suddenly deceased. We're talking massacre with a capital M."

Keyes had never seen Wiley so grim, or heard his voice so leaden. He wondered if Wiley meant Jenna, or Cab, or friends from the newspaper.

"Brian, if we do things my way, on my schedule, the violence will be minimized—I promise. If all goes well, in a few weeks the whole truth can be told. But not now—it's too early. My name would be nothing but a distraction, a liability to the organization. So my role here—well, let it be our little secret for a while. The rest of the saga is yours to tell. In fact, that's why we invited you here. Can I offer you some softshell-turtle stew?"

Keyes said: "Let me get this straight. I'm supposed to go back to Miami and scare the shit out of everybody."

"Exactly," Wiley said.

"With what, Skip? A halter top and a dime-store medallion?"

Wiley shook his head. "Those are just freebies for the cops, old pal. No, the most significant thing you'll carry back to civilization tomorrow is *testimony*."

Keyes was getting tired. His arms ached, his wrists hurt, and invisible insects were feasting in his crevices.

"Okay, Skip, I'll go back and tell the cops that a gang of crazed radicals dragged me out of a canoe, tied me to a tree, and gave me tea that tasted like goat piss. Is that what you want?"

"Not quite," Wiley said. The smile was thin, the eyes cheerless. "We want you to go back and tell everyone that you witnessed a murder."

Keyes went cold.

Wiley stood up and smoothed his pseudo-African smock. "Tommy! Jesús! Viceroy!" he called. "Go get Mrs. Kimmelman."

The morning actually had started off well for Ida Kimmelman. The arrival of the Social Security checks was always a good omen, and then her sister called from Queens to say that Joel, Ida's youngest nephew, had finally gotten into law school. It wasn't a famous law school—someplace in Ohio, with two names—but Ida went out and bought Joel a card anyway. Basically he was a good young man, a little disrespectful perhaps, but deserving of encouragement.

The truth was that Joel, as most of Ida's blood relations, couldn't stand her. They had all been fond of Lou Kimmelman, a sweet little fellow with a teasing sense of humor, but for years the clan had puzzled over how Lou could put up with Ida's tuba voice and her incredible charmlessness. Around the apartments the same was true: Lou was popular and pitied, while Ida was barely tolerated.

When Lou finally passed on, the social invitations

dried up and the fourth-floor bridge club recruited a new couple, and Ida Kimmelman was left all alone with her dog Skeeter in apartment 4-K at Otter Creek Village. Somehow the U.S. government had overlooked Lou Kimmelman's death and continued to mail a $297.75 Social Security check every month, so Ida was making out pretty well. She'd bought herself a spiffy red Ford Escort and joined a spa, and every third Tuesday she would drive Skeeter to Canine Canaan and get his little doggy toenails painted blue. Of course Ida's Otter Creek neighbors disapproved of her extravagance and thought it tacky that she boasted of her double-dipping from Social Security. Ida knew they were jealous.

She was truly ambivalent about Lou's death. On some days she felt lonely, and guessed it must be Lou she was missing. Who else had shared her life for twenty-nine years? Lou had been an accountant for a big orthopedic shoe company in Brooklyn. He had been a hard worker who had saved money in spite of Ida; Ida, who'd never wanted children of her own, who was always scheming for a new car or a tummy tuck or a new dinette. When it came time to retire, the Kimmelmans had argued about where they would go. Everyone on the block was moving to Florida, but Ida disliked everyone on the block and she didn't want to go. Instead she wanted to move to Southern California and make new friends. She wanted a condo on the beach in La Jolla.

But Lou Kimmelman had been a shrewd accountant. One painful evening, two weeks before the shoe company gave him the traditional gold Seiko sendoff, Lou had sat Ida down with the Chemical Bank passbooks and the Keogh funds and demonstrated, quite conclusively, that they couldn't afford to move to California unless they wanted to eat dried cat food the rest of their lives. Reluctantly, Ida had accepted the inevitability of Florida. After all, it was unthinkable not to go *somewhere* after your husband retired.

So they'd bought a small two-bedroom unit at Otter Creek, three doors down from the Seligsons, and Lou Kimmelman soon became captain of the fourth-floor shuffle-board team and sergeant-at-arms of the Otter Creek Home-owners' Association.

One thing Ida Kimmelman didn't miss about Lou, now that he was gone, was how he'd sit there in his madras slacks and blinding white shoes, watching TV in their new living room (which was hardly big enough for a family of squirrels), and ask, "Now aren't you glad we moved down here after all?"

Lou Kimmelman would say this three or four times a week, and Ida hated it. Sometimes she'd wonder bitterly if she hated Lou, too. She'd squeeze out on the balcony, which was actually more of a glorified ledge, and gaze at the parking lot and, beyond that, the emptiness of the Everglades. In these moments Ida would imagine how great it would be to have a town house on a bluff in La Jolla, where you could sip coffee and watch all those brown young men on their candy-colored surfboards. *That* was Ida Kimmelman's idea of retirement.

Instead she was stuck in Florida.

After Lou died, Ida had gathered all the bankbooks and E. F. Hutton statements and got the calculator to add up their worldly possessions—only to discover that Lou Kimmelman, damn his arithmetic, had been absolutely correct. Southern California was no more affordable than Gstaad.

So Ida laid her dream to rest with Lou, and vowed to make the best of it. Never would she admit to her Otter Creek neighbors that her unhappiness was anything but a widow's grief, or that sometimes, especially during Florida's steambath of a summer, she longed to be back up North, in the city, where one could actually walk to the grocery without an oxygen tank.

December, with its cooler nights, wasn't so unbearable. The snowbirds were trickling south and the condominium was a much livelier place than in August, when nothing moved but the mercury. Now Otter Creek Village was awakening slowly, soon to be clogged with other couples who'd discovered Florida as long-ago tourists or honeymooners and returned to claim it in their old age.

The center of social life was the swimming pool. Not much swimming took place, but there was a lot of serious floating, wading, and talking—by far the most competitive of all condominium sports.

When Ida went down to the pool, which wasn't often, she'd usually end up dominating some debate about the perilous traffic, the impossible interest rates, or the criminally high hospital bills. Each outrage was a harbinger of financial ruination, which was the favorite poolside topic at Otter Creek. Lately, since she'd discovered Lou's Social Security checks were still coming, Ida's stock speech on the economy had lost some of its fire and she'd avoided the daily discussions. Ida loved to express her opinions, but she loved her spa, too.

On the morning of December 8, Ida Kimmelman followed her morning routine: hot bagels, two cups of coffee, six ounces of prune juice, David Hartman, and the Fort Lauderdale *Sun-Sentinel,* which had terrific grocery coupons. By ten Ida was usually made-up and ready to walk Skeeter, but on this day she was running late because she had to go to Eckerd Drugs to buy a card for her nephew Joel the law student.

Ida returned to the apartment at ten-thirty to find a nasty little present from Skeeter on the shag in the bedroom. This was another reason she missed Lou, because Lou would always clean up after the dog; he never clobbered Skeeter or threatened to put him to sleep the way Ida did.

She was so mad about the mess in the bedroom that she hooked Skeeter to his leash and dragged him, yelping, down four flights of stairs. She led the dog out to the canal behind Otter Creek Village, near the Everglades dike, and unfastened the leash to let him run.

Ida noticed there was nobody out by the pool. She thought: These people! A touch of cold weather and they run indoors. The breeze felt good, too, although it puffed her new hairdo.

After fifteen minutes Ida Kimmelman got goose bumps and wished she'd brought a light sweater. She clapped her hands and shouted for Skeeter in a baritone that seemed to carry all the way to Orlando.

But Skeeter didn't come.

Ida picked up her pace along the canal, careful not to get too close. She called for Skeeter again, expecting any moment to see his beautifully barbered, AKC-registered poodle face hopping through the high grass along the banks of the canal.

But there was no sign of the little dog.

Ida trudged on, hollering, calling, cooing, thinking: He's just mad about what happened upstairs. He'll be back.

Soon she found herself standing in a field of scrub and palmetto, a full mile from Otter Creek. The sandspurs stuck to her slacks, and she cried out when a fat coppery ant chomped on her big toe.

"Skeeter darling," Ida Kimmelman cried, the great voice fading, "come home to Momma! Momma loves you!"

Suddenly she heard a commotion and turned to see two men waist-deep in the scrub; one black and ominous, the other small and dark. Nothing frightened Ida Kimmelman so much as the fact that the small man wore an undershirt, the mark of a true desperado.

"Have you seen my doggie?" Ida asked nervously.

The black man nodded. "Skeeter had an accident," he said. "You'd better come quick."

"What kind of accident?" Ida Kimmelman cried, forgetting her own safety and clumping after the men. "I said, what kind of accident?"

"An eagle," the black man said. "A fish eagle, ma'am."

And when Ida Kimmelman saw what was left of poor Skeeter, presented in a shoebox by the man in the undershirt, she fainted dead away. The next time she opened her eyes was in the airboat.

Standing before Brian Keyes was a plainly terrified woman in her late sixties, slightly overweight, lacquered with rouge and mascara. Her mouth was covered with two-inch hurricane tape, and her hands were tied with rope. Her shiny wine-colored hair was piled in a tangled nest on one side of her head. She was doing plenty of talking with her eyes.

Jesús Bernal cut Keyes loose and stood him up.

Skip Wiley said, "Brian, this is Mrs. Kimmelman."

"Skip, are you nuts?" Keyes said. "This is kidnapping! You and your merry men are gonna wind up at Raiford."

"Mrs. Kimmelman and her late husband discovered South Florida in 1962," Wiley said, "when they spent two weeks on gorgeous sun-drenched Miami Beach. Stayed at the Beau Rivage, shopped at Lincoln Road. Went to see a Jackie Gleason show live, right, Mrs. Kimmelman?"

Ida Kimmelman nodded.

"Had such a good time, they came back again and again," Wiley said, "and when Mr. Kimmelman, rest his soul, retired, they moved down here for good. Bought a unit out at Otter Creek Village, forty-two-five at twelve percent. A very tasteful place, Mrs. Kimmelman, I must say."

"Mmmmmm," Ida Kimmelman protested through the tape.

"Skip, let her go."

"Can't do that, Brian."

Viceroy Wilson held one of Ida Kimmelman's pale arms, and Tommy Tigertail the other. Wiley jerked his head and they led her out of the clearing into the darkness.

"Skip, I don't need to see any more. Let her go and I'll do what you want. I'll go back and tell the cops you mean business."

"No, I think you need to be convinced," Wiley said.

"I know *I* would. Skeptics, you and I both, Brian. Take nobody's word for anything. First law of good journalism: if your mom says she loves you, check it out first."

Jesús Bernal handed Brian Keyes his trousers and said something sternly in Spanish.

"Put your pants on," Wiley translated, "and follow me."

In great strides Wiley crashed through the brush while Keyes struggled to keep up. Sawgrass and grape-sized pine burs bit into his bare feet, but Jesús Bernal stayed close enough to prod him with his beloved knife whenever Keyes faltered.

Ahead Wiley broke from the shelter of the hammock and took a ragged trail through an open, flat expanse of swamp. A juggernaut of noise, he was just as easy to track by sight, the cream-colored smock fluttering in the gray night.

Keyes found himself trotting faster to escape the insects, but dreading what awaited him. Jesús Bernal gave no clues, grunting with each step.

After ten minutes the sprint ended abruptly at water's edge. Keyes caught his breath and studied the scene by yellow lantern light: Mrs. Kimmelman, whimpering on the ground where they had laid her; Wiley, looking haunted but anticipatory; Viceroy Wilson, cool, unexerted, and bored; Tommy Tigertail, up to his knees in the water, his back to the light; and Jesús Bernal, swatting bugs off his sweaty arms.

"Tommy," Wiley said, panting, "do the honors, please."

Tommy Tigertail splashed the water with both hands and began to clap.

"Skip?" Keyes whispered.

"Shhhh!"

Tommy cupped his hands to his mouth and barked in a deep gravelly voice: "Aaaarkk! Aaaarkk!" He slapped the water at his feet.

Skip Wiley extended the lantern and peered into the marsh. "Here, boy!" he sang out.

"Oh God," said Brian Keyes.

A massive shadow cut a clean V in the silky water and made no noise as it swam. Its eyes shone ruby-red, and the snaking of its prehistoric tail cast a roiling wake.

Now Brian Keyes knew what had happened to Sparky Harper.

"His name is Pavlov," Wiley said. "He is a North American crocodile, one of only about thirty left in the entire world. He's a shade over seventeen feet and weighs about the same as a Porsche 915. All that tonnage with a brain no bigger than a tangerine. Isn't nature wonderful, Brian? Who said God doesn't have a sense of humor?"

Keyes was awestruck. He watched Tommy Tigertail lean over to stroke the giant reptile's armored snout. From where he stood Keyes could hear its breath hissing.

"Is it . . . tame?"

Wiley laughed. "Lord, no! He knows Tommy brings the food but there's no loyalty there, Brian. See, crocodiles are different from alligators. Tommy grew up around gators and he could tell you better than I."

Without taking his eyes off the beast, Tommy said, "Crocs are meaner, more aggressive. Gators get fat and lazy."

Wiley said, "You won't ever see a Seminole wrestle a crocodile, will you, Tommy?"

"Never," Tommy agreed. "Have to be crazy."

Keyes was afraid that anything he said might hasten the ceremony, so he said nothing. If only Wiley would keep jabbering, maybe the damn crocodile would get bored and swim away. Meanwhile Ida Kimmelman was sobbing and Jesús Bernal hovered watchfully, in case she tried to get up and run. Keyes wondered if Ida had figured out the plan by now.

"This is not murder," Wiley declared, "it's social Darwinism. Two endangered species, Pavlov there and Mrs. Kimmelman, locked in mortal combat. To the victor goes the turf. That's how it ought to be, Brian."

"It's not fair, Skip."

"Fair? There are nine million Mrs. Kimmelmans between here and Tallahassee, and thirty fucking crocodiles. Is that fair? Who has the legitimate right to be here? Who does this place really belong to?"

Wiley was hitting warp speed. Keyes backed off and tried another strategy.

"Mr. Wilson," he said, "please don't let this happen."

Viceroy Wilson just wanted the whole thing to be over so he could go back to the campfire and sleep off a couple joints. It wasn't his idea to do it quite this way; this was something cooked up by Wiley and the Indian. Viceroy Wilson went along to expedite the revolutionary process and also to avoid irritating the Indian, who, after all, was very generous with his Cadillac.

So Viceroy Wilson said to Keyes: "You don't like it, close your goddamn eyes." Which was exactly what Viceroy Wilson planned to do.

As for Pavlov, he seemed to drift leisurely in the pond

not far from Tom Tigertail's ankles. The leviathan's eyes, two burning barbecue coals, gave nothing away. Keyes imagined he saw bemusement there—as if the carnivorous dinosaur were just playing along with Skip Wiley's schemes.

At Wiley's instruction, Jesús Bernal tore the hurricane tape from Ida Kimmelman's mouth and cut the ropes on her wrists. Immediately she began bellowing so loudly that the crocodile was drawn closer to shore.

"Please be quiet!" Wiley commanded.

"Who do you think you are—"

"Shut up, Mrs. Kimmelman! This is going to be a fair contest, despite what Mr. Keyes says. You and Pavlov are going for a swim. If you survive, you can go home."

"But what's the meaning of this?" Ida cried.

Wiley clenched his jaw and rubbed at his temples. "It is a contest, pure and simple. You and Pavlov have laid claim to the same territory"—he waved his hand at the Glades—"and always such disputes must be settled by battle. Two primitive animals fighting for elemental needs. It's the natural order. How's that for *meaning?*"

"But I can't swim!" Ida Kimmelman said.

"So what? Pavlov can't play bridge. Sounds like you're even to me." Wiley snapped his fingers. "Viceroy!"

Viceroy Wilson seized Mrs. Kimmelman by the shoulders and firmly guided her toward the water. Tommy Tigertail stepped out of the pond, drying his arms with the towel.

"Brian, this may get a little rough," Wiley cautioned. "You'd better sit down."

Keyes felt shaky and nauseated. He opened his mouth but nothing came out. He took one queasy step toward Viceroy Wilson, then another, and finally a scream came to his throat and he was able to launch himself at the football player.

He grabbed on with both hands, snarling as he dug his fingernails into the jet flesh. By the look on his face, Viceroy Wilson obviously was surprised at Keyes's strength.

Keyes felt the athlete's neck cords tighten in his grip, and saw Mrs. Kimmelman wilt to the ground between them. The lantern strobed, and then came shouting: "No, Jesús! Stop!"

Skip Wiley's voice, but not in time.

Keyes felt the fiery rip beneath his right armpit and, on the inside, something metal scrape his ribs. His hands turned to cork and he fell back, gasping. A rush of heat drenched his flank. Even with Wiley and the Cuban on his back, Keyes somehow held his balance until Viceroy Wilson put him down with a vengeful right cross to the jaw.

Crumpling after the punch, Keyes dearly hoped that Wilson had knocked him out. He was hoping to awake later, when it was over, in daylight and sanity.

But Brian Keyes was not unconscious.

He lay curled on his right side, sticky with blood, looking out across the misty, lantern-lit pond. Keyes watched helplessly while Viceroy Wilson and Jesús Bernal carried Mrs. Kimmelman to the water's edge. Pavlov slowly submerged, leaving a cheerful bubble on the pond. In dread Keyes watched as the Cuban took Mrs. Kimmelman's feet and the football player grabbed her arms and they swung her twice and let go—like at a fraternity pool party. She landed in a tangle and floundered on the surface, spluttering in an enormous voice.

"Oh, stop that!" Wiley scolded, playing swim coach. "Kick your legs and keep your head up."

Recklessly Mrs. Kimmelman windmilled toward shore, flailing the swamp to a froth. The giant crocodile was nowhere to be seen, but ominous clouds of bottom mud stained the water. Then the silky surface of the pond seemed to bulge.

"Help!" Mrs. Kimmelman yelled.

"Keep swimming," Wiley counseled. "You're doing quite well."

Brian Keyes closed his eyes when the water finally exploded.

As Ida Kimmelman went under, she thought: Damn you, Lou, are you happy now?

TWELVE

Brian Keyes shivered on the deck of a speeding airboat and watched dawn bleed across the pale Everglades sky. High on the driver's platform sat Tommy Tigertail, his black hair dancing in spikes.

Keyes lifted his head with a groan, but the Indian couldn't hear him over the din of the engine. Tommy wore a serene look as he steered deftly through the sedge.

If Skip Wiley was the ebullient nerve of *Las Noches de Diciembre*, Tommy Tigertail was the soul. He was a man of unusual temperament—taciturn, sometimes brooding, yet outwardly gracious, even warm. He was quiet not because he was shy or queer, as Jesús Bernal would whisper; Tommy was quiet because he was watchful. Never relax, never look away, never trust a white soul—the expensive lessons of history. Tommy Tigertail did not carry the pain of his ancestors for strangers to see; he carried it in his heart and dreams, which haunted him. He was tormented by the nightmare of his great-great-grandfather, Chief Tiger Tail, dying in the dank misery of a New Orleans prison barrack. Tiger Tail, who had never quit like Coacoochee, or been duped into capture like the eloquent Osceola; Tiger Tail, who had spurned the Army's demand to abandon godforsaken Florida with its fever and mosquitoes and rebuild the Seminole nation in Arkansas, of all places. Arkansas! Tiger Tail, who from the beginning had sensed the white man's mendacity and fought back brilliantly until the end, when there were virtually no warriors left. Tiger Tail, who had been captured in the battle at Palatka and shipped to a dungeon on the Mississipi, where he soon died, tubercular, homesick, and broken.

Growing up, Tommy Tigertail had memorized the broken treaties—Camp Moultrie, Payne's Landing, Fort Gibson, and the rest. These were the devices that had swept from paradise all but three hundred unconquerable Seminoles, among them Tommy's great-grandfather, then a teenager, who had hidden and fought and never touched a quill to a U.S. treaty.

Viceroy Wilson had read up on the Seminoles, who impressed him as some of the craftiest motherfuckers ever to raise a rifle. The more he read, the more Wilson was persuaded that Tommy's people had just as much fury to burn as American blacks. Viceroy Wilson was waiting for the day when the Indian's hatred percolated into raw violence or sinister magic, but so far Tommy Tigertail had kept it under rein. Moderation and manners served him well. He weaved as effortlessly through the white man's labyrinth of high finance as he did through the knotted trails of the Big Cypress. It was Tommy Tigertail who had turned the inane bingo fetish of Florida's senior citizens into a Seminole bonanza: soon after gambling was ruled to be legal on the Indian reservations, Tommy converted some old airplane hangars into the world's biggest bingo halls. Ingeniously he tailored them for the various South Florida markets:

Yiddish bingo, Cuban bingo, Brooklyn bingo, and redneck bingo. The tribe got rich, and Tommy Tigertail became a tycoon without even trying. It was bingo money that bankrolled *Las Noches*, but Tommy didn't seem to care how it was spent. He said little, and carried out Skip Wiley's extravagant orders with dispassionate obedience. Around the midnight campfires it was Wiley who did the fulminating, who put the anger and the passion into words, but it was Tommy Tigertail whose spirit seemed to dominate; it was in Tommy's burntwood eyes that Skip Wiley found a pure purpose for his crusade.

As his airboat sliced through the morning mist, Tommy Tigertail thought for the hundredth time: It is too bad Great-great-grandfather didn't have one of these babies. They'd never have caught him.

"Slow down!" Brian Keyes croaked, teeth clicking.

Tommy Tigertail glanced down at his prisoner.

Keyes mouthed the words: "Help me."

The Indian cut the engine, and the airboat coasted to a stop. The silence seemed sudden and immense.

Tommy hopped off his perch and bent over Keyes.

"I'm bleeding to death," Keyes said, fingering his sticky shirt.

"No," Tommy Tigertail said. "I dressed the wound myself. And gave you medicine."

"I don't remember."

"Button snakeroot and willow shavings." Tommy lifted Keyes's shirt and studied the knife wound. Gently he put his hand on Keyes's belly. "You're very cold," he said. "We'll wait a few minutes then." He opened a moleskin canteen and tipped it to Keyes's mouth. The liquid was hot and smoky-tasting, stronger than any coffee known to man.

"Black tea," explained Tommy Tigertail, "to stop the madness."

"Too late for that," Keyes said with a sign.

The Seminole wore a long-sleeved flannel shirt, denims, and western boots – the same damn boots from Wiley's cabin. Tommy Tigertail looked like no other Florida millionaire Brian Keyes had ever met.

The Indian surveyed the swamp. "We are four miles from the road." He climbed into the driver's seat and pointed toward the sunrise.

"When I was a boy," he said, "a herd of white-tailed deer lived here. Three bucks, many does. The fawns you seldom saw. In the winter, when the water disappeared, I could always find the deer grazing on the edge of this basin. When I was fifteen it was time to kill one, and I did."

Keyes sat up, bolstered by the strange tea. Under different circumstances Tommy's version of *Bambi* would have touched him, but Keyes could scarcely listen. He was preoccupied with the selfish notion that he should be taken to a hospital as soon as possible.

Tommy Tigertail said: "Three years ago the deer died. Five white men in a half-track ran them into the high water and killed them with shotguns. The fawns, too. I watched from this spot." The Indian described the slaughter with no outward emotion, as if it were something he'd been expecting his whole life. It gave Keyes a fresh chill.

The Seminole said, "You were wondering what I'm doing with Mr. Wiley. You didn't ask, but you wondered just the same. So this is my answer: your friend Mr.

Wiley says there's a chance to put things right, to make those who don't belong here go away forever."

"But it's fantasy," Keyes said.

Tommy Tigertail smiled handsomely, his caramel face brightening. "Of course it's a fantasy. Of course it is!" He laughed softly, a laugh full of irony. "Ask anybody," Tommy said. "Florida is the place where fantasies come true. Now, lie down, Mr. Keyes, and we will go."

With that the Indian cranked the propeller and the two of them were drowned in noise. The airboat rocketed out of the sawgrass, and the wind shocked Brian Keyes to the spine. He huddled down, cheek to the cool aluminium deck, and counted out the miles in his pounding head.

Shortly after noon on the ninth of December, the head nurse of the emergency room at Flagler Memorial Hospital was notified by a policeman that "a school bus with serious injuries" was on its way to the hospital.

Assuming the worst, which is the only sane way to function in Miami, the nurse immediately declared a Code Orange and scrambled every available surgeon, anesthesiologist, scrub nurse, and lab tech in the hospital. The other patients—miscellaneous gunshot victims, drug overdoses, and screeching teenagers in labor—were shuffled out of the way and told to manage as best they could. Flagler Memorial braced for full-scale carnage and catastrophe.

In no time the E. R. filled with TV crews, newspaper reporters, photographers, and personal-injury lawyers. After about an hour of waiting, everyone got cranky and wanted to know what was the damn story with this busload of mangled orphans. Where were the choppers? And the ambulances? Where the hell were the grieving parents?

The head nurse was getting baleful glares from the orthopedic surgeons ("It's Sunday, for Chrissakes!") when the bus finally clattered up to the emergency-room door.

It was not a school bus, though once it might have been. And in fairness to the cop who radioed it in, the bus had the right colors, yellow and black; the yellow being paint and the black being rust.

The driver, a phlegmatic fellow with a Budweiser in one hand, seemed extremely surprised to be met by bright lights and Minicams and an army of tense-looking people dressed in white. Drunk as he was, the driver could sense their collective disappointment.

For the bus was not packed with seriously injured children, but perfectly healthy migrant workers—Jamaicans, Haitians, Dominicans, and Mexicans, all sweaty and dusty and peeved that their day in the tomato fields had been cut short.

"I don't understand," the nurse said, scanning the dark faces. "Where's the emergency?"

"There's your fuckin' emergency," the bus driver said, waving a stubby arm. "Up top."

The nurse stood on the tips of her white shoes and saw what the driver was talking about: a young man strapped to the rack on top of the bus. He looked damp and half-conscious, his clothes soaked with blood. For some reason a briefcase had been placed under his lolling head.

"Humph!" said the nurse, turning to face the throng. "Relax, everybody."

A pair of orderlies clambered atop the bus and untied Brian Keyes. As they placed him on a stretcher and carried him into the hospital, the emergency room emptied with a groan. Only one reporter hung around to ask questions, and that was Ricky Bloodworth.

Nobody bothered to retrieve the briefcase from the top of the migrant bus. Miraculously it remained there, unsecured, almost halfway back to Immokalee, until the bus accidentally struck an opossum crossing Route 41. The jolt launched the briefcase—containing all Skip Wiley's vital evidence—off the roof of the bus into the Tamiami Canal, where it sank unopened into a gator hole.

Al García was in a bellicose mood. He hated the night shift if he couldn't be out on the streets, and he couldn't be on the streets if he was running the motor pool. The motor pool was a terrible place for a detective; there was nothing to investigate. The highlight of the evening was when one of the K-9 guys drove in with chunks of dead cat all over the backseat of the squad car. The cop said the cat had gone crazy and attacked his K-9 German shepherd and the dog didn't have a choice but to fight back—it was just a terrible thing to see. García said sure, pal, and wrote it up anyway, musing over the sick possibilities.

Al García did not want his career to end this way, in a stale little office on a parking lot full of police cars.

He was still furious about the two goons from I.A.D. who had foraged through his house, hunting for a type-writer that wasn't there. They'd each carried Xerox copies of the *El Fuego* letters to compare with anything they found. But all they'd discovered was a bunch of hand-scrawled hate letters García had once written to Lee Iacocca, the president of Chrysler Motors. For some reason almost every cop car in America is made by Chrysler, and Al García calculated that he'd spent at least forty thousand hours of his life riding in Chrysler-made automobiles: Furies, LeBarons, Diplomats, Monacos, Darts, you name it. Al García was an expert on Chryslers, and he hated the damn things. Hated the steering, hated the shocks, hated the brakes, hated the radios. García especially hated the seats. He had hemorrhoids the size of bell peppers and it was all Lee Iacocca's fault. So García had dashed off a few appropriate missives, which he wisely never sent. Typically the letters would begin: "Dear Shit-for-Brains." For some reason the guys from I.A.D. found this fascinating. They sealed the letters in a plastic bag and exchanged congratulatory whispers. García gave them the finger on their way out the door.

He didn't really expect to see the I.A.D. boys again anytime soon, so he was mildly surprised when one of the assholes appeared that night at the motor pool. García remembered that his name was Lieutenant Bozeman. He was very young to be a lieutenant, and much too sharply dressed to be a good cop.

"I hope you need a car," García said. "You like cats?"

Bozeman helped himself to a seat. He took a notebook from his coat.

"Just a few questions, sergeant, if you don't mind."

"I *do* mind, dipshit. I'm very busy right now, in case you didn't notice. I got six marked units waiting to have the tires rotated, I got a rear bumper missing off a paddy wagon, and the transmission just dropped out of an undercover car in the middle of the Rickenbacker Causeway. Much as I'd love to help you, I got no time."

Bozeman said, "Harold Keefe thinks you wrote the *Fuego* letters."

"Why would I do a stupid thing like that?"

"To make him look bad."

"Hal doesn't need my help."

Bozeman scribbled something in the notebook. "Weren't you passed over for a promotion last year?"

"Yeah," García said. "Failed the swimsuit competition. So what?"

Scribble, scribble. The scratch of the pen jangled García's nerves.

"You don't like Detective Keefe very much, do you, García?"

"I love Detective Keefe," García said. He leaned over and beckoned Bozeman with a fat brown finger. "I love Hal very much," García whispered. "In fact, I *want* him."

"That's not funny," Bozeman said stiffly.

"You're right, it's very sad. See, Hal doesn't want me . . . what did you say your first name was?"

"I didn't."

Bozeman started jotting again. García firmly took him by the wrist. "I like you, too, lieutenant."

"Stop it!"

"Please don't be shy. Are you married?"

"Sergeant, that's enough."

García frowned. "You don't want me either?"

"No!"

"Then why are you getting a lump in your pants, you little fruit!"

Bozeman pulled away, as if burned on a stove. García wheezed with laughter and pounded on the desk.

"You!" Bozeman tried very hard to look icy, Bronson-style, but was betrayed by his crimson blush. "You're nothing but a psychopath, Sergeant García."

"And you're nothing but a well-dressed sack of shit." García stood up and exhaled straight into the lieutenant's face. "Now get out of here before I launch that Bic pen up your Brooks Brothers ass. And put this in your notebook: whoever wrote those *Fuego* letters is crazier than me, and he's for real."

After the I.A.D. guy left, García didn't have much to do so he scrounged up a police manual and looked up "moral turpitude." The definition wasn't so bad but, Christ, those two words really jumped off the page. Especially *turpitude*, which inspired images of Great Danes and Reddi Wip and double-jointed cheerleaders. Certainly wouldn't go over very big back at the homestead. If I.A.D. dumps on me, García thought, maybe they'll have the decency to go with simple "insubordination." With a creep like Bozeman, who could tell.

Ricky Bloodworth's story began like this:

A local private investigator was stabbed and left for dead along an Everglades highway Sunday.

Police said Brian Keyes, 32, was attacked and dumped on the Tamiami Trail about fifteen miles east of Naples. Keyes was spotted by a passing bus driver and transported to Flagler Memorial Hospital, where he was listed in stable condition following surgery.

Keyes, a former Miami newspaper reporter, told the *Sun* that he was on a canoe trip when he was abducted, robbed, and stabbed by two Slavic men wearing wigs and Halloween masks.

Bloodworth finished typing and took the story to Cab Mulcahy's office. Mulcahy sat behind the desk, dictating letters, trying to conceal his wretchedness. He wore an expensive knit sports shirt—a classy lemon pastel, not a crease anywhere.

The old boy never came in on weekends; Bloodworth wondered what was up.

"You said you wanted to see this?"

"Yes, Ricky, have a seat." Mulcahy took the story and read it. It took him a long time; he seemed to read each sentence twice.

"Is it the byline?" Bloodworth asked worriedly.

Mulcahy glanced up. "What?"

"My byline. I changed it." Bloodworth walked around the desk and pointed over the editor's shoulder. "See? Richard L. Bloodworth. Instead of Ricky."

"Oh yes."

"I think it looks better," Bloodworth said. "More professional."

What had really happened was this: Ricky Bloodworth had eaten breakfast with a correspondent from the *New York Times*, who explained that the *Times* simply didn't hire people named *Ricky*. How about just plain Rick? Bloodworth had asked. Well, *Rick* was a swell name for a Little League coach, the reporter had said, as kindly as he could, but it was hardly appropriate for a world-class journalist. Bloodworth was devastated by this revelation because he'd spent half his adult life sending résumés to Abe Rosenthal without even a post-card in reply. Now he knew why. He pressed the *Times* man for more tips and the fellow told him that everybody on the *Times* used middle initials in their bylines because surveys showed that middle initials enhanced credibility twenty-three percent among newspaper readers.

Ricky Bloodworth thought this was a great idea, and he'd quickly fallen in love with the way *Richard L. Bloodworth* looked on the screen of his word processor.

"So, you like it?" he asked Mulcahy.

"It's fine," Mulcahy said, paying no attention whatsoever. Personally he didn't care if Bloodworth called himself *Richard L. Douchebag*. Mulcahy was more concerned about Brian Keyes.

"What else did he say?"

"Not much. They gave him a shot at the hospital and he got real spacey," Bloodworth said. "Kept asking for Jenna."

Mulcahy groaned inwardly. "Did he mention anyone else?"

"No. It sure is a strange tale. What do you suppose he was doing way out there in a canoe?"

"I've got no idea." Mulcahy handed Bloodworth the story. "Good job, Richard L. The new byline looks splendid."

"Thanks," Bloodworth said, beaming. "I'm gonna use it on the column, too."

Cab Mulcahy's ulcer quivered. "Ricky, I meant to tell you: the column's been put on hold for now. We need you on general assignment."

"Sure, Cab," Bloodworth said in a wounded voice.

Then, rebounding: "Tell you what. I'm gonna go see Brian again tomorrow. Try to get a blow-by-blow."

Mulcahy shook his head. "Let him rest."

"But it'd be a terrific second-day feature—"

"The man just got his thorax stitched back together. Give him a break, okay? Besides, somebody gets stabbed every thirty seconds in Miami. It's not news anymore. Maybe in Spudville, Iowa, but not here."

Not news. That was all Ricky Bloodworth needed to hear.

He retreated to his desk and practiced typing his new byline. He even experimented with different middle initials, just to gauge the effect: Richard A. Bloodworth, Richard B. Bloodworth, Richard C. Bloodworth and so on. There was something about having a vowel for a middle initial that struck Bloodworth as impressive, and he wondered if his mother would get upset if he changed his middle name from Leon to Attenborough.

Bloodworth was still mulling the notion an hour later when an editor handed him a police bulletin about some old lady who'd turned up missing from her Broward condominium. As he skimmed the police report about Mrs. Kimmelman's disappearance, Ricky Bloodworth suddenly remembered something else Brian Keyes had whispered from his Demerol fog on the stretcher, something even odder than the business about the Slavic kidnappers.

"Ida is dead," Keyes had told him.

Richard L. Bloodworth emptied his typewriter and started working the phones like a dervish.

THIRTEEN

Skip Wiley had a plan.

That's what he told them—the Indian, the football player, and the Cuban—whenever they got restless.

Trust me, boys, I have a plan!

And he was such a convincing eccentric that they usually calmed down. Wiley overpowered them—even Viceroy Wilson, who thought Wiley would've made a righteous TV preacher. Of all *Las Noches de Diciembre*, only Wilson was absolutely certain of Wiley's sanity. As much as he hated honkies, Wilson found Skip Wiley vastly amusing.

Jesús Bernal, on the other hand, was not amused. He thought Wiley was a reckless lunatic, and wasted no opportunity to say so. Bernal believed discipline was essential for revolution; Wiley, of course, believed just the opposite.

Usually it was Viceroy Wilson who was left to suffer the Cuban's ravings because the Indian just ignored both of them. Without Wiley around, Tommy Tigertail invariably climbed into his airboat and roared into the Everglades without a word. Viceroy Wilson didn't mind, as long as Tommy left the keys to the Cadillac.

On the morning of December 10, Skip Wiley was gone and the Indian had vanished, leaving Viceroy

Wilson alone with Jesús Bernal. At Wiley's instruction, the two of them were driving to Miami on an important mission.

"He's *loco*," Bernal was saying. "Did you see his eyes?"

"He just drank a six-pack," Wilson reminded him.

"Crazy fucker. All this work and what do we have to show for it? *Nada*. Remember all the publicity he promised? NBC! Geraldo Rivera! *Mother Jones!* Ha!"

Jesús Bernal no longer spoke Spanish in the presence of Viceroy Wilson because Wilson had promised to kill him if he did. The mere sound of people speaking Spanish gave Viceroy Wilson a terrible headache. Opera had the same effect.

"The man's got a plan," Wilson said, "so chill out."

"What plan? He's a fucking nut!" Bernal nervously knotted the tail of his undershirt. "We're all going to wind up in prison, except him. He'll be at the Betty Ford Clinic while you and me do twenty-five at Raiford, getting butt-fucked in the showers."

"Be a good experience for you."

"Don't tell me about *plans*," the Cuban groused.

Viceroy Wilson slid Lionel Richie into the tape deck.

"Oh, man, turn the jungle drums down—" Jesús Bernal reached for the volume knob but Wilson forcefully intercepted his arm. "Okay, okay! Christ, take it easy." Bernal couldn't see Viceroy Wilson's eyes behind the Carrera sunglasses; it was just as well.

"So tell me about Dartmouth," Wilson said in a phony Ivy League tone. "Did you excel?"

"That wasn't me, that was another Jesús Bernal. I'm a different person now."

"Too bad," Wilson said. "Tell me about the First Weekend in July Movement."

"Never!"

Wilson chuckled dryly. He'd done a little checking at the Miami Public Library.

"Why'd they kick you out?"

"They didn't kick me out, *coño*, I quit!"

Viceroy Wilson didn't like the sound of *coño*, but he let it slide. He was having too much fun. He'd been waiting for this since the first time Jesús Bernal had flashed his switchblade. Jesús was a bully, his mean streak carefully rehearsed; Viceroy Wilson would have loved to play football against Jesús Bernal. Just one play. Thirty-one Z-right.

"So tell me about the bombs."

Bernal sneered.

"Come on, Jesús. I read where you were in charge of munitions."

"I held the title of defense minister!"

"Yeah, that was later. I'm talking about 1978, June 1978."

Bernal's upper lip twitched. He stared out the car window and started humming "All Night Long," drumming on his knee.

Viceroy Wilson said, "June 15, 1978."

"Turn up the music."

This is what had happened on the afternoon of June 15, 1978: Jesús Bernal manufactured a letter bomb which was meant to kill a well-known Miami talk-show host. This TV celebrity had been foolhardy enough to suggest that the United States should send emergency medical supplies to a rural province in Cuba, where a deadly strain of influenza had afflicted hundreds of children.

The talk-show host had actually made this appeal for Cuba on the air. In Dade County, Florida.

Jesús Bernal, munitions man for the First Weekend in July Movement, saw the talk show and flew into action. It had taken only two hours to fashion an inconspicuous letter bomb with gunpowder, C-4, glass, wire, gum, and blasting caps. He'd addressed the package to the talk-show star at the television studio, and put it in a mailbox at Southwest Eighth Street and LeJeune Road (the same intersection where, years later, poor Ernesto Cabal would peddle his mangoes and cassavas).

At 4:10 P.M. on June 15, 1978—ten minutes after Jesús Bernal had deposited the lethal package—the mailbox blew up. No one was killed. No one was injured. It wasn't even a particularly loud explosion, by Miami standards.

Jesús Bernal knew he was in trouble. Frantically he'd telephoned seven Cuban radio stations and announced that the First Weekend in July Movement was responsible for the bombing. They all wanted to know: what bombing?

Two days later, on orders from above, Jesús Bernal had tried again. Another letter bomb, another mailbox. Another premature detonation. This time it had made the newspapers: *Feds Seek Postal Prankster.*

When Jesús Bernal had translated this headline for the *comandante* of the First Weekend movement, the old man had erupted in fury, waving the newspaper with a scarred and trembling fist. We are terrorists, not pranksters! And you, Jesús, are a *maricón!* Make another bomb, a big one, and kill the *coño* on TV...

or else. The *comandante* was a revered veteran of the Bay of Pigs, and was to be obeyed at all costs. Jesús worked swiftly.

It was the third bomb that made the pages of *Time* and *U.S. News & World Report*, where Viceroy Wilson read about it years later in the stacks of the public library. The third bomb was a delicate yet extremely powerful device that was meant to blow up a car. Jesús Bernal spent four days building the bomb in the kitchen of a Little Havana rooming house. He had personally transported the device to the television station, where he'd meticulously affixed it to a forest-green El Dorado which, in the darkness of the night, appeared identical to the one driven by the seditious TV talk-show host.

Unfortunately, the El Dorado was not identical; in fact, it was not the right automobile. The El Dorado that blew up on the Dolphin Expressway on June 22, 1978, actually belonged to a man named Salvatore "The Cleaver" Buscante, a notorious loan shark and pornographer who had often played gin with Meyer Lansky.

The headline the next day said: *Anti-Castro Terrorists Claim Credit for Mob Hit; Feds Puzzle Over Cuban Connection.*

Jesús Bernal immediately was expelled from the First Weekend in July Movement, and ordered at gunpoint to leave Florida. He spent ten miserable months in Union City before being recalled by the *comandante*, who had come to miss Bernal's public-relations acumen. So what if he'd bombed the wrong guy? He got press, didn't he?

Over the protests of almost all the First Weekend in July's hardcore soldiers, the *comandante* had promoted Jesús Bernal to defense minister and bought him an

IBM Selectric. From then on, the First Weekend was known for having the most impeccable press releases in the hemisphere. In his new role Jesús Bernal was an innovator: he even sent communiqués on embossed letterheads—italic for bombings, boldface for political assassinations. Even the most skeptical commandos had to admit that the kid from Dartmouth had style. Soon the First Weekend in July became the preeminent anti-Castro group in the United States.

In the summer of 1981, under Bernal's inspired guidance, the terrorists launched an ambitious PR campaign to discredit Fidel Castro. Although this effort again won national publicity, it also led to Jesús Bernal's second and final banishment from the First Weekend in July.

The linchpin of the campaign had been a "letter" from a renowned Swiss doctor reporting that President Castro was dying of a rare venereal disease transmitted by poultry. The malady supposedly was manifested by a number of grotesque symptoms, the mildest of which was drooling insanity. Of course the Swiss letter had been invented by none other than Jesús Bernal, but the document was accepted in Miami so unquestionably, and with such patriotic fervor, that Bernal decided to unleash it in Cuba as well. He hatched a daring scheme and persuaded the *comandante* to donate $19,022—a sum which, sadly, represented the entire treasury of the First Weekend in July Movement.

Not surprisingly, Jesús Bernal picked the first weekend of July in 1981 as the time of attack: the weekend Fidel would finally fall. In Little Havana, the air filled with intrigue and jubilation.

But not for long. On July 4, 1981, a low-flying DC-3 cargo plane dumped six metric tons of anti-Castro leaflets on the resort city of Kingston, Jamaica. The townspeople were baffled because the literature was printed in Spanish; only the words *Castro* and *syphilis* seemed to ring a bell among some Jamaicans. One of the leaflets was shown to the island's prime minister, who immediately cabled Fidel Castro to express sorrow over the president's unfortunate illness.

Later, under scornful grilling by the *comandante*, Jesús Bernal admitted that no, he'd never studied aerial navigation at Dartmouth. Bernal argued that it had been an honest mistake—from thirteen thousand feet, Kingston didn't look *that* different from Havana. Then Jesús had flashed his trump card: a copy of the *New York Times*. Three paragraphs, page 15a, in the International News roundup: *Tourist Bus Damaged by Falling Air Cargo*.

But the *comandante* and his men were not mollified: Jesús Bernal was purged forever from the First Weekend in July Movement.

"I know all about the bombs," Viceroy Wilson said as they drove to Miami, several years later. "You're just doing this to redeem yourself."

"Ha! I am a hero to all freedom fighters."

"You're a pitiful fuck-up," Wilson said.

"Look who's talking, goddamn junkie spook."

"What you say?"

Thank God the music was up so loud.

"Nothing," Jesús Bernal said. "You missed the damn exit." He was getting mad at Viceroy Wilson. "You never even said thanks."

"Thanks for what?" Wilson asked from behind his sunglasses.

"For slicing that guy back in the swamp when he tried to strangle you."

Wilson laughed. "A mosquito, man, that's all he was."

"You looked pretty uptight when that mosquito grabbed your neck. Your eyeballs almost popped out of your chocolate face, that little mosquito was squeezing so hard."

"Sheee-iiit."

"Yeah, you owe me one, *compadre*."

"You're the one should be thanking *me*. You been waitin' your whole Cuban life to stab somebody in the back and now you did it. Guess that makes you a man, don't it? Say, why don't you call up your old dudes and see if they'll take you back." Viceroy Wilson grinned nastily. "Maybe they'll make you minister of switch-blades."

Jesús Bernal scowled and mumbled something crude in Spanish. "I spit on their mothers," he declared. "If they got on their knees I wouldn't go back. Never!"

This was a total lie: Jesús Bernal yearned to abandon Skip Wiley's circus and rejoin his old gang of dedicated extortionists, bombers, and firebugs. In his heart Jesús Bernal believed his special talents were being wasted. Whenever he thought about Wiley's crazy plan he got a sour stomach that wouldn't go away. Somehow he couldn't visualize the masses ever mobilizing behind *El Fuego;* besides, if Wiley had his way, there'd be no masses left to mobilize—they'd all be heading North. These doubts had begun the day Ernesto Cabal hanged himself; guilt was a deadly emotion for a stouthearted terrorist, but guilt is what Jesús Bernal felt. He didn't feel particularly good about feeding strangers to crocodiles, either. It wasn't that the Cuban sympathized with *gringo* tourists, but Wiley's peculiar method of murder did not seem like the kind of political statement *Las Noches de Diciembre* ought to be making. And if nothing else, Jesús Bernal considered himself an expert on political statements.

"This is the place," Viceroy Wilson announced.

Great, thought Jesús Bernal. He wished Wiley would just let him alone with the typewriter and plastique.

Wilson parked the car in front of a two-story office building on Biscayne Boulevard at Seventy-ninth. A sign out front said: "Greater Miami Orange Bowl Committee."

"Comb your hair," Wilson grumbled.

"Shut up."

"You look like a damn *Marielito*."

"And you look like my father's yard man."

The lady at the reception desk didn't like the looks of either of them. "Yes?" she said with a polite Southern lilt unmistakable in its derision.

"We're here about the advertisement," Viceroy Wilson explained, shedding his Carreras.

"Yes?"

"The ad for security guards," Jesús Bernal said.

"Security guards," Wilson said, "for the Orange Bowl Parade."

"I see," said the Southern lady, warily handing each of them a job application. "And you both have some experience?"

"Do we ever," said Viceroy Wilson, smiling his touchdown smile.

*

When Brian Keyes awoke, the first thing he noticed was a woman on top of him in the hospital bed. Her blond head lay on his shoulder, and she seemed to be sleeping. Keyes strained to get a glimpse of her face, but every little movement brought a fresh volt of pain.

The woman weighed heavily on his chest; his ribs still ached from the surgery. Keyes stared down at the soft hair and sniffed for fragrant clues; it wasn't easy, especially with the tube up his nose.

"Jenna?" he rasped.

The woman on his chest stirred and gave a little hum of a reply.

"Jenna, that you?"

She looked up with a sleepy-eyed hello.

"You sound just like George Burns. Want some water?"

Keyes nodded. He let out a sigh when Jenna climbed out of bed.

"Where'd you get the nurse's uniform?"

"You like it?" She hitched up the hem. "Check out the white stockings."

Keyes sipped at the cold water; his throat was a furnace.

"What time is it? What day?"

"December 10, my love. Ten-thirty P.M. Way past visiting hours. That's why I had to wear this silly outfit."

"You'd make a spectacular nurse. I'm getting better by the second."

Jenna blushed. She sat at the foot of the bed. "You looked so precious when you were asleep."

Keyes shut his eyes and faked a snore.

"Now stop!" Jenna laughed. "You look precious

anyway. Aw, Brian, I'm so sorry. What happened out there?"

"Skip didn't tell you?"

She looked away. "I haven't talked to him."

Keyes thought: She must think I've had brain surgery.

"What happened out there?" she asked again.

"I got knifed by one of Skip's *caballeros*."

"I don't believe it," Jenna said.

Pausing only for gulps of water, Keyes related the sad tale of Mrs. Kimmelman. For once Jenna seemed to focus on every word. She was curious, but unalarmed.

"That poor woman. Do you think she died?"

Keyes nodded patiently. "I'm pretty sure."

Jenna stood up and walked to the window. "The weather got muggy again," she remarked. "Three gorgeous days with a little winter, and then poof, Sauna City. My folks already had three feet of snow."

"Jenna?"

When she turned to face him, her eyes were moist. She was trying to keep it inside, trying to recoup like the magnificent actress she was.

"I'm s-s-so sorry," she cried. "I didn't know you'd get hurt."

Keyes held out his hand. "I'm all right. C'mere."

She climbed back into bed, sobbing on his shoulder. At first the pain was murderous, but Jenna's perfume was better than morphine. Keyes wondered what he'd say if a real nurse walked in.

Jenna sniffed, "How's Skip?"

"Skip's a little crazy, Jenna."

"Of course he is."

"Slightly crazier than usual," Keyes said. "He's killing off tourists."

"I figured it'd be something like that. But it's not really murder, is it? I mean *murder* in the criminal way."

"Jenna, he fed an old lady to a crocodile!"

"He sent me a Mailgram," she said.

"A Mailgram?"

"It said: 'Dear Jenna, burn all my Rolodex cards at once. Love, Skip.' "

Keyes asked, "Did you do it? Did you burn the Rolodex?"

"Of course not," Jenna said, as if the suggestion were preposterous. "The message obviously is in code, which I haven't yet figured out. Besides, he keeps the Rolodex inside that darned coffin, which gives me the creeps."

Keyes grimaced, not from pain.

"Look at all these tubes," Jenna said. "There's one in your chest and one up your nose and another stuck in your arm. What's in that bottle?"

"Glucose. Tomorrow I'm back on solids and in three days I'll be out of here. Jenna, where's Skip now?"

"I've no idea."

"You've got to find him. He's killed four people."

"Not personally he hasn't." Jenna pulled back the sheet. "Let me see your stitches."

Keyes turned to one side and lifted his right arm.

"Oh, boy," said Jenna, whistling.

"Nasty, huh?"

"Looks like a railroad track." She traced the wound with a finger, light as a feather. Keyes shivered pleasurably.

"Did the knife hit your lung? Or was it a knife?" Jenna asked.

"Nicked it," Keyes said.

"Ouch," Jenna whispered. She stroked his forehead and smiled. "How do you feel? I mean *really*."

Keyes flushed. He knew what she meant. Really.

"Woozy," he said, thinking: Something extraordinary is happening here; maybe Wiley's under the bed.

"Too woozy? What if I took this one away . . . would you be all right? Could you breathe?"

"Well, let's find out," Keyes said. Of course she couldn't be serious. Not *here*. He removed the oxygen tube and took three breaths.

"Okay?" Jenna asked.

Keyes nodded; it was pain he could live with.

Jenna slid out of bed and unbuttoned her starched nurse's uniform. Suddenly she was standing there in bra and panties and white hospital hose. She had a deliciously naughty look on her face. Keyes didn't think he'd seen that particular look before.

"I think we should make love," Jenna announced.

Keyes was stupefied. Considering what had happened the last few days, maybe he was due for a miracle. Maybe this was God's way of balancing fate. Or maybe it was something else altogether. Keyes didn't care; it was bound to be his last spell of infinite pleasure until Skip Wiley was caught or killed.

"It's possible I still love you, Brian," said Jenna, slipping out of her bra. "Mind if I lock the door?"

"What about the nurses?"

"We'll be oh-so-quiet." Jenna stepped out of her panties. She looked radiant, her new tan lines providing a phenomenal lesson in contrasts. Keyes had never seen her velvet tummy so brown, or her breasts so white.

He said: "I'm a wreck. I need to shave."

Then he said: "I don't know if I can do this."

And then he decided to just shut up and let things happen, because he really couldn't be sure that this wasn't some splendid Dilaudid dream, and that Jenna wasn't just your usual breathtaking nude mirage in white hospital stockings.

She studied him from an artist's pose, arms folded, a finger on her lips. "This is going to be tricky. I guess I'd better get on top." And she did.

Smothered in delight, Keyes kissed Jenna's neck and throat and collarbone and whatever else he could get his mouth on. He half-hugged her, using the arm that wasn't attached to the intravenous tube, and played his fingers down her spine. Jenna seemed to enjoy it. She arched, then pressed down hard with her hips. Her aim was perfect.

"Have you missed me, Brian?"

"Yup." Which was all the breath he had left.

Jenna sat up, straddling him. Her eyes were liquid and, for once, not so far away. She swayed gently with a hand on each bed rail, as if riding a sled.

"Am I hurting you?" she asked with one of those killer smiles. "I didn't think so."

Partly out of passion and partly to get the weight off his tortured diaphragm, Keyes pulled her down. He kissed her lightly on the mouth and right away she closed her eyes. At first she was tentative, maybe even nervous, but soon she started doing all the amazing things she used to do when they were lovers; things he'd never forgotten but never thought he'd experience again.

Lovemaking with Jenna had always been an emotional workout for Brian Keyes—shock therapy for the heart. True to form, his brain shut down the moment she pressed against him. He totally forgot where he was and why he was there. He forgot his stitches, he forgot his collapsed lung, and he forgot the tube gurgling out of his side. He forgot the nurse, who was pounding on the door. He even forgot Ida Kimmelman and the goddamn crocodile.

He forgot everything but Jenna and Wiley.

"What about Skip?" he whispered between nibbles. "I thought you were madly in love with Skip."

"Hush now," Jenna said, guiding his free hand. "And try not to kick the I.V."

FOURTEEN

Jesús Bernal finally got a chance to build another bomb, thanks to Ricky Bloodworth.

On the morning of December 12, the Miami *Sun* published its first front-page story about *Las Noches de Diciembre*. It was not a flawless piece of journalism but it stirred excitement at Skip Wiley's Everglades bivouac.

The lead of the story focused on the ominous *El Fuego* letter discovered in Ida Kimmelman's condominium mailbox. A trusting Broward County detective had read the contents to Ricky Bloodworth (*Dear Otter Creek Shuffle-board Club: Welcome to the Revolution!*) and Bloodworth realized he had a hot one. He worked the phones like a boiler-room pro, pestering every cop he knew until he unearthed the fact that this *Fuego* letter was the fourth of its kind. Thus the murder of B. D. "Sparky" Harper finally was linked to the disappearance of the Shriner, the abduction of the Canadian woman at the Seaquarium, and now the unsolved kidnapping of Ida Kimmelman. Of course, neither the police nor Ricky Bloodworth knew precisely what had happened to the last three victims—who could have guessed?—but it was still quite a list. Especially if you tacked on the savage stabbing of private investigator Brian Keyes.

This front-page attention thrilled Skip Wiley, and in a brief campfire ceremony he thanked his fellow radicals for their patience. "Remember ye this day!" he told them. "On this day we are born to the eyes of America. Today the Miami *Sun*, tomorrow *USA Today*!"

None of the conspirators were identified in Bloodworth's story, and Brian Keyes's description of his "Slavic" abductors was repeated as if it were an established fact. Wiley admired the yarn as a stroke of originality.

There was one significant error in Ricky Bloodworth's story which, when read aloud by Jesús Bernal, made Skip Wiley roll his eyes, Viceroy Wilson laugh out loud, and Tommy Tigertail shrug. It was a shrug Tommy saved for extremely stupid behaviour by white people. Somehow Ricky Bloodworth had managed to screw up the name of Wiley's group and referred to it throughout the story as *Las* Nachos *de Diciembre*, which translates exactly as one might suppose. Skip Wiley had been in the newspaper business too long not to be tickled by this mistake, but Jesús Bernal was apoplectic. "Nachos!" he shrieked. "This is your brilliant publicity coup? We are now world-famous nachos!" With that Jesús Bernal shredded the newspaper and declared that he'd never experienced such humiliation in all his days in the underground. Skip Wiley suspected that, more than anything, Bernal resented the Mexican insinuation.

"Relax," he told Jesús. "We'll straighten this out soon enough, won't we?"

Several persons were deeply displeased to see Ricky Bloodworth's story. One was Cab Mulcahy, who sensed

Skip Wiley's demented hand behind the *El Fuego* caper. Mulcahy could see disaster looming. For the newspaper. For himself. For all Miami. He shriveled at the vision of a handcuffed Wiley being led up the steps of the Dade County Courthouse—wild-eyed and foamy-mouthed, bellowing one of his dark axioms. Every major paper in American would cover the extravaganza: *Columnist Goes on Trial as Mass Murderer.* It would be better than Manson because Skip Wiley was more coherent. Skip Wiley was a hell of a quote.

Despite his premonitions, Cab Mulcahy knew there was little he could do until he was absolutely sure.

Another person who cringed at the sight of Richard L. Bloodworth's byline was Detective Harold Keefe, who'd nearly succeeded in convincing the police hierarchy that a renegade cop had dreamed up those crazy letters. Harold Keefe had refused to speak with Bloodworth the night before and now was sorry he hadn't. Keefe could have used the opportunity to drop the dime on Al García and derail all this freaky *Las Noches* crap. Now it was too late, a veritable disaster. The chief was furious, I.A.D. was on red alert, and the Chamber of Commerce was handing out cyanide capsules.

As Harold Keefe studied the front page of the Miami *Sun*, he decided to retaliate swiftly, utilizing the police department's vast apparatus for equivocation. He would compose a public statement to put the whole Nacho case in a sober perspective. The wording would be dicey, considering the publicity, but Keefe would stick to the original platform: The murder of B. D. Harper is unrelated to the subsequent disappearance of tourists . . . No evidence of foul play . . . The *Fuego* letters are a sick hoax perpetrated by a disgruntled policeman (for support, quote from Dr. Remond Courtney's report to the chief) . . . Close by saying the whole matter remains under investigation . . . an *internal* investigation. Pretty tidy, Keefe thought.

He recorded two versions of the statement, a thirty-second loop for radio and two fifteen-second sound bites for TV. The tapes were copied and the cassettes distributed to broadcast reporters in the lobby of police headquarters. Full texts of the press release (in English, Spanish, and Creole) were hand-delivered to all Miami newspapers; a studio eight-by-ten of Harold Keefe was conveniently included in the package.

Keefe's statement was released just in time for the noon news on radio and television.

Tommy Tigertail was driving east on Alligator Alley when he heard the broadcast. He turned around and cruised back to tell Skip Wiley.

"I'll be damned, a cover-up!" Wiley exclaimed. The Indian had found him fishing near the secret campsite. Wiley was dressed in a buckskin jacket and Fila tennis shorts; he wore an Australian bush hat with a red emblem on the crown. He listened closely to Tommy Tigertail's account of the police press release, and winced at the mention of Dr. Remond Courtney.

"I wonder what happened to Brian," Wiley said irritably. "He was our ace in the hole, our smoking gun. I even gave him the briefcase—it was all the proof those moron cops would ever need."

"So what do we do?" the Indian asked.

"Strike again," advised Jesús Bernal, who had wandered out of the hammock to eavesdrop. "Strike again, and strike dramatically."

Wiley's bestubbled face cracked into a grin. "Jesús, *mi hermano*, do you still have some C-4?"

"*Sí.*"

"*Bueno*," said Wiley, humoring him with Spanish. "Make me a bomb."

"Yes, sir!" Bernal said, scarcely concealing his rapture. "What kind of bomb?"

"A bomb that goes off when it's supposed to."

"*Claro*! Do not worry."

"Please don't blow up my car," Tommy Tigertail said.

Among those who had no intention of waiting for a bomb were the residents of Otter Creek Village, where the abduction of Ida Kimmelman had set off a minor panic. Newly hired security guards now patrolled the shuffleboard courts until midnight—security guards with guns! Furthermore, the Otter Creek Safety Committee declared that all condominium owners should henceforth walk their dogs *en masse*, for protection. This was a drastic measure that only promoted more hysteria at Otter Creek—a herd of yipping, squatting miniature poodles dragging scores of Sansa-belted retirees across the landscaping. Fearful of kidnappings, some of the oldsters armed themselves with sharp umbrellas or canisters of Mace, which they often used on one another in the heat of competition for shrubs and hydrants. Indelible terror seized the residents when the actual text of the *El Fuego* letter appeared in the newspaper; within hours forty-seven units at Otter Creek were put up for sale. Contracts on fourteen other apartments, including a penthouse with a whirlpool, were canceled. Overnight the parking lot seemed to fill with mustard-colored moving vans and station wagons with New York tags.

This was the first wave out of Florida.

It was exactly the way Skip Wiley had dreamed it.

One morning Brian Keyes looked up and saw the round, friendly face of Nell Bellamy. For a second he thought he was back on the sidewalk outside Pauly's Bar.

"Hello again."

"Hi," Keyes said.

"I read about your accident."

"It wasn't exactly an accident," Keyes said. "Why are you whispering?"

"It's a hospital. I always whisper in hospitals." Nell Bellamy looked embarrassed.

Keyes said, "It was nice of you to come."

"How are you feeling? The nurses said you had a little setback."

"Tore a few stitches the other night. One of those things." The cost of Jenna's heavenly visit; the next morning he'd felt like a gutted carp.

Nell tucked another pillow under his head. "Did you see the paper? They think it's a gang of . . . maniacs."

Brian Keyes knew why Nell Bellamy had come, and it was time to tell the truth. As a reporter, he'd always tried to do these melancholy chores over the phone, never in person. On the phone you could just close your eyes and take a deep gulp and say, "Ma'am, I'm sorry to have to tell you this, but—" and then the rotten news. Your little boy got hit by a truck. Your sister was a passenger on that 727. They found your daughter's body, Mrs. Davenport. Sometimes Keyes couldn't bring himself to do it, and he'd play the line-is-busy game with his editor. *Sorry, can't get a comment from the family. The line's been busy all afternoon.* And then if the editor persisted, Keyes would dial his own phone number and hold the receiver away from his ear, so the busy signal would be audible.

Unfortunately, Nell Bellamy wasn't on the other end of a telephone. She was standing intently at the rail of the hospital bed, bracing for what her ace private investigator was about to say.

"Mr. Keyes, I've a feeling you found out something important."

Keyes couldn't bear to look in her eyes, so he concentrated on the buttons of her crisp blouse. "Mrs. Bellamy, I'm sorry to have to tell you this, but your husband is dead. I think he was murdered."

Nell Bellamy sat down, neat and plump, in a chair by the window. "Oh, Teddy," she said softly.

At that moment Brian Keyes could have murdered Skip Wiley, could have grabbed his wild blond mane and snapped his neck. In his derangement Wiley had come to see his own life as a headline, getting bigger and more sensational each day. Everything *El Fuego* said and did, or ordered done, was devised with one test: how it would look in print. Sparky Harper gagging on a rubber alligator, for instance—masterful, in a way. For days Keyes had been thinking about Wiley's macabre front-page reality. Now he thought: Skip ought to be here to watch this woman cry.

"I think it was the same people who stabbed me," Keyes said. "They're very dangerous, Mrs. Bellamy. They're fanatical."

"The Nachos?" Nell Bellamy asked. "But why would they kill my husband? He's just a realtor."

"They're killing off tourists," Keyes said.

Nell nodded as if she understood, as if Florida was finally making sense. "Well, the police warned me not to believe the newspaper."

"The police are wrong, Mrs. Bellamy."

"A detective told me Teddy must've drowned. He said there's no such thing as The Nachos."

"They had Teddy's swimming trunks," Keyes said.

"Oh no," Nell said, stricken. "What did they do to him? I mean, how . . .?"

Keyes felt terrible. He held out his hand and Nell Bellamy took it. "They told me it was quick and painless," he said. "I'm very sorry."

From nowhere Nell produced a handful of pink Kleenexes and dabbed at her eyes. "You're a brave man, Mr. Keyes. Risking your life the way you did." She composed herself and took a paisley checkbook from her purse. "How much do I owe you?"

"Put that away," Keyes said. "Please, Mrs. Bellamy."

"You're very kind."

No, I'm not, Keyes said to himself.

"Is there any chance," Mrs. Bellamy said, "of finding Teddy's body?"

"None," said Keyes, thinking of Pavlov the crocodile.

The door opened and the two beefy Shriners came into the room. They wore business suits and mauve fez hats.

"You're a popular fellow," Burt the Shriner said. "Lots of visitors. Mr. Mulcahy from the newspaper was here. So was Detective Keefe. Later there was a Sergeant García, kind of a rude fellow. Also some television types asking for an interview. One of those Live-Eye jobs."

"We told them to come back another day," said the Shriner named James, "when you were up to snuff."

"I asked Burt and James to keep an eye on the door," Nell Bellamy explained. "Hope you don't mind."

"Not at all. Thank you." Keyes knew what García and the other visitors had wanted: a firsthand account of his *noche* with *Las Noches*. Cab Mulcahy doubtlessly had figured out the Wiley connection. Keyes wondered what the old boy would do now.

"We knew it'd be like Grand Central Station up here after that newspaper article," Burt said. "We thought you'd appreciate a little peace and quiet." He looked at Mrs. Bellamy and said, "So what's the verdict, Nellie?"

"Mr. Keyes says the newspaper was right."

"Slavic murderers! Wearing wigs!"

"No," Brian Keyes said, "That part was wrong."

"But the part about Ted being killed, that was true," Nell told the Shriners. "They stole his bathing trunks."

"Lord God," Burt said, "those bastards."

James put a meaty arm around Nell Bellamy's shoulders and she went for the Kleenex again.

Burt waited a decent interval, then asked: "What are the chances that the police will catch these people?"

"Fifty-fifty," Keyes replied, without conviction.

"Not good enough," James said.

"Piss poor," Burt concurred. "Mr. Keyes, what's your timetable? Are you going to stick with this case?"

"Absolutely."

"Good. We'd like to tag along."

"Nellie's going back to Evanston," James said protectively. "Tonight."

"But not us, no sir, we've got a score to settle," Burt declared. "What about it, Mr. Keyes? We're not professionals, not like you, but we can take care of ourselves. I'm pretty good with a handgun—"

"*Pretty* good!" James interjected. "Jeez."

"And James himself has some martial-arts experience. Black belt, yellow belt, you name it. Plus a pilot's license. What about it, Mr. Keyes, think you could use some help?"

Well hell, thought Brian Keyes, why not?

"I'd be grateful," Keyes told them.

"Good, then it's settled."

"Just one thing."

"Yes, Mr. Keyes?"

"About those hats. You have to wear them all the time?"

There was an awkward moment of silence, as if Keyes had breached some sacred Shriner wont. Burt and James glanced at one another, and even Nell Bellamy looked up, her face mostly hidden by a mask of pink tissue.

"It's a fez," Burt said, touching the purple crown. "What about it?"

"Would you like one?" James offered. "Maybe without a tassel."

"Never mind," Keyes said. He pressed the button to ring for a nurse. It was time to check out.

The annual competition for Miami's Orange Bowl queen had attracted the usual chorus line of debutantes, fashion models, ex-cheerleaders, and slick sorority tarts.

Jesús Bernal, who'd spent the whole day building a bomb, was overwhelmed. As far as he was concerned, this was a dandy way to take your mind off plastique.

"You ever seen this much pussy?" he asked Viceroy Wilson.

"Sure," Wilson said. "Dallas. Super Bowl Eight."

Two touchdowns, three blow-jobs, and a cowgirl sandwich. God, he was such a lowlife in those days. All hard-on, no purpose. Wilson shook his head at the memory and lighted a joint.

"Not here!" Bernal snapped. "Remember, we're supposed to be security guards."

"Well, I feel so secure I'm gonna smoke some weed."

They stood in darkness at the rear of the Civic Center. The stage was bathed in kliegs. It was dress rehearsal and the auditorium was empty, except for a skeleton orchestra, some TV technicians, and the contestants themselves. The women milled onstage, tugging at their gumdrop-colored swimsuits and poofing their hair. The air conditioning was running full blast, and Jesús Bernal had never seen so many erect nipples in one congregation.

"The fourth one from the left," Bernal said. "Her name is Maria."

"No way," said Viceroy Wilson. He really couldn't see a damn thing with the sunglasses on.

"How about the redhead? Rory McWhat's-her-face."

"Forget it, Hay-zoos. She don't have a prayer. Freckles look rotten on TV."

"She made it to the semifinals," Bernal said.

"Sympathy vote. Mark my words."

Viceroy Wilson was having as good a time as his abstemious revolutionary ethic would allow. Whenever Wilson found himself distracted by lust, he sublimated rigorously. And whenever he sublimated, he was struck by a vestigial urge to run with a football. Right now he wanted to run down the center aisle, hurdle onstage, and steamroller the emcee. The emcee had a voice that could take the paint off your car.

"They're going to fire your ass for smoking," Bernal scolded. "You'll wreck everything."

"Know what you need? You need about eight Quaaludes. Calm your Cuban ass right down."

Jesús Bernal was appalled at the lack of regimentation within *Las Noches de Diciembre*. Viceroy Wilson, who personified this insubordination, wouldn't have lasted ten minutes with the First Weekend in July. Using drugs during a mission! The Cubans would have wasted him immediately.

"Any sisters make the semis?" Wilson asked.

"*Nadie*," Jesús Bernal reported. "Seven Anglos, three Cubans."

"God damn, that figures."

Jesús Bernal could no longer see Viceroy Wilson's face, only a sphere of bluish smoke behind the sunglasses. Bernal knew that Wilson was worried about the Indian's Cadillac, which they'd double-parked in front of the Hyatt Regency. Bernal himself was anxious about the car, and for the same reason. The double-parking had nothing to do with it.

Skip Wiley had ordered them to interrupt their mission and stop at the Civic Center. A scouting assignment, Wiley had explained, extremely important.

Drive carefully, Wiley had added. Very carefully.

Which only reinforced Jesús Bernal's belief that Wiley was especially crazy when it came to risking other people's asses. A reputable terrorist simply would not dally in downtown Miami with a freshly assembled bomb in the trunk of his Cadillac. Bombs, like pizzas, are made for speedy delivery.

"Straighten up," Wilson said, stubbing out the joint. "Somebody's coming."

A man with a walkie-talkie charged up the aisle. He was the chief of security for all Orange Bowl festivities.

"What's that smell?" he demanded, looking straight at Jesús Bernal.

"*No sé*," Bernal replied.

"Caught some kids smoking dope in the back row and threw 'em out," Wilson said. "Broke their fingers first."

"Good work, Mr. Wilson."

The security chief was a big Dolphins fan, so he was overjoyed to have the legendary Viceroy Wilson on his staff.

"So, you enjoying the pageant?" he chirped.

"Loving it," Wilson said. "Who's your pick?"

"Rory McAllister, Little redhead with the nice ass. Second from the right."

"*Sí, es muy bonita*," Jesús Bernal said.

"Tell me, my man, why don't I see any black women up on that stage?"

The security chief lost his locker-room grin and wilted back a few steps. "Gosh, I don't know. That's a stumper. Want me to ask the judges?"

"Yeah," Viceroy Wilson said. "Do that."

"Right away, Mr. Wilson. And, hey, good work rousting those dopers!" The security chief hurried away.

Jesús Bernal and Viceroy Wilson strolled to the foot of the stage and stared up at the beauty contestants, who were practicing the winner's walk. Back straight, boobs out, buttocks tight, big smile. To Jesús Bernal each of the women seemed six feet tall, perfect and impenetrable.

"Number five," Wilson said in a disinterested tone. "That's your winner."

Jesús Bernal found a program and read aloud: "Kara Lynn Shivers. Sophomore, University of Miami. Majoring in public relations. Hobbies: Swimming, mime, and French horn. Hair: blond. Eyes: hazel."

"Height?" Wilson said.

"Five-eight."

"She weighs one-twenty."

"One hundred ten," Bernal said "That's what it says here."

"Vanity," Wilson coughed. "The bitch is lying."

Bernal shrugged. "Whatever you say. Is one-twenty too heavy?"

Wilson smiled, thinking of all those NFL linebackers. Somebody yelled "Cut!" and the emcee swaggered across the stage, trailing a microphone cord. He leaned over and spoke to Wilson and Bernal. "You guys are too close to the action. We got the top of your heads in that last shot."

The emcee sounded quite annoyed. Viceroy Wilson had never seen such large bright teeth on a white person. You could tile a swimming pool with teeth like that.

Jesús Bernal stuck out his chest and tapped the badge that was pinned to the pocket of his gray security-guard uniform.

The emcee said, "Hey, I'm super-impressed, okay? Now, get away from the stage. You're making the girls nervous and you're fucking up the take. *Comprende*?"

From somewhere inside Viceroy Wilson came a wet growling noise. Jesús Bernal seized him by the arm and tried to pull him away from the stage, but it was too late. Wilson reached up and grabbed one of the emcee's black nylon ankles.

"Let go, you!" the emcee cried.

"Let go, Viceroy," Jesús Bernal pleaded.

"Aarrrummmm, rrmmmmm," Viceroy Wilson said.

Then the emcee was a blur, the microphone flying one way, a black shoe flying the other. The emcee's blow-dried head hit the stage with a crack that carried to every corner of the acoustically perfect auditorium. A few of the beauty contestants shrieked "Oh Jerry!" and ran to the young man's aid; others just stared with pained expressions at the prone tuxedo.

The security chief sprinted down the aisle and bounded onstage. "My God, what happened here? Back off, girls, give him air. Give him air."

Jesús Bernal glanced at Viceroy Wilson and thought: The dumb spade just ruined everything.

"The man slipped on a puddle," Bernal told the security chief.

"Naw, it was an epileptic attack," said Viceroy Wilson.

"Get a doctor!" the security chief hollered into his K-Mart walkie-talkie. "Somebody get a doctor."

"An epilepsy doctor," advised Viceroy Wilson.

Kara Lynn Shivers gracefully dropped to her knees and cradled the emcee's head. Discreetly she removed some tissue from the left cup of her bathing suit and began dabbing the emcee's forehead. The injured man gazed up at Kara Lynn's perfect sophomore breasts with a stunned but tranquil look.

"I told you she's gonna win," Viceroy Wilson whispered. "This'll be so damn easy."

"Let's move," Jesús Bernal said, commando style. "We've got to find the golf course before it gets dark."

"Hay-zoos, lemme tell you something," Wilson said, taking his time. "If your little box of Tinker Toys goes off before we get there, just 'member the last thing you're gonna see on this earth is my black face— and I'll be chewing on your fuckin' guts all the way to hell."

FIFTEEN

Like all terrible golfers, Dr. Remond Courtney believed that nothing was too extravagant for his game. He wore Arnold Palmer sweaters and Tom Watson spikes, and carried a full set of Jack Nicklaus MacGregors, including a six-wood that the Golden Bear himself couldn't hit if his life depended on it.

And like all terrible golfers, Dr. Courtney preferred to play very early in the morning, embracing the myth that golf balls fly farther in cool weather. Since he had no true friends at the Palmetto Country Club, Dr. Courtney often recruited his patients to play golf with him. This worked out fine if the patients were fairly stable, but occasionally one would go completely berserk. This usually happened on the back nine, which was lousy with water hazards, and Dr. Courtney would wave the other golfers to play through while he took an hour to tranquilize his partner. Some Thursdays a round of golf for Dr. Courtney was almost as grueling as a day at work, which is why he had no qualms about writing off all his MacGregors as a hefty tax deduction.

On December 13, Dr. Remond Courtney hitched up his pretentious tweed knickers and teed off at 7:08 A.M. The foursome included one of his patients—a vastly improved schizophrenic named Mario Groppo—and two total strangers from Seattle. The strangers were engineers for Boeing, the aerospace company, and they tended to shank the ball off the tee. Predictably, Mario Groppo would hook the ball on one hole and slice the ball on the next. Nobody in the foursome could putt worth a damn.

As for Dr. Remond Courtney, his golf swing was so unusual that from a distance he appeared to be beating a snake to death. It was a very violent golf swing for a psychiatrist. He managed an eight on the first hole and still won it by two strokes. It looked like it was going to be a long morning.

By the fifth tee, Dr. Courtney had become confident enough in his partners' ineptitude that he'd started betting on every hole. Poor Mario Groppo promptly dropped thirty dollars and appeared headed for a major anxiety attack; the Seattle tourists went to the bourbon flask early and lost their amiable out-of-towner dispositions. Every time Dr. Courtney would bend over a putt, one of them would fart or sneeze in flagrant violation of golf etiquette. The psychiatrist haughtily ignored this rudeness, no matter how many strokes it cost.

The foursome made the turn with Dr. Courtney leading the Seattle engineers by four and seven strokes respectively, while Mario Groppo sweated bullets somewhere around twenty over par.

Weatherwise it was a fine Florida day. The sky was china blue and a light breeze fought off the lethal humidity. As they strolled down the twelfth fairway, the psychiatrist sidled up to Mario and said, "So how are we feeling today, Mr. Groppo?"

"Just fine," replied Mario, fishing in his golf bag for a five iron.

"Come now," Dr. Courtney said. "Something's troubling you, isn't it?"

"I'm lying three in the rough. That's all that's troubling me."

"Are you sure? I've got some Thorazine in my golf bag."

"I'm fine," Mario said impatiently. "Thanks anyway."

Dr. Courtney patted him on the back and gave a doctorly wink. "When you want to talk, just let me know. I'll set aside some time."

Dr. Courtney and the Boeing engineers put their shots smack on the green, while Mario Groppo dumped his five-iron in the back bunker.

"Too much club," the psychiatrist remarked.

"Too much mouth," sniped one of the guys from Boeing.

Dr. Courtney snorted contemptuously and marched toward the green, his putter propped like a musket on his shoulder.

While the other golfers lined up their putts, poor Mario Groppo waded into the sand trap, a canyon from which he could barely see daylight.

"I'll hold the stick," Dr. Courtney called.

Over the lip of the bunker Mario could make out the tip of the flagstick, Dr. Courtney's pink face and, beyond that, the visors of the two Seattle tourists, waiting their turns.

The psychiatrist kept shouting advice. "Bend the left knee! Keep the club face open! Hit behind the ball!"

"Oh shut up," Mario Groppo said. He grimaced at

the idea of surrendering another ten bucks to Remond Courtney.

Mario glared down at the half-buried Titleist and grimly dug his spikes into the sand. He took one last look at the flag, then swung the wedge with a mighty grunt.

To everyone's surprise, Mario's golf ball leapt merrily from the sand trap, kissed the green, and rolled sweetly, inexorably toward the hole.

"All right!" exclaimed one of the Seattle tourists.

"I don't believe it," sniffed Dr. Courtney as Mario's ball dropped with a plunk.

At that instant the twelfth green of the Palmetto Country Club exploded in a hellish thunderclap. The bomb, hidden deep in the cup, launched the flagstick like a flaming javelin. The air crackled as a brilliant orange plume unfurled over the gentle fairways.

There was no time to run, no time to scream.

His face scorched and hair smoldering, poor Mario Groppo found himself lost in a crater. Haplessly he weaved in circles, using his sand wedge as a cane. "Holy God!" he mumbled, squinting through the smoke and silicate dust for some sign of the doomed threesome. "Holy Jesus God!" he said, as the sky rained wet clumps of sod and flesh, twisted stems of golf clubs, and bright swatches of Izod shirts.

Mario sat down in the dirt. In a daze he thought he heard a man's voice, and wondered if one of the other golfers had been spared.

"Hello! I'm right here!" Mario cried. "Over here!"

But the voice that replied was much too far away, and much too sonorous. The voice rose in proclamation from a stand of tall Australian pines bordering the thirteenth fairway.

"*Bon voyage*, Dr. Goosefucker!" the voice sang out. "Welcome to the Revolution!"

Jenna stood at the door, hands on her hips. "Boy, everybody in Miami's looking for you!" She wore an indigo Danskin and a white terrycloth headband. Her forehead was damp; the Jane Fonda workout video was on the television.

"May I come in?" Brian Keyes asked.

"Of course. I'm making granola bars. Come sit in the kitchen and talk."

Jenna was in her element, and Keyes knew he'd have to take it slowly. One wrong move and it was lights out.

"Cab called. He's hunting all over for you."

"I'll bet."

"What about these cops?" Jenna emptied a box of raisins into a mixing bowl. "Cab says the cops want to talk to you about what happened. Hey, are you feeling okay? How come you left the hospital so soon?"

"I got better," Keyes said, "thanks to this incredible nurse."

No reaction. Jenna stood at the kitchen counter with her back to him. She was stirring the granola mix.

"You're really something," Keyes said playfully. "I got in all kinds of trouble, you know."

"What kind of trouble?"

"The doctors chewed me out, moved me to a private room. They said we violated about five hundred hospital rules. The whole wing was talking about it."

"Yeah? You like carobs? I'm gonna add some carobs."

"I hate granola bars."

"These are homemade." Jenna's stirring became rhythmic.

"I talked to Skip today." She glanced over her shoulder at Keyes. "He wanted me to tell you how sorry he was about the Cuban. He said the little fellow means well; he just gets carried away with the knife. I told Skip you were doing better and he was quite relieved. He wanted me to tell you it won't happen again."

"How thoughtful," Keyes said acidly. "Where is the Madman of Miami, anyhow?"

"We didn't talk about that," Jenna said. She was padding around the kitchen in jazz exercise tights and no shoes. "Skip made a bunch of new rules," she said. "Rule number one: Don't ask where he is. Rule number two: Don't use his name over the telephone. Rule number three: No more horny love letters."

"Jenna, you've got to help me find him."

"Why? He's done nothing wrong. He told me he's got a clear conscience. Here, want a taste of this?" She thrust a wooden spoon in his mouth. "See, that's good stuff."

"Not bad," Keyes said, thinking: She's at it again.

Jenna poured the granola batter into a pan, and put the pan in the oven. She took a bottle of white wine from the refrigerator and poured herself a glass.

"Fewer calories than you think," she said, her green eyes sparkling through the wine crystal.

"You sure look great."

"As soon as the granola bars are done, I'm leaving town," Jenna announced.

Keyes said nothing.

"I'd ask you to stay for dinner, but I've got to catch a plane."

"I understand," Keyes said. "Where you going?"

"Wisconsin. T'see my folks."

No hesitation; she had it all worked out. Keyes admired her preparation. If he didn't know her so well he might've believed her. He tried to stall.

"May I have some wine?"

"Unh-unh," Jenna said. "Better not. You know how you get."

"Sleepy is how I get."

"No, sexy and romantic is how you get."

"What's wrong with that?"

"Tonight it's wrong."

"It wasn't wrong in the hospital, was it?"

"Not at all," Jenna said. "It was perfect in the hospital." She kissed him on the forehead; a polite little kiss that told Keyes his time was running out. She might as well have tapped her foot and pointed at the clock.

He stood up and took her hands. "Please help me."

"I can't," Jenna said firmly. She looked him straight in the eyes, and Keyes realized that, for her, this was no dilemma. She wasn't torn over loyalties. Skip Wiley came first, second, and third.

Keyes guessed how it must have started: a spark of an idea—maybe Jenna's, maybe Skip's—something mentioned over dinner, maybe even in the sack. A fantastic notion to turn back time, to drive out the carpetbaggers, to reclaim the land by painting it as treacherous and uninhabitable. And to do it all with sly tricks and egregious pranks—Armageddon, with mirrors. Wiley would have embraced the idea, embellished it, talked it to life, and made it all seem possible.

And Jenna, having started the spark or at least fanned it, would have slipped back to watch her passionate genius turn the whimsy into reality—watching with love and amazement, but not paying quite enough attention. So that when the killing started, and she finally understood how far he had carried the scheme, there was nothing to do but let him finish. The alternative was betrayal: to destroy Skip and orphan this dream, the thing they had created together.

"Is he going to stop this craziness?" Keyes asked.

"I don't think so," Jenna said, looking away.

"Then he'll be caught," Keyes said, "or killed."

"Oh, I doubt that." She removed her headband and plucked off her tiny gold earrings. "I know Skip, and he's way ahead of everybody. Even you, my love. Now, scoot out of here and let me pack. I've got a ten-o'clock plane."

Brian Keyes retreated to the living room and sat dejectedly on the coffin-turned-coffee-table.

"What are you doing?" Jenna asked from the kitchen doorway. "Brian, it's time to go."

"Did you hear what happened today? Today it was a goddamn bomb. Three people blown to bits. You think that's cute? The old Wiley sense of humor—you find bombs amusing?"

"Not particularly." Jenna paused, frowning briefly, and something crossed her face that Keyes seldom had seen. Guilt, remorse . . . something. "Don't jump to conclusions about Skip," she said finally. "That shrink had lots of enemies."

"This isn't a game of Clue," Keyes said. "Your boyfriend has become a murderer."

"It's not like you to get so melodramatic," Jenna said

impatiently. "Why can't you just leave it alone? Get busy on your other cases and forget about it. You did your job: you found Skip. When he's ready to come back, he will. That's what I told Cab this morning, but he's just like you. He thinks Skip has some kind of crazy death wish. Nothing could be sillier, Brian. I'm really disappointed in you guys." She was twirling the headband on her index finger, and looking very self-assured.

"Brian, you've got two problems Skip doesn't have."

"What's that?" Keyes asked, sensing defeat.

"Your ego and your heart."

"Well, pardon me." Now it was time to go. He didn't have to take this Joyce Brothers shit from a woman who bakes her own granola bars.

Halfway out the door he turned and said, "Jenna, what about the other night in the hospital? What *was* all that?"

"That was a moment, Brian, yours and mine." She smiled; the first soft smile of the whole evening. "It was one lovely moment, and that's all. Why does there have to be more? Why do you guys think there's always a Big Picture? Honest to God, Brian, sometimes I think the newspaper business fucked you up forever."

Jenna hardly ever used the word "fuck." Keyes figured she really must be agitated.

"Have a good trip," he said. "Give your parents my best."

"Aw, you're sweet," Jenna said. "You get some rest while I'm gone. Forget about Skip, forget about me, forget about the Big Picture. Everything's going to work out fine."

*

Ninety minutes later she left the house carrying a canvas travel bag and a tin of hot granola bars. She wore tight jeans, a loose long-sleeved blouse, and white heels. Her hair was pinned in a prim bun.

The drive to the airport was vintage Jenna—no recognition or regard for curbs, stop signs, traffic lights, or pedestrians. Brian Keyes kept a distance of two or three blocks, wincing at Jenna's close calls. He had borrowed a rental car from one of the Shriners because Jenna surely would've recognized the MG, by sound if not by sight.

She parked in the long-term garage at Miami International. Slouching low in the driver's seat, Keyes whizzed right past her and found a spot on the next level. He bolted from the car, raced down the stairwell, and caught sight of Jenna disappearing into the elevator. He ran all the way to the terminal building and waited.

Even in a crowd she was impossible to miss. She had a classic airport walk, sensual but aloof; men always moved out of the way to watch Jenna's jeans go by, back and forth, a divine natural metronome.

Keyes followed her until she stopped at the Bahamasair ticket counter. He hid behind a pillar, scouting for Skip Wiley.

"Want us to take over?"

Keyes wheeled around. "Jesus Christ!"

"Didn't mean to frighten you."

It was Burt the Shriner.

"Where'd you come from?" Keyes asked.

"Right behind you. Ever since you came in."

"And your pal?"

"He's around the corner. Keeping an eye on your lady friend."

Keyes was impressed; these guys weren't half-bad.

"She's on her way to Nassau," Burt reported. "Her ticket was prepaid."

"By whom?"

"The Seminole Nation of Florida, Incorporated. Does that make any sense, Mr. Keyes?"

"I'll explain later."

Keyes peered around the pillar at the Bahamassair counter, but Jenna was gone.

"Shit!"

"Don't worry," Burt said. "James is close behind."

"We're too damn late." Keyes broke into a run.

Because of the phenomenal number of airplane hijackings from Miami, the FAA had installed sophisticated new security measures designed to prevent anyone with bombs, guns, or invalid coach-class tickets from entering the flight concourse. The most effective of all these security steps was the hiring of squads of fat, foul-tempered, non-English-speaking women to obstruct all runways and harass all passengers.

In tracking Jenna, James the Shriner made it no farther than Concourse G, where a corpulent security guard named Lupee pinned him to the wall and questioned him relentlessly in Portuguese. The focus of her concern was the fez that James was wearing, which she tore off his head and ran through the X-ray machine several times, mashing it in the process. In the meantime Bahamasair Flight 123 to Nassau departed.

"I blew it," James apologized afterward in the coffee shop. "I'm sorry."

"Don't worry," Keyes said. "You didn't have a chance."

"Not one-on-one," Burt agreed. "Mr. Keyes, our

information says that your lady friend is traveling alone."

Somehow Burt had secured a printout of the passenger manifest (he wouldn't say how, and Keyes could only assume a fraternal Masonic connection with one of the ticket agents). With the Shriners staring over his shoulder, Keyes ran his finger down the passenger list. Wiley wouldn't be using his own name, nor would he settle for a simple Smith or Jones as an alias.

"Who are we hunting?" Burt asked.

"A very cunning fruitcake."

"What did you say his name was?"

"I didn't," Keyes said.

He found whom he was looking for, assigned to seats 15-A and 15-B:

"Karamazov, Viceroy."

"Karamazov, Skip."

Keyes crumpled the passenger manifest into a ball and disgustedly tossed it over his shoulder. The Shriners smoothed it out and studied the names.

"A real wiseass," Burt said. "This friend of yours, he seems to be enjoying all this, doesn't he?"

"Sure looks that way," Keyes grumbled, trying to remember where the hell he'd left his passport.

SIXTEEN

They found Skip Wiley snoring beneath a baby-blue umbrella on Cable Beach. He wore ragged denim cutoffs and no shirt. A pornographic novel titled *Crack of Dawn* was open across his lap. A half-empty bottle of Myers's rum perspired in a plastic bucket of ice, protected by the shade of Wiley's torso.

Brian Keyes removed the rum and dumped the ice cubes over Wiley's naked chest.

"Christ on a bike!" Wiley sat up like a bolt.

"Hello, Skip."

"You're one cruel fucker." Wiley reached for a towel. "Introduce me to your friends."

"This is Burt and this is James."

"Love the hats, guys. Sorry I missed the sale." Wiley shook hands with the Shriners. "Pull up some beach and have a seat. Terrific view, just like on *Love Boat*, huh?"

Burt and James silently agreed; they had never seen the ocean so glassy, so crystalline blue. It truly was a tropical paradise. The cabdriver had said that one of the James Bond movies had been filmed in this cove, and from then on the Shriners had felt they were on a great adventure. They didn't know what to make of this fellow under the beach umbrella, but they'd already agreed to let Brian Keyes do the talking.

"Where's Jenna?" Keyes asked. He liked to start with the easy questions.

"House hunting," Wiley said. "I can't stand this goddamn hotel. Full of American rubes and geeks pissing away Junior's college fund at the blackjack tables. It's pathetic." Wiley poured himself an iceless rum and cranberry juice. "How're the ribs, Brian?"

"Getting better." Keyes was scouting the shoreline.

"Relax, he's not here."

"Who?"

"Viceroy, that's who! So you can unpucker your asshole. I sent him on some errands because I wanted privacy. Now you show up with these burly bookends."

"They're friends of Theodore Bellamy."

"I see," Wiley said, scratching his head. "So we're here for vengeance, are we? Brian, I hope you explained to your companions that they are now on foreign soil and treading in a country that takes a dim view of kidnapping and murder. A country that respects the rights of all foreign nationals and adheres to the strictest legal tests for extradition."

"Meaning what?" Burt demanded.

"Meaning you and your bucket-headed partner are on your way to Fox Hill Prison if you fuck with me," Skip Wiley said, waving his rum glass. "I'm a guest here, an honored guest."

This problem had occurred to Brian Keyes as soon as he set foot in Nassau. He had no idea how one would go about kidnapping Skip Wiley and hauling him back to Florida. By boat? Barge? Private helicopter? And if one succeeded, then what? No charges had been filed against Wiley in the States because no one, besides Keyes and possibly Cab Mulcahy, knew the true identity of *El Fuego*.

"Did you kill Dr. Courtney?" Keyes asked.

"Ho-ho-ho."

"Why'd you do it?"

"Please," Wiley said, raising a hand, "we've been through all this."

"You need help, Skip."

"I've got all the help I need, Ace. Look, you're lucky I'm still talking to you. I gave you everything you'd need to turn the cops loose like a bunch of bloodhounds."

"I lost the briefcase."

"Swell, just swell." Wiley laughed sourly. "Some fucking private eye you turned out to be. I will admit one thing: that was a great line you fed Bloodworth about Slavic crazoids in fright wigs. Just the right nuance of xenophobia."

"I was hoping nobody'd believe it."

Wiley's cavernous grin disappeared and his lively brown eyes hardened. "Tell your friends to take a stroll," he said under his breath. "I want to talk to you."

Keyes motioned to the Shriners and they trudged down the beach, glancing over their shoulders every few steps.

"So talk," Keyes said to Wiley.

"You think I'm just a deranged egomaniac?"

"Oh no, Skip, you're completely normal. Every newspaper has at least one or two reporters who moonlight as mass murderers. It's a well-known occupational hazard."

Wiley sniffed scornfully. "Let me assure you, my young friend, that I'm not crazy. I know what I'm doing, and I know what I've done. You're fond of the word *murderer*—fine. Call me whatever you want. Zealotry can be grueling, that's for sure; don't think it doesn't take a toll on the psyche—or the conscience. But just for the record, it's not my name that's important, it's the group's. Recognition is damned essential to morale, Brian, and morale is vital to the cause. These fellas deserve some ink."

"But a revolution? Skip, really."

"Revolution?—perhaps you're right; perhaps that's hyperbole. But Jesús and Viceroy are fond of the imagery, so I indulge them." Wiley tossed his rum glass into the sand. "So there'll be no revolution, in the classic sense, but chaos? You bet. Shame. Panic. Flight. Economic disaster."

"Pretty ambitious," Keyes said.

"It's the least I can do," Wiley said. "Brian, what is Florida anyway? An immense sunny toilet where millions of tourists flush their money and save the moment on Kodak film. The recipe for redemption is simple: scare away the tourists and pretty soon you scare off the developers. No more developers, no more bankers. No more bankers, no more lawyers. No more lawyers, no more dope smugglers. The whole motherfucking economy implodes! Now, tell me I'm crazy."

Brian Keyes knew better than to do that.

Wiley's long hair glinted gold in the Bahamian sun. He wore a look of lionly confidence. "So the question," he went on, "is how to scare away the tourists."

"Murder a few," Keyes said.

"For starters."

"Skip, there's got to be another way."

"No!" Wiley shot to his feet, uprooting the beach umbrella with his head. "There ... is ... no ... other ... way! Think about it, you mullusk-brained moron! What gets headlines? Murder, mayhem, and madness—the cardinal M's of the newsroom. That's what terrifies the travel agents of the world. That's what rates congressional hearings and crime commissions. And that's what frightens off bozo Shriner conventions. It's a damn shame, I grant you that. It's a shame I simply couldn't stand up at the next county commission meeting and ask our noble public servants to please stop destroying the planet. It's a shame that the people who poisoned this paradise won't just apologize and pack their U-Hauls and head back North to the smog and the blizzards. But it's a proven fact they won't leave until somebody lights a fire under 'em. That's what *Las Noches de Diciembre* is all about. *'Cops Seek Grisly Suitcase Killer'* ... *'Elderly Woman Abducted, Fed to Vicious Reptile'* ... *'Golf Course Bomb Claims Three on Tricky Twelfth Hole'* ... *'Crazed Terrorists Stalk Florida Tourists.'*" Wiley was practically chanting the headlines, as if he were watching them roll off the presses at the *New York Post*.

"Sure, it's cold-blooded," he said, "but that's the game of journalism for you. It's the only game I know, but I know how to win."

"The old hype button," Keyes said.

"You got it, Ace!" Wiley slapped him on the shoulder. "Let's go find your funny friends."

They walked up Cable Beach. Keyes sidestepped the wavelets but Wiley crashed ahead, kicking water with his enormous slabs of feet. He cocked his head high, chin thrust toward the sun.

"If you hate tourists so much," Keyes said, "why'd you come here, of all places?"

"Sovereignty," Wiley replied, "and convenience. Besides, the Bahamas is different from Florida. The A.Q. here is only forty-two."

A.Q., Keyes remembered, stood for Asshole Quotient. Skip Wiley had a well-known theory that the quality of life declined in direct proportion to the Asshole Quotient. According to Wiley's reckoning, Miami had 134 total assholes per square mile, giving it the worst A.Q. in North America. In second place was Aspen, Colorado (101), with Malibu Beach, California, finishing third at 97.

Every year Skip Wiley wrote a column rating the ten most unbearable places on the continent according to A.Q., and every year the city editor diligently changed "Asshole Quotient" to "Idiot Quotient" before the column could be published. The next day Wiley would turn in a new column apologizing to his readers because he'd neglected to count one more total asshole, that being his own editor. And of course Wiley's editor would immediately delete *that*, too. After a few years it was obvious that even Skip Wiley couldn't get the word *asshole* into the Miami *Sun*, but the whole newsroom looked forward to the annual struggle.

"The great thing about the Bahamas," Wiley was saying, "is that they don't let the tourists stay. Trying to buy property here is like trying to get a personal audience with the pope. Damn near impossible without the right connections. So, Mr. and Mrs. Mickey Mouse Ears from Akron can come and tinkle away all their money, but then it's bye-bye, leavin' on a jet plane.

Punch out at immigrations. Too bad they didn't think of this system in Florida."

"Florida's not an island, Skip."

Wiley hopped over two Bahamian children who were wrestling in the water. His gravelly, melodic laughter mixed with their giggles and carried into the surf.

"Don't you think this has gone far enough?" Keyes asked.

"I was waiting for you to say that," Wiley said, marching ahead. "Mr. I'm-Only-Trying-to-Help, that's you. A real killjoy."

Keyes stopped walking. The blue water curled over his tennis shoes. "I hate to see people die, that's all," he said to Wiley.

"I know you do," Wiley said, looking back. "So do I. Believe it or not." He didn't need to say any more. They were both remembering little Callie Davenport.

Up ahead a crowd of bathers gathered noisily in a circle under some slash pines. Keyes and Wiley heard the sound of men shouting and, in the distance, a siren.

Keyes thought of Burt and James and started running, his sneakers squishing in the sand. Wiley put on a sudden burst of speed and caught him by the arm.

"Wait a minute, Ace, better let me check this out."

On the fringe of the mêlée Keyes counted four Bahamian policemen, each wearing a pith helmet and crisp white uniform. They carried hard plastic batons but no sidearms. Wiley strolled up and started chatting with one of the cops; he came back with the bad news.

"I'm afraid your friends had to learn the hard way."

From a distance Keyes watched the Bahamian officers lead Burt and James away from the beach. The purple fez hats were easy to follow, bobbing above the jolly crowd.

"What the hell happened?" Keyes asked, contemplating a rescue attempt.

"Stay here," Wiley cautioned, "unless you're into bondage."

What had happened was this: on their reluctant trek down Cable Beach, the keen-eyed Shriners had spotted none other than Viceroy Wilson, the fugitive football star, coming toward them. As usual Wilson was wrapped safely behind his Carrera sunglasses and, as usual, he was stoked to the gills, having scored some primo Jamaican herb off a busboy at the hotel. Viceroy Wilson had never been to the islands, and the striking display of Bahamian womanhood along the beach had seriously diverted his attention from the revolution. Wilson was so preoccupied that he hadn't noticed the two husky purple-hatted honkies in gray suits stalking him among the bathers.

The Shriners had struck swiftly, with a sinister rustle of polyester. Burt had seized Viceroy Wilson's left arm and James had grabbed the right, pivoting and twisting in a very sophisticated karate maneuver. Unfortunately, the people who invented karate never got to practice on 235-pound former NFL fullbacks with sequoia-sized arms. Viceroy Wilson had disrespectfully flattened the Shriners and broken hard for the hotel. Robbed of agility by the marijuana, he'd tripped on an Igloo cooler and gone down. The Shriners had been upon him quickly, puffing and grunting and attaching themselves to his powerful torso. Somehow Viceroy Wilson had risen to his feet and galvanized his famous legs. The old reflexes had taken command; with Shriners clinging to his thighs, Wilson churned along the beach. It was a memorable sight, and several quick-witted tourists had turned their home-movie cameras toward the combat. Viceroy Wilson was all elbows and knees and speed, and the Shriners had fallen away, tassels spinning. Eventually the police had arrived and arrested Burt and James for assault. The officers apologized profusely to Skip Wiley, for they specifically had been recruited to keep watch over Wiley's entourage, a commitment guaranteed by a generous cash gratuity.

"I told your bookends to behave," Wiley said reproachfully as they watched the police van drive off.

Keyes asked wearily, "Are they going to jail?"

"Naw, to the airport. They'll be deported as undesirables. Certainly can't argue with that."

They returned to the shade of the blue umbrella. Keyes sat down in the cool sand. Wiley stretched out on the patio chair.

"They're going to figure out it's you," Keyes said. "The cops, the press. Somebody'll put it together."

"Not for a while." Wiley squinted into the sun. "You weren't thinking about squealing, were you?"

Keyes shook his head and looked away, out at the gentle waves. *Of course I'm thinking about it, you jerk.*

"Because I meant what I said before," Wiley said. "If the cops catch on to me too soon, we're in trouble. And if they do catch on, I'll know it was you. Nobody else."

"But, Skip, there's all kinds of clues. Wilson and the Cuban, they're leaving a trail—"

"Fine, no problem. That we can survive. Besides, they're secretly dying to be famous again. Me—I've got to work in the background right now. Too much planning to be done, juking here and there. I can't have Metro Homicide sniffing after me; it plays hell with the creative process. See, if I'm exposed as *El Fuego*, I'll lose my leverage with the troops. It'll mean I'm not so shrewd, not so clever, not so irreplaceable. They'll stop listening to me, Brian, and that's big goddamn trouble. Some of the things these fellas want to do, some of the people they want to snuff! Lose me and you lose the voice of reason. Then it's Bloodbath City, old pal, and that ain't standard Wiley hyperbole. That's a goddamn fact."

Keyes studied his unraveled friend and thought of the Ida Kimmelman ceremony. Skip's threat of a massacre seemed deadly serious.

Keyes said, "If you've got them so mesmerized, convince them to call it off."

Wiley answered with a snort. "Never! The cause is just. The dream is pure." He pointed a finger at Keyes. "It's up to you and Cab and the others to end the violence. How? Accept the Nights of December as a legitimate terrorist cell. Give us a forum. Pass the message that we're serious, that we'll continue the campaign until the exodus is fully under way. Ha! Imagine: bumper-to-bumper from Key West to Jacksonville: U-Hauls, Winnebagos, Airstreams, station wagons, moving vans, buses, eighteen-wheelers. All north-bound!" Wiley sat up animatedly. "Brian, in the last hour we've been talking, 41.6 morons moved into the state of Florida. They are arriving at the rate of a thousand a day. One thousand each and every day!

There is *no place to put them!* The land is shriveling beneath us, the water is poison, the air is rancid." Wiley threw back his head. "Lord, such a simple equation. Nature's trying to tell us it's time to move on."

"The last of the Malthusians," Keyes said.

"Hell, Malthus only *dreamed* a nightmare like Interstate 95. He never had to drive the fucking thing."

Keyes thought: He seems to have his mind made up. Maybe I'll have to kill him after all. Certainly not now, not on a crowded beach in the afternoon. But maybe soon.

Wiley propped his fuzzy chin on his knuckles and grew silent. He watched the arrival of a gleaming cruise ship across the harbor. Its alabaster decks were lined with bright specks of tourists snapping pictures and flailing idiotic hellos toward the peddlers on the dock. Wiley looked quite amused. Brian Keyes wished he could penetrate his old friend's twisted swamp of a brain; he felt more helpless than ever.

Wiley said: "I suppose you want to hear what's next."

"You bet."

"It's a real beaut."

"Let's have it."

"Okay," Wiley said. "We're going to violate the most sacred virgin in all Miami."

"Can you be a little more specific?"

"'Fraid not, Brian. You're a bright young man, you figure it out."

"When you say violate, you mean rape."

"Hell no!" Wiley was indignant. "I can't believe you'd think such a thing. All the years we've known each other—Christ, do I look like a rapist?"

213

Keyes didn't answer because sometimes Skip Wiley *did* look like a rapist.

"The word 'violate'—"

"Dust off your dictionary, Ace. We're going to desecrate an immaculate princess. That's all the clues for you."

Wiley dug into his jeans and came up with a silver traffic whistle, which he blew three times, loudly.

"What the hell is that?" Keyes asked, realizing that it was too late.

"Time for you to say good-bye to Goombayland."

Keyes caught sight of four starch-shirted Bahamian cops running down the beach, kicking up sand with their black boots, and waving batons.

"Oh shit," Keyes muttered.

"Look at them move," Wiley marveled. "Isn't bribery wonderful?"

Keyes quickly reviewed his options. Physical resistance was out of the question; the policemen looked like four scowling black locomotives. Running also seemed futile—there was nowhere to go where he wouldn't shine like a two-hundred-watt bulb. He considered plunging into the surf and swimming for freedom, but was dissuaded by the probability of being mortally gnawed by a bull shark, or mowed down by a ski boat. In the end, Keyes meekly presented himself to the Bahamian officers. The tropical sunshine seemed to evaporate as they encircled him.

"Take it easy, men," Skip Wiley said, unfurling from the beach chair. "He's obviously harmless."

Eight rock-hard hands clamped onto Brian Keyes.

"I guess this means you and Jenna aren't inviting me up for conch chowder."

"'Fraid not, Brian." Wiley yawned, stretching his ropy brown arms. "Have a safe trip home."

"When am I gonna see you again, Skip?"

"Soon," Wiley said. "On national TV. Now, if you'll excuse me, I'm late for my windsurfing lesson."

SEVENTEEN

"Kara Lynn."

"Yes, Mr. Mayor."

"What do you think about famine?"

Kara Lynn Shivers considered the question carefully. "Which famine, Mr. Mayor?"

"World famine," the mayor said, "in general."

"Well, in general," Kara Lynn said, "I think famine is a truly terrible thing."

"If you were selected our Orange Bowl queen," the mayor went on, "would you work to end world famine?"

"Tirelessly, Mr. Mayor."

The other judges nodded approvingly. They liked Kara Lynn Shivers better than the other semifinalists, and they'd already made up their minds. If only the mayor would hurry up with the last interview.

"How would you do it?" the mayor asked.

"Do what?" Kara Lynn said.

"Stop famine."

"I didn't say I could stop it," Kara Lynn said with a trace of sarcasm. In the third row she spotted her father, grimly making a slashing motion across his throat.

"But I'd certainly try," she said, softening. "As you know, I'm majoring in public relations, Mr. Mayor, and

I could use those special skills to bring the world's attention to the plight of its starving children. I would consider that my first priority as Orange Bowl queen."

The mayor beamed. Kara Lynn's father let out a sigh of relief.

"Thank you, Kara Lynn," the mayor said. "We'll adjourn until tonight."

"Thank you, Mr. Mayor," Kara Lynn said. Then, nodding sweetly toward the other judges, "Thank *all* of you."

And now, she thought, you can all go back to the Hyatt and whack off.

Kara Lynn Shivers, nineteen years old, blond, hazel-eyed, five-foot-eight, one hundred twenty pounds (Viceroy Wilson was on the money), had become a cynical young woman. She despised beauty pageants and all the fraudulent insouciance they required. Though she had won many titles—Little Miss Mass Transit, Miss Anglo Miami and, of course, Stone Crab Queen—each new tiara only added to Kara Lynn's deepening misery. Offstage she had no smiles, no charms, no patience. She was all used up.

It was her father's fault. He was the one who'd made her learn "Eleanor Rigby" on the French horn. "The judges'll love it," he'd said, and they always did.

It was her father who made her, at age six, change her name from Karen Noreen because "Noreen belongs in the 4-H, not Atlantic City."

It was her father who dragged her to Geneva, at age nine, to be ministered by "the greatest ambidextrous orthodontist in all Europe."

Kara Lynn Shivers suspected there was something seriously hinky with her father—not for wanting his little princess to be a star (a harmless fantasy), but for suggesting that no price was too high.

It was her father who'd mailed off a stack of bikini Polaroids to *Playboy* magazine, then to *Penthouse*, then *Oui*, and after countless rejections announced that Kara Lynn needed bigger breasts. Kara Lynn didn't want bigger breasts. Her little breasts were just fine; round, perky, very cute. No one ever complained about her breasts except her father, who hadn't seen them naked since she was a kid anyway.

One afternoon, a few months before the Orange Bowl pageant, Kara Lynn's father secretly invited a renowned plastic surgeon to the house. Kara Lynn had just returned from exercise class in a pink body stocking. She was in the kitchen, fixing a pitcher of iced tea, when the two men slipped up behind her.

"Well, what do you think?" her father had asked.

"No sweat," the surgeon had said. "B-cup, or C?"

"Stay away from my tits!" Kara Lynn had cried, reaching for a steak knife.

"But, buttercup, I'm only trying to help."

"They're my tits, Dad. You stay away!"

"Forty million people watch that parade on New Year's Eve. Don't you want to make a good impression?"

Kara Lynn's mother was no help.

"Your father just wants the best for you," she'd said. "What's so wrong with that?"

"Mother!"

"It'll be a lovely Christmas present."

"But I don't want new boobs for Christmas," Kara Lynn said, "I want a Volkswagen."

On the night of December 16, Kara Lynn Shivers and

her original breasts charmed a small but enthusiastic crowd at the Civic Center, and the judges unanimously crowned her Miami's Orange Bowl queen. A surprise guest, Julio Iglesias, presented Kara Lynn with a bouquet of roses. She smiled expertly and accepted Julio's kiss, but her heart was not aflutter. After the television lights went dark, Jerry, the oily emcee, thanked Kara Lynn for reviving him after his altercation with the black security guard. Jerry told Kara Lynn he was "wiped out emotionally" by her rendition of "Eleanor Rigby," and asked if she'd join him for a drink.

"You just want a blow-job," Kara Lynn said. "What's that got to do with world famine?"

Kara Lynn Shivers decided that the Orange Bowl would be her last beauty pageant. She was right.

The week of December 16 was the busiest yet for *Las Noches de Diciembre*. Three more tourists vanished, a drunken college kid was eaten alive by a wild crocodile, and the bucolic Hibiscus Kennel Club was the grisly scene for what became known as the Trifecta Massacre. The national wire services were slowly awakening to Florida's newest crime wave, and no less an authority than the *New York Times* published its own priceless account: *Abductions of Florida Tourists Trouble Some Authorities*.

It was the worst week in the entire life of Detective Harold Keefe.

With Skip Wiley out of the country, Jesús Bernal went hog-wild with bombs. He built three of them, and typed up a preliminary list of targets:

1. Detective Harold Keefe.
2. Anyplace with lots of tourists.
3. Anyplace with lots of Communists.

The first bombing was not a total success.

On the morning of December 17, Harold Keefe left his house at the usual time and took his usual route to the Metro-Dade Police Department. From keen surveillance Jesús Bernal knew that between 7:38 and 7:46 A.M., Detective Keefe would pass through the toll plaza on the Dolphin Expressway. He also knew that Keefe would use the lane marked Trucks-Change-Receipts. Jesús Bernal was ready. He got to the toll booth at 7:25 A.M., tied up the cashier, and watched for Harold Keefe's unmarked black Plymouth Volare.

Harold Keefe was not at his most observant early in the morning. He scarcely glanced at the lean Cuban cashier who dropped his change—"Sorry, meester!"—and crawled under his car, groping (Kccfc assumed) for the quarter. And he paid no attention to the faint plink of metal on metal.

Which was the sound of Jesús Bernal attaching the remote-control bomb.

"Have a nice day!" Bernal waved as Harold Keefe drove away.

Sixty seconds later the bomb exploded, lifting the black Volare out of rush-hour traffic and dropping it into a drainage culvert.

Harold Keefe was not killed. The Miami *Sun* described his wounds as "massive foot injuries," which is another way of saying that the detective's toes were blown off, every single one; other than that, Harold Keefe hopped away without a scratch. It was one of the strangest bombings anyone could remember, and it was not what Jesús Bernal had in mind.

The second bomb was more powerful, and its results more spectacular. It blew up on the night of December 18, during the first race at the Hibiscus Kennel Club before a record crowd of 14,501 spectators (including two-thirds of the county commission). The kennel club bomb actually was a small land mine, a rudimentary imitation claymore, which Jesús Bernal had buried on the second turn of the track. The greyhound that triggered the mine was a speedy dam named Blistered Sister who went off at 20-to-1. Literally. One second there were eight lank dogs churning along the rail, and the next they were airborne, inside-out. It was a mess. The blast took out a sixty-foot stretch of racetrack and disrupted betting for hours. Blistered Sister, whose brindle carcass landed closest to the finish wire, was ruled the winner and paid out $40.60 on a $2 ticket. As the kennel crews repaired the mangled track with a backhoe and shovels, a taut, unfamiliar voice rang out of the public address system:

"*Hola*, Pari-Mutuel Wagerers," the voice said. "Welcome to the Revolution!"

Only the county commissioners seemed alarmed.

The third bomb was the one Jesús Bernal saved. He'd looked all over Miami for a gathering of Communists to blow up, but found none. He knew they were there— they *had* to be. Bernal didn't want to waste this bomb because it was a real masterpiece; his ticket back to the First Weekend in July. He decided to save the bomb until some Communists popped up. If worse came to worst, he could always plant it at ACLU.

While Jesús Bernal scurried around town with his

C-4 and blasting caps, Tommy Tigertail and Viceroy Wilson (back from Nassau, still celibate) picked off three more tourists.

"We need the stats," Skip Wiley had urged by telegram.

"Stats?" mumbled the Indian.

Viceroy Wilson understood perfectly.

The kidnappings were nothing fancy: a young surfer at the Pompano Pier, lured to a waiting Cadillac with a lid of fresh Colombian red; and a middle-aged couple from White Plains who mysteriously vanished from their front-row table during Jackie Mason's second show at the Diplomat.

At midweek, Tommy Tigertail delivered some grim news.

"Pavlov is sick," he told Viceroy Wilson at the Everglades campsite.

"I'll bet it was that goddamned surfer," Wilson said.

"No," the Indian said, "it's the water. He needs salt water."

Viceroy Wilson scanned the pond for the ominous brown log that was Pavlov's snout. From a distance—a safe distance—the monster looked just fine.

"This is a North American crocodile. His habitat is salt water," Tommy explained. "He's been out here two weeks and now he needs to go home."

"Fine with me," Viceroy Wilson said.

The second they got the ropes on Pavlov, Viceroy saw what the Indian was talking about. The big croc was listless and cloudy-eyed. Even its hiss sounded anemic.

Hauling Pavlov from the bowels of the Glades to the shores of Biscayne Bay turned out to be a day-long endeavor. Even in a state of lethargy the crocodile was formidable cargo, and its disposition did not improve as the trip wore on. The Indian had rented a tractor-trailer for the journey, but there wasn't enough room in the cab for all three commandos. Viceroy Wilson decided that Jesús Bernal, by virtue of his switchblade prowess, was best equipped to ride in back with the giant reptile. Every time Tommy Tigertail took a sharp corner the trailer came alive with muffled hissing and Spanish invective.

At dusk they pulled off the Seventy-ninth Street Causeway, dragged Pavlov out of the rig, and prodded him into the salty shallows of Biscayne Bay. The croc swam east, never looking back, propelled by that massive rhythmic tail. Pavlov did not stop swimming for thirty hours. He crossed the bay, entered the Atlantic through Haulover Cut, and churned north along the Gold Coast. It was as if, Skip Wiley mused later, the great beast somehow had been imbued with the spirit of *Las Noches;* as if it had drawn inspiration from its captors.

To Viceroy Wilson, the explanation was more elementary: Seminole magic. The damn Indian had worked a spell.

Pavlov stopped swimming when he reached the famous Ft. Lauderdale beachfront. There, in darkness, he dragged his thousand pounds ashore and made for the party lights of the Barbary Coast Hotel. Later, in daylight, beachgoers would trace the crocodile's lethal path by the trench in the sand.

Wiley's mystical notions aside, what probably happened was that the croc merely grew tired of fighting the ocean currents and came ashore to rest. Once on land, its nostrils got wind of the Barbary's luxuriant saltwater swimming pool, and Pavlov had decided to enjoy himself.

Besides being young, drunk, and stupid, Kyle Griffith (University of Georgia, Class of '87) had no good reason to be in that swimming pool at four in the morning. A bad reason for being there—nude, save for a foam-rubber hat that said "Go Bulldawgs!"—was that Griffith's dithering Sigma Nu brothers had dared him to jump thirty feet from the balcony of the hotel room to the warm pool, which lay in darkness so complete that even a seventeen-foot crocodile could be invisible.

Having eaten prodigiously in recent days, Pavlov was not very hungry. A snack would have been fine, perhaps a coot or a small garfish. But once Kyle Griffith hit the water, Pavlov's dinosaural instincts took over. The crocodile seized the bewildered Sigma Nu by the legs and submerged to the bottom of the swimming pool, where the beast lay motionless for several minutes, as if contemplating the wisdom of its own gluttony. In the end, of course, the college kid was consumed, though Pavlov regurgitated the silly rubber hat.

This onslaught of violent and weird events destroyed Detective Harold Keefe's hoax theory (not to mention his career) and convinced the civic leaders of Dade County that a ruthless band of psychopaths was indeed roaming the streets.

Toeless and sullen, Keefe was spared the shame of a demotion and allowed to take a generous disability leave from the police department.

On the morning of December 20, while Brian Keyes

was on the phone to the U.S. State Department, three uniformed police officers arrived at his office and politely requested his company downtown. Keyes had been expecting the visit, and was in no mood to argue. He had spent the week dodging Ricky Bloodworth and trying to negotiate the release of the two Shriners from a Bahamian prison, where they were being held on vague charges of espionage and lobster poaching. Keyes sent word to Skip Wiley that enough was enough, the joke was over, but all he got back was a cable that said: "Don't you have work to do?" Eventually Burt and James were fined five thousand dollars each and placed on a nonstop Nassau-to-Chicago flight. Keyes had been playing dumb with the State Department when the cops showed up.

At police headquarters Keyes was led to a soundproof conference room and told to wait. The windowless suite was newly carpeted and smelled like paint. On the wall hung a blackboard on which someone had chalked the words: "*Las Noches de Diciembre?* Nights of December?" After a few minutes Al García strolled in, grinning like a whale.

"No more motor pool!" he chortled. "Welcome to the big time."

"Big time, Al?"

"My very own task force. Can you believe it, Brian, they put *me* in charge."

"In charge of what?"

"In charge of solving the *Las Noches* murders."

"No offense, Al," Keyes said, "but why you?"

"Well, the gang has a Spanish name. I'm a Spanish cop." García laughed until he turned red. He sat down at the head of a long table and lit a cigarette. "It's all top secret, this task force, and let's keep it thataway. We don't want to cause a panic, close the hotels, God forbid. It's the season, y'know."

García was still chuckling. Keyes knew he didn't give a shit about the hotels.

"How big is your task force?"

"Four detectives, including me, plus a guy at the FBI if we need him. We got a real code name and everything: Fuego One."

"I like it," Keyes said. Almost time for the big decision. García was finished circling.

"So, my friend, you've had quite a time of it, eh?"

"Quite a time," Keyes agreed.

"Let's talk about it." García fished a spiral notebook from his rumpled jacket. "What do you know about this outfit?"

"I know they set up Ernesto Cabal for a fall. The poor putz had nothing to do with Sparky Harper's death, just like I tried to tell you weeks ago."

García frowned. "I'm sorry, man. Really. He looked hot, and he was all we had at the time."

"And that's it? *Adiós*, Ernesto."

"What do you want, five Hail Marys? I said I was fucking sorry, and I am. Don't forget I didn't kill Cabal, Brian, he killed himself. A little more patience and the *hijo de puta* mighta walked out of jail a free man."

Keyes said, "He was scared, that's all."

"Yeah, man, well, I'm kinda scared too. I'm scared these nuts are gonna murder more innocent people. And I'm scared that I'm going to have to look at more legless dead bloated bodies. But most of all I'm scared of what my wife's going to do when I tell her I have to work through Christmas! So, rest in peace and forgive me,

Ernesto"—García made a perfunctory sign of the cross—"but I got to get busy."

"I'll try to help, Al."

"Excellent. You can start by telling me who you saw out there in the Glades. Anybody interesting?"

"Guy named Jesús Bernal."

"Hey, our bomber! Sloppy fucker, too. Left his fingerprints all over the piping. Buys the wire in Hialeah." García jotted in his notepad. "He the one who jammed the shiv in your ribs?"

"I think so," Keyes said.

"What about your pal from Pauly's joint, the football hero?"

"Viceroy Wilson. Yeah, him too."

"He must be *El Fuego*."

Keyes thought: There it is. Time to shut up or throw in Wiley. Once it was done, there'd be no going back.

"Al, I'm not sure."

"About what?"

"*El Fuego*. See, there were four of them, and they never mentioned it."

García cigarette toggled excitedly. "Four of them! Who were the other two?"

"There was an Indian."

"A raghead Indian or a Tonto Indian?"

"A Seminole. Tommy Tigertail, they call him."

"The man with the Cadillac," García said. He jotted down Tommy's name and asked, "How about number four?"

"White male, late thirties." Keyes shrugged. "It was dark, like I said." So that was the decision: to get Skip Wiley himself. Keyes knew he stood a better chance of finding him quietly, with no police sirens. Most of all he was worried about Wiley's threat of a bloodbath; what had seemed unthinkable three weeks ago seemed imminent now.

García sat back and folded his puffy hands. "Something's bothering me, *amigo*. I think to myself, why the hell would these maniacs snatch mild-mannered Brian Keyes, of all people? I mean, if they weren't gonna kill you, then why take the risk? They just want to chat or what?"

"They wanted me to witness a murder," Keyes said.

"And did you?"

"Yes, I think so. Ida Kimmelman was the woman's name."

"The Broward condo queen," García muttered, writing intently.

"They fed her to a crocodile," Keyes said.

"Who?"

"Wilson and Bernal. They threw her in a pond—why are you looking at me like that?"

Al García capped his pen. "Go on, Brian."

"I'm not making this up. They threw her in the water and a crocodile ate her."

Lost in thought, García gnawed on a thumbnail. He'd heard about the college kid who got gobbled up in Lauderdale and pondered the connection—after all, how many crocodiles could there be?

Keyes said: "They did it for effect. For headlines, that's all."

"Why didn't you report this a week ago?"

"And read about it on the front page? No way, that's exactly what they wanted. I wasn't about to let them use me."

"Very noble," García said caustically. "Really showed

'em who's boss. By the way, hotshot, you been reading the fucking newspaper this week? Your pals out there in the swamp make Richard Speck look like Soupy Sales."

"For God's sake, Al, it's not like I've been on vacation. What do you think I've been working on?"

"Tell me more."

"I'd like to."

"Excellent." García tapped his pen on the table.

"Al, they're planning something big." Without naming Skip Wiley, Keyes recounted the enigmatic threat to "violate the most sacred virgin in all Miami."

"Sounds like Rape City."

"I think it's worse than that."

"Maybe you could find that camp again."

"Not in a million years," Keyes said. He was telling the truth.

"I'll get a chopper and we'll take a SWAT team."

"How about the National Guard?"

"Don't laugh," García said. "They've promised whatever I need."

"Find the Cuban and the football player," Keyes advised, "and that'll be the end of it. No more kidnappings."

"Brian, I get the feeling you're holding back." García peered over the top of his reading glasses. "Tell me you're not holding back."

"Al, I don't remember much. I was busy losing three units of blood."

"Yeah, well, maybe something'll come back to you." García waved good-bye with the cigarette. "We'll talk again. Sanchez will give you a lift downtown."

Keyes started to get up from the table.

"By the way," García said, "that was a helluva funny piece in the *Sun* today. D'you see it?"

"My paper was in a puddle."

"Well, I got it in my coat somewhere. Clipped it out. Here it is . . . I hate to admit it, but I actually started to miss this asshole's column while he was out sick."

"May I?" Keyes asked. Apprehensively he lifted the folded newspaper clipping from García's brown paw. He opened it at arm's length, as if it were radioactive.

"Go ahead, read it," Al García said. "It's funny as hell. All about his vacation in the Bahamas. The guy's got a regular way with words."

"So he does," said Brian Keyes, trying not to appear dumbfounded by what he saw.

In print.

With a studio photo.

Under a headline that said:

Wiley Returns.

EIGHTEEN

*Nassau—**The worst** thing about visiting the Bahamas is Americans like me. The hotels are lousy with us.*

Americans with terrible manners.

Americans who talk like the rest of the world is deaf.

And dress like the rest of the world is blind.

I come here seeking solitude, an oasis for recuperation, and all I get is a jackhammer sinus headache that won't go away. From Bay Street to the baccarat salons, there's no escaping this foul plague of tourists.

In Florida we've grown accustomed to their noisome behavior (and tolerate it, as avarice dictates we must), but there is something obscene about witnessing its infliction upon the people of a foreign country.

Frankly, we ought to be ashamed of ourselves.

Perhaps it's basic pioneer spirit that compels Americans each vacation season to evacuate their hometowns and explore new lands. Fine. But how do you justify fluorescent Bermuda shorts? Or E.T. beach sandals? What gives us the right to so offend the rest of civilization?

Ah, but look who's talking.

The other day I tried windsurfing, an absurd sport that requires one to balance perilously on a banana-shaped piece of fiberglass while steering the seas with a flimsy canvas sheet.

Windsurfing lessons in the Bahamas cost $45, a bargain for vacationing yahoos who firmly believe that the more dangerous an enterprise, the more you should pay for it. And for a thirty-seven-year-old degenerate in my addled condition, windsurfing is fraught with exciting little dangers: lacerations, compound fractures, groin pulls, spinal paralysis—not to mention toxic jellyfish, killer sharks, sea urchins, and sting rays.

Windsurfing probably is not as dangerous as, say, flying a slow U-2 over Cuba, but there isn't a jock pilot in the whole damn Air Force who's ever had to worry about losing his swimtrunks (and self-esteem) before a beachload of gawking, tittering, shrimp-skinned tourists.

Which is what happened to me at high noon yesterday when I was blindsided by a thunderous breaker.

My Bahamian windsurfing instructor, Rudy, had every right to laugh; it was a stupendous moon job.

After my spill (and near-drowning), I loudly accused him of supplying faulty equipment. Replied Rudy: "De only 'quipment dat fawlty, mon, is you drunken old body."

He was right. You can't surf with a bottle of Myers's under your arm. Stupid bloody tourist.

Wiley Returns.

"How could you print that crap?" Brian Keyes demanded.

"Calm down," said Cab Mulcahy, "and close the door."

But Keyes could not be calm, not with Wiley's elongated face leering from the pages of the Miami *Sun*. That the newspaper would revive his column was beyond belief, a monstrous gag. Wiley had the gun, and Mulcahy had just handed him the bullets, gift-wrapped.

"Cab, you don't know what you're getting into."

"I'm afraid I do." Mulcahy looked chagrined. "Skip's involved with these terrorists, isn't he?"

"He's not just *involved*, Cab, he's running the whole damn show. He's the Number One Nacho."

"You're certain, Brian?"

"Absolutely."

The editor closed his eyes. "How bad?"

"Imagine General Patton on acid."

"I see."

They sat in morose silence, pretending to gaze out Mulcahy's office window. On Biscayne Bay the waves had turned to slate under pickets of bruised thunderclouds, advancing from the east. It was probably raining like hell in the Bahamas.

"He called yesterday from Nassau," Mulcahy began. "Said he was feeling better. No more visceral rage, he said; back to big-league journalism. He sent the column by telex—totally harmless, no preaching, no politics. You've got to admit, it's good for a chuckle. I told Skip we'd run it after he came back to Florida and we had a long talk, to which he replied: 'In due time.'"

"So you published the damn thing anyway."

"I was outvoted," Mulcahy said.

"By whom?"

"By the only one who matters."

"Cardoza?" Keyes asked.

Cardoza was the publisher.

"The prince himself," Mulcahy said. "Two weeks is a long time without your clean-up hitter, Brian. I told him Skip was still under the weather, suffering from exhaustion, the whole nine yards. But Cardoza read the column and said Skip sure didn't *write* like he was exhausted so we might as well print the column. And that was it, end of argument. Listen, we were getting a lot of mail, a *lot*, including some cancellations. You would've thought we yanked *Doonesbury* or *Peanuts*."

Keyes said, "Did you tell Cardoza everything?"

"About as much as you told the cops."

Keyes shrugged. *Touché.*

"This is grand," Mulcahy said sardonically. "Here we are, two truth-seekers who for once actually get hold of the truth. So what do we do? We hide it. Swallow it. Smother it. You should be telling the police, and I should be telling my readers, but look at us—the original chickenshit twins. We're both worried about that crazy sonofabitch—as if he deserves our concern—and we're both telling ourselves that there's got to be another way. Except there isn't, is there? It's gone too damn far. People are dead, the cops are rabid, and the city's in an uproar. Meanwhile our old pal Wiley is hiding somewhere out there, dreaming up a punch line for this hideous joke."

"What do you want to do?" Keyes asked.

"Go to the cops," Mulcahy said. "Right now."

Keyes shook his head. "Skip said there'd be a bloodbath if his name got out."

"Bloodbath—he used that word?" Mulcahy asked incredulously.

"Yep. 'Massacre,' too, if I'm not mistaken. We've got to think about this carefully, Cab. Think about what they've already done—the kidnappings, the bombings. Look what they did to Dr. Courtney and that detective, Keefe. I don't think Wiley's bullshitting when he talks bloodbath. They've got the credentials now." Keyes didn't mention his fear for Jenna or for Mulcahy himself.

"All right, suppose we tell the police but embargo all the press."

"Be serious," Keyes said. "Once the cops heard Wiley's name they'd leak like the Haitian navy. And when the radio and TV folks get wind of it, the *Sun* will have no choice. You'll have to go with the story. Out front, too."

"We have to get him back from the Bahamas," Mulcahy asserted. "I'm going to try the embassy."

"It won't work, Cab. Skip's untouchable over there. I found out he entered the island on a fake passport, but nobody in Nassau seems to care. Apparently he's bribed everyone but the prime minister."

"So what the hell do we do?"

Keyes said, "I think we've got to play rough. You've got the one thing he cares about, that column."

"Yeah," Mulcahy said, "and every damn word goes through me."

Keyes thought about that.

"I know a little something about the Bahamas government," he said. "They're hypersensitive about their national image."

"What are you suggesting?"

"Suppose you rewrote Skip's next column."

"Suppose I let Bloodworth try it," Mulcahy said.

"Oh boy." In Wiley's words, rewriting was a mortal sin, punishable by castration. Spray-painting the Sistine Chapel, he used to call it.

Keyes thought he noticed the old boy's eyes twinkle.

"Suppose I gave it to Bloodworth and told him to punch up the lead. Make it more hard-hitting. Asked him to tinker with some of Skip's more energetic passages."

"Might turn into something the Bahamians wouldn't like," Keyes mused. "Might wear out Skip's welcome real quick."

"I can't believe we're talking about this."

"Suppose it works," Keyes said. "Let's say he comes back to Miami. Then what?"

"Intercept him at the airport," Mulcahy said. "Turn him in, take him out of circulation. Get him some professional help."

"He could always plead insanity."

"I'm considering it myself," Mulcahy muttered. "After twenty-two years you'd think I could spot a psychopath in my own newsroom."

"On the contrary," said Keyes. "The longer you're in the business, the harder it gets."

Mulcahy was one of those rare editors who'd gone into newspapers for all the right reasons, with all the right instincts and all the right sensibilities. He was a wonderful fluke—fair but not weak, tough but not heartless, aggressive but circumspect. The Wiley situation was tearing him up.

Mulcahy toyed with a memo, shredding the edges. "I pulled his personnel file today, just for kicks. Jesus

Christ, Brian, it's full of wild stuff. Stuff I'd forgotten all about."

The episodes had escalated in gravity:

December 13, 1978. Skip Wiley reprimanded for impersonating National Security Adviser Zbigniew Brzezinski in an effort to obtain box seats to an NFL playoff game.

April 17, 1980. Wiley reprimanded after filing an IRS return listing his occupation as "prophet, redeemer, and sage."

July 23, 1982. Wiley suspended two days with pay after using obscene cunieform symbols to describe Senator Jesse Helms of North Carolina.

March 7, 1984. Wiley suspended five days with pay after telling a radio-talk-show audience that Florida's entire supply of drinking water had been poisoned by Bolivian drug dealers.

October 3, 1984. Wiley suspended three days without pay for allegedly assaulting a Jehovah's Witness with a long-handled marlin gaff.

"I guess I wasn't paying attention," Mulcahy said, "on purpose." He leaned forward and dropped his voice to a whisper. "Brian, do you really think he's crazy? I mean, *crazy* crazy?"

"I'm not sure. Skip is no drooling yo-yo. If he were, we'd have nothing to worry about. You could let him write all he wants—who'd give a shit? Whatever he wrote wouldn't make sense anyway—if he were *crazy* crazy."

"Are you saying—"

"He makes some sense, yes," Keyes said. "Wiley's goddamn plan makes sense because it seems to be working. He's got the entire Gold Coast terrified, your venerable newspaper included. I saw where the big Teamsters' convention was moved to Atlantic City—"

Mulcahy nodded lugubriously.

"And *The Battle of the Network Bibos* or whatever—switched from Key Biscayne to Phoenix, of all places."

"Tucson," Mulcahy corrected.

"You see my point."

"It'll wear off," Mulcahy said. "Panic always does."

"Not if the tourists keep disappearing."

"He's wiring us a new column tomorrow afternoon. I'll give it to Ricky for a good butchering and we'll publish it Sunday. See if *that* doesn't bring the bastard back from his tropical vacation."

Keyes said, "If it doesn't, we'll have to think of something else." He made the *something else* sound ominous.

Mulcahy sighed. "I'd still hate to see him die."

Keyes had saved the worst for last. "Skip's planning something horrendous," he told Mulcahy. "I don't know the details, but it's going to happen soon. He said they're going to violate a sacred virgin, whatever that means."

Mulcahy mulled the possibilities.

"The mayor's wife?"

"Naw, not Skip's type," Keyes said.

"A nun, then—you think they'd snatch an actual nun?"

"I doubt it, Cab. Skip's very big on symbolism. I think a nun is off the mark."

"How about a celebrity? Hey, Liza Minnelli is playing the Eden Roc this month."

"Skip can't stand Liza Minnelli," Keyes noted.

"There you go!"

"The most sacred virgin in all Miami—Liza Minnelli?"

"Well, shit," Mulcahy said. "You got a better idea?"

Brian Keyes did have an idea, but it wasn't one that Mulcahy especially wanted to hear. Keyes hoped that Cab might think of it on his own.

"If you were Skip and you wanted to get the world's attention," Keyes said, "you'd try something drastic, something beyond the realm of merely heinous."

"Don't try to cheer me up."

"And if you were Wiley," Keyes went on, "you'd want—no, you'd *demand*—maximum exposure."

Mulcahy's chin came off his chest. "Maximum exposure?"

"We're talking television," Keyes said. "Network television." That's what Skip had promised at Cable Beach.

"Oh no." Mulcahy sounded like a man whose worst nightmare was coming true.

"Cab, what's the most fantastic spectacle in Miami, the event watched every year by the entire country?"

"The Orange Bowl Parade, of course."

"And who's the star of the parade?"

"Holy shit," Mulcahy groaned. He thought: If Brian's right, this is even worse than a nun.

"The Orange Bowl queen."

"Right," Keyes said, "and when is the Orange Bowl Parade?"

"The last night of December!" Mulcahy exclaimed.

"The very last night of December," said Brian Keyes. "*La Ultima Noche de Diciembre.*"

NINETEEN

The conference table had been carved into the likeness of a Florida navel orange. A big one. The table filled the Chamber of Commerce with its roundness and orange-ness. And at the crown of the orange, where the stem had been hewn, sat the chairman of the Orange Bowl Committee.

"Have a seat, Mr. Keyes," he said.

Brian Keyes slipped into a leather chair. He couldn't take his eyes off the damn table. Once upon a time it must have been a beautiful slab of white walnut, before they'd varnished it into such a florid atrocity.

"You know most everyone here," the chairman said.

Keyes scanned familiar faces: the Miami chief of police, the Dade County chief of police, two vice-mayors, a few ruddy Chamber of Commerce types (including the late Sparky Harper's successor), Cab Mulcahy, looking dyspeptic, and, of course, Al García from the newly mobilized Fuego One Task Force. García was sitting at the giant orange's navel.

The air was blue with cigarette smoke and sharp with the aroma of fresh coffee. Everyone had their own ashtray, their own glass of ice water, and their own packet of press clippings about the tourist murders. The mood of the group was funereal.

"Let's start with Sergeant García." the Orange Bowl chairman said, consulting a legal pad. "Did I pronounce that correctly?"

"Yes, sir." The words hissed through clenched teeth. García had promised the chief he'd be polite. The Orange Bowl chairman was a doughy white-haired Florida cracker who was still getting used to the whole idea of Cubans.

"The name of the gang is *Las Noches de Diciembre*, or the Nights of December," García began. "It's an extremist organization but we're not sure about its politics or its motives. We do know they use murder, kidnapping, torture, and bombing. So far they haven't asked for a ransom or anything else. All they seem to want is publicity. Their targets are mainly tourists, although we think they also whacked Mr. B. D. Harper."

"Whacked?" said the chairman.

"Murdered," Keyes explained.

"Yes, murdered," Al García said, "with a capital M. These bozos mean business."

"Bozos?" the chairman said tentatively, glancing around the table.

"The bad guys," Keyes explained.

"*Las Noches*," García said.

That was the extent of García's formal presentation. He hated meetings like this; they reminded him of *Sesame Street*. García took off his tinted reading glasses and fished in his pockets for a cigarette.

The Orange Bowl man cleared his throat and said, "Sergeant, do we know exactly who these people are?"

"Some of them."

García took his time with the Bic lighter.

"The gang has at least four members. A white male,

mid-thirties, identity unknown." García gave a sideways glance toward Keyes. "There's a young Seminole Indian named Tigertail. The bomber, the one who did the Palmetto Country Club job—he's an old acquaintance. A Cuban right-winger named Jesús Bernal."

"How do you spell that?" the chairman asked, pen poised over the legal pad.

"J-e-s-ú-s," García said impatiently.

"Oh. Just like *our* Jesus, only pronounced different."

"Yeah," García said. "And the last name is B-e-r-n-a-l."

"What does that mean?" the chairman asked. "In English."

"It means 'Jesús Bernal,' " García grumbled. "It's his fucking name, that's all."

The Dade County police chief looked sick to his stomach.

García said, "The fourth suspect you all know. His name is Daniel Wilson, AKA Viceroy."

"Oh no," said the chairman. "One of the Dolphins."

"Old number thirty-one," one of the vice-mayors lamented.

Everyone at the orange table was a big football fan, and the mention of Viceroy Wilson's name ignited a paroxysm of nostalgia.

"It's hard to understand," the chairman said sadly. "Our town was very good to that boy."

Brian Keyes didn't need the NAACP to tell him there were no black faces sitting at the orange table.

"Well," García said. "Mr. Wilson apparently has a beef against society. A serious beef. They all do."

"Which one is *El Fuego?*" somebody asked.

"Don't know," García replied.

"What does that mean, *El Fuego?*" the chairman asked.

"The Fire. The Flame. Take your pick." García was annoyed. He hadn't come to teach Spanish 101.

"When can you arrest these men?" the chairman demanded.

"When I find 'em." García motioned toward Cab Mulcahy. "There'll be a story in tomorrow's newspaper that ID's the three known suspects and asks for the public's help in locating them. We sent over some mug shots this morning with Mr. Bloodworth."

"We're running the pictures," Mulcahy said, "on the front page."

"That'll help," García said. "But somehow I don't think these guys are going to sit still and let us find them. I think we're going to have to wait till they appear. And they *will* appear. Mr. Keyes here is a private investigator, a pretty good one. As you know, he was abducted by *Las Noches* a couple of weeks ago and roughed up pretty good. Brian, tell 'em the good news."

Keyes said, "We have reason to believe that they plan to kidnap the Orange Bowl queen."

Everyone at the table sat back in their chairs like they'd been punched in the chest. There was plenty of nervous whispering.

"That's the craziest stunt I ever heard," said somebody in a bright blazer. Actually, several of the men wore identical bright blazers. The blazers were orange.

"We're taking this threat very seriously," interjected the Dade County police chief, always jittery among civic-leader types.

"We think it's going to happen during the parade,"

Brian Keyes said, touching off another round of white-establishment gasping.

"Good Lord!"

"They're going to kidnap the Orange Bowl queen in the middle of the parade?"

"On national goddamn TV? In front of Jane fucking Pauley?"

"And Michael Landon?"

"'Fraid so," Al García said.

Jane Pauley and Michael Landon were scheduled to host the King Orange Jamboree Parade from an elevated booth on Biscayne Boulevard. Jane Pauley and Michael Landon were big celebrities, but García tapped his cigarette ashes all over the orange walnut to let everyone know he didn't give a shit about that. Brian Keyes admired the way García had taken over the meeting from the guys in the blazers.

One of the vice-mayors turned to Keyes and said, "You've met these people. What do you think—would they listen to reason?"

"Doubtful," said Keyes. "Very doubtful." If necessary, he was prepared to tell them what happened to Ida Kimmelman, just so they'd give up the idea of trying to bargain with *El Fuego*.

"Mr. Keyes," a vice-mayor said, "what is it they want?"

"They want us to leave," Keyes said.

"All of us," García added, "from Palm Beach to Key West."

"I don't understand," the vice-mayor said.

"They want Florida back," Keyes said, "the way it was."

"The way it was *when?*"

"When it wasn't fucked up with so many people," García said.

The table erupted in snorts and sniggering, and the men in the blazers seemed to shake their heads gravely in syncopation. "Why doesn't this kind of shit ever happen to Disney World?" one of them said mournfully.

The Orange Bowl chairman decided he'd heard enough dire news from the private eye and the rude detective, so he turned to the police chiefs for encouragement.

"Gentlemen, surely you're not just going to sit and wait for these outlaws to show up and disrupt the parade. They must be arrested as soon as possible, before New Year's Eve. It's bad enough that the press already knows about them."

"It's pretty tough to keep the lid on mass murder," remarked the Miami police chief. "God knows we've tried."

"We're doing all we can to find these people," added the Dade County police chief. "We've got every available detective working the case, but it's tough. Especially around Christmas. Half the department's on leave."

The Orange Bowl chairman said grumpily, "I don't want your excuses. I want to hear exactly what you're doing to catch these killers!"

The police chiefs turned to Al García, who'd been waiting patiently for the ball to bounce back his way.

"Right now we've got six undercover guys in Little Havana looking for Jesús Bernal," García said. "We've got eight more over in Liberty City searching for Viceroy Wilson. The Indian—well, he's a problem. Looks like he just disappeared off the planet. Anyhow, we got

245

plenty of reward money out on the street—just how much, I can't say, but it's more than my whole damn pension. We've doubled the patrols at every big South Florida tourist attraction—the Seaquarium, Ocean World, Six Flags, the racetracks, the beaches. There was a rumor that the Monkey Jungle might be next so we've got a sniper team waiting upwind. What's more, we got choppers and airboats searching the Glades for *El Fuego's* camp. We even hired our own Indian guide."

A nearsighted Miccosukee, García noted silently, but he was better than nothing.

One of the vice-mayors suggested that warnings be posted in all the major tourist hotels.

"Are you out of your mind?" screeched Sparky Harper's Chamber of Commerce successor. "Are you *trying* to cause panic?"

"No one would panic," the vice-mayor said defensively, "if the warnings were worded properly."

"Perhaps in small type," the chairman suggested.

"And perhaps in Chinese," said Al García.

The chairman glowered. "Sergeant, you don't seem to understand what's at stake here."

"Human lives," the detective said, raising his hands. "That's all, far as I'm concerned."

"It's much more than that," the Orange Bowl chairman snapped. "NBC is here! Let's not forget that. And let's not forget the theme of this year's parade: 'Tropical Tranquillity.' "

Brian Keyes desperately looked across the table at Cab Mulcahy. The managing editor's eyelids closed slowly, like a dying iguana's.

"Look," García said, "you guys have to put on a parade and I have to solve murders. Maybe even prevent 'em, if possible. So listen real good 'cause here's the plan: we're gonna have cops crawling all over Biscayne Boulevard on New Year's Eve. We're gonna have the Orange Bowl queen so completely surrounded by police that you might as well paint a badge on her goddamn float. I don't care what it looks like on television. Fuck NBC. Fuck Jane Pauley. Fuck Alf Landon."

"*Michael* Landon," Keyes whispered.

"Him, too."

The Orange Bowl chairman looked like he'd have killed for a Maalox. He said, "Sergeant, that's the worst plan I ever heard. It would be a catastrophe, image-wise."

"I agree," said Sparky Harper's successor.

"This is not a military parade," scoffed another Chamber of Commerce man.

"Now, wait a minute," said one of the orange-blazer guys. "Maybe we can compromise. Suppose we have the police wave batons and march in lockstep behind the queen's float! I'd say that would look mighty darn impressive. And no one would suspect a thing."

"How about screw the batons," said Al García.

"Then plainclothes," suggested the Dade County police chief.

"Maybe," García said.

"And have them hiding in the crowd," the Orange Bowl chairman said. "Not in the blessed parade."

"Won't work," Keyes said. "I've been stuck in that crowd before, when I covered the parade for the *Sun*. You can't move—it's like acres of human taffy. Something happens and it'd take you five minutes to reach the float, and that's too long."

The Orange Bowl chairman was not persuaded. He

scrunched his blackberry eyes and said, "There will be no police marching in this parade! We're selling Tropical Tranquillity, not *Dragnet*."

"Okay, if that's the way you want it," García said. "How about we just stash a midget with a MAC-10 underneath the queen's gown?"

"Al, please," groaned the Dade County police chief.

"No one would notice a thing," García said mischieviously, "except maybe the midget."

"Don't you have another plan?" pleaded one of the blazers.

"Yeah, matter of fact, I do." García winked at Brian Keyes. "I sure do."

Skip Wiley's Christmas column arrived from Nassau by telex on Saturday, December 22.

Cab Mulcahy read it carefully before he summoned Ricky Bloodworth to his office.

"You've been doing a fine job on the terrorist story," Mulcahy said. This was a shameless lie, but Mulcahy had no choice. Bloodworth was a sucker for phony compliments.

"Thanks, Cab," he said. "Did you hear? *Time* magazine called."

"Really."

"Yup. Wanted all my clips on *Las Nachos*."

"*Las Noches*," Mulcahy corrected.

"Right. But isn't that great? About *Time* magazine?"

"Terrific," Cab Mulcahy said, thinking: Does this chowderhead really believe *Time* magazine wants to hire him?

"Ricky, I need your help."

Bloodworth's squirrelly features furrowed. "Sure, Cab, anything at all."

"I got this column from Skip Wiley"—Mulcahy waved the telex—"and, frankly, it's not up to par."

Ricky Bloodworth didn't say anything immediately, but his eyes brightened with an it's-too-good-to-be-true look.

"You want to substitute one of mine!"

"Not exactly," Mulcahy said.

"I've already got a Christmas column worked up," Bloodworth persisted. "Christmas in Palm Beach. I interviewed Rose Kennedy's butler. It's a nice little story, Cab. Rose Kennedy bought the butler a Chevrolet last Christmas, and you know what he got for her? You'll never guess."

"Probably not."

"Two tickets to *Torch Song Trilogy*."

"Ricky . . ."

"Don't you think that's a good Christmas story?"

"Very moving, but not precisely what I had in mind."

God forgive me, thought Cab Mulcahy as he handed Wiley's column to Ricky Bloodworth.

"I want you to punch up Skip's piece," Mulcahy said. "Really make it sing."

Bloodworth skimmed the column warily. "Geez, Cab, I don't know about this."

"Do it as a favor," Mulcahy said, "for me."

"But what's Skip going to say?"

"Let me worry about that."

"He can get pretty nasty, Cab. He punched me once," Bloodworth said, "in the groin area."

"Skip punched you?"

Bloodworth nodded. "He said I burned one of his sources."

"Did you?"

"It was a misunderstanding. I didn't know the guy was off-the-record. Anyway, he gave me a helluva quote."

"So," Mulcahy said, "you printed his name in the story."

"Right."

"What happened?"

"I think the guy got fired."

"I see."

"And possibly indicted," Bloodworth said.

"Hmmm." Mulcahy thought: When it's all over, I'm getting rid of this asshole. Send him up to the Okeechobee bureau to cover Cucumber Jubilees for the rest of his life.

"The whole thing was just a misunderstanding, but Skip was totally irrational about it. He blamed me for everything."

"Did he now?" Mulcahy's ulcer was shooting electric messages.

Bloodworth said, "The point is, I don't want Skip to go on the warpath again. He's a violent man."

"Ricky, let me worry about it. Just take a crack at the column, all right?"

It had arrived as a lovely little piece, one of Wiley's traditional holiday tearjerkers. It began like this:

Rollie Artis rowed out to sea last Thursday dawn.
You could watch him from Cable Beach, paddling out Nassau harbor, his thick black arms flashing at the oars.

Rollie went to hunt for conchs, which was his livelihood, as it was his father's. And, as his father, Rollie Artis was a splendid diver with strong lungs and sharp eyes and an instinct for finding the shellfish beds.

But on Thursday the winds were high and the water was ferocious, and the other conch divers had warned Rollie not to try it.

"But I got to," he had said. "If I don't go fishin', there be no Christmas for my babies this year."

At dusk Rollie's wife Clarisse waited on the dock behind the Straw Market; waited, as she always did, for the sight of the bright wooden skiff.

But Rollie Artis never returned. The next morning the seas calmed and the other fishermen searched for their friend. Not a trace was found. A few of the men were old enough to remember that the same thing had happened to Rollie's father, on another winter's day. An act of God, the old divers said; what else could explain such tragic irony?

Yesterday, at Rollie's house in Queen's Park, Clarisse put up a yule tree and sang to her two small children. Christmas carols. And the song of a fisherman.

Ricky Bloodworth took Wiley's column to his desk and slaughtered it. It took less than an hour. Cab Mulcahy was surprised at Bloodworth's aptitude for turgidity; it came naturally to the kid.

This, unedited, is what he brought back:

The Bahamas Coast Guard has some real explaining to do.

Nassau fisherman Rollie Artis disappeared from sight last Thursday and nobody except his fishing pals seem to give a hoot.

In our country, Artis would have been the object of a massive air-and-sea rescue effort. But in the Bahamas, nobody lifts the first helicopter. Is it money? Manpower? Equipment? Makes you wonder where all those tourist tax dollars are going—especially when you consider what they're gouging for a decent hotel room these days on Paradise Island.

It also makes you wonder about a supposedly modern government that fails to enforce basic safety regulations for boaters. If a law had forced Rollie Artis to carry life jackets, he might be alive today. And if his boat had been properly equipped with an outboard motor, he might have made it back to port.

He might have been home for Christmas.

Ever since its independence the Bahamas has been telling the world community what a prosperous advanced nation it has become. Well, it's time to start acting like one. It's time this little country, which so loves rich foreigners, took an equal interest in the fate of its own people—especially the poor and feckless.

Cab Mulcahy nearly gnawed through his upper lip as he read Ricky's rewrite.

"I thought Skip was being a little too sentimental," Bloodworth explained. "I think he really missed the big picture."

"Yes," Mulcahy said pensively. "You've turned a sentimental anecdote about a missing fisherman into a blistering indictment of a friendly foreign government."

"Exactly," Bloodworth said proudly. "The column's got some guts to it now."

"Guts."

"Cab, isn't that what you wanted?"

"Oh yes. This is perfect."

"You know," Bloodworth said, "normally I'd ask for a byline on the column, since I rewrote it and all. But under the circumstances, I think I'd like to leave my name off. Just keep it our secret."

"Smart move," Mulcahy said.

"Otherwise Skip might get the wrong idea."

"I understand."

"Because if he gets upset—"

"I told you, I'll handle it. Don't worry."

"Thanks, Cab."

Forty minutes after Richard L. Bloodworth left, Mulcahy had not moved from his desk. He looked rumpled and dispirited.

The city editor strolled in and said, "I hear Ricky's polished up Wiley's column."

Listlessly Mulcahy handed it to him.

The city editor didn't know what to say. He was the one who'd always said Bloodworth showed promise. Consequently, he felt duty-bound to offer something positive.

"Well," the city editor said, not taking his eyes off the page, "Ricky certainly doesn't pull any punches, does he?"

"He's an insensitive cretin. A menace."

"He's a pretty good police reporter, Cab."

"I never said he wasn't."

"So what do you want me to do?"

"Smooth the wrinkles and run it Monday."

"But that's Christmas Eve," the city editor said. "I thought we were using it Christmas Day."

"I refuse to do that to our readers," Mulcahy said. "Not on Christmas."

"But what'll I run in Wiley's slot Christmas Day?"

"I don't know," Mulcahy said. "A prayer would be nice."

TWENTY

The Shivers family lived in a beautiful old home next to a golf course in Coral Gables. It was a two-story house, white Florida stucco with a red barrel-tile roof. An ancient ficus tree cloaked the front lawn. In the driveway were a BMW, a Lincoln, and a new Volkswagen. Brian Keyes parked behind the VW.

A short man with a fresh tan and a pointy chin answered the door. He was trim, almost youthful, and dressed stem-to-stern in L. L. Bean. He definitely belonged to the BMW.

"Reed Shivers," he said with a collegiate handshake. "Come in, Mr. Keyes."

They sat in an elegant living room with plenty of soft camel furniture. In one corner stood a tall, woodsy-smelling Christmas tree; some of its ornaments were made of blown glass.

"Pumpkin!" Reed Shivers called. "Come here!"

At first Brian Keyes thought Shivers might be shouting to a pet beagle.

"My daughter," Shivers said. "She'll be down in a minute, I'm sure. Would you like coffee?"

"Thanks," Keyes said. "No sugar."

"Not in this house," Shivers said. "We watch our diets. You'll see for yourself."

Shivers poured the coffee from a silver pot.

"So you're a private detective."

"Yes," Keyes said restlessly.

"I'm a tax lawyer, myself."

"So I heard."

Shivers waited, thinking the private eye would ask about what it's like to be an important tax attorney in Miami. Keyes sipped at his coffee and said nothing.

"I'm just curious," Shivers said. "How much money do private investigators make?"

"At least a million a year," Keyes said. "Sometimes two million. I lose track."

Reed Shivers whistled. "Wov! You've got good shelters, I presume."

"The best."

"Oil, right?"

"Concrete."

"Hmmm-mmm," said Reed Shivers.

Keyes wondered how this clown ever made it through Yale Law.

"Pumpkin pie!" Shivers hollered again. "I don't know what's keeping her, Mr. Keyes."

"Before your daughter gets here, I'd like to offer some advice."

"Certainly."

"Don't let her ride that float in the Orange Bowl Parade."

"You're joking."

"Not at all," Keyes said. "The people who've made this threat are very violent. And ingenious. No one knows what they might do."

"Sergeant García said it was a kidnapping plot."

"It's a bit more complicated than that."

"You think they might try to harm Kara Lynn?"

"It's very possible," Keyes said.

"But there'll be cops all over the place!"

Keyes put down his coffee cup, aiming for a linen doily. "Mr. Shivers, I just want you to be aware of the risks. The risks are substantial."

Reed Shivers looked annoyed. "Some risk. An Injun, a Cuban, and a washed-up spade ballplayer. Don't tell me a hundred well-armed policemen can't stop a bunch of losers like that!"

"Mr. Shivers, losers get lucky. If one nut can shoot the damn President in Dealey Plaza, a whole gang of nuts can sure as hell snatch your precious little Pumpkin off Biscayne Boulevard."

"Shhhh."

Kara Lynn Shivers stood at the French doors.

"Sugar doll! Come here and meet Mr. Keyes."

Reed Shivers whispered. "Isn't she spectacular?"

She was. She wore tight jeans, white sneakers, and a gray Miami Hurricanes sweatshirt. Kara Lynn Shivers greeted Brian Keyes with an expert smile. It was one of the best smiles he'd seen in a long time.

"So you're my bodyguard," she said.

"It wasn't my idea," Keyes said.

"I can think of worse assignments," Reed Shivers said with a locker-room wink.

Keyes said, "Kara Lynn, I'm going to tell you what I told your dad: I think you ought to drop out of the parade next week. I think you're in serious danger."

Kara Lynn looked at her father.

"I already told him," Shivers said. "It's out of the question."

"Do I get a choice?"

"Of course, buttercup."

"Then I want to hear what Mr. Keyes has to say."

Kara Lynn Shivers was quite beautiful, which wasn't surprising; one did not get to be Orange Bowl queen by looking like a woodchuck. What did surprise Brian Keyes was the wit in Kara Lynn's gray-green eyes and the steel in her voice. He had expected a chronic case of airheadedness but found just the opposite. Kara Lynn seemed very self-assured for nineteen, and canny—light-years, ahead of her old man. Still, Keyes was wary. He had stopped falling in love with beauty queens when he was twenty-six.

"One reason Sergeant García asked me to keep an eye on you," Keyes said, "is because I'm the only person who's seen the terrorists face-to-face. At least, I'm the only one still alive. They're treacherous and unpredictable. And clever—I can't overemphasize that. These guys are damn clever. Now, your father's right: there will be scores of plainclothes police all up and down the parade route. You won't see them, and neither will the folks watching on TV, but they'll be there, with guns. Let's hope *Las Noches* know it; then maybe they'll think twice before trying anything."

"Dad, suppose something happens," Kara Lynn said.

"We pay the ransom, of course. I've already called Lloyd's about a kidnap policy and arranged the very best—the same one all the top multinationals have on their executives."

"That's not what I meant," Kara Lynn said sharply. "Suppose there's a shoot-out during the parade, with all those little kids in the crowd. Somebody might get killed."

"Now, darling, these police are expert marksmen."

"Mr. Shivers," Keyes said, "you've been watching way too much TV."

Kara Lynn started to smile, then caught herself.

"In the first place, this gang doesn't ask for ransoms. They don't need your money," Keyes said. "And your daughter's absolutely right about the shooting. Once it starts, somebody's going to die. As for all those cops being crack shooters, I guarantee you that half of them couldn't hit the SS *Norway* with a bazooka at ten paces."

"Thank you, Mr. Keyes," Reed Shivers said acidly, "for your reassurance."

"I'm not paid to give pep talks."

"Dad—" Kara Lynn said.

"Sweetie, it's the *Orange Bowl Parade*. Forty million people will be watching, including all the top talent agents in Hollywood and New York. Jane Pauley's going to be there. In person."

Kara Lynn knew the forty-million figure was a crock.

"Dad, it's a parade, not a moon shoot."

Reed Shivers' voice quavered. "It's the most important moment in your whole life!"

"And maybe the last," Keyes said. "But what the hell. It'd be worth it just to see little Pumpkin's face in *People* magazine, right?"

"Shut up, you creep!" Pink in the face, Shivers bounced to his feet and assumed a silly combative stance. With one hand Brian Keyes shoved him back into the folds of the camel sofa.

"Don't be an asshole," Keyes said. "This is your daughter's life we're talking about."

Reed Shivers was so angry his body seemed to twitch.

It was not an image the L. L. Bean people would have chosen for the spring catalog.

"If it's so damn dangerous," Shivers rasped, "why won't they just cancel the parade?"

Keyes chuckled. "You know Miami better than that. Christ himself could carry the cross down Biscayne Boulevard and they'd still run the Orange Bowl Parade, right over his body."

"Mr. Keyes," Kara Lynn said, "can I talk to my father for a minute, alone?"

Keyes walked out to the game room, which was walled in chocolate-brown cork. It was Sunday so there was nothing but football on the wide-screen television; Keyes turned it off. He counted sixteen golfing trophies in one maple bookcase. On the bar was a framed color photograph of Reed Shivers with his arm around Bob Hope. In the picture Shivers looked drunk and Bob Hope looked taxidermied.

Keyes went to the billiard table and glumly racked up the balls. Guarding the girl had been García's idea; Keyes wasn't thrilled about it but he'd taken the job anyway. With Skip Wiley out of reach in the Bahamas there wasn't much else to do. No fresh tourist corpses had popped up and even the Trifecta Massacre had turned into a dead end, the bomber having made a clean getaway. Now it was a waiting game, and Kara Lynn was the bait.

Keyes scratched the cue ball just as she walked in. She closed the door behind her.

"Look, don't get mad, but I've decided to go ahead and be in the parade."

"Swell," Keyes said. "I hope your father knows probate."

"You're really trying to scare me. Well, I'm scared, okay? I honestly am." She really was.

"Then don't be stubborn." Keyes propped the cue stick in a corner.

"Look," Kara Lynn said, "if I drop out, they'll just get somebody else, one of the runners-up. Let me tell you, Mr. Keyes, some of those girls would ride in that parade no matter what. They'd *pay* to do it. So if I quit, it won't change a thing. The Nights of December will still have somebody to kidnap, or try to. It might as well be me."

"Besides," Keyes said, "it'll make great television."

Kara Lynn glared at him. "You think I like this whole setup?"

"Don't you want to be a star?"

"I'd much rather be alive." Kara Lynn shrugged. "My dad wants to see his little girl on NBC. Let him have his moment, Mr. Keyes. He says it's safe."

"Your dad's a real piece of work."

"I told you not to get mad."

Keyes smiled in spite of himself. It wasn't easy, being a tough guy. "Okay, I'm not mad."

"Good." Kara Lynn went to the bar and fixed herself a club soda. She tossed a cold can of Coors at Keyes. He caught it one-handed.

"I've never had a bodyguard before," she said. "How does this work?"

"Well, for the next week or so, it's just you and me, with some discreet assistance from Dade County's finest. The most important thing is that you're never alone when you're out of this house. We want the bad guys to see that you're not a sitting duck, that you've got protection—though I use the term loosely. You want to go shopping, I'll carry the groceries. You want to play tennis, I'll carry the rackets. You want to go to the beach, I'll carry the Coppertone."

"What if I want to go on a date?"

"No dates."

"Says who?"

"The eminent Orange Bowl Committee. They would prefer that you not go anywhere at night. I think that's a good idea."

"Oh, just a great idea."

"Your boyfriend can come by the house to visit. Watch TV. Play Trivial Pursuit. Smoke dope. Doesn't matter to me."

"Can we make love?"

Keyes reddened. "If you're quiet about it," he said. "I need my sleep."

Kara Lynn laughed. "I'm just kidding. I don't have a boyfriend; we broke up after I won this stupid contest. Mr. Keyes—"

"It's Brian, please. I get a new gray hair every time a pretty girls calls me mister."

"All right . . . Brian, will you carry a gun?"

"Sometimes. And a nifty Dick Tracy police radio."

"What kind of gun?" asked Kara Lynn.

"Never mind." It was a Browning nine-millimeter. Keyes hated the damn thing. The holster bled all over his shirts.

"Can I ask you something?" she said. "I don't want to hurt your feelings, but when they told me about a bodyguard I expected somebody . . ."

"A little larger?"

"Yeah. More imposing."

"Imposing is my specialty," Keyes said. "But you want to know why they didn't send a big gorilla cop instead of a skinny private eye."

Kara Lynn nodded. Her eyes were just dynamite.

Keyes said, "The eminent Orange Bowl Committee felt that it would be a catastrophe, image-wise, if it became known that the Orange Bowl queen was under police protection. The eminent Orange Bowl Committee felt that the scoundrels of the press would seize upon such a nugget and blow it way out of proportion. They feared that surrounding a beauty queen with heavily armed police would create the wrong kind of publicity. Detract from their splendid program. Make people too scared to come to the parade. So the civic fathers decided to hide the cops and hire a freelance undercover baby-sitter. Me."

"Unbelievable," Kara Lynn said. "Those jerks."

"I know you'd feel safer with Clint Eastwood," Keyes said. "So would I."

"You'll do fine."

"Your dad doesn't like me."

"But I do," Kara Lynn said, "and I'm the queen, remember? When do you start?"

"My stuff's in the car."

"The gun, too?"

"Would you forget about the gun!"

"As long as *you* don't forget whose adorable little ass is on the line here." Kara Lynn patted her blue-jeaned rump. "Mine! I know you're no Dirty Harry, but promise me that you actually know how to use the gun, Brian. Promise me that much, please?"

*

The next day was Christmas Eve, and Skip Wiley assembled three-fourths of the Nights of December in his rented villa near Lyford Cay, on the outskirts of Nassau.

Tommy Tigertail had elected to stay deep in the Everglades, tending to bingo business, but Jesús Bernal and Viceroy Wilson had jumped at the chance to get out of South Florida, particularly since their photographs had been published on the front page of the Miami *Sun*. To be sure, neither picture bore much resemblance to the two men sitting on Skip Wiley's sundeck. The photograph of Jesús Bernal with a Snidely Whiplash mustache had been taken in 1977 after his arrest for illegal possession of a surface-to-air missile. He looked about fourteen years old. The picture of Viceroy Wilson was no better; it actually had been clipped from an old Miami Dolphins yearbook. Wilson was decked out in his aqua jersey and shoulder pads, pretending to stiff-arm an invisible tackler. He was wearing the same phony scowl that all the bubblegum companies want football players to wear in their pictures; Viceroy Wilson's real scowl was much more effective.

No photograph of the Indian had appeared in the Miami media because no photograph was known to exist.

Skip Wiley didn't seem too concerned about the mug shots as he cracked jokes and handed out cold Heinekens to his visitors.

Viceroy Wilson peered over the rims of his sunglasses. "How come the papers don't mention your name?" he asked Wiley.

"Because Mr. Brian Keyes apparently is covering up

for me. Don't ask me why, boys. A misguided act of friendship, I suppose."

"The cops searched my mother's house this morning," Jesús Bernal blurted angrily. "My sister's house, last night. They're all over Little Havana, like rats, those cops."

"An occupational hazard," Wiley said. "You should be used to it by now."

"But they broke down her door!" Bernal cried. "Fucking animals. This guy García, he's going to pay. 'Scum of the earth,' he called us. It was in the papers. *Scum of the earth!* Cubans know how to deal with traitors like that."

"Here we go again," Viceroy Wilson said. "The Masked Avenger."

"You shut up!"

Wilson laughed and attacked a plate of johnnycake.

"Go easy on the bread," Wiley said. "Remember, you've got to drop ten pounds this week."

Viceroy Wilson shoveled a thick slice into his cheeks.

"And who the fuck are you," he said, spitting crumbs, "Don Shula?"

"Aren't we testy this morning? You boys must have had a bumpy flight." Wiley festively stacked the empty green beer bottles. "I know just the thing to cheer you up. Jenna's doing a plum pudding!"

"Count me in," said Viceroy Wilson.

"And I think there might be a little something for both of you under the Christmas tree."

"No shit?" Jesús Bernal said brightly. "Well, God bless *Las Noches de Diciembre*, each and every one."

But the Nights of December never got to open their gifts. Hitting the newsstands of Nassau that afternoon was the Miami *Sun*, featuring Skip Wiley's doctored Christmas column. Within thirty minutes the prime minister himself called an emergency cabinet meeting and declared that the story about the fisherman Rollie Artis was "an insult to the sovereignty and self-respect of the Bahamas." The minister of home affairs immediately drafted a deportation order, to which each cabinet member affixed his signature. At approximately six P.M., just as Jenna's plum pudding ignited, six uniformed Bahamian immigration officers burst into Wiley's palatial manor house and ordered him out of the commonwealth forever. No amount of proffered cash or traveler's checks would change their minds.

It wasn't until much later, on the midnight flight to Haiti, that Jenna got up the courage to show Skip Wiley what had been done to his column.

"Bloodworth!" he gasped. "That wretched nematode!"

"It sure was a mean trick," Jenna allowed.

"Sacrilege!" Wiley said, his brown eyes smoldering.

"But clever," Jenna remarked. "Wouldn't you say?"

"Well, now it's our turn to be clever," Wiley said, slipping the column into his jacket. "Jenna, as soon as we get to Port-au-Prince, send a message to Tommy back at camp. Have him Federal Express me the Nielsens from last New Year's Eve. And the Arbitrons, too, if he can get his hands on 'em."

"What now, Skip?"

"Don't worry, darling, the strategy stays the same." Wiley patted her knee. "Full speed ahead."

TWENTY-ONE

From a bare-bulb warehouse off Miami Avenue, Jesús Bernal placed a phone call to the secret headquarters of the First Weekend in July Movement.

"*El Comandante, por favor,*" he said.

From the other end came thick Cuban voices, the sound of chairs scraping, a door opening. The telephone clanged as if someone had dropped it into a steel drum.

"Hey!" Jesús Bernal said angrily. "*Oye!*"

"*Qué pasa, chico?*" It was the Mixmaster rasp of the *comandante* himself. In his mind's eye Jesús could picture the old bastard sucking on a wet cigar, his strained twisted fingers like a vulture talon clutching the receiver. Jesús Bernal could picture those mean brown eyes, narrowing at the sound of his voice.

"It's me," Jesús said in Spanish. "Have you seen the newspapers, *Comandante?*"

"*Sí*"

Proudly Jesús said, "I am famous."

"So is Ronald McDonald."

"I was expelled from the Bahamas," Jesús declared.

"For what? Stealing coconuts?"

Jesús began to fume. "It is important work."

"It is girl's play."

"I bombed a Miami policeman!"

"You bombed his fucking feet," the *comandante* said. "I read the papers, *chico*. All these years and you are still the worst bomber I ever saw. You couldn't blow up a balloon."

After a pause, the old man said. "Tell me, who is this *El Fuego*?"

"I am *El Fuego*," Jesús answered.

The *comandante* cackled. "You are a shit-eating liar," he said, again in Spanish.

Jesús grimaced. "All right. *El Fuego* is a powerful Anglo. He is also a crazy man, he wants to give Florida back to the Indians and the raccoons. He recruited me for the dirty work."

"And to write the communiqués."

"*Claro.*"

"It is the one talent you seem to have."

Jesús Bernal smiled hopefully. There was a long silence on the other end. He heard the sound of a match striking wood; the old man's damn cigar had gone out.

"The FBI has been asking about you," the *comandante* growled. "It's a bad idea, you calling me."

Jesús Bernal swallowed hard. "I want to come back to the movement. My work here is finished. This organization, it is not disciplined, *Comandante*. There is drug use . . . and liquor. And the crazy man, *El Fuego*, he's always making jokes."

"I'm not surprised. It is all very funny."

"Please, *Comandante*, read the papers! Haven't I proven myself?"

"You bombed a fucking golf course," the old man said.

"A vital strategic target," Jesús countered.

"*Coño!* A Russian freighter is a strategic target, but

a golf course is . . . a goddamn golf course. And these were not Communist soldiers you killed, they were rich Americans. I'm surprised Fidel himself didn't send you a medal."

By now Jesús was trembling. His voice skipped like a teenager's. He cupped his hand over the mouthpiece so Viceroy Wilson couldn't hear him begging.

"Please, *Comandante*, I've committed many bombings, kidnappings, even murders—all in the name of The Cause. What must I do to convince you to take me back?"

"Do something serious," the old man said, his chest rattling. "And do it right."

Jesús Bernal slammed down the phone and cursed. He returned to the sawhorse where Viceroy Wilson was working, snatched a hammer, and started whaling on a two-by-four. The warehouse was hazy with sawdust and marijuana smoke.

"So you didn't get the job," Wilson said through a mouthful of nails.

"I thought you didn't understand Spanish," Bernal snapped.

"In 1977 we had a placekicker named Rivera," Wilson said. "From Mexico, I think. Used to give Spanish lessons on the team plane. One Sunday in Kansas City the motherfucker missed four straight field goals inside the thirty and we lost the game. That night a bunch of us got together and called Immigration."

"You had him arrested?"

"The next day at practice." Viceroy Wilson shrugged. "Football's a tough sport, man."

"So now you're going to tell Wiley I want out."

"Naw," Wilson said. "Not if you stay through New Year's. After that, I don't give a fuck what you do."

"I'm thinking of starting my own group," Jesús Bernal confided.

"What you gonna call it?"

"I haven't decided."

"How about: The Ernesto Cabal Cabal."

"Go to hell," said the Cuban, still sensitive on the Ernesto issue.

"This new group," Viceroy Wilson said, "what's the mission this time?"

"Invade Havana."

"Naturally." With switchblades, no doubt. Viceroy Wilson started hammering again. Every once in a while he'd step back to see how the thing was taking shape.

Tommy Tigertail sat on a blanket in the corner, beneath a somber daguerreotype of Thlocko-Tustenugee, Chief Tiger Tail. Tommy's eyes were open but unfocused; fresh from an Everglades passage, he had only just learned that Pavlov had been shot the week before in a beachfront swimming pool by the Fort Lauderdale SWAT team. Grief had robbed the Indian of all energy, and he had dropped his hammer and sat down in a trance. He feared it would be a night of dreams, when his fingers again would claw the wet bars of the dungeon where his great-great-grandfather had perished. On such nights Tommy's soul wandered, keeping company with his warrior ancestor. Tommy knew what would happen if his soul should not return from its journey by dawn: He would forever become part of his own nightmare, and never awake from it. This was the fate of many anguished Seminoles, whose souls suddenly fled in the night; for Tommy Tigertail, such a death would be infinitely worse than anything the white policemen might do to him.

"Look at that crybaby," Jesús Bernal said, scowling at the heartsick Indian. "Somebody shot his pet lizard."

"You shut up," Viceroy Wilson hissed at the Cuban, "or I'll nail your nuts to your nose."

Tommy Tigertail was the closest thing to a brother that Viceroy had found in the Nights of December. Between them was an unspoken bond that had nothing to do with the use of the Cadillac; it was a bond of history. In his post-heroin library days Viceroy Wilson had studied the Seminole Wars, and knew that Tommy's people had fought not just to keep their land, but to protect the runaway slaves who had joined them on the Florida savannas. The magnificence of that struggle was not lost on Viceroy Wilson; he knew Tommy would never give him up. Viceroy had never trusted anyone so completely.

Jesús Bernal sensed that it was unwise and perhaps dangerous to make fun of the Indian, so he changed the subject.

"I'm going to show the *comandante* a thing or two," he said determinedly.

"That's cool," said Viceroy Wilson, turning back to his work, "long as you wait till after New Year's."

"We'll see about that, *negrito*," Jesús said bravely, after Viceroy Wilson had cranked up the circular saw and could not possibly hear him.

TWENTY-TWO

Brian Keyes never thought of himself as lonely, but there were times when he wondered where all his friends had gone. As a rule private detectives are not swamped with party invitations and that part Keyes didn't mind; he wasn't a lampshade-and-kazoo type of guy. But there were nights when a phone call from any sociable non-felon would have been a welcome surprise on the old beeper. It wasn't loneliness, really; aloneness was more like it. Keyes had felt it as soon as he'd quit the *Sun*; it was as if the quintessential noise of life had suddenly shrunk by fifty decibels. On some days the quiet tortured him; the office, the apartment, the stake-outs. Sometimes he wound up talking to the car radio; sometimes the damn thing talked back. Two years away from the *Sun* and Keyes still longed for the peculiar fraternity of the city room. It ruled your whole damn life, the newspaper, and even if it made vulgar cynical bastards out of everybody, at least the bastards were there in the empty times. Day or night you could walk into the *Sun* and find somebody ready to sneak out for a beer or sandwich. These days Keyes ate alone, or with clients so scuzzy he wanted to gag on the corned beef and rye.

Which is why he came to enjoy guarding Kara Lynn Shivers. The first couple days she'd treated him with the same frostiness and suspicion she held for most men, but gradually she had warmed up. The less they talked about the beauty-queen racket, the happier Kara Lynn seemed. She was good company, nothing like Keyes had expected. It seemed a miracle that she had emerged from the cloying parentage of Reed Shivers so independent, unspoiled, and classy. It also was amazing that her sense of humor had survived, as had some soft and thoughtful edges. Talking to Kara Lynn was so easy that Keyes had to remind himself that this was not prom week, it was a serious assignment, and the package did not include true confessions. He was getting paid a small truckload of money to do one job: deliver Kara Lynn Shivers safe, pristine, and magnificent aboard the queen's float.

Two days after Christmas, five days before the big parade, Kara Lynn came downstairs wearing a sassy lemon-yellow tennis skirt and a matching knit vest. She handed Brian Keyes one of her father's expensive boron tennis rackets and said, "Come on, Marlowe, we're going to the club."

Keyes wasn't in a clubby mood. He'd spent a second straight morning at the airport, watching Customs in case Wiley tried to slip through. As usual, Miami International was a zoo—and there'd been no sign of Skip.

"I'm beat," Keyes told Kara Lynn. "Besides, I'm lousy at tennis."

"Not with those legs," Kara Lynn said. "Now, come on."

They took her VW. It was only a ten-block ride, a winding circle around the Coral Gables golf course. Keyes drove. In the rearview, two cars back, was a Cadillac Seville with tinted windows. It was the worst tail job Keyes had ever seen—if that's what it was. On an open stretch Keyes coasted the VW and the Caddy backed off by half a mile. Then it turned off and disappeared.

Kara Lynn was very cool; she hadn't turned around once.

"Do you have your own gun?" she asked casually.

"It's in the trunk."

"There is no trunk."

"There is too," Keyes said, "in the MG."

"Brilliant," she said. "How much did you say they were paying you?"

Keyes gave her a that's-very-funny look.

"Who do you think was following us?"

"Maybe nobody. Maybe the bad guys."

"They wouldn't try anything now, not before the parade."

"Who knows," Keyes said. "We're dealing with a special brand of fruitcake." He pulled into the clubhouse parking lot.

Kara Lynn asked, "How are you going to play tennis in those ratty sneakers?"

"Badly, I'm sure." The shoes weren't the worst of it. Keyes was wearing raggedy cutoff jeans and a Rolling Stones concert T-shirt.

"Take my arm," Kara Lynn said, "otherwise they'll think you're a caddy."

Keyes dragged himself around the tennis court for a solid hour, volleying like a madman, all speed and no finesse. His stitches throbbed constantly and his right lung was on fire. The only thing that kept him going was the long-legged sight of Kara Lynn rushing the net, her lips set intently, cheeks flushing pink, blond hair shimmering with each step. When it came to tennis, she was a very serious young lady. Nothing fancy, no power to speak of, but clean precise strokes. Tricky, too.

She beat him 6–4, 3–6, 7–6. A drop shot got him. He made a valiant stab, but wound up straddling the net. He was too exhausted to feel embarrassed.

Afterward Kara Lynn led him into the clubhouse lounge. Keyes took a quick survey and concluded that he was the only person in the whole joint without an alligator on his shirt. Even the bartender had one. Keyes thought he'd died and gone to Preppie Heaven.

Several fragrant young men stopped Kara Lynn for a peck on the cheek. Kiss, kiss. Howya doing. Looking great. Bye now. Keyes himself got a few curious stares.

"You ever see *Goodbye, Columbus*?" he said to Kara Lynn when they sat down. "I feel just like the shmuck in that movie, and you're the Ali MacGraw part."

"Oh please."

"It was before your time. Forget about it."

"I like the Rolling Stones," Kara Lynn volunteered.

"Yeah?"

"Your T-shirt's pretty pitiful, but the Stones are all right."

She ordered a club soda. Keyes asked for a draft.

"I was kidding about the shirt," Kara Lynn said.

"And my sneakers."

"No, I was serious about the sneakers." She gave his arm a little pinch. Keyes grinned. He was starting to feel warm and comfortable and incredibly witty. Time to watch out. Book of Jenna, Chapter One.

"Why'd you leave the newspaper?" Kara Lynn asked. Some weight-lifter-type with an enormous head of curly blond hair waved at her from across the lounge and pointed to his drink. She shook her head no, and turned away.

"You want to join him, it's okay," Keyes said. "I'll sit up at the bar."

"Oh no you won't. Tell me why you quit the newspaper."

Keyes gulped the beer. "Because I made a mistake."

"Everybody makes mistakes."

"Not big ones. Not in that business."

"Oh, come on. How bad could it be?"

"The worst." Keyes set down the mug and leaned forward. "Let me explain something. Your dad's a bigshot lawyer. If he goofs up, he waltzes into court, files a new motion, and fixes it. The client never knows. If a surgeon screws up, he digs a little deeper, adds a few extra stitches, and makes it all right. In most jobs it's like that—there's always a way out. But what I did, I can't fix. It's done forever. Once the paper rolls off the press, that's it. Sure, you can publish a correction or a bloody apology, but there's no guarantee that the right people will see it. Some folks will only remember what you wrote the first time, and if what you wrote was wrong, that's how they'll remember it."

"Did you get fired?"

"I resigned. My boss never knew why."

"You were scared to tell him."

"No, I was scared to hurt him."

Kara Lynn twirled the ice cubes in her club soda.

"Do you miss it?"

"Sometimes," he said, "I miss the people. Some of the smartest people I know work in that business. And some of the screwiest. That's what happens when you chase the truth for too long; you finally catch up with it and you're never the same. Screwed up for life." He was thinking of Skip Wiley.

Kara Lynn was a terrific listener. She was *too* good. Keyes wondered if she was petrified with boredom.

But then she said: "Tell me about being a private eye."

"One thrill after another: *Mr. Keyes, here's two grand. Find out if my wife's sleeping with her psychiatrist. Take some pictures, too.*"

"Still chasing the truth," said Kara Lynn.

"Yeah. But it's a cheap grimy truth. Gets in your hair, your clothes. Under your goddamn fingernails. I never felt like this when I was a reporter, honest to God."

"You're pretty unhappy, Brian."

"That makes two of us, Cinderella."

"Why, whatever do you mean? I'm the Orange Bowl queen, remember? I've got a thousand-dollar savings bond, a new wardrobe, a singing coach, and a four-year scholarship." Kara Lynn shook loose her ponytail and struck a haughty profile. "What more could a girl want?" Then she cracked up laughing.

Keyes laughed too.

The gorilla with the curly blond hair was waving again.

"I think Hercules wants to buy you a drink," Keyes said.

"Yeah, time to go." Kara Lynn signed the tab. Keyes didn't feel the least bit odd about it; Reed Shivers would find a way to write it off.

"Do me a favor, Brian."

"Sure."

"When we walk out of here, would you hold my hand?"

"Why?"

"Because it's more polite than saying, 'fuck off.' Which is what I'd like really to tell these jerks, but I can't. Not here at Dad's club."

As they rose from the table, Keyes tucked the tennis racket under his left arm and put his right arm around Kara Lynn's shoulders. They walked out that way, right past the Old Spice preppies. It felt just fine.

"You're a good sport," Kara Lynn said when they got to the car. "and I was right about your legs. You ran me ragged out there."

Brian Keyes wasn't listening.

The Seville was parked across the street, in the shade of a banyan tree. A thin dark man in an undershirt sat on the fender, drumming his hands on the side of the car. The man wasn't paying attention; he wasn't doing what he'd been told.

"Get in the car," Keyes said to Kara Lynn. "The police radio's under the front seat. Try to call García."

Kara Lynn got in the driver's side of the VW and rolled down the window. "Where are you going?"

"That's the asshole who stabbed me."

"Brian—"

But he was already gone, strolling across the parking lot. He looked perfectly calm, a tennis bum on his way home. Kara Lynn could hear him whistling a song. "Yesterday," it sounded like. She saw Keyes slip the leather sheath off her father's tennis racket.

"Oh no," Kara Lynn said.

Jesús Bernal did not recognize Brian Keyes immediately. He wouldn't have been looking for him, anyway. Jesús Bernal's mission was to scout for cops; Skip Wiley had wanted to know if there were policemen assigned to the girl. So far, Bernal hadn't seen the first patrol car; the lunatic Wiley was wrong again, as usual. Bernal was just about ready to call it quits and cruise back to the warehouse when the tennis player ambled up to him.

"Hey, *muchacho*, remember me?"

Bernal looked hard at the boyish face and, after a moment or two, remembered.

But not fast enough.

Keyes swung the tennis racket and hit Jesús Bernal flush in the face. A nicely timed forehand smash. Broke three strings on the racket.

The Cuban's head bounced off the Cadillac's bumper. He landed faceup on the pavement, snorkeling his own blood. The undershirt hung in shreds from the hood ornament.

Keyes bent over Jesús Bernal and whacked him again, this time a solid backhand to the throat. The Cuban kicked his legs and made a sound like a garbage disposal.

"Gggrrrnnnn," he burbled.

"You should see my serve," said Brian Keyes.

Kara Lynn Shivers pulled the VW alongside the Cadillac. Keyes got in and she stomped the accelerator.

"God Almighty, you killed him!"

"No such luck. You get hold of the cops?"

"No, the radio—" She was too excited to talk.

"Find a phone booth," Keyes said.

"Brian, he looked . . . really . . . dead!"

"He wasn't. Not by a long shot. I gotta call García. Find a goddamn phone booth."

She nodded, and kept nodding, like a dashboard puppy. She was scared as hell.

"Was he one . . . of . . . them?" Kara Lynn spoke in

breathless gulps, as if she'd been crying, but she hadn't. Her knuckles were red on the steering wheel.

Keyes touched her arm, felt her flinch.

"Kara Lynn, it'll be all right." But he was thinking: Maybe this means Wiley's back.

"It's scary," Kara Lynn said shakily, staring hard at the road ahead. "It's insane."

"Honest to God, it'll be all right."

TWENTY-THREE

When Sergeant Al García's squad finally got to the country club, all they found beneath the banyan tree were radial tire tracks, a syrupy puddle of blood, and several kernels of corn, which turned out to be human teeth. The police searched all night for the Seville. They roared in convoys through Coral Gables and Little Havana, stopping every Cadillac in sight, rousting every poor sap in an undershirt.

Yet the Fuego One Task Force did not find the injured Jesús Bernal, and by eight o'clock the next morning Al García's phone was ringing off the hook. Reed Shivers. The chief. The Orange Bowl chairman. Ricky Bloodworth. The Chamber of Commerce. Even NBC, for Christ's sake.

García carried three Styrofoam cups of black coffee to his office and locked the door behind him. He dialed the Shivers house and Brian Keyes picked up on the first ring.

"He got away," the detective said.

"You don't say."

"Hey, it's not our fault Shirley Temple couldn't figure out the police radio."

"She was scared stiff," Keyes said. "I was on the phone five minutes later. Five lousy minutes."

"That's all it takes," García said. "If it makes you feel any better, the sonofabitch leaked pretty good. He's got to be hurting."

Hurt or not, it was unimaginable that Jesús Bernal would turn up at a hospital; he was probably out in the Glades drinking Tommy Tigertail's home-brewed medicines. Which meant he was probably going to recover.

Brian Keyes figured Jesús Bernal probably could make a career out of getting revenge.

"Al, they've got to call off the parade."

"Not in a billion years," García said.

"But this clinches it—it proves these idiots are serious about taking Kara Lynn. After yesterday they're going to try twice as hard."

"We'll be ready." García slugged down the coffee; he figured he'd need a gallon of caffeine to brave the waiting shitstorm.

"How's the queen holding up?" he asked.

"Mildly terrified. All of a sudden she's not sure who's more dangerous, *Las Noches* or me. She wants to call the whole thing off but Daddy's leaning hard. It's been a very lively morning."

García asked, "Did you call your Shriner pals up North?"

"Yeah. They're on board."

"Excellent! Remember, *chico*, not a word to a soul."

"You got it."

"The dudes in the orange blazers, they'd have a stroke."

"Not to mention your badge," Keyes said.

*

Jesús Bernal lay shirtless on a blue shag carpet remnant. His eyes were shut and his breath whistled through raw gums. His throat shone purple and swollen. Every once in a while his hands tremored and drew into bony fists. Macho dreaming, Viceroy Wilson thought. Intermittently he checked on Bernal, then went ahead hammering and sawing and drilling as if he were alone in the warehouse, which was no bigger than a garage.

Time was running out. The Indian had sent lumber and palmetto trimmings, but no manpower. Wilson had been working like hell, living on wheat germ milkshakes; he'd dropped five pounds in two days.

The sound of an automobile outside startled him. It wasn't the Seville, either; Wilson knew the hum of the Caddy like he knew his own mother's voice. Stealthily he set down the tools and picked up a sawed-off shotgun. He heard footsteps at the warehouse door. The lock rattled. Wilson brought the gun to his shoulder.

The door opened and Skip Wiley stalked in.

"A little jumpy, aren't we?" he said.

Tommy Tigertail stood behind him.

They stared at Viceroy Wilson until he lowered the sawed-off. Wiley came up and gave him a hug. "You're doing damn fine," he said. "Damn fine."

Viceroy Wilson was not wild about hugs; a handshake would have sufficed. "So you're back from the tropics," he said to Wiley, "looking tanned and tough."

"Horseshit. I look like hell." But he didn't. Wiley's face was bronze and his beard was golden-red from the sun. He was wearing a brightly striped soccer jersey with the words "Cap Haitien" printed across the front pocket.

"D'you join a fucking spa?" Wilson said.

"Hardly." Wiley stopped over the snoring, sawdust-sprinkled form of Jesús Bernal. "Looks meaner with no teeth, doesn't he?"

"Sorry sack of shit," Wilson said.

"I know, I know. That's Item One on the agenda."

Skip Wiley removed his panama hat and prowled the small warehouse, examining Viceroy Wilson's creation in the bleak light of the bare sixty-watt bulb. Tommy Tigertail stood in a corner, his features unreadable in the shadow. Viceroy Wilson popped a can of Heineken and waited for the fun to begin; he needed a breather, anyway.

Wiley sat down on a sawhorse and folded his arms. "Wake him up," he told the Indian.

Tommy prodded Jesús Bernal with the hard toe of his boot. The Cuban moaned and rolled over, burying his face in the crook of an elbow. Tommy poked him again, decisively. Jesús sat up snuffling and rubbing his eyes. His fractured nose was the shape of a question mark and the rest of his face was a grid: the perfect imprint of a Spalding tennis racket.

"How you feeling?" Skip Wiley asked.

"Thiddy," the Cuban said. "Damn thiddy."

"I'll get you some new teeth," Wiley promised.

"Mank a mot." Jesús sounded like he was talking through a mouthful of marbles.

Wiley clasped his hands evangelically. "Well," he said, "I'm delighted we're all here. The rainbow coalition, together again. And only four days left!"

"Mank God," muttered Jesús Bernal. "Idth aah turding duh thid." *It's all turning to shit*, is what Jesús was trying to say.

Skip Wiley took a loud breath and stared down at

the dusty floor. All at once the cheeriness seemed to drain from his expression; his mouth, always on the verge of smiling, suddenly turned thin and severe; the merry brown eyes shrank and turned dull. The transformation was so palpable and so volcanic that even Jesús Bernal was moved to silence.

"The reason I came back," Wiley said somberly, "is to prevent disaster. To save us from international ridicule."

As he looked up, the pale light snared his chin, the ridge of his long nose, the blond crest of his forehead. The others were struck by Wiley's flickering visage. He reminded Jesús Bernal of a priest in the confessional, and Viceroy Wilson of a Basin Street scat singer. And when Tommy Tigertail looked at Wiley, he was reminded of an animal spirit he had once encountered at the sacred Green Corn dance.

"Our moment is at hand," Wiley told them. "And this is no time to be losing ground or getting careless. We've had a rotten week. First we're booted out the Bahamas—humiliating, but not calamitous—and then yesterday we nearly blow it for good. Yesterday"—he glanced down at the Cuban—"we had extreme major fuckage."

"Unngh," Bernal remarked defensively.

"The whole idea," Wiley said, his voice building, "of surveilling Kara Lynn Shivers was to determine if she was under police protection. I assumed we all understood that it was vitally important to remain invisible."

The word *invisible* seemed to snake through the warehouse and wrap around the Cuban's neck.

"Now, Jesús," Wiley went on, "since your teeth got knocked out and your larynx looks like an avocado, I'm not going to make you tell me precisely what happened. Not now, anyway. Today I want you to rest, and I want you to stay here until I tell you to leave. Because, as we speak, every police officer in Dade County is out looking for you. If you were captured—and I realize that might appeal to your grandiose appetite for martyrdom—but *if* you were captured, there's no telling what they'd do to make you talk."

"No mucking way," Bernal said.

"Let's not take the chance. You stay put," Wiley said. "Gentlemen, we've had a major setback: we've lost the element of stealth."

"But Keyes already knew the plan," Tommy Tigertail said.

"Of course, of course—but look . . ." Wiley was trying to come up with a good Seminole-type metaphor. "Tommy, it's the difference between knowing there's a panther hiding in the swamp, and seeing that panther with your own eyes. What's more frightening: wondering where it is, or finding it?"

The Indian didn't need it spelled out for him. Neither did Viceroy Wilson. They knew the magnitude of Bernal's transgression.

"Judging by the paper this morning, yesterday's clumsy episode has taken some of the luster from our mission," Wiley said sardonically. "In all my life I've never heard of a professional terrorist being subdued by a putz with a tennis racket."

"Eaaamy," replied Jesús Bernal, probably in Spanish.

"Lucky he didn't kill you," Viceroy Wilson said.

"Lucky's the right word," Wiley added. "Lucky all we lost is a car."

"What?" Wilson cried.

"I'm sorry, old man, but the cops put a BOLO out on the Caddy so I had Tommy get rid of the darn thing."

"No!"

"I dumped it in a rockpit," the Indian said.

With the roar of a wounded grizzly, Viceroy Wilson hurled himself upon Jesús Bernal and began pummeling him ferociously in the ribs and kidneys.

"Ged ob me, you addhoe!" the toothless Cuban howled. "Hep!"

With great effort Tommy Tigertail was able to pull Viceroy Wilson away from Jesús Bernal. Once separated, the two revolutionaries glowered at each other, panting like leopards.

Skip Wiley rose to his feet. "Look what's happening here! Ten days ago *Las Noches* was unstoppable, fearless, indivisible. Now we're trying to maim and mutilate each other. Last week we were front-page news and today the paper's making fun of us. Did you see the *Sun*? Did you see the bloody cartoon? Bearded guy supposed to look like Che Guevara, with a beret and machine gun, except he's got a tennis racket smashed over his head! Funny, huh? Vaudeville terrorists, that's us. That's the Nights of December. And instead of going out to redeem ourselves with some serious extremism, what do we do? We sit in this rathole and hold our own tag-team wrestling match. Don't you see, this is exactly what they want! They're trying to destroy us from within!"

Tommy Tigertail thought Wiley was giving García and the other white men entirely too much credit. Brian Keyes was the only one who worried Tommy.

"The sad truth is, we've lost our psychological

advantage," Skip Wiley said, "and we've got to get it back. That's why I've divined a new plan."

"What new plan?" asked Viceroy Wilson. He couldn't bear the thought of learning a whole new plan; he thought the old plan was all right.

"Nupid! Mus plain nupid!" Jesús Bernal whined. Not only was it stupid, it was downright suicidal to change the plan so late in the game; it went against all basic terrorist training. It was unthinkable.

"Lighten up, comrades," Skip Wiley said. "We're not tossing out the old plan, just embellishing it."

"Tell them," the Indian said. "Tell them your idea."

So Wiley told them all about it. "Not just one princess, but two!" he concluded merrily. "Double your pleasure, double your fun!"

Viceroy Wilson liked what he heard; the new plan was Wiley's cleverest yet. Phase One would wreak bedlam, knock everybody off-balance; the perfect setup. Phase One also required a helicopter, and Viceroy Wilson had always wanted to ride in a helicopter. Tommy Tigertail approved of the plan too, mainly because it afforded him a couple days of working deep in the Everglades, alone with his people.

Only Jesús Bernal opposed Skip Wiley's new plan. He lay on the warehouse floor, carping unintelligibly, growing more and more miserable as Wiley issued orders. The beating he'd gotten from that *maricón* Keyes and the cruel scolding he'd gotten from *El Fuego* had plunged Jesús Bernal into a familiar well of self-pity. Unable to be understood in any language, he found himself ignored. And worse, patronized. That Wiley had decided upon such a reckless change of strategy without consulting him—him, the most seasoned of all the terrorists!—infuriated Jesús Bernal. It was infamy repeating itself; it was the First Weekend in July Movement all over again.

When it came time for the Cuban's assignment, Skip Wiley announced that *Las Noches* once again would be needing Bernal's unique skills at the Smith-Corona; there were historic communiqués to be written! Jesús assented halfheartedly, hoping that in the dim light the other conspirators could not see the disloyalty in his eyes, or his sneer of contempt. Jesús Bernal made a private and fateful decision: he would proceed with a plan of his own. He would humble them all: the arrogant Indian, the stoned-freak nigger and the *culebra* cop García. Keyes, too; Keyes would suffer in failure. And when it was over, on New Year's Day, *El Comandante* would beg Jesús Bernal to return and lead the holy struggle against the Bearded One. It would be most satisfying to watch the old man grovel. Ha!

And Wiley, damn him—who said he was such a genius? If Wiley was so smart, Jesús thought, how could he have forgotten about the third bomb, the most powerful of all? How could he forget to inquire what had become of it? What kind of leader was so careless to let such a thing pass?

So tonight when it becomes an issue, thought Jesús Bernal, I can look him square in the eye, on the way out the door, and say: *But, El Fuego, you never asked. You never asked.*

Richard L. Bloodworth had spent the day at the Metro-Dade police station, lying in wait for Sergeant Al García. Bloodworth could be excruciatingly patient. He passed the time introducing himself to secretaries and patrolmen, upon whom he proudly foisted newly printed business cards on which the "Ricky" had been replaced with the staid "Richard L." Most of those who received Bloodworth's business card tore it up the minute he was out of sight, but a few tucked it away in a drawer or a wallet. Someday, Bloodworth hoped, one of these drones would call with a hot tip, maybe even a ticket to the front page.

At first Al García had no intention of letting Ricky Bloodworth slither within striking distance. Their last exchange had been brief and unfortunate:

Bloodworth: Sergeant, these terrorists act like real scum of the earth, don't they?

García: Yeah. Get out of my office.

The next morning the detective had picked up the paper and seen this impolitic headline: *Cop Labels Terrorists Scum of Earth.*

Al García believed that no good could ever come from a newspaper interview, and that only idiots spoke to newspaper reporters. He explained this to the chief when the chief phoned to ask why the Miami *Sun* was getting jerked around. As often happened, the chief did not agree with Al García's philosophy and remarked on the detective's poor attitude. The chief argued that it was vital for the head of the Fuego One Task Force to keep a high law-and-order profile until the Orange Bowl Parade. That meant cooperating with the press.

So Ricky Bloodworth finally got an audience with the sergeant. The reporter came in wearing a lawyerly three-piece suit. He said hello to García and shook hands amiably, as if being forced to wait seven and a half hours was the most natural thing in the world.

Bloodworth took out a notebook, uncapped a red pen, and jotted García's name at the top of a page. The detective watched the ritual with a sour face.

"Before I forget, I'd like you to have one of these." Bloodworth handed García a business card.

"I'll treasure it always," García said. "What's the L. stand for?"

"Lancelot," Bloodworth said. That was one of the drawbacks about the new byline; people were always asking about the middle initial. Leon was such a nerdy name that Bloodworth had scrapped it. Lancelot was more fitting.

Bloodworth asked his first question.

"Sergeant, exactly what happened last night?"

"The suspect escaped."

"Jesús Bernal, the famous terrorist?"

"Yeah."

"What about the vigilante with the tennis racket?"

"We're waiting," García said, "for him to come forward." Bloodworth scrawled in the notebook.

"Do you intend to press charges?"

"What for?"

"Assault, of course. According to witnesses, he simply walked up to Mr. Bernal and beat him senseless with the tennis racket, without any provocation."

García said, "That's still under investigation."

Bloodworth scribbled some more. He was starting to remind García of that young shithead Bozeman from Internal Affairs.

"Any idea what Mr. Bernal was doing in Coral Gables?"

"Nope," García said.

Bloodworth dutifully wrote "NO IDEA" in his notebook.

"Sergeant, I'm still puzzled about how this went down."

García hated it when jerks like Bloodworth tried to talk like cops.

"What do you mean *went down?* Down where?" García said.

"I mean, how could it happen? Here's one of the most wanted men in Florida lying unconscious in a pool of blood on a busy public street—and the police still manage to lose him. How in the world did he get away?"

García shrugged. He thought: Let's see you *quote* a shrug, asshole.

"It seems simply . . . inconceivable," Bloodworth remarked.

Al García realized that, in effect, he'd just been called a Jell-O-brained moron. That was the beauty of a snotty word like *inconceivable*.

"The one thing everybody wants to know," Bloodworth continued, "is where the Nights of December are going to attack next."

"I'd like to know, myself."

"You have no idea?"

"Nope," García lied.

Again Bloodworth wrote, "NO IDEA."

"Let me burn a cigarette," the detective said.

"Sorry, but I don't smoke."

"Then what's that in your vest? It looks like a pack of cigarettes."

Bloodworth smiled sheepishly and took out a small

Sony Pearlcorder. "A tape recorder," he explained unnecessarily.

"Oh," García said. "Is it on?"

"Well, yes."

"Can I see it?"

Ricky Bloodworth handed the miniature recorder to García.

"Quite a little gadget," the detective said. "You keep the First Amendment in here, do you?"

"Very funny." Bloodworth's bluish mouth opened in a round ratlike smile, all incisors.

García set the Pearlcorder flat on the desktop, its tiny reels still spinning. He reached into his holster and took out his Smith and Wesson service revolver.

"What are you going to do?" Bloodworth asked.

"Watch."

With the butt of the pistol, García pounded the Sony to tiny pieces. He gave the pieces back to Bloodworth, along with a tangle of brown ribbon.

"Don't ever tape me again," García said, "not without asking."

Bloodworth stared in disbelief at the expensive Japanese debris.

"What's the matter with you?" he cried. "Everybody uses tape recorders. It's just a tool, for God's sake . . . for accuracy . . . to make me a better reporter."

"Brain surgery wouldn't make you a better reporter," García said. "Now get out of here before I have you strip-searched." So much for cooperating with the press.

"This is . . . an outrage," Bloodworth stammered.

"Simply inconceivable," García agreed.

For half an hour Bloodworth sat on the steps of the

police station and morosely flipped through his note-book. García had given him practically nothing, not one damn usable quote. It had been a dry week, too, newswise. Until last night, *Las Noches* had been quiet: no more kidnappings or murders to goose the story back to page one. Bloodworth was getting itchy. He wondered if Cab Mulcahy would let him do a column about Al García and the bumbling Fuego One Task Force. He wondered what García's boss would say if he found out about the tape-recorder incident.

A local TV crew marched up the steps, around Blood-worth, into police headquarters. He thought: What if García had given them an interview, too? What if the detective actually said something important on tele-vision? Identified *El Fuego*, for instance? Bloodworth's flesh turned clammy. Christ! He'd completely forgotten to ask Sergeant García about *El Fuego*.

In a panic, Bloodworth dashed back up the steps. He couldn't go back to the newsroom empty-handed, too much was riding on this story—a raise, his very own column, maybe even a job with the *New York Times*. The stakes were too fantastic to let an oafish Cuban cop ruin everything.

Bloodworth hopped off the elevator at Homicide, but the TV crew was nowhere in sight. He scurried from office to office, unimpeded. At the end of a long hall, he finally spotted the bright TV lights.

It was too late. Through the window of a soundproof interview room, Bloodworth saw Al García talking expansively to a pretty brunette television reporter. She was holding a microphone and he was smiling like it was cocktails at the Four Seasons. The camera rolled.

Bloodworth watched in wretched helplessness,

struggling to read the detective's lips. García glanced at Bloodworth's face in the window and mouthed three words: "Up your ass."

In a fury, Bloodworth retreated to García's empty office, where he fumed and cursed and looked at his wristwatch every thirty seconds. How long could it last? What could he be telling her? Bloodworth felt a damp stripe settle down the back of his shirt. He was getting beaten, beaten badly. By a TV bimbo.

A man with a plastic badge that said "Mail Room" came in and piled papers and packages on García's desk.

As soon as the messenger left, Bloodworth slid over and sifted through the goodies. A two-page memo on weapons training. A ten-page memo on pensions. An invoice for softball uniforms.

Crap!

Next he sampled the unopened mail, scanning the return addresses. He found something from the FBI fingerprint section in Washington and held it to the light, without success; the clever Feebs used opaque envelopes.

Underneath the stack of letters was a brown box the size of a toaster.

A bright red courier sticker was glued to the box: Same-day service, fourteen bucks. Oddly, whoever had sent the parcel had tied a luxurious bow in the twine, the kind of bow you'd see on a Fifth Avenue Christmas package.

The address label had been typed neatly:

> To Sgt. Alberto García, Maggot and Traitor
> Metro-Dade Police Pig Department
> Miami, City of Pigs, Florida

Ricky Bloodworth excitedly opened his notebook and copied everything.

In the upper-left-hand corner, on the top of the box, the sender had written:

"*De un guerrero y patriota.*"

From a warrior and patriot.

Ricky Bloodworth went to the door and peered down the hallway. Amazingly, the TV lights were still blazing away. God Almighty, he thought, not even Joe Wambaugh yaps this much.

Bloodworth returned to the desk and picked up the brown box. It was much lighter than he expected. Bloodworth shook it cautiously at first, then briskly. Nothing. It was packed solid.

Bloodworth trembled at the thought of what he was about to do.

We're talking felony, he told himself. This is police evidence, no doubt about it.

But screw García—he busted my tape recorder.

Ricky Bloodworth put the box under one arm and hurried out of the Homicide office. He went down three flights of stairs and came out in the Traffic Division, which was deserted. He found an empty rest room and locked himself in a stall that reeked of ammonia and bad cologne.

The reporter sat on a toilet and set the box on his lap. He propped his notebook on the tissue rack. He stuck the red pen behind his left ear.

Bloodworth's heart was drumming. He actually felt himself getting hard—that's how much he loved this job. Ricky savored his coup: a treasure chest of clues from the Nights of December. An exclusive, too . . . that was the part that gave him a hard-on.

He had already decided what he would do. As soon as he was done peeking, he'd send the package right back to García. He'd wrap it exactly the same and steam the labels—who would ever know?

Lovingly Ricky Bloodworth rubbed the smooth brown paper, fingered the frayed twine.

Then he pinched one end of the magnificent bow and pulled, pulled on it until the knot popped.

And a savage furnace swallowed him.

Tore the air from his lungs.

And the flesh from his cheeks.

Until the universe turned molten white.

TWENTY-FOUR

It had always puzzled Cab Mulcahy that Mr. Cardoza took such an ardent personal interest in the Miami *Sun*. Traditionally publishers love to meddle with the news operation (because that's the most exciting part of a newspaper, the only part worth dicking around with), but Cardoza was not a typical publisher. He had little understanding of the tenets of journalism with no paternal affection for the newspaper, for his fortunes did not singularly rise or plummet with the *Sun*. Rather, Cardoza was a boundless entrepreneur, a man who loved the variety of making money; a man with dozens of incongruous irons in the fire. He owned a soccer team in St. Kitts, a stock car in Darlington, a chain of family cinemas, four butcher shops, a Liberian oil tanker, three thousand coin-operated condom machines, and a phosphate mine. Any single one of those enterprises, Cab Mulcahy thought, was infinitely more amusing as a money toy than the frequently struggling Miami *Sun*, of which Cardoza owned fifty-one percent. Which automatically made him publisher and meddler-for-life.

On the evening of December 28, a Friday, Cab Mulcahy was summoned from an opulent pre-Orange Bowl cocktail party to explain to Mr. Cardoza why Skip

Wiley's column had not appeared in the paper since Christmas Eve.

The publisher did not particularly wish to see Mulcahy in person, and he certainly had no intention of visiting the newsroom. Cardoza preferred to do business office-to-office, by telephone—distance yields perspective, he liked to say. Also, he got a kick out of hanging up on people.

At the appointed hour, Cardoza dialed Mulcahy's desk.

"I didn't think much of that Christmas Eve column," he began.

"Me neither," Mulcahy said.

"Who gives a shit about some native fisherman who can't swim? It seems to me Mr. Wiley can do better."

"He's still not himself," Mulcahy said.

"He gets paid to be himself." Cardoza said. "A small fortune, he gets paid. And here it's Christmas week, tourist season, when our circulation's supposed to shoot sky-high, and where's our star clean-up hitter? Every day I pick up the newspaper, and nothing. No Skip Wiley. The *Sun*'s dead without him. Lies there like a dog turd on my front lawn."

Mulcahy said, "Really, Mr. Cardoza, I wouldn't go that far."

"Oh you wouldn't? You'd like to hear the cancellation figures, maybe. Or take a few hours to read some of the mail we've been getting."

"That's not necessary."

For years Cab Mulcahy had tried to tell Cardoza that he overestimated Wiley's popularity, that no single writer could pull enough support to significantly boost or bust the circulation numbers. Whether that was

299

true or not, it was what Mulcahy chose to believe. However, as a pure businessman Cardoza felt that he appreciated the concept of a Good Product far better than some ivory-tower editor. And in Cardoza's predominant and immutable view, what made the Miami *Sun* a Good Product were Skip Wiley, Ann Landers, and Dagwood Bumstead. On some days Wiley alone was worth the twenty-five cents.

"Where the hell is he?" Cardoza demanded.

"I don't know," Mulcahy said. "I expected him back in town on Christmas Day."

"Send someone to Nassau," Cardoza barked through the speaker box. "Do whatever you have to do."

Mulcahy rubbed the back of his neck and closed his eyes. It was fortunate that Cardoza couldn't see him. "Skip's not in the Bahamas anymore," he said. "Apparently he was deported from the islands on the twenty-fourth."

"Deported!" Cardoza huffed. "For what?"

"It's quite a long list, sir."

"Give me the high points."

"Attempted bribery, possession of a controlled substance, and behaving as an undesirable, whatever that means. For what it's worth, the embassy says Wiley was set up. Apparently that column about the fisherman didn't go over too well with the Bahamian government."

"Now everybody's a goddamn critic," Cardoza said.

"All I know is that they put him on a plane," Mulcahy said. "At gunpoint."

"Why didn't we think of that?"

Though miserly with compliments, Cardoza privately held great admiration for Cab Mulcahy; he couldn't imagine anyone trying to manage so many deeply disturbed individuals as there were in the newsroom. It was a disorderly place where eccentricity, torpor, petulance, even insubordination were tolerated, so Cardoza stayed far away, where it was safe. He stayed near the money.

"God knows I'd never tell you how to run that operation, Cab, but I do want to see Skip Wiley in my newspaper again. That means you'd better find him. I want a New Year's column from that crazy sonofabitch, you understand? Don't tell me he's sick and don't tell me he's exhausted, and don't fucking tell me that he's not himself. Just tell me that he's writing again, understand?"

"Yes, sir, but apparently—"

And Cardoza hung up.

All week long Cab Mulcahy had been waiting for the phone call or telegram, waiting for that familiar profane foghorn greeting. Waiting in vain. He couldn't believe that Skip Wiley had docilely accepted the butchery of the Christmas column; he couldn't believe that Wiley had suppressed what must have been a colossal homicidal rage.

Was Skip that far gone?

In the meantime, the Nights of December had fallen quiet and dropped off the front page, much to the relief of the men in the orange blazers. Scores of suspects had been rounded up, including a few men who might have vaguely resembled Jesús Bernal or Daniel "Viceroy" Wilson; all were released or charged with unrelated crimes. There was also talk of a summit with Seminole tribal elders to seek assistance in locating Tommy Tigertail, but the Seminoles refused to go near the police station and the cops refused to enter the reservation, so the meeting never materialized.

The morning edition of the *Sun* had carried four stories about the upcoming Orange Bowl festivities (including a color photograph of twenty newly arrived Shriners, jovially polishing their Harleys), but in the whole newspaper there was only one item about *Las Noches de Diciembre*. It was a short feature story and a cartoon, beneath a headline that said: *Tennis Buff Boffs Bomb Suspect.*

It was only now, rereading it in print, that Cab Mulcahy realized how trenchantly the presentation of Ricky Bloodworth's article—the tone, the headline, the slapstick cartoon—struck at the very manhood of the Nights of December. It worried Mulcahy. Coupled with Wiley's ominous silence, it worried him profoundly.

He looked out at the newsroom just in time to see a lean figure running toward the office, weaving through the desks and video-display terminals. It was Brian Keyes.

"He called!" Keyes said breathlessly. "Twenty minutes ago. The bastard left a message on my beeper."

"What did he say?"

"He said he's gonna phone here, your office. Wants to talk to both of us."

"It's about damn time," Mulcahy said, feeling a little better about the prospects. He took off his black dinner jacket and hung it over a chair.

As they waited for the phone to ring, Mulcahy busied himself by brewing a fresh pot of coffee. His hands shook slightly as he poured it. Keyes scooped a handful of peppermint candies from a jar on the secretary's desk and ate them mechanically, one by one.

"What are we going to say?" Mulcahy asked. "When he calls, what the hell are we supposed to say?"

"We've got to convince him it's all over," Keyes said. "Tell him we know the whole plan. Tell him if he tries anything at the parade, *Las Noches* are as good as dead. Tell him it'll make Bonnie and Clyde look like Sunday at the beach."

Mulcahy nodded neutrally. Might work, might not. With Skip, who the hell could ever tell?

"I think we ought to concede some minor points," Mulcahy suggested. "He'll never give up if he thinks it's been a total loss."

"You're right," Keyes said. "Congratulate him on all the ink they got. The newsmagazines, the *Post, USA Today.* Tell him the Nights of December made their point. They got everybody's attention."

"Which is true."

"Of course it's true."

"But is it enough for Skip?"

Keyes and Mulcahy looked at each other with the same answer.

"What are we going to do," Keyes asked, "when he tells us to go beat our meat?"

Mulcahy stroked his chin. "We could talk to Jenna."

"Forget it," Keyes said sharply. "Lost cause."

"Then it's over. Bloodbath or not, we go to the cops."

"Yup." Keyes glanced at the telephone.

"Imagine the headlines, Cab."

"God help us."

The phone rang. Once. Twice. Mulcahy swallowed hard and answered on the third ring.

"I see," he said after a few seconds.

Keyes excitedly pointed to the speaker box. Mulcahy shook his head unhappily. Then he hung up. His face was like gray crepe.

303

"That wasn't him," Mulcahy said. "It wasn't Wiley."

"Then who was it?"

"Sergeant García," he said gravely. "Apparently the Nights of December just blew up the one and only Richard L. Bloodworth."

The bomb that exploded in Ricky Bloodworth's lap was powerful by Little Havana standards, but not utterly devastating. To build it, Jesús Bernal had hollowed a round Styrofoam lobster float and packed the core with generous but unmeasured amounts of Semtex-H, C-4, and old gunpowder. Then he ran a fuse through the middle and plugged the ends with gasoline-soaked Jockey shorts and two Army blasting caps. Next Bernal had meticulously embedded into the Styrofoam ball hundreds of two-penny nails (the sharp ends facing out), as well as assorted slivers of rusty cola cans and soup tins. It was not a bomb designed to wipe out embassies or armored limousines; this was, in the terrorist vernacular, an antipersonnel device. Bernal had packed the bristling lobster buoy into an empty one-gallon paint drum and threaded the fuse through a hole in the lid. The fuse became part of the magnificent bow that adorned the deadly brown box—an inspired touch of which the Cuban was especially proud.

Yet, as always, Jesús Bernal had a problem with quality control. He had envisioned a weapon that would fire shrapnel in all directions at an equal force, leaving no square centimeter of human flesh unpunctured. The paint can, Bernal had determined, would itself disintegrate into jagged fragments and become part of the lethal payload.

Fortunately for Ricky Bloodworth, that is not what happened. Fortunately, Jesús Bernal had failed to seal properly the bottom of the paint can, which blew off at the instant of explosion and gave the bomb something it was never supposed to have: rocket thrust.

In what the Metro-Dade Bomb Squad calculated was no more than two-thousandths of a second, Jesús Bernal's prize package blasted off from Ricky Bloodworth's lap on a nineteen-degree trajectory, passed cleanly through three ply-wood toilet stalls, and detonated in the men's urinal. The rest room was gutted.

An hour later, when Cab Mulcahy and Brian Keyes arrived, men in white lab coats were balanced on stepladders, scraping what appeared to be chunks of pink bubble gum off the charred rest-room ceiling.

"Mr. Bloodworth's fingertips," Al García explained. "We've found seven out of ten, so far."

"How is he?" Mulcahy asked.

"He's got a nosebleed like Victoria Falls," the detective said, "but he'll make it."

Luckily, the police station was only five minutes from Flagler Memorial Hospital. Ricky Bloodworth had arrived in the emergency room semiconscious and suffering from hand injuries, lacerations and second-degree burns over his face and groin.

"The tip of his cock got fried—don't ask me how," García said. "He's also deaf, but the doctor says that might be temporary."

Mulcahy stepped gingerly through the smoky chamber, his shoes crunching on a carpet of broken mirror, splintered wood, and powdered tile. Pretzeled by the blast, naked water pipes sprouted from the walls and floor, dripping milky fluid.

Brian Keyes knelt next to the bomb-squad guys as they picked through the ceramic ruins of the urinal. "Look at all these damn nails," Keyes said.

"Two hundred seven," said one of the bomb experts, "and still counting."

Keyes looked up and saw Mulcahy with his black tie loosened and French sleeves rolled up. He had a notebook out, and was descending on Al García. Keyes had to grin: the old boy looked right at home.

Mulcahy asked García: "How do you know this was the Nights of December?"

"Your Mr. Bloodworth's been working on the story, right? That makes him a prime target." García eyed the notebook uneasily. "Besides, the boys here tell me this looks like another Jesús Bernal special."

"What was Ricky doing down here?" Keyes said.

"Probably taking a dump," García said.

"Come on, Al, this is Traffic. Why wouldn't he be upstairs in Homicide?"

"'Cause I kicked his sleazy ass out when I caught him trying to tape-record me. Had one of those little James Bond jobs tucked in his vest."

Mulcahy frowned. "I'm sorry about that, Sergeant. That's strictly against newsroom policy."

"Fucking A."

"When you saw him last," Keyes said, "did he have a package?"

"Nope," García said. "But here's my theory, Brian. After I chase him out of here, he goes home, finds this hinky package in the mailbox, freaks out, and comes racing back to show me. On the way upstairs he stops in the john and bang!"

"How'd he get the box past the security desk in the

lobby?" asked Mulcahy. A damn good question, Keyes thought.

But García just chuckled. "You could waltz a Pershing missile by those bozos downstairs and they'd never look twice."

At first Keyes didn't want to believe that Bloodworth himself had been the target, or that Skip Wiley might have ordered his execution. It was something Wiley had threatened for years around the newsroom, but then so had almost every other reporter. Bloodworth was always on somebody's shit list.

Yet Keyes couldn't deny that the bombing made perfect sense, considering what Bloodworth had written about *Las Noches*, and considering what had happened to Wiley's Christmas column. Keyes felt guilty about his role in the Bahamas scheme; Cab Mulcahy felt much worse. Across the rubble the two men exchanged anguished glances and shared the same chilling thought: Skip wasn't kidding about a bloodbath. Imagine a bomb like this, in a crowd. . . .

If this was Wiley's way of warning Keyes and Mulcahy to keep their silence, it worked.

With a gloved hand, one of the bomb-squad guys displayed a twisted scrap of tin which still bore a red-and-white soup label. "Minestrone," he announced. "This baby was sharpened with a diamond file."

"Cute," Mulcahy said, pocketing the notebook. "Come on, Brian, let's go see Ricky."

Within minutes of the explosion, the emergency room of Flagler Memorial had been occupied by a clamorous army of journalists, each resolved to make Richard L.

Bloodworth a hero of the Fourth Estate. News-wise, it would have been a better story (and certainly less work) if Ricky had been killed outright, but near-martyrdom was better than nothing. The mere fact that the Nights of December had bombed a news reporter guaranteed international headlines, and the event was sure to draw the Big Boys from New York—the networks, the *Times* and *Sixty Minutes*, all of whom would do anything to get out of Manhattan in the winter. The locals realized that now was the time to score the big interview, before Diane Sawyer strolled into town and scooped them all.

Two policemen escorted Brian Keyes and Cab Mulcahy through the mob and hustled them into a laundry elevator. Five minutes later they stood at the door of Bloodworth's private tenth-floor room.

The hospital's official press release had listed Ricky in satisfactory condition, but in no sense of the word did he seem satisfactory. He looked like he'd stuck his head into a bonfire—burnt ears curled up like fortune cookies, hairless eyelids swollen tight, the seared nose and cheeks stained burgundy with surgical antiseptic. He looked like a barbecued mole.

Cab Mulcahy quaked at the sight of his wounded reporter. Like a stricken father, he stood at the side of the bed, lightly touching Bloodworth's arm through the sheets.

Bloodworth made a singsong noise and Keyes edged closer. It was hard to tell through the bruised slits, but Ricky's eyes seemed to be open.

"Grunt if you can hear me," Keyes said.

Bloodworth made no sound.

"Brian, he's deaf, remember?"

"Oh yeah." Keyes made an "okay" signal with his thumb and forefinger. Bloodworth smiled feebly.

"Good boy," Mulcahy said. "You're going to be just fine. We'll take care of everything."

Bloodworth raised his right hand to return the gesture, a poignant if somewhat palsied effort. Keyes noticed that each of Ricky's fingers was bandaged to the second joint; in fact, the fingers seemed oddly stubbed. Keyes lifted the sheet and checked Bloodworth's left hand—same thing. Al García wasn't kidding: Jesús Bernal's bomb had sheared all Ricky's fingertips. Not even the thumbs had been spared. Evidently he had been holding the box at the moment of explosion.

"Oh brother," Keyes said, replacing the sheet.

"Everything's going to be just fine," Mulcahy said to Bloodworth.

"He's never gonna type again," Keyes whispered.

"Ssshhhh!"

"Or bite his nails, for that matter."

"We'll get the best plastic surgeon in Miami," Mulcahy vowed. He was wondering what in the world to do with a deaf reporter with no fingertips. For his suffering Ricky certainly deserved something, Mulcahy thought, something generous but safe. Perhaps a lifetime column on the food page—even Bloodworth couldn't screw up a casserole recipe.

"Too bad he can't tell us what happened," Keyes said.

Ricky Bloodworth had no intention of telling anyone what had happened; even an elephant-sized dose of painkillers had not dulled his sense of survival. Maimed or not, he knew he'd be fired, perhaps even indicted, if it ever became known that he'd snatched the brown package from Sergeant García's desk. It was better to let the world think the bomb had been meant for him—better for his career, better for the story. And why should that lout García get any attention, anyway?

Through a haze, Bloodworth saw Cab Mulcahy holding up a notebook. On it the editor had written: "You are going to make it okay."

Bloodworth smiled and, with one of his nubs, gave a tremulous thumbs-up.

Keyes took the notebook and wrote: "Where did you get the package?"

Bloodworth shrugged lamely.

"I guess he doesn't remember much," Mulcahy said.

"Guess not."

Next Keyes printed: "Are you strong enough to write a note for the cops?"

Bloodworth squinted at the pad, then shook his head no.

"We'd better let him rest," Mulcahy said.

"Sure."

"I don't know what to tell the wolf pack downstairs," Mulcahy fretted.

"Hell, Cab, they're the competition. Don't say a damn thing."

"I can't do that."

"Why not? You're the *Sun*'s reporter on this one, aren't you? So just keep your mouth shut and write the story. Write the hell out of it, too."

Amused, Mulcahy said, "Well, why not?"

He winked at Bloodworth and turned for the door. Bloodworth grunted urgently.

"He wants to say something," Keyes said. He laid

the notebook on Ricky's chest and fitted the pen into his gauzed claw.

Bloodworth wrote laboriously and in tall woozy letters:

"PAGE ONE?"

Keyes showed the notebook to Mulcahy and said, "Can you believe this?"

A nurse came in and gave Ricky Bloodworth an enormous shot. Before drifting off, he saw Keyes and Mulcahy waving good night.

Outside the hospital, Keyes said, "It's getting late, Cab, I'd better head back to the house." Dismally he wondered what a nail bomb could do to Reed Shivers' cork billiard room.

"Go on ahead," Mulcahy said. "If our pal calls, you'll be the first to know."

Back in the newsroom, the other reporters and editors were surprised to see Cab Mulcahy sit down at a video-display terminal and begin to write. Before long his presence seemed to galvanize the whole staff, and the Friday-night pace of the newsroom quickened into something approaching gusto.

The spell was interrupted by the city editor, who, after circling reluctantly, finally stepped forward to give Cab Mulcahy the message.

"From Wiley," the city editor said uneasily. "He phoned while you were out."

Mulcahy's ulcer twinged when he saw the message.

"I say yes, you say no," it read. "You say stop, and I say go, go, go."

TWENTY-FIVE

From the hospital Brian Keyes drove straight to Coral Gables to check on Kara Lynn. He rang the bell three times before Reed Shivers opened the door.

"Nice of you to show up," Shivers said archly. He wore a monogrammed wine-colored robe and calfskin slippers. A walnut pipe bobbed superciliously in the corner of his mouth.

"Nice to see you, too, Mr. Hefner."

"Don't be a wise guy—where've you been? You're getting big bucks to be a baby-sitter."

"There's been another bombing," Keyes said, brushing past him. "A newspaper reporter."

"The Nachos again?" All the Anglos in Miami had started calling Wiley's gang the Nachos because it was so much easier to pronounce than *Las Noches de Diciembre*.

"Where's Kara Lynn?" Keyes asked.

"Out in the game room working her fanny off. Try not to interrupt."

Keyes examined Reed Shivers as he would a termite. "After all this, you still want your daughter to ride in that parade?"

"They have dogs, Mr. Keyes, dogs trained to sniff out the bombs."

"You're incredible."

"We're talking about a career decision here."

"We're talking murder, Mr. Shivers."

"Not so loud!"

Keyes heard music coming from the game room. It sounded like the Bee Gees. *Stayin' alive, stayin' alive, oooh-oooh-oooh-oooh.* The bass guitar thumped through the wall.

"Jazz aerobics," Shivers explained. "Since Kara Lynn can't go out to class, the teacher came here. I thought that was damned considerate."

Keyes went into the game room. The stereo was extremely loud. The pool table had been rolled to one wall. In the middle of the carpet, Kara Lynn was stretched out, grabbing her heels.

Keyes smiled.

Then he looked up and saw Jenna.

"Oh God, no," he said, but the words were lost in the music. Jenna and Kara Lynn were so absorbed that neither noticed him standing there gaping.

Their choreography was enthralling; each woman gracefully mirrored the other, stretching, dipping, arching, skipping, kicking. Keyes was transfixed by the vision—the two of them in sleek leotards and practically nothing else, both with their blond hair up in ponytails. Of course there was no mistaking one for the other: Jenna was bustier, fuller in the hips, and she had those gold earrings. Kara Lynn was taller, with long thorough-bred legs. Tennis legs.

Brian Keyes could not have dreamed up a more stunning, or baffling, apparition. He turned off the stereo, leaving the dancers stranded in mid-jumping jack.

"Whoa!" Jenna said, dropping her arms to her sides.

"Hey! What's the idea?" Kara Lynn was a little annoyed.

"I'll explain," Keyes said.

Jenna turned around and stared. "Brian!" She seemed shocked to see him.

"Hey there," Keyes said. "Since when do you make house calls?"

"Oh boy."

Kara Lynn looked quizzically at Jenna, then back at Keyes. The prickly silence gave it all away.

"So you two know each other," said Kara Lynn.

"Long time ago," Keyes said.

"Not so long," said Jenna, talking with her eyes.

Kara Lynn looked embarrassed. "I'm going to get some lemonade."

When she was gone, Jenna said, "How'd you find me here?"

"Don't flatter yourself. I wasn't even looking." Keyes felt rotten. And angry. "Tell me what's going on," he said.

Jenna dabbed her forehead with a towel that matched her pink lipstick. "Kara Lynn's been a student of mine for two years. She's a good dancer and quite athletic, in case you didn't already know."

Keyes let that one slide.

"She said she couldn't come to class this week—something about a parade curfew—so I offered to stop by here for a short workout. I don't know what you're being so snotty about."

"Where's Skip?" The eternal question; Keyes wondered why he even bothered.

"I'm not sure. This is some room, huh?"

"Jenna!"

"Time for sit-ups."

"Stop."

But in an instant she was supine, arms locked behind her neck. "Hold my legs. Please, Brian, don't be a pill."

He got down on all fours and braced her ankles with his hands. He thought: She really is on another planet.

"One . . . two . . . three . . ." She was as limber as a whip.

"Where's Wiley?" Keyes asked.

"Seven . . . eight . . . I got one for you . . . what are *you* doing here?" With each sit-up Jenna emitted a soft round cry, half-moan and half-grunt. Keyes was intimately familiar with the sound.

"I've been hired to keep an eye on Kara Lynn," he said.

"You? Come on, Bri . . ."

"Your deranged boyfriend plans to kidnap her during the Orange Bowl Parade, or didn't you know?"

"Fourteen . . . fifteen . . . Jeez, I said *hold* my legs, don't fracture them . . . you're wrong about Skip. . . ."

"Did he send you here?" Keyes asked.

"Don't be silly . . . he doesn't even know I'm back in the country . . . supposed to be house-hunting in Port-au-Prince. . . ."

"Holy Christ." Keyes couldn't imagine Skip Wiley loose on the streets of Port-au-Prince. The government of Haiti was not known for its sense of humor.

"Twenty-four . . . twenty-five . . . Tell me the truth, Brian, are you sleeping with this kid?"

"No." Why did he answer?—it was none of her damn business. "Jenna, I just don't want her to get hurt."

"Skip wouldn't do that . . ."

"No? He blew up Ricky Bloodworth tonight."

"Mmmm . . . all the way?"

"He's still breathing, if that's what you mean."

Jenna was tiring, but not much.

"Thirty-nine . . . forty . . . Skip promised he wouldn't hurt the girl . . . ease up a little on the left leg . . . hey, you still miss me?" She caught his eye, beamed. Full of confidence, like she could jerk the leash anytime she wanted.

"Do you want Skip to die?" Keyes said tonelessly. He'd had about all he could take.

"Forty-six, forty-seven . . . 'course not . . . do you?"

"No." But don't ask me why not, Keyes thought, because the bastard richly deserves it.

"Brian . . . don't let anything happen to him."

That was it. One the count of forty-nine he stopped her, slipped a hand behind her head and held her there, in a sitting position. Probably with more firmness than was necessary.

"Just one more!" Jenna protested.

"Know what he said, Jenna? He said there'd be a bloodbath if I told the cops about him. Said lots of people would die."

"Baloney." She strained against his grip. "He's just bluffing."

Keyes said, "Look here at my clothes—what do you suppose that is?"

"A-1 Sauce?"

"It's blood, you bubblehead! Human blood. I knelt in a big warm puddle of it tonight over at police headquarters. You should have been there, the place looked like Beirut."

"Let me go," Jenna said.

"So what do you make of all these darned murders?" he said. "Pretty hilarious, huh?"

"Brian, just stop it."

"No, goddammit, look at me!" But she wouldn't.

"Look at these bloodstains and tell me Wiley's a big hero," he said angrily. "Tell me how proud you are, go ahead, Jenna. The man's a genius, all right. Takes a real visionary to bomb a moron in a toilet."

She squirmed loose and shot to her feet. Her face was pink and she was breathing hard.

Keyes said, "Jenna, you can end all this—it's not too late. Do everyone a favor and turn him in."

She shook her head once and spun away, out the door.

"I'm going for pizza," Kara Lynn announced.

"Not alone you're not," Keyes said.

"It'll make you chubby," Reed Shivers added. "The only Orange Bowl queen with a mozzarella tummy."

"That's enough, Daddy. I'm hungry."

"Then we'll get it delivered," Keyes said. He picked up the telephone in the game room and stared at it. The phone was made out of an actual bottle of Seagram's; Reed Shivers had ordered it specially from a golf catalog.

"What do you like on your pizza?" Keyes asked.

Kara Lynn shrugged. "Mushrooms, anchovies."

"No pizza!" her father said. "Pumpkin, we've got publicity stills tomorrow, remember?"

"Screw it," said Kara Lynn.

"That's the spirit," Keyes cheered.

"But it's *swimsuit*," Shivers pleaded.

"And I'll look sensational, Daddy. Tiny tits and all."

Keyes changed his mind about having the pizza delivered. Kara Lynn obviously needed to get out of the house.

"You ever been to Tony's?" he said. "Great pizza."

"Let's go."

"At least go easy on the cheese," Reed Shivers said, pouting into his pipestem.

They took the MG. It was a chilly night, full of stars. The brisk air whistled through a rusty hole in the floorboard, and the car got cold quickly.

"The heater's busted," Keyes said. "I got an extra sweater in the back."

"I'm okay." Kara Lynn cupped her hands and blew into them softly. Keyes could see the gooseflesh on her bare arms.

"How far to Tony's?" she asked.

"I've got no idea," Keyes said. "I made it up."

"Oh."

"To get us away from Professor Higgins."

"Daddy's not a bad guy," Kara Lynn said, "but he can be such a pain in the ass."

Keyes drove north down LeJeune Road. Just for the hell of it, he squared the block at Miracle Mile to make sure they weren't being followed again.

"Is the Pizza Hut okay?"

"Sure," Kara Lynn said.

They got a booth in the corner, away from the jukebox and video games. Keyes ordered a pizza with mushrooms, pepperoni, and anchovies. Kara Lynn looked like she was freezing in her dance tights, so Keyes went out to the car and got his spare sweater, a gray cotton pullover.

With a nod of thanks, she slipped it on over the leotard. Keyes wondered why she was so quiet; it wasn't a hostile silence, or even a sulk. It reminded him of the first few days at the house, when she was sizing him up. Kara Lynn was a pro when it came to withdrawal, a real blank page when she wanted to be.

"What's on your mind?" he finally asked.

"I was just wondering about you and Jenna."

"Ancient history."

"Go on."

"Very boring."

"I'll bet."

"And painful."

"Oh." She took a sip of diet cola, a concession to her father. "Didn't mean to pry."

"Forget it," Keyes said. "But do me a favor: no more aerobics classes until after the parade."

"How come?"

"Call it a security precaution."

"For heaven's sake, you're not saying Jenna's dangerous!"

You don't know the half of it, Keyes thought. "Did Jenna ever say anything about the Orange Bowl?"

"Sure. She wished me luck before the pageant—even sent a bouquet of wild sea oats to the dressing room."

"She would have made a great florist."

"Actually she's the one who convinced me to enter the contest. To be honest, I was burned out on the darned things. Besides, I didn't think I had a chance— you should've seen some of the other girls. But Jenna said to give it a try. Strike a blow for small-breasted women, she said."

"A great florist and a great psychologist," Keyes

said. So Jenna was in on it from the beginning. What the hell did he expect? He decided to leave it at that, though. Jenna wouldn't be back, and there was no use scaring Kara Lynn.

"She says I look like her, ten years ago."

"Maybe a little," Keyes said. It wasn't the beauty they had in common, so much as the aura—an aura of absolute control. The ability to conquer with a shy glance or the slightest of smiles.

"I hope I look that good when I'm twenty-nine," Kara Lynn remarked.

"You will."

A waitress brought the pizza, hot and pungent. They attacked it hungrily. Keyes got tomato sauce on both his sleeves. Kara Lynn rolled her eyes, pretending to be mortified.

"Have you had many girlfriends?" she asked.

"Thousands. I was once engaged to half the Rockettes."

"You don't like this subject, do you?"

"Look, I never asked you what it's like to be the Stone Crab queen, with a dozen greaseball contest judges staring up your crotch. I never asked because it seemed personal and none of my business, and I knew you wouldn't want to talk about it."

"You're right. It's awful, that's why."

"It *looks* awful," Keyes said. "I don't know how you do it."

Kara Lynn plucked an anchovy from the pizza and dropped it neatly on a napkin; a little anchovy graveyard. "It's easy to become Stone Crab queen," she said. "All you have to do is get some black heels and a bikini and learn to play 'Eleanor Rigby' on the French horn."

"You got my vote."

"I hate it. All of it."

"I know."

"Half the girls get boob jobs and butt tucks," Kara Lynn said. "Nobody does anything about it."

"What happens to them when there's no more beauty pageants?"

"Two, three years of modeling. A few local TV commercials if you're lucky. Guy once offered me three grand to lie on the hood of a Dodge truck and say: *I got my Ram Charger at Cooley Motors.* Real Shakespearean television. Daddy had a seizure when I turned it down."

"What do you really want to do, Kara Lynn?"

"Stop world famine, of course."

Keyes laughed. "And after that?"

"See Europe."

Keyes cut another slice of pizza but it surrendered grudgingly. A web of cheese hung elastically from his mouth to the platter.

"What about you, Brian? Your life all mapped out?"

Keyes chewed pensively.

"Someday I'm going to buy a sailboat," he said. "Move down to Islamorada, live off seaweed and lobsters. Let the sun fry me so brown that my hide gets tough as a turtle shell. I think I'd make a helluva good sea turtle—hey, don't look at me like that."

"But you're serious!"

"A turtle's got no natural enemies," Keyes said.

Kara Lynn felt warm. She liked the cozy smell of the sweater. "Can I come visit you down there?"

"You bet. Fix up a nice big plate of sargassum. We'll pig out."

Kara Lynn watched him so closely that Keyes began to feel a little uncomfortable. She was zeroing in on something. The old Jenna antennae started to twitch.

"What do you think about me, Brian?"

"I like you," he said. "I like you very much."

"She really hurt you, didn't she?"

Out of the blue. Just when he'd started to relax.

"Who?" he said inanely.

"Jenna. One look at the two of you together—"

"Forget the two of us together."

"I'm sorry. No more soap opera, I promise." She folded her arms and sat back. Her gray-green eyes captured him, froze him in one place. Nineteen years old, no one should have a look that good, Keyes thought.

"I can't figure out what I like so much about you," Kara Lynn said. "But I think it's your attitude."

"I've got a miserable attitude."

"Yeah, you come on that way but it's bullshit, isn't it, Marlowe? Some of it's an act."

"Until I grow my turtle shell."

"What I like," said Kara Lynn, "is your attitude toward me. You're the first man who hasn't treated me like a porcelain doll. You don't pamper, you don't drool, and you don't try to impress me."

Keyes smiled wanly. "Somehow I knew there was no danger of that."

"And I like the way you tell the truth," she said. "For instance, I think you told the truth just now when you said you liked me. I think you really do."

"Sure."

"I think you wouldn't mind if I kissed you."

Keyes opened his mouth but nothing came out. He felt a little shaky. Like prom night, for God's sake.

Kara Lynn reached over and took his arm. She pulled him gently. "Meet you halfway," she said.

They kissed across the table. It was a long kiss, and Keyes nearly got lost in it. He also managed to plant his left elbow in the pizza.

"You're nervous," she said.

"You're a client. That makes me nervous."

"Naw. Pretty girls make you nervous."

"Some of them, yeah."

In the MG on the way home, she sat much closer.

"You're worried about me," Kara Lynn said.

"I don't want you in this stupid parade."

She held onto his right arm with both hands. "I've got to do it. It's either me or some other girl."

"Then let it be some other girl."

"No, Brian."

Things were changing—all of a sudden the stakes couldn't be higher. The harrowing parameters of his nightmare had become perceptible; and locked inside them, Kara Lynn Shivers and Skip Wiley.

Keyes wondered if the maniac had phoned Cab Mulcahy, like he promised.

"You're frightened, aren't you?" Kara Lynn asked.

"Yup."

"We'll be all right," she said. Like Jenna used to say.

The house was dark when Keyes pulled into the driveway. The shaggy-headed palms hung still in the crisp night. Grackles bickered high in the old ficus tree. From the flowerbed a disinterested calico cat watched them come up the walk.

Keyes waited on the second step while Kara Lynn unlocked the front door. He went in first, switched on a small lamp in the hall, checked around.

"Everything's fine," he said. And out of habit took a step toward the guest room where he slept.

"No," Kara Lynn whispered, taking his hand. "Come upstairs."

TWENTY-SIX

Skip Wiley stormed into the warehouse shortly after noon on the twenty-ninth of December, the day after the bombing at police headquarters.

"Where is Jesús?" Wiley demanded.

"Don't know," Viceroy Wilson said.

"He was gone when we got here," said Tommy Tigertail.

Both men were shirtless, with leather carpentry belts strung from their waists. The Indian had a red bandanna around his neck, and his caramel chest was beaded with perspiration. Viceroy Wilson wore gray sweatpants and faded aqua wristbands, which kept his hands dry.

They had worked unceasingly since dawn, and the skeletal contraption had grown to fill the warehouse from floor to ceiling.

"It's coming along," Wiley said halfheartedly. "You're doing fine."

He paced with agitation, gnawing his lower lip, hands crammed in the pockets of his jeans. With each step his track shoes squeaked on the dusty concrete—a noise that only added to the tension. *El Fuego* was on the threshold of eruption; Viceroy Wilson and Tommy Tigertail could sense it.

In slow motion Skip Wiley picked up an iron mallet.

He studied it methodically, weighed it in each hand, then began to pound the aluminium door like a gong. With every swing came a new expletive. "That crazy-cretinous-brainless-shitheaded putz of a Cuban!" he grunted. "Worthless-misguided-suicidal-goddamn miscreant!"

Viceroy Wilson flinched each time the mallet landed, the noise amplified in his skull by forty freshly ingested milligrams of methamphetamine.

"Why didn't he tell me about this?" Wiley cried. "Who ordered him to go bomb that reptile Bloodworth?"

"Maybe he thought it would make up for the tennis thing," Tommy Tigertail said.

"Rubbish! Even after my lecture on solidarity, he pulls a silly stunt like this! No wonder the other crazy Cubans kicked him out. I should have known better—I should have listened to you guys."

Viceroy Wilson resisted the temptation to rub it in. Actually he was somewhat puzzled by Skip Wiley's anger. He figured that after all that had happened, Wiley ought to be elated to see Ricky Bloodworth go up in smoke. And if a new wave of counterpublicity was what Wiley sought, the bombing had been a bonanza: *Las Noches* were all over the morning papers and TV. But Viceroy Wilson listened unquestioningly to the harangue because he simply couldn't bring himself to defend Jesús Bernal. He'd warned the little bastard to chill out until after New Year's.

"Insubordination!" Wiley bellowed. "A group like ours can't survive with insubordination. You know what this is? A test, that's what. That slippery hot-blooded weasel is trying to push me as far as he can.

He thinks I'm not tough enough. He wants *mucho macho*. He wants machetes and machine pistols and nightscopes. He wants us to dress in fatigues and crawl through minefields and bite the necks off live chickens. That's his idea of revolution. No subtlety, no wit, no goddamn style."

Wiley was getting hoarse. He dropped the iron mallet. Viceroy Wilson handed him a jar of cold Gatorade.

"We need to find him," the Indian said.

"Damn soon," added Wilson.

Wiley wiped his mouth. "Any clues?"

Viceroy Wilson shook his head. In one corner of the warehouse, on Bernal's pitiful carpet remnant, sat the Smith-Corona typewriter. It was empty.

"He won't be back," Tommy Tigertail said.

"A loose cannon," growled Wiley, subsiding a bit.

Viceroy Wilson decided there was no point in keeping Jesús Bernal's secret. "The other night he was on the phone to his old dudes. Trying to get back on the A-team."

"The First Weekend in July?"

"They told him no way," Wilson said.

"So he decided to put on a one-man show," Wiley said.

"Looks that way."

"Well, that's gratitude for you."

"Let's try to find him," Tommy Tigertail repeated, with consternation.

"Hopeless," Skip Wiley said. "Anyway, he'll crawl back when he gets lonely—or when he can't stand the heat from García."

"Oh fine," Viceroy Wilson grumbled. "Just what we need."

Wiley said, "Besides, I hate to completely give up on the guy." What he really hated was the thought that anyone could resist his charisma or so blithely spurn his leadership. Recruiting a hard-core case like Jesús Bernal had been a personal triumph; losing him stung Skip Wiley's ego.

"Look, I've got to know," he said. "Are you boys still with the program?"

"Tighter than ever," Viceroy Wilson said. The Indian nodded in agreement.

"What about the chopper?"

"Watson Island. Nine tonight," Wilson said. "The pilot's cool. Freelance man. Does some jobs for the Marine Patrol, the DEA and the blockade-runners, too. Long as the price is nice."

"And the goodies?" Wiley asked.

"Safe and sound," Tommy Tigertail reported.

"Nobody got hurt?"

The Indian smiled—these white men! "No, of course not," he said. "Everybody had a ball."

Wiley sighed. "Good, then we're on—with or without our Cuban friend." He reached into a pocket and came out with something in the palm of his hand. To Viceroy Wilson the object looked like a pink castanet.

"What the hell," Wiley said. He carefully placed the object on the keyboard of Jesús Bernal's abandoned typewriter. "Just in case he comes back."

It was a brand-new set of dentures.

*

Cab Mulcahy had waited all night for Skip Wiley to call again. He'd attached a small tape recorder to the telephone next to the bed and slept restlessly, if at all. There was no question of Wiley reaching him if he'd wanted—Skip knew the number, and had never been shy about calling. Back when he was writing in full stride, Wiley would phone Mulcahy at least once a week to demand the firing or public humiliation of some mid-level editor who had dared to alter the column. These tirades normally lasted about thirty minutes until Wiley's voice gave out and he hung up. Once in a while Mulcahy discovered that Skip was right—somebody indeed had mangled a phrase or even edited a fact error into the column; in these instances the managing editor would issue a firm yet discreet rebuke, but Wiley seldom was satisfied. He was constantly threatening to murder or sexually mutilate somebody in the newsroom and, on one occasion, actually fired a speargun at an unsuspecting editor at the city desk. For weeks there was talk of a lawsuit, but eventually the poor shaken fellow simply quit and took a job with a public-relations firm in Tampa. Wiley had been remorseless; as far as he was concerned, anyone who couldn't weather a little criticism had no business in journalism anyway. Cab Mulcahy had been dismayed: firing a spear at an editor was a sure way to bring in the unions. To punish Wiley, Mulcahy had forced him to drive out to the Deauville Hotel one morning and interview Wayne Newton. To no one's surprise, the resulting column was unprintable. The speargun episode eventually was forgiven.

As a habit Skip Wiley called Mulcahy's home only in moments of rage and only in the merciless wee hours of the morning, when Wiley could be sure of holding the boss's undivided attention.

Which is why Cab Mulcahy scarcely slept Friday night, and why he was so fretful by Saturday morning when Skip still hadn't phoned. Keyes called twice to see if Wiley had made contact, but there was nothing to report; both of them worried that Skip might have changed his mind. By midafternoon Mulcahy—still unshaven, and rambling the house in a rumpled bathrobe—was battling a serious depression. He feared that he had missed the only chance to reason with Wiley or bring him in for help.

He was fixing a tuna sandwich on toast when the phone finally rang at half-past five. He hurried into the bedroom, closed the door, punched the tape recorder.

"Hello?"

"You viper!"

"Skip?"

"What kind of snake would let Bloodworth sodomize a Christmas column!"

"Where are you, buddy?"

"At the Gates of Hell, waiting. I told 'em to save you a ringside seat at the inferno."

Mulcahy was impressed by Wiley's vitriol; not bad for a five-day-old rage. "I'm sorry, Skip. I should never have done it. It was wrong."

"Immoral is what it was."

"Yes, you're right. I apologize. But I don't think morality is your strong suit, at the moment."

"Whoa," Wiley said. "Blowing up Ricky Bloodworth was *not* my idea, Cab. It was one of those things that happens in the fever of revolution. Corrective measures are under way."

"He's going to recuperate. You're damn lucky, Skip."

"Yeah, I paid a visit to the hospital."

"You did? But there's supposed to be a police guard!"

Wiley said, "Don't get all upset. The kid was thrilled to see me. I brought him a stuffed skunk."

Mulcahy decided to make his move. A conversation with Wiley was like a freight train: you either got aboard fast or you missed the whole damn thing.

"If you're in town, why don't you stop by the house?"

"Thanks, but I'm extremely busy, Cab."

"I could meet you somewhere. At the club, maybe."

"Let's cut the crap, okay?"

"Sure, Skip."

"Keyes isn't as smart as he thinks."

"Oh."

"Neither are you."

"What do you mean?"

"In due time, old friend."

"Why are you doing this?" The wrong thing to say— Mulcahy knew it immediately.

"Why am I doing this? Cab, don't you read your own newspaper? Are you blind? What do you see when you stare out that big bay window, anyway? Maybe you can't understand because you weren't here thirty years ago, when it was paradise. Before they put parking meters on the beach. Before the beach disappeared. God, Cab, don't tell me you're like the rest of these migratory loons. They think it's heaven down here as long as the sun's out, long as they don't have to put chains on the tires, it's marvelous. They *think* it's really paradise, because, compared to Buffalo, it is. But, Cab, compared to paradise . . ."

"Skip, I know how you feel, believe me. But it'll never work."

"Why not?"

"You can't evacuate South Florida, for God's sake. These people are here to stay."

"That's what the cavemen said about tyrannosaurus."

"Skip, listen to me. They won't leave for a bloody hurricane—what makes you think they'll move out after a few lousy bombs?"

"When the condos fail, the banks fail. When the banks fail, it's bye-bye lemmings." Wiley sounded impatient. "I explained all this to Keyes."

"Okay, I understand it," Mulcahy said. "I understand perfectly. Just tell me, what's this business about 'violating a sacred virgin'? How does that fit into your theory?"

"I thought you smartasses had it all figured out."

"Well, if it's the Orange Bowl queen, forget it. The police are everywhere."

"Maybe, maybe not."

Mulcahy said, "Skip, you're going to get yourself shot."

"I'm not planning on it."

"What *are* you planning?"

"To be on the front page of your newspaper again tomorrow."

"Tomorrow?" Mulcahy found it difficult to sound nonchalant. "But the parade's not for two days."

"This is a little preview, Cab."

Mulcahy was flustered. "What kind of preview?"

Wiley said, "You'll have to wait and see. As a courtesy, I'm advising you to budget some space for tomorrow's front page."

Mulcahy took a deep breath. "No, Skip."

There was a pause; then Wiley laughed disbelievingly. "What do you mean *no?*"

"I won't put the Nights of December on page one. I'll bury the story, so help me God."

"You can't," Wiley said, sounding vastly amused. "Don't you see, you're powerless. You can't ignore the news unless you're ready to forsake the public trust—and you're not, Cab. I'll bet on it. You're too honorable, too ethical, too everything. The integrity of that newspaper is sacred to you, probably the only thing sacred in your life. Diddling around with my column is one thing, but censorship's another. You wouldn't do it, not in a million years. You're at the mercy of the news, old friend, and right now the news is me."

"Skip, I still run this paper," said Mulcahy, his voice taut. He was choking the phone with both hands.

"And you do a swell job running the paper," Wiley said. "But if you don't think I know how to make the front page after all these years, then it's *your* brain that's turned to Rice-a-Roni. Now I've really got to sign off. My schedule is extremely tight."

"No, Skip, hold on just a second. I want you to please, please stop killing these innocent people—"

"Dammit, I haven't. Not one. Not innocent."

"Just stop the murders, please. As a friend I'm begging you. The cops are going to figure it out and they'll track you down. Why don't you end this thing and turn yourself in. You need—"

"What do I need? Help? I need help? Come on, Cab,

lighten up. Melodrama doesn't suit you. I've got to run."

"Skip, if you hang up, I'm calling García. I'm going to give him your name, tell him everything."

"Brian didn't explain the rules."

"I can't go along anymore, threats or not. Bloodbath, my ass—I mean, what more can you do, Skip? You even blew up one of my reporters."

"So you're going to put all this in the newspaper?"

"Absolutely."

"Then do me a favor," Wiley said seriously.

"What?"

"Make sure you run a good picture. I'm partial to the right-side profile, the one where I'm wearing the corduroy jacket. The dark brown one."

"Yeah, I remember," Mulcahy said dejectedly.

"What about Cardoza?"

"He's next on my list, after the cops."

"S'pose he wants his New Year's column."

"Don't even think about it," Mulcahy said.

"Fine. Be that way. The paper's dull as dishwater."

"I'll handle Cardoza," Mulcahy said.

"I'm sure. But in the meantime, Cab, watch the heavens."

"What do you mean?"

"Watch the heavens! Got that?"

"Yes," Mulcahy said. He didn't like the sound of things. He would have preferred that Wiley not bother giving any more clues. "Look, Skip, why don't you call Brian?"

"He's busy nymphet-sitting."

"Talk to him!"

"Nah."

"Okay, then he wanted me to tell you something. He wanted me to tell you that it's hopeless, that what you're doing is sheer suicide. He wanted me to tell you that whether you know it or not, it's all over."

"Ho-ho-ho," Skip Wiley said, and hung up.

Right away Cab Mulcahy put in a call to Al García, but the entire Fuego One Task Force was out in the Everglades on a tip. A deer hunter had stumbled into a fresh campsite that looked promising; García wasn't expected back in the office until morning. Mulcahy left an urgent message.

Next he tried Keyes, but Brian was gone too. There was a photo session out on the beach, Reed Shivers explained—the Orange Bowl queen at sunset. The languid look, very artsy. Keyes had tagged along to keep an eye on things; took the gun but not his beeper.

"Shit," Mulcahy said.

Cardoza was strike three. The publisher was attending the Palm Beach premiere of a new Burt Reynolds movie. Afterward was a cookout at Generoso Pope's.

Cab Mulcahy fixed himself a pitcher of martinis, sat down with Mozart on the stereo, and waited for the telephone to ring. It was the lousiest Saturday night of his life, and it was about to get worse.

One of Sparky Harper's only legacies was the annual pre-Orange Bowl Friendship Cruise. Each year, on the Saturday evening before the Monday parade, a large contingent of visiting dignitaries, politicians, VIPs and wealthy tourists set sail from the Port of Miami for a two-day junket to Freeport and Key West. Sparky

Harper had inaugurated the Friendship Cruise as a goodwill gimmick, and also as a secret favor to one of his ex-wives' brothers, who ran a lucrative catering firm for the cruise lines. For the first few years, the Orange Bowl queen contestants had been invited along on the cruise, as had all the Orange Bowl football players. However, the Chamber of Commerce quietly discontinued this policy in the late 1970's following an unseemly episode involving a lifeboat, a young beauty queen, and three University of Oklahoma sophomore linebackers. Once the beauty contestants and the football players had been banned from the ship, Sparky Harper had found himself with loads of empty chairs and four hundred pounds of surplus Gulf shrimp. It was then he had gotten the idea to invite journalists— but not just any journalists: travel writers. Sparky Harper and the Greater Miami Chamber of Commerce adored travel writers because travel writers never wrote stories about street crime, water pollution, fish kills, beach erosion, refugees, AIDS epidemics, nuclear accidents, cocaine smugglers, gun-runners, or race riots. Once in a while, a daring travel writer would mention one of these subjects in passing, but strictly in the context of a minor setback from which South Florida was pluckily rebounding. For instance, when huge tracts of Miami Beach began to disappear into the ocean, leaving nothing but garish hotels at water's edge, a decision was made to hastily build a new beach out of dredged-up rock, shells, and coral grit. Once this was done, Sparky Harper mailed out hundreds of impressive aerial photographs to newspapers everywhere. Sure enough, many travel writers soon journeyed to Miami and wrote about the wondrous new beach without ever mentioning the fact that you needed logger's boots to cross it without lacerating the veins of your feet. As a rule, travel writers wrote only about the good stuff; they were A-okay in Sparky's book. So, with the endorsement of the Chamber of Commerce, in 1980 Sparky Harper invited fifty travel writers from newspapers all across North America to come to Miami during Orange Bowl Week and sail the Friendship Cruise. Of course, 1980 was the year of the Liberty City riots and the Mariel boatlift, so only nine travel writers showed up, several of them carrying guns for protection. The following year the turnout was much better, and the year after that, better still. By the time of Sparky Harper's death, the Friendship Cruise was widely regarded by American travel writers as one of the premier junkets in the business.

This year the Chamber of Commerce unanimously had voted to dedicate the event to Sparky Harper's memory. On the night of December 29, four weeks after Sparky's murder, a crowd of 750 gathered at the Port of Miami and listened as the mayor of Miami read a brief tribute to the slain public-relations wizard. Afterward the crowd streamed up the gangplank and boarded the SS *Nordic Princess*, where an orgy of eating and drinking and banal joke-telling commenced.

The SS *Nordic Princess* was a sleek cruise liner, and nearly brand-new. Built on a fiord in Norway, she was 527 feet long and carried a gross tonnage of 16,500. She had seven decks, four hundred cabins, two heated swimming pools, five restaurants, eight bars, a spa, a library, a bowling alley, fifty slot machines, and a video arcade. There was also a branch of Chase Manhattan on the gambling mezzanine. The *Nordic Princess* was served by a crew of three hundred, mostly Dominicans and Haitians, with a few obligatory white Englishmen to serve as bell captains and maître d's.

Many of the passengers on the Friendship Cruise had never before sailed on an ocean liner. One of them was Mack Dane, the new travel writer from the Tulsa *Express*. Dane was a spry and earnest fellow in his midsixties who had spent most of his newspaper career trying to cover the oil industry. As a reward for his thirty-two years of service (and also to get him out of the way to make room for a young reporter), the *Express* had "promoted" him to the travel beat. The Orange Bowl was his first assignment, the Friendship Cruise his maiden voyage.

Like most of the guests aboard the *Nordic Princess*, Mack Dane was tickled to be in Miami in December. He had just spoken to his daughter back in Oklahoma and learned that there was three feet of fresh snow and a wind chill of forty-two below, and that the dog had frozen to the doorstep.

As the ship glided out of Government Cut, Mack Dane found his way to the top deck and strategically positioned himself near a tray of fresh stone crabs and jumbo shrimp. Christmas lights were strung festively from the ship's smokestacks, and a live *salsa* band was performing a medley of Jimmy Buffett tunes in a fashion that no one had ever dreamed possible. A strong breeze blew in from the ocean, pushing clouds and a promise of light rain. Mack Dane grabbed another banana daiquiri. He was having a grand time. He wondered if any of his fellow travel writers were young and pretty.

Two tourists stood at the rail and waved at the tiny figures of snook fishermen out on the jetty. Mack Dane watched the tourists for a few minutes and decided to interview them for his story. They looked like a reasonable couple.

"The Gilberts," they said warmly. "Montreal."

Sam Gilbert was about forty years old. He wore pale yellow slacks and an expensive toupee that was having a rough go of it with the wind. Other than that, he was a handsome-looking gentleman with a pleasant smile. His wife appeared to be in her later thirties. She was dressed in a tasteful beige pantsuit, a sheer silk scarf tucked around her neck. Her hair was so unnaturally blond that it was attracting fireflies, but other than that Mrs. Gilbert looked like a friendly and decent person.

"This your first cruise?" Mack Dane asked.

"Yes," Mrs. Gilbert said. "We had to book four months in advance. This is a very popular trip."

Mack Dane told them he was a travel writer, and a guest of the Chamber of Commerce.

"You didn't have to pay?" Mrs. Gilbert said.

"Well, no."

"What a great job," said Sam Gilbert.

"First trip to Miami?" Mack Dane asked.

"Right," Gilbert said. "We're here to see the Irish stomp the Huskers." Notre Dame was playing the University of Nebraska in the Orange Bowl football game on New Year's Day. According to many sportswriters, the game would determine the national collegiate football championship.

"I don't like football," Mrs. Gilbert confided. "I'm here for the sunshine and shopping."

"We just bought a winter home in Boca Raton," Sam Gilbert said. "Not a home, actually, a condominium."

"Sam's a doctor," Mrs. Gilbert explained.

Mack Dane felt like another drink. The *Nordic Princess* was out to sea, rocking ever so lightly in the northeast chop. Behind her, the skies of Miami glowed a burnished orange from the sodium anticrime lights.

"So it's safe to say you're really enjoying this trip," Mack Dane said.

"Oh yes." Mrs. Gilbert noisily attacked a stone-crab claw. Mack Dane wondered if she'd considered removing the shell first.

"Put in your article," she said, "that Dr. and Mrs. Samuel Gilbert of Montreal, Canada, are having the time of their lives."

Sam Gilbert said, "I wouldn't go that far."

"Mr. Dane, could you do us a favor? Could you take our picture?"

"Sure." Mack Dane put away his notebook and wiped his hands on a cocktail napkin that was decorated with the seal of the State of Florida. Mrs. Gilbert handed him a small thirty-five-millimeter camera with a built-in flash and built-in focus and built-in light meter.

The Gilberts posed arm-in-arm against the rail of the ship. Sam Gilbert wore his doctor face while Mrs. Gilbert kept reaching up and fiddling with his toupee, which, in the strong wind, had begun to resemble a dead starling.

Mack Dane squinted through the viewfinder and tried to frame the Gilberts romantically, with the lights of Miami shining over their shoulders. At first it was a perfect picture—if only there'd been a full moon! Then something went wrong. Suddenly Mack Dane couldn't see the Gilberts anymore; he couldn't see anything through the camera except a white light. He figured something broke on the focus.

But when he took the camera away from his face, Mack Dane realized that the white light was real: a beam piercing down from the heavens. Or from something *in* the heavens. Something that hovered like a dragonfly high above the SS *Nordic Princess*.

"A helicopter," Mack Dane said. "A big one." He knew the sound of a chopper. He'd flown them lots of times out to the oil rigs.

The Gilberts craned their necks and stared into the sky, shielding their eyes from the powerful search beam. The other partiers crowded together, pointing. The *salsa* band took a break.

Mack Dane said, "It's coming down."

The helicopter did seem to be descending slowly, but it was no longer in a hover, it was flying in a slow arc. Trailing behind the chopper was a long advertising banner.

"This is really tacky," Sam Gilbert said.

Mack Dane put on eyeglasses and turned in circles, trying to read the streamer. In four-foot letters it said: "AVAST AND AHOY: WELCOME TO THE REVOLUTI—"

"Revoluti?" puzzled Sam Gilbert.

"Maybe it's a new perfume," said his wife.

Mack Dane wondered if some letters had fallen off the advertisement.

The helicopter dropped lower and lower, and soon the partiers aboard the Friendship Cruise found themselves drowned to silence by the rotor noise. When the chopper was no more than one hundred feet above the deck, the banner was cut loose. It fluttered into the sea like an enormous confetti. The crowd ooooohhhed, and a few even applauded.

Mack Dane noticed that the top deck—the Royal Sun Deck, according to the ship's guide—was filling with tourists and VIPs and travel writers who had come up from below to investigate the commotion. Before long, people were packed elbow to elbow. In the meantime, the captain of the SS *Nordic Princess* had grown concerned about the reckless helicopter and cut his speed to eight knots.

"Hello, folks!" said a brassy male voice. Somebody on the helicopter had an electric bullhorn.

"Having a good time in Florida?" the voice called.

"Yeaaaah!" shouted the partiers, their faces upturned brightly. Some of the stuffy civic-leader types—the mayor, the Orange Bowl committeemen, the Chamber of Commerce life members—were miffed at the interruption of the cruise but, not wanting to spoil anyone's fun, said nothing.

The loud voice in the helicopter said: "How would all of you like some genuine Florida souvenirs?"

"Yeaaaah!" shouted the partiers.

"Well, here you go!" the voice said.

A door on the side of the helicopter opened and a white parcel plummeted toward the deck of the *Nordic Princess*. It was followed by another and another. At first Mack Dane thought the objects might be miniature parachutes or beach towels, but when one landed near his feet he saw that it was only a shopping bag from Neiman-Marcus. Soon the deck was being rained with shopping bags from all the finest department stores—Lord and Taylor, Bloomingdale's, Macy's, Burdine's, Jordan Marsh, Saks. Once the travelers realized what was happening, the Friendship Cruise quickly dissolved into a frenzied scrabble for the goodies.

Mack Dane thought: This is some advertising gimmick.

To her credit, Mrs. Gilbert held her own against stiff competition. She outmuscled a jewelry dealer from Brooklyn and the vicious wife of a Miami city commissioner to capture three of the prized shopping bags.

"Look, Sam!"

"Really," Sam Gilbert muttered.

"What did you win?" Mack Dane asked.

"I'm not sure," Mrs. Gilbert said. The shopping bags were stapled shut. She ripped one open and fished inside.

Her hand came out with a bracelet. The bracelet had a pattern of pale yellow chain, and looked like rubber. The odd thing was, it appeared to be moving.

It was a live snake.

Mrs. Gilbert was speechless. Her eyelids fluttered as the snake coiled around her creamy wrist. Its strawberry tongue flicked in and out, tasting her heat.

"Jesus Christ," said her husband.

It was not a big snake, maybe three feet long, but it was dark brown and fat as a kitchen pipe. The snake was every bit as bewildered as the Gilberts.

Behind Mack Dane a woman shrieked. And across the deck, another. A man yelled out, "Oh my God!" and fainted with his eyes open. As if jarred from a trance, Mrs. Gilbert dropped the brown snake and back-pedaled; her jaw was going up and down, but nothing was coming out.

By now each of the shopping bags (exactly two

hundred in all) had been opened with the same startling results.

The sundeck of the *Nordic Princess* was crawling with snakes. King snakes, black snakes, blue runners, garter snakes, green snakes, banded water snakes, ring-necked snakes, yellow rat snakes, corn snakes, indigo snakes, scarlet king snakes. Most of the snakes were harmless, except for a handful of Eastern diamondback rattlers and cottonmouth water moccasins, like the one in Mrs. Gilbert's prize bag. Skip Wiley had not planned on dropping any poisonous snakes—he didn't think it necessary—but he'd neglected to tell Tommy Tigertail and his crew of Indian snake-catchers. The Seminoles made no distinction, spiritual or taxonomical, between venomous and nonvenomous snakes; all were holy.

As the reptiles squirmed across the teakwood, the crowd panicked. Several men tried to stomp on the snakes; others rushed forward brandishing deck chairs and fire extinguishers. Many of the snakes became agitated and began snapping in all directions.

Mrs. Gilbert, among others, was bitten on the ankle. Her husband the doctor stood there helplessly.

"I'm just a radiologist," he said to Mack Dane.

The captain of the *Nordic Princess* looked down from the wheelroom and saw bedlam on his ship. To restore order, he blew the ship's tremendous horn three times.

"What does that mean?" cried Sam Gilbert, who was carrying his wife around on his back.

Mack Dane did not care to admit that although he was a travel writer, he knew nothing about ocean liners. So he said: "I think it means we abandon ship."

"Abandon ship!" screamed Mrs. Gilbert.

And they did. They formed a flying wedge, hundreds of them, and crashed through the rails and ropes of the upper deck. The Gilberts were among the first to go, plunging seventy feet into the Atlantic Ocean, leaving the ship to the damnable snakes.

As soon as he hit the water, Mack Dane was sorry he'd said anything about jumping overboard. The water was chilly and rough, and he wondered how long he could stay afloat. It also occurred to him, in hindsight, that sharks might be infinitely worse than a bunch of frightened snakes.

The *Nordic Princess* came dead in the water, towering like a gray wall above the frantic swimmers. Fire bells rang at both ends of the ship. Mack Dane could see crew members on every deck throwing life preservers and lowering the dinghies. The ocean seemed full of shrieking people, their heads bobbing like so many coconuts.

Mack Dane noticed that the mystery helicopter was circling again, firing its hot-white spotlight into the water. Occasionally the beam would fix on the befuddled face of a dog-paddling tourist.

From the helicopter drifted a melody, muted by the engines and warped by the wind. It was not a soothing song, either. It was Pat Boone sounding like Brenda Lee. It was the theme from the motion picture *Exodus*.

A good-looking man in a business suit who was treading water near Mack Dane raised up a fist and hollered at the helicopter: "You sick bastards!"

Mack Dane recognized the man as the mayor of Miami.

"Who are those guys up there?" Mack Dane asked.

He was thinking about the story he'd have to write, if he survived.

"Fucking Nachos," the mayor said. He kicked hard and swam off toward the SS *Nordic Princess*.

Mack Dane watched the chopper climb sharply and bank east, against the wind. The white spotlight vanished and the cabin door closed. In a few moments all that was visible were three pinpoints of light—red, green, and white—on the fuselage, although the racket of the propellers remained audible, dicing the night air.

An empty lifeboat drifted toward Mack Dane and he pulled himself aboard. He peeled off his blazer and laid it on his lap. As he was helping a young couple from Lansing, Michigan, climb in, Mack Dane saw a diamondback rattlesnake swim by. It looked miserable and helpless.

"What a night," said the man from Lansing.

Something about the sound of the helicopter changed. Mack Dane looked for the lights and spotted them about a mile east of the ship, and low to the purple horizon. The rotor engines sounded rough, the pitch rising.

"Something's not right," Mack Dane said.

The next sound was a wet roar, dying among the waves. Then the sky turned quiet and gray. The helicopter was gone. A plume of smoke rose off the water, marking the grave as surely as a cross. A few minutes later, the rain came.

TWENTY-SEVEN

Miraculously, none of the voyagers from the *Nordic Princess* perished in the Atlantic Ocean. Many had snatched life jackets before leaping overboard; others proved competent if not graceful swimmers. Some of the tourists were too drunk to panic and simply lolled in the waves, like polyester manatees, until help arrived. Others, including the Gilberts, were saved by strong tidal currents that dragged them to a shallow sandbar where they waited in waist-deep water, their hair matted to pink skulls, each of them still wearing a plastic nametag that said, "Hi! I'm—" Luckily a Coast Guard cutter had arrived swiftly and deployed inflatable Zodiac speedboats to round up the passengers. By midnight, all 312 missing persons had been retrieved. The rescue had unfolded so quickly that all thirteen victims of poisonous snakebites made it to the hospital with time to spare and only transient hallucinations. A survey of other casualties included one possible heart attack, seven broken bones, four man-of-war stings, and a dozen litigable whiplashes.

Although the thrust of the rescue efforts concentrated around the cruise ship, a small contingent of Coast Guardsmen launched a separate search for the mystery helicopter one mile away. A slashing rain and forty-mile-per-hour gusts made the task dangerous and nearly impossible. As the night wore on, the waves grew to nine feet and the searchers reluctantly gave up.

The next morning, in a misty sprinkle, a sturdy shrimp trawler out of Virginia Key came upon a fresh oil slick a few miles off Miami Beach. Floating in the blue-black ooze was a tangle of debris: two seat cushions and a nest of electronic wiring from the helicopter, an album sleeve from an old Pat Boone record, a bloodied white-and-aqua football jersey, an Australian bush hat with a red emblem on the crown, and two dozen empty plastic shopping bags from Saks Fifth Avenue. Judging by the location of the slick, the helicopter had gone down in 450 feet of water. When the skies cleared, the Coast Guard sent two choppers of its own, but no more wreckage was found. A forensics expert from the Navy later reported to the Fuego One Task Force that no one could have survived the crash, and that there was virtually no chance of recovering any bodies. The water, he said, was full of lemon sharks.

Terrorist Believed Dead After Aerial Assault on Cruise Ship.

Skip Wiley had been right. The wild saga of the *Nordic Princess* appeared in sixty-point type across the front page of the Miami *Sun* the next morning. Cab Mulcahy had been left with no choice, for Wiley had shrewdly selected the day of the week with the most anemic competition for news space—the President was giving a speech on abortion, a bus filled with pilgrims crashed in India, and a trained chimpanzee named Jake upchucked in the space shuttle. The sensational story of *Las Noches* got big play all over the country, and wound up on the front pages of the *Washington Post*, the Atlanta *Journal* and *Constitution*, the Los Angeles *Times*, the Chicago *Tribune* and the Philadelphia *Inquirer*. The version that appeared in the Miami *Sun* was the most detailed by far, though it made no mention of Wiley's role; Mulcahy was still trying to reach Al García to tell him.

Only one other newspaper devoted as much space to the *Nordic Princess* story as did the *Sun*, and that was the Tulsa *Express*. (Old Mack Dane had outdone himself, dictating thirty-eight breathtaking inches of copy to the national desk over a Coast Guardsman's marine-band radio.) As for the broadcast media, NBC had capitalized on its extra Orange Bowl manpower and diverted camera crews to the Port of Miami, Coast Guard headquarters, and Flagler Memorial Hospital. Heroes, victims, witnesses, and distant relatives flocked to the bright television lights, hoping to be interviewed by Jane Pauley or someone equally glamorous. By Sunday noon, much of the United States had heard or seen the story about killer snakes from the sky and the gang of South Florida crazies known as the Nights of December.

The chairman of the Orange Bowl Committee didn't know whether to laugh or blow his brains out. In the space of forty-eight hours at the apogee of the tourist season, homicidal lunatics had detonated a newspaper reporter and launched an aerial attack against a domestic ocean liner. That was the bad news. The good news was: the bastards were dead. The parade was saved.

At 8:30 A.M. on Sunday, December 30, a press

conference was staged at the office of the Greater Miami Chamber of Commerce, in the hallowed room with the table shaped like a giant navel orange. Sitting around the table's upper hemisphere were the chairman of the Orange Bowl Committee (at the stem), then Sergeant Al García, Sparky Harper's successor at the Chamber of Commerce, the mayors of Miami and Dade County, the police chiefs of Miami and Dade County, and an officer from the Coast Guard, who wished he were someplace else. The lower half of the table was occupied by reporters and cameramen, including a crew from the CBS *Morning News*.

The Orange Bowl chairman stood up and spoke nervously into a microphone at a portable podium. He read from a prepared statement:

"Ladies and gentlemen, thank you for coming on such short notice. At approximately 9:16 last night, the cruise ship SS *Nordic Princess* was accosted by an unmarked, unidentified helicopter off the coast of Miami Beach, Florida. At the time of the attack, the cruise ship was under lease to the Greater Miami Chamber of Commerce as part of the Orange Bowl Jamboree festivities. As a result of hostile actions undertaken by occupants of the helicopter, more than three hundred persons were forced to abandon the ocean liner in an emergency Mayday. I am happy to report that all those passengers, including myself and several others in this room, were safely rescued. All of us wish to extend our heartfelt thanks to Commander Bob Smythe and the United States Coast Guard for their quick and decisive action."

Commander Bob Smythe smiled wanly as a half-dozen motor-drive Nikons went off in his face. He couldn't wait for his transfer to Charleston to come through.

"Shortly after the incident involving the *Nordic Princess*," the Orange Bowl man continued reading, "the suspect helicopter flew away from the cruise ship in an easterly direction. At approximately 9:21 P.M., the aircraft experienced engine trouble and apparently went down at sea. No radio contact was ever made with the helicopter, so the nature of its distress may never be known."

The Orange Bowl chairman paused for a drink of water. He was unhappy with the tone of the press release, which had been composed hastily by a high-priced public-relations man. The PR man was a former Washington magazine editor who was reputed to be the model of glibness in crisis situations, but the Orange Bowl chairman was unimpressed. The press release sounded stiff and tedious, like it had come out of the Pentagon. The Orange Bowl chairman didn't know much about good writing, but he knew "Tropical Tranquillity" when he saw it—and this wasn't it. He wondered why it was so hard to find a good cheap hack.

"At approximately 6:07 this morning, a commercial fishing vessel discovered fuel residue and evidence of helicopter wreckage approximately six miles off Miami Beach. Navy and Coast Guard personnel searched the area throughly and found no signs of survivors. Because of the preponderance of carnivorous deep-water marine species, it is highly unlikely that any human remains will be recovered.

"However, one item found in the debris has been conclusively identified as the property of Daniel Wilson, age thirty-six, a former professional football player who had been sought as a suspect in several recent kidnappings."

The Orange Bowl chairman reached into a brown grocery bag and pulled out the dark-stained Miami Dolphins jersey belonging to Viceroy Wilson. At the sight of the number 31, the photographers became frenzied.

"According to Sergeant Al García of the Metro-Dade police, Mr. Wilson was an active member of a small terrorist group known as *Las Noches de Diciembre*. This organization, also known as the Nights of December, has claimed credit for several recent kidnappings, homicides, and bombings in the Miami area, including the so-called Trifecta Massacre at the Hibiscus Kennel Club. The Nights of December are also prime suspects in a bombing incident two days ago in which a local journalist was seriously injured. We have strong reason to believe it was Mr. Wilson and three other members of this radical cell who carried out last night's attack on the *Nordic Princess*, and who died in the subsequent helicopter crash. While every effort is being made to verify this information, we feel confident that a sinister and senseless threat to our community has been removed, and that the people of South Florida can celebrate the New Year—and the Orange Bowl festival—without fear or worry. Thank you all very much."

The Orange Bowl chairman sat down and wiped the back of his neck with a crisp white handkerchief. He had no intention of uttering another word, or doing anything to ruin his slick job of delivering the press release. He'd even improvised a bit, changing the distasteful and tourist-repellent phrase "oil slick" to "fuel residue" in the third paragraph.

As soon as the reporters began firing questions, the Orange Bowl chairman motioned Al García to the podium.

The detective approached the long-necked microphone with extreme caution, as if it were a flamethrower.

"What about Jesús Bernal?" a TV reporter shouted.

"No comment," García said. He felt like having a cigarette, but the chief had ordered him not to smoke in front of the cameras.

"Where did all the snakes come from?" someone asked.

"I've got no idea," said Al García. The sound of two dozen scribbling felt-tip pens clawed at his nerves.

"What about the banner?" a radio reporter said. "Did you find the banner?"

"No comment."

"Where did the chopper come from?"

"No comment."

Several reporters began to complain about all the *no comments* and threatened to walk out of the press conference. The Dade County mayor excitedly whispered something to the chief of police, who leaned across and excitedly whispered something to Al García. The detective glared at all of them.

"Seems I've been authorized to answer your questions," García told the reporters, "as long as it won't interfere with the investigation. About the helicopter—we haven't traced it yet. It was a rebuilt Huey 34, probably stolen up in Lauderdale or Palm Beach."

"What about Jesús Bernal?" asked a man from a Cuban radio station.

Al García decided to give the guys in the orange blazers something to think about. "We have no evidence that Mr. Bernal was aboard the helicopter last night," he said.

The Orange Bowl chairman shot to his feet. "But he probably was!"

"We have no such evidence," García repeated.

"What about the banner?" the radio reporter asked.

"We recovered it this morning, tangled up in a sword-fish line. The streamer was rented yesterday afternoon from Cairo Advertising at the Opa-locka Airport. Three individuals were seen attaching the letters. A white male, bearded, late thirties, wearing an Australian bush hat; a black male, approximately the same age but heavyset, wearing a football jersey; a younger, dark-skinned male, clean-shaven, described as either a Mexican or a native American Indian. The banner on the chopper basically said the same thing as all the previous communiqués—'Welcome to the Revolution' et cetera."

"Those men seen at the airport," a TV reporter said, "those were The Nachos?"

"*Las Noches*," García snapped.

"Who paid for the banner?" somebody shouted.

"Apparently the white male."

"How much?"

The Orange Bowl chairman sensed that it had been a tactical mistake to let Al García stand at the micro-phone. The idiot was actually answering the journalists' questions. The more García talked, the more frenetically the reporters wrote in their notebooks. And the more they wrote in their notebooks, the more stories would appear in the newspapers and the more airtime the dead Nachos would get. More was not what the Orange Bowl Committee wanted to see.

The chairman stood up and said with a smile, "I think that's all for now." But he was completely ignored by everyone, including Al García.

"The white male suspect paid three hundred dollars cash for use of the advertising streamer," García said.

"Could that man have been *El Fuego?*" a reporter asked.

"It's possible, yeah."

"Did he give a name at the airport?"

"Yes, he did," García said.

Then all at once, like a flock of crows: "What?"

García glanced over at the police chief. The chief shrugged. The Orange Bowl chairman waved a chubby hand, trying to get somebody's attention.

"The suspect did use a name at the airport," García said, "but we believe it was an alias."

"What was it?"

"In fact, we're ninety-nine percent sure it was an alias," the detective said, fading from the microphone.

"What was it, Al? What?"

"Well," García said, "the name the suspect gave was Hugo. Victor Hugo."

There was a lull in the questioning while the reporters explained to each other who Victor Hugo was.

"What about motive?" somebody shouted finally.

"That's easy," García replied. "They attacked the ocean liner for the same reason they marinated Sparky Harper in Coppertone. Publicity." He smiled with amusement at all the busy notebooks. "Looks to me like they got exactly what they wanted."

The press conference had taken a perilous turn, and the Orange Bowl chairman could no longer contain his rising panic. Squeezing to the podium, he discreetly placed a stubby hand between García's shoulder blades and guided the detective to the nearest available chair. Then the Orange Bowl man boldly seized the neck of the microphone himself. "Ladies and gentlemen," he said cordially, "wouldn't you rather hear the mayor's firsthand account of his escape from the *Nordic Princess*?"

Brian Keyes watched the press conference on a television in Kara Lynn Shivers' bedroom. Her father was out playing golf and her mother was eating quiche with the Junior League.

Kara Lynn was curled up on the bed in bikini panties and a lemon T-shirt. Keyes wore cutoffs. He squeezed her hand as they listened to Al García talking to the reporters. When the mayor got up and started to tell about the helicopter attack, Keyes punched the remote control and switched to a basketball game.

For a long time he didn't say anything, just stared at the TV screen. Kara Lynn put her arms around him and kissed him on the neck.

"It's really over," she whispered.

"I don't know," Keyes said distantly. He kept visualizing that crackpot Wiley, strolling into the Opa-locka Airport with his bush hat and two hundred bags of wild snakes. Keyes tried to imagine the scene later, aboard the Huey, Wiley and his portable record player; Wiley trying to explain *Exodus* to Viceroy Wilson.

"The only one left is that Cuban," Kara Lynn said.

"Maybe." Keyes tried to think of Skip Wiley as dead and could not. The obstacle was not grief; it was plain disbelief. It was not beyond Wiley to have rented an aged and dangerously unreliable helicopter, or to have hired an inept pilot. What was uncharacteristic was for Wiley to have placed himself so squarely in jeopardy. All through December he had kept a safe distance from the actual terrorism, sending Wilson or Bernal or the Seminole to take the big risks. Why the sudden bravery? Keyes wondered. And what a convenient way to die. He had felt a little guilty that he could summon so little sadness for his old friend—but then again, maybe it was too soon for mourning.

"The late Victor Hugo," Keyes mused. Wiley must have known how his friends would smile at that one; he was forever edifying his own legend.

"*Les Misérables*," Kara Lynn said. "Sounds like Mr. Fuego had a sense of humor."

"Sick," Keyes said. "Sick, sick, sick." Wiley would be better off dead, he thought, before the incredible dismal truth were known. With Wiley dead, Kara Lynn would be safe. So would the newspaper; Cab Mulcahy could return to the world of honest journalism. It would be better for almost everybody if Wiley were lost at sea, everybody except Jenna—Jenna was another issue. She hadn't been aboard that helicopter. Keyes knew it instinctively. Jenna's talent was creating catastrophes, then avoiding them.

"I want this to be the end," Kara Lynn said quietly.

"Well, maybe it is."

"But you don't believe they're really dead," she said.

"The way it happened, it's too perfect."

"The Prince of Cynics. You don't believe life can ever be perfect?"

"Nope," Keyes said. "Death, neither."

Later, when Kara Lynn was in the shower, Al García phoned.

"It's about damn time," Keyes groused.

"Been kinda hectic around here," the detective said. "I saw this stack of messages from you and Mulcahy. Figured your conscience finally woke up."

"We had our reasons, Al. Now it's time to talk."

"Oh, I can't wait. But it just so happens I already got a line on *El Fuego*."

So García knew.

Keyes felt lousy about not telling him in the first place, but Wiley's threats had seemed serious and, in retrospect, believable. García would have to understand.

"When we were doing routine checks on Wilson and Bernal, I had a pal search the morgue at the newspaper," the detective said. "Easy, really. I guess it's all on computer now. Funny thing, Brian. About four months ago your asshole buddy Wiley does this story on whatever happened to Daniel Viceroy Wilson, the famous football star. Very sympathetic. Hard-times-for-the-troubled-black-athlete number. Typical liberal shit. Anyway, three weeks later, guess what? Guy does a column about Jesús Bernal. *Our* precious Jesús. *Fire burns in the breast of a young Cuban freedom fighter*—that's how the story starts off. Makes me sick, too, I gotta tell you. Nearly tossed my black beans. So I'm thinking, what a weird coincidence this is: two of the four Nights of December getting a big ride in the newspaper just before the ca-ca hits the fan. So, for the hell of it, what d'you suppose I do?"

"Pull all Wiley's columns."

"Right. Big stack of 'em, and they're full of geeks and cons and losers . . . shit, if you threw them all together you'd have the scariest nest of bizarros in the history of the planet Earth. Took me a week to wade through that crap, too—hey, the guy can write, I told you that. He can put the words together okay, but it's his attitude that hacks me off. Such an arrogant hump. Anyway, out of all these columns, guess who pops up next? Your Indian, Brian, the guy with the airboat, Tommy Tigerpaws or whatever the hell it is. A fuck-ing full-blooded gator-wrestling white-hating Seminole Indian. I got more stuff out of Wiley's column than I've been able to squeeze out of the whole Seminole tribe. Turns out ole Tommy's richer than your average Colombian snowbird. And he's also very bitter about all the bad shit to come down on his ancestors—for that I can't blame him, Brian. That was *your* people, too. The Cubans had nothing to do with screwing the Indians out of Florida."

"Al, let's—"

"I'm almost done, *amigo*. So after all this I look on my desk and what have I got? I got an angry black racist football player, a crazy bomb-happy Cuban revol-utionary, and a filthy-rich Indian with a bingo chip on his shoulder. Three of the four. So the rest was easy, even for a dumb cop like me—the trick was to read everything Wiley wrote for the last two years. *Cristo!* What a strange guy."

"Funny you didn't mention all this at the press conference," Keyes said.

"Gee, guess I forgot."

Which meant García wasn't ready to buy the chopper crash.

"It bugs me," he said. "I think to myself, why would *El Fuego* pick a stunt like this to show his face?"

"If only they'd found some bodies," Keyes said. The words sounded stark and bloodless, but he meant them. He said to García: "What do we do now?"

"The smart guys in the suits say it's all over."

"What do you say, Al?"

"I say we wait till after the parade before we open the fucking champagne."

"Good idea. In the meantime, I'll stick with the queen."

"One more thing, Brian. Since I'm nice enough not to immediately throw your ass in jail for obstruction, the least you could do is stop by later and tell me about your crazy batshit friend."

"Yeah," Keyes said, "I guess I'd better."

TWENTY-EIGHT

As Al García hung up, he chided himself for not hollering more at Brian Keyes. He didn't know why Keyes had held back about Skip Wiley all these weeks, but he certainly would find out. The gamesmanship of trading information always irritated García, but he accepted it as essential to the job. Reporters, cops, politicians, private detectives—all gifted in the coy art of you-tell-me, I-tell-you. Afterward you felt like either an oracle or a whore.

García assumed there was a compelling reason for what Keyes had done. There better have been. A trade-off of some sort, maybe even extortion. Wiley seemed capable of anything.

Besides, the question had diminished in urgency since the helicopter crash. No sooner had the Sunday press conference ended than the chief had slipped García a terse note: "Consider disbanding Fuego One Task Force. We could have a press release ready by tomorrow A.M."

García had acknowledged the suggestion without committing to it. As all good detectives, he had learned to subsist on the bittersweet. Good guys, bad guys, you had to watch your step. He'd met crooks to whom he'd entrusted his life, and cops who'd steal crackers from the blind. García was seldom moved by the wisdom of his superiors, and more often dazzled by the cleverness of the criminal mind. The *Fuego* case had been a peculiar challenge; all along he had felt as if he were battling two sides, *Las Noches* and the Miami establishment.

The detective was ambivalent about the mysterious helicopter crash. Part of him wanted to believe that the Nights of December was dead. It had nothing to do with the Orange Bowl or civic boosterism or preserving the tourist trade. Rather, it seemed a marvelous example of bad guys getting their due; justice in the biblical sense. And as a practical matter, there was no tidier way to solve a homicide than to have all your suspects suddenly croak. God knows the small fortune it would save the taxpayers.

On the other hand was the tug of professional pride: García didn't like the Chamber of Commerce opening and closing his murder cases. The self-congratulatory tone of the TV press conference had been farcical; the truth was, García's crack squad never had come close to finding, much less capturing, *Las Noches de Diciembre*. It had been a frustrating assignment for a cop unaccustomed to being outwitted, and García didn't like the taste of it. To see Skip Wiley and his weird crew vanquished by a sputtering old Army helicopter seemed mundane and anticlimactic. From García's view, it would have been immensely more satisfying to have tracked the bastards to their Everglades hideout and smoked them in a blazing firefight.

Which is why he wasn't ready to call it quits.

Intuition told García that the ending didn't fit. A bunch of crazy Cubans or Nicaraguans?—sure, that's the sort of fuck-up you'd expect, running a chopper clean out of fuel. But from the very first victim, the

Nights of December had been different. They had approached each act of violence with a certain selectivity and élan. Choking Sparky Harper with a toy alligator was more than murder; it was terrorism with imagination. It was the stamp of a blade like Wiley.

Wiley—who, in Al García's opinion, was too damn smart to flame out over the deep blue sea. It'd be just like that cagey sonofabitch to fake his own death, lull everyone to sleep, then swoop down on the Orange Bowl parade and snatch the queen—just like he'd planned all along.

The detective crumpled the chief's directive and dropped it into a trashcan. He flipped through a stack of clippings until he came to the infamous hurricane column:

> *What South Florida needs most is a killer hurricane, sudden and furious, an implacable tempest that would raze the concrete shorelines and rake away the scum and corruption ...*

As he read it for the second time, García felt the hairs prickle on the back of his neck.

> *The tidal surge, a swollen gargoyle of a wave, is born beyond the Gulf Stream. Gaining size and thunder by the minute, it races under a deafening wind toward Florida's sleeping coastline. In purple darkness it pulverizes Miami Beach with a twenty-foot wall of water, flooding Carl Fisher's billion-dollar island of muck. Picture it: corpses upon corpses, clogging the flooded lobbies of once-majestic condominiums; dead dreamers, swollen, blue-veined, carplike.*

> *They will die in bewilderment, in the fierce arms*
> *of the beloved ocean that brought them here in the*
> *first place. Fools! the wind will scream, fools all.*

García thought: These are the words of a pathologi-
cally bitter man, if not a certified fruitcake. He was
dying to hear what Keyes could tell him about the guy.

Somebody rapped lightly on the door.

"Come on in, Brian," García said.

The door flew open with a crash.

García's left hand found the butt of his revolver but
he changed his mind. Nothing like a sawed-off shotgun
to argue for prudence.

"*Buenas noches*," the detective said to the man in
the soiled undershirt.

"Hello, maggot," said Jesús Bernal. "Let's go for a
ride, just you and me."

Since spurning the Nights of December, Jesús Bernal
had slipped into a desperate and harried state. He had
pinned his grandiose hope of redemption on his last
homemade bomb, only to see it claim the wrong victim,
some goofball news reporter. Once again serendipity
had taunted Bernal, reducing his most passionate and
calculated crimes to slapstick. His long career as a terrorist had been marred by such misfortune, and he had
come to fear that he might be forever cheated of his
place in radical history, that he had blown his last big
chance. That morning's press conference had pitched
the little Cuban into an orgy of self-pity—he had
screeched at the television screen, pummeled the walls,
kicked holes in the doors of his motel room. He *knew*

364

that the helicopter stunt was a frivolous idea, that the first plan had been the best. He had *tried* to teach the others about discipline and efficiency, about the fatal dangers of impetuosity. But that fuckhead Wiley was beyond reason, and the dope-wasted nigger and the creepy Seminole Indian had trailed along like zombies. They were babies playing a man's game. Now they were dead, and so for all practical purposes was *Las Noches de Diciembre*, leaving Jesús Bernal an orphan of the cause. Wretchedly he wondered what his ex-comrades in the First Weekend in July Movement were saying about him; he could hear the *comandante*'s sneering laughter. Who could blame the old fart? For all the fanfare about *Las Noches*, nothing historic had been proven, nothing of permanence achieved. So there was no point calling the old man to beg again for readmission.

Bernal knew his options were limited. Strategically, it would be futile to revive the name of the organization—as far as the world was concerned, the Nights of December no longer existed. Even the fucking stationery was useless.

One possibility was to start his own underground terrorist movement. To hell with the crazy Wileys and the feeble old Bay of Piggers; it was time for daring new blood. Yet there was still the problem of credibility, and shedding the stigma of recent failures.

Which was why Jesús Bernal sneaked into Metro-Dade police headquarters on Sunday evening, December 30.

If all went as planned, Jesús figured he'd never again have to worry about his future; he would be the Reggie Jackson of South Florida terrorism, a free-agent superstar-assassin. The First Weekend in July, Omega Seven, Alpha 66—they'd all be knocking down his door. Then maybe he *would* form his own gang, recruiting only the best from the others and leaving the faggots and doddering old men to their Eighth Street parades.

Even before the helicopter accident, Jesús Bernal had unilaterally decided to select a new victim. To impress the *comandante*, the target would have to be a person of prominence and formidable authority. And most important, the chosen prey must represent an abhorrence to The Cause—either compromise, complicity, or total apathy.

Bernal's brightest hope was Sergeant Al García.

The chubby turncoat had invited trouble during the press conference by noting there was no evidence of Jesús being aboard the ill-fated Huey. In his emotionally bruised and paranoid state, Bernal perceived this remark as a slur, something meant to portray him as a sniveling coward who cringed in the background while his brethren risked their lives. In fact, García had mentioned Jesús Bernal only to annoy the guys in the orange blazers; he never thought it would precipitate this kind of visit.

"Take the back stairs," Bernal commanded.

The police station was all but empty on a Sunday night and they saw no one on the stairwell. The two men emerged from a doorway on the northwest side and crossed the jail parking lot, concealed by a tall hedge. Bernal walked stiffly, the shotgun pointed down and held close to his right leg; from a distance he looked like a man with a slight limp.

García's unmarked police car was parked on

Fourteenth Street. "You drive," Bernal said. "And stay off the freeways."

They headed south, crossed the Miami River drawbridge, and stopped at the busy traffic light at Northwest Seventh Street.

"Which way?" García asked.

Jesús Bernal hesitated. "Just a second." Across his lap lay the shotgun, its barrel gaping from the crook of his arm. The gun was an over-and-under model, cut back to fourteen inches. Al García didn't need the training manual to figure out what a sawed-off could do. It was pointed at his kidneys.

"Turn right," Bernal said hoarsely. García could make out the faint cross-hatch imprint of the tennis racket on his abductor's face. He also noticed that Bernal's nose was badly broken, though his teeth were straight and gleaming.

They spoke Spanish to each other.

"Where we going?" García asked.

"Why, you worried?" Bernal said tautly. "You think a badge and a gun makes you a hero! Makes you a genuine American! I beg your pardon, Mr. *Policía*. You are no hero, you're a coward. You turned your back on your true country."

"What do you mean?" García asked, biting back anger.

"Do you not have family in Cuba?"

"An uncle," the detective replied. "And a sister."

Bernal poked the shotgun into García's neck. The barrel was cold and sharp. "You abandoned your own sister! You are a shit-eating worm and I should kill you right now."

"She chose to stay behind, my sister did."

"*No creo*—"

"It's true," García said. "She married a man in the army."

"Such shit! And your uncle—what lie have you invented for him?"

"He is a doctor in Camaguey, with a family. Four children. This is not a lie."

"Such shit!"

"Put the gun down before somebody sees it," García warned.

Reluctantly Jesús Bernal lowered the sawed-off. He held it across his knees, below the dashboard.

"You think it was easy for me?" García said. "You think it was easy to leave, to start over? I came here with nothing."

Jesús Bernal was unmoved. "Why are you not fighting for your family's liberation?" he demanded.

Rather than say something he might eternally regret, García said nothing. Psychology was not his strong suit; he was a firm believer of the fist-in-the-face school of criminal therapy.

Jesús Bernal was a mangy bundle of nerves. He smelled like he hadn't bathed for a month and his black hair was a dull curly mat. His high-topped sneakers tapped the floorboard, while his free hand knotted and reknotted the tail of his threadbare undershirt. He fidgeted like a little kid whose bladder was about to burst.

"What do you think about this, Mr. *Policía?* Me catching you, instead of the other way around!" Jesús flashed his new dentures. "Cut over to the Trail and we'll head for the Turnpike."

"But you said no freeways."

"Shut up and do as I say." Bernal reached over and

ripped the microphone from García's police radio. He threw it out the window. "You get lonely, you talk to me."

García shrugged. "Nice night for a drive."

"Hope you got plenty of gas," Bernal said. "García, I want to ask you something, okay? How does a scum like you sleep at night? What kind of lullabies does a *buitre* sing? When you close your eyes, do you see your sister and your uncle in Cuba, eh? Do you feel their torture and suffering, while you get fat on American ice cream and go to jai-alai with your Anglo pals? I have often wondered about traitors like you, García.

"When I was very young, my job was to visit the businessmen and collect contributions for *La Causa*. I had four blocks on *Calle Ocho*, three more on Flagler Street downtown. A man named Miguel—he owned a small laundry—once gave three thousand dollars. And old Roberto, he ran *bolita* from a café. *Zorro rojo*, the red fox, we called him; Roberto could well afford to be a generous patriot. Not all these businessmen were happy to see me at their door, but they understood the importance of my request. They hated Fidel, with their hearts they hated him, and so they managed to find the money. This is how we survived, while traitors like you ignored us."

"Chickenshit shakedowns," García muttered.

"Shut up!"

García picked up the turnpike at the Tamiami Trail and drove south. Traffic thinned out and, on both sides of the highway, chintzy eggshell apartments and tacky tract-house developments gave way to pastures, farmland, and patches of dense glades. García now had no doubt that Bernal planned to kill him. He guessed, cynically, that it would probably be a simple execution; kneeling on the gravel of some dirt road, mosquitoes buzzing in his ears, the shotgun blast devoured by the empty night. The fucking turkey buzzards would find him first. The *buitres*.

Maybe it wasn't such a bad idea to piss the little runt off. Maybe he'd get excited, maybe a little careless.

"So what about your pals?"

"Idiots!" Bernal said.

"Oh, I'm not so sure," García said. "Some of that stuff was ingenious."

"That was mine," Bernal said. "The best stuff was mine. The kennel club bombing—I thought it up myself."

"A pile of dead dogs. What the hell did *that* prove?"

"Quiet, *coño*. It proved that no place was safe, that's what it proved. No place was safe for tourists and traitors and carpetbaggers. Any idiot could see the point."

García shook his head. Carpetbaggers—definitely a Skip Wiley word.

"Dead greyhounds," García said mockingly. "I'm sure Castro couldn't sleep for days."

"Just drive, goddammit."

"I never understood your stake in the group," García went on. "I think, what the hell does a hardcore like Jesús care about tourists and condos? I think, maybe he just wants his name in the papers. Maybe he's got nowhere else to go."

Bernal made a fist and pounded the dash. "See, this is why you're such a dumb cop! Figure it out, García. What really happened to the movement? Everyone in Miami got fat and happy, like you. Half a million

Cubans—they could stampede Havana anytime they wanted, but they won't because most of them are just like you. Greedy and prosperous. Prosperity is killing anti-communism, García. If our people here were starving or freezing or dying, don't you think they'd want to go back to Cuba? Don't you think they'd sign up for the next invasion? Of course they would, by the thousands. But not now. Oh, they are careful to wave flags and pledge money and say *Death to the bearded one!* But they don't mean it. You see, they've got their IRAs and their Chevrolets and their season tickets to the Dolphins, and they don't give a shit about Cuba anymore. They'll never leave Florida as long as life is better here, so the only thing for us to do is make life worse. That's exactly what the Nights of December had in mind. It was a good plan, before the great Señor Fuego cracked up, a good plan based on sound dialectic. If it came to pass that all the snowbirds fled north—chasing their precious money—then Florida's economy would disintegrate and finally our people would be forced into action. And Cuba is the only place for us to go."

García's patience was frayed. He knew all about Jesús Bernal Rivera, born in Trenton, New Jersey, son of a certified public accountant and product of the Ivy League; a man who had never set foot on the island of Cuba.

"You're a phony," García told him, "a pitiful phony."

Bernal raised the stubby shotgun and placed the barrel against the detective's right temple.

García pretended not to notice. He drove at a steady sixty-five, hands damp on the wheel. Bernal would never shoot him while the car was going so fast. Even with the gun at his head García was feeling slightly more optimistic about his chances. For ten miles he had been watching a set of headlights in the rearview mirror. Once he had tapped his brakes, and whoever was following had flashed his brights in reply. García thought: Please be a cop.

After a few tense moments Bernal put the shotgun down. "Not now," he said, seemingly to himself. "Not just yet." García glanced over and saw that a crooked smile had settled across the bomber's griddled features.

The Turnpike ended at Florida City, and the MG was running on fumes. Brian Keyes coasted into an all-night service station but the pumps were off and he had to wait in line to pay the attendant. He watched helplessly as the taillights of Al García's car disappeared, heading toward Card Sound.

Catching up would take a miracle.

Keyes had arrived at police headquarters just as Jesús Bernal and García were getting in the car. He had spotted the shotgun, but there had been no time to get help; all he could do was try to stay close and hope Bernal didn't see him.

Everything was going smoothly until he'd checked the gas gauge.

Keyes hurriedly pumped five dollars' worth. He ran back to the bullet-proof window and pounded on the glass.

"Call the police!" he shouted at the attendant. The man gave no sign of comprehending any language, least of all English.

"A policeman is in trouble," Keyes said. He pointed down the highway. "Get help!"

The gas station attendant nodded vaguely.

"No credit cards," he said. "Much sorry."

Keyes jumped into the MG and raced down U.S. Highway One. He turned off at Card Sound Road, a narrow and seemingly endless two-lane lined with towering pines. The road ahead was black and desolate, not another car in sight. Keyes stood on the accelerator and watched the speedometer climb to ninety. Mosquitoes, dragonflies, and junebugs thwacked the car, their jellied blood smearing the windshield. Every few miles the headlights would freeze a rabbit or opossum near the treeline, but there was no sign anywhere of human life.

As the road swung east, Keyes slowed to check some cars at a crab shanty, then at Alabama Jack's, a popular tavern, which had closed for the night. At the toll booth to the Card Sound Bridge, he asked a sleepy redneck cashier if a black Dodge had come through.

"Two Cubans," she reported. "'Bout five minutes ago. I 'member cause they didn't wait for change."

Keyes crossed the tall bridge at a crawl, studying the nocturnal faces of the crabbers and mullet fishermen lined along the rail. Soon he was on North Key Largo, and more alone than ever. This end of the island remained a wilderness of tangled scrub, mahogany, buttonwood, gumbo-limbo, and red mangrove. The last of the North American crocodiles lived in its brackish bogs; this was where Tommy Tigertail had recruited Pavlov. There were alligators, too, and rattlers, gray foxes, hordes of brazen coons, and the occasional shy otter. But mostly the island was alive with birds:

nighthawks, ospreys, snowy egrets, spoonbills, limp-
kins, parrots, blue herons, cormorants, the rare owl.
Some slept, some stalked, and some, like the scaly-
headed vultures, waited ominously for dawn.

Keyes turned off on County Road 905, drove about
half a mile, and parked on the shoulder. He rolled down
the window of the MG and the tiny sports car immediately filled with insidious bootblack mosquitoes. Keyes
swatted automatically, and tried to listen above the
humming insects and the buzz of the nighthawks for
something out of place. Perhaps the sound of a car door
slamming, or human voices.

But the night surrendered no clues.

He went another mile down the road and parked
again; still nothing but marsh noises and the salty smell
of the ocean. After a few minutes a paunchy raccoon
waddled out of the scrub and stood on its hind legs to
investigate; it blinked at Keyes and ambled away,
chirping irritably.

He started the MG and headed down 905 at high
speed to blow the mosquitoes out of the car. He was
driving so fast he nearly missed it, concealed on the east
side of the highway, headfirst in a dense hammock. A
glint of chrome among the dark green woods is what
caught Keyes's eye.

He pumped the brakes and steered off the
blacktop. He slipped out of the sports car and popped
the trunk. Groping in the dark, he found what he was
looking for and crept back to the spot.

The black Dodge was empty and its engine nearly
cold to the touch.

*

The two men stood alone at the end of a rutted lime-stone jetty, poking like a stone finger into the sea. A warm tangy wind blew from the northeast, mussing García's thin black hair. His mustache was damp from sweat, and his bare arms itched and bled from the trek through the hammock. The detective had given up all hope about the car in the rearview mirror; it had turned off in Florida City.

Jesús Bernal seemed not to notice the cloud of mosquitoes swarming around his head. García thought: perhaps they don't sting him—his blood is poisoned and the insects know it.

Fevered with excitement, Bernal's face glistened in the water's reflection. His eyes darted ratlike and his head jerked at each muffled animal noise from the woods behind them. In one hand Bernal clutched the sawed-off shotgun, and with the other waved a heavy police flashlight, lacing amber ribbons in the blackness.

Jesús was already contemplating the journey back to the car, alone. The shotgun probably would be empty by then, useless. He grew terrified just thinking about the ordeal—what good was a flashlight against panthers! He imagined himself imprisoned all night by the impenetrable hammock; at first disoriented, then panicked. Then lost! The sounds alone might drive him insane.

For Jesús Bernal was scared of the dark.

"What's the matter?" García asked.

"Nothing." Bernal ground his dentures and made the fear go away. "This is where we say *adiós*."

"Yeah?" García thought it seemed an odd place for an execution. The jetty provided no concealment and the echo of gunfire would carry for miles across the water. He hoped a boat might pass soon.

Jesús Bernal fumbled in his khaki trousers and came out with a brown letter-sized envelope, folded in half.

"Open it," he wheezed. "Read it aloud." He aimed the flashlight so García could make out the document, which had been typed neatly. It appeared much longer than any of the communiqués from the Nights of December.

"What is this, you writing a book?" the detective grumbled.

"Read!" Bernal said.

García took his eyeglasses from a shirt pocket.

There were two identical sections, one in English and one in Spanish:

"I, Alberto García Delgado, hereby confess myself as a traitor to my native country of Cuba. I admit to the gravest of crimes: persecuting and harassing those brave revolutionaries who would destroy the dictator Castro, and who would liberate our suffering nation so that all Cuban peoples may return. With my despicable crimes I have dishonored these patriots and shamed my own heritage, and that of my father. I deeply regret my seditious behavior. I realize that I can never be forgiven for using my police authority to obstruct what was good and just. For this reason, I have agreed to accept whatever punishment is deemed fitting by my judge, the honorable Jesús Bernal Rivera—a man who has courageously dedicated his life to the most noble of revolutionary callings."

García thrust the document back at Jesús Bernal and said, "I'm not signing it, *chico*." He knew time was short.

"Oh, I think you'll reconsider."

"No way."

García lunged forward, his arms reaching out for the shotgun. Jesús pulled the trigger and an orange fireball tore the detective off his feet and slammed him to the ground.

He lay on his back, staring numbly at the tropical stars. His head throbbed, and his left side felt steamy and drenched.

Jesús Bernal was a little wobbly himself. He had never before fired a shotgun, and discovered that he had not been holding the weapon properly. The recoil had hammered him squarely in the gut, knocking the wind out. A full minute passed before he could speak.

"Get up!" he told García. "Get up and sign your confession. It will be read on all the important radio stations tomorrow."

"I can't." García had no feeling on his left side. He probed gingerly with his right hand and found his shirt shredded and soaked with fresh blood. Jagged yellow bone protruded from the pulp of his shoulder. He felt dizzy and breathless, and knew he would soon be in shock.

"Get up, *traidor!*" Jesús Bernal stood over the detective and waved the gun like a sword.

García thought that if he could only get to his feet he might be able to run to the woods. But when he tried to raise himself from the gravel, his legs convulsed impotently. "I can't move," he said weakly.

Jesús Bernal angrily stuffed the document into his pocket. "We'll see," he said. "We'll see about this. Are you prepared to receive your sentence?"

"Yeah," García groaned. "What the hell."

Bernal stalked to the tip of the jetty. "I chose this spot for a reason," he said, pointing the gun across the Atlantic. "Out there is Cuba. Two hundred miles. It is nearer than Disney World, Mr. *Policía*. I think it's time you should go home."

"I don't believe this," said Al García.

"Are you much of a swimmer?" Jesús Bernal asked.

"Not when I'm fucking paralyzed."

"Such a baby. But, you see, this is your sentence. The sentence which—you have agreed—befits your treasonous crimes. Alberto García, maggot and traitor, I hereby command you to return at once to Cuba. There you will join the underground and fight the devil in his own backyard. This is how you will redeem yourself. Perhaps you may someday be a hero. Or at least a man."

"How about shark food?" García said. Even with two good arms he was a rotten swimmer. He knew he'd never make it as far as Molasses Reef, much less Havana harbor. It was a funny idea, really. García heard himself laugh out loud.

"What's so goddamn hilarious?"

"Nothing, commander."

The detective began to think of his family. Dreamily he pictured his wife and his children as he had last seen them. At dinner, two nights ago. They all seemed to be smiling. He thought: I must have done *something* right.

He opened his eyes and turned his head to see the tops of Jesús Bernal's moldy sneakers.

"Up!" Bernal cried. He kicked at García, once, twice, three times, until the detective lost count. They were not hard kicks, but diabolically aimed.

Bernal bent down until their faces were inches apart.

"Get your stinking ass off the ground," Bernal said, his breath sour and sickening.

Once more García tried to sit up, but rolled sideways instead. He nearly passed out as his full weight landed on his mangled arm.

Bernal resumed kicking and García rolled again, the limestone and coral digging into his flesh.

"Go!" Bernal shouted, prodding with his feet. "Go, go, go!"

García landed in the water with a muted splash. The salt scoured his wounds and a sudden coldness seized his chest, robbing him of all breath. García did not know how deep the water was, but it didn't matter. He could have drowned in a saucepan. Somehow he clawed to the surface and slurped air.

He looked up toward the jetty and saw Bernal's stringy silhouette, the shotgun raised over his head in triumph. Jesús played the flashlight across the waves.

"You'd better get started!" he called exuberantly. "Head for Carysfort Light. It's a good place to rest. By daybreak you'll be ready to go again. Hurry, *mi guerrero*, onward to Cuba! She is not as far as you think."

García was too weak to float, much less swim. Hungrily he gulped breath after breath, but it was not enough. A marrow-deep pain began to smother his conscious thought, and he sensed himself slipping away. He paddled mindlessly with his good arm; he didn't care that he was going in circles, as long as his head stayed above water.

"You look like a fool!" Jesús Bernal yelled giddily. "A fat little clown!"

Another gunshot split the night and Jesús Bernal commenced a curious dance, hopping like a marionette.

In his deepening fog Al García thought: The idiot is shooting into the sky, like frigging New Year's Eve.

Still another shot went off, and then more, until the crackles blended to a dull resonance, like a church bell. García wondered why he saw no firebursts from the mouth of the sawed-off.

Jesús Bernal's queer dance became palsied. Suddenly he stopped hopping, bent over double and emitted a horrific wail. The shotgun and the flashlight clattered to the rocks.

But García himself was out of strength. His arm felt like cement, and his will to save himself evaporated under a warm wave of irrepressible fatigue. He was sliding downward into euphoria, away from all pain. The ocean took him gently and closed his tired eyes, but not before he saw a final shot shear the crown of Jesús Bernal's head and leave him twitching in a heap on the jetty.

TWENTY-NINE

"**Nice shooting, Ace,**" Al García said feebly.

"I hate that damn gun." Brian Keyes had needed six rounds from the Browning to put a bullet where he'd wanted. His hands still tingled from the shots.

"Which hospital is nearest?"

"Homestead," García said, shivering. "Call my wife, would you?"

"When we get there."

"I'm pissed you didn't tell me about your pal Wiley."

"He said he'd kill lots more people if I did."

García coughed. "It couldn't have been much worse than it was."

"Oh no? You saw what that bomb did to the john—now imagine the same thing at the parade, with all those kids. A holocaust, Al. He seemed capable of anything."

"You shoulda told me anyway," García said. "Shit, this hurts. I'm gonna sleep for a while." He shut his eyes and sagged down in the passenger seat. Soon Keyes could hear his breathing, a weak irregular rasp.

Keyes drove like a maniac. Droplets of salt water trickled from his hair into his mouth and eyes; he was soaked to the skin. García's blood dappled his shirt and pants. As he wheeled the MG back onto Highway One, a sharp pain pinched under his right arm. Keyes wondered if he had torn open the old stab wound while carrying García piggyback through the hammock.

The trip to Farmer's Hospital from Key Largo took twenty minutes. García was unconscious when they arrived at the emergency room, and was immediately stripped and taken to surgery.

Keyes telephoned García's wife and told her to come down right away, Al had been hurt. Then he tried Jenna. He let it ring fifteen or twenty times but no one picked up. Was she gone? Hiding? Dead? He considered driving up to the house and breaking in, but it was too late and he was too exhausted.

He made one more phone call, to Metro-Dade Homicide. He told them where to find Jesus Bernal's body. Soon the island would be crawling with reporters.

Keyes looked up at the clock and smiled at the irony; two-thirty in the morning. Too late to make the morning papers.

The phone jarred Cab Mulcahy from his sleep at seven-thirty.

"I got a message you called. What's up?" It was Cardoza.

Mulcahy sat round-shouldered on the edge of the bed, rubbing sleep from his eyes. "It concerns Skip Wiley," he said fuzzily.

He told Cardoza about Wiley's criminal involvement with the Nights of December, omitting nothing except his own knowledge.

"Goddamn!" Cardoza exclaimed. "Maybe that explains it."

"What?"

"Wiley sent me a New Year's column yesterday but I damn near tossed it out. I thought it was a fake, some asshole playing a joke."

"What does it say?" Mulcahy asked. He was not surprised that Wiley had ignored the chain of command and appealed directly to the publisher. Skip knew how much Cardoza loved his stuff.

Cardoza read part of the column aloud over the phone.

"It sounds like a confession," Mulcahy said. It was actually quite remarkable. "Mr. Cardoza, we have to write about all this."

"Are you kidding?"

"It's our job," Mulcahy said.

"Making a blue-chip newspaper look like a nut-house—that's our job?"

"Our job is printing the truth. Even if it's painful and even if it makes us look foolish."

"Speak for yourself," Cardoza said. "So what exactly do we do with this column? It's not the least bit funny, you know."

"I think we run it as is—right next to a lengthy story explaining everything that's happened the last month."

Cardoza was appalled. In no other business would you wave your stinky laundry in the customers' faces; this wasn't ethics, it was idiocy.

"Don't go off half-cocked," Cardoza told Mulcahy. "I heard on the radio that the whole gang is dead. I assume that means Mr. Wiley, too."

"Well, tonight's the big parade," Mulcahy said. "Let's wait and see."

Cardoza was stunned by the revelation about Skip Wiley. Of all the writers at the paper, Wiley had been his favorite, the spice in the recipe. And though he had never actually met the man, Cardoza felt he knew him intimately from his writing. Undoubtedly Wiley was impulsive, irreverent, even tasteless at times—but homicidal? It occurred to Cardoza that a newspaper this size must be riddled with closet psychopaths like Wiley; the potential for future disasters seemed awesome. Expensive disasters, too. Lawyerly-type disasters.

"You sure we have to print this?" Cardoza said.

"Absolutely," Cab Mulcahy replied.

"Then go ahead," the publisher growled, "but when the calls start pouring in, remember—I'm out of town."

The crusty businessman in Cardoza—which was to say, *all* of Cardoza—immediately thought of selling the newspaper, getting out before they straitjacketed the whole building. Just last week he'd had an excellent offer from the Krolman Corporation, makers of world-famous French bidets. A bit overcapitalized, but they'd cleared thirty million last year after taxes. Cardoza had been impressed by the bottom line—thirty mil was a lot of douching. Now the Krolman boys were looking to diversify.

The publisher's fingers were flying through the Rolodex even as he hung up on Cab Mulcahy.

Reed Shivers pounded loudly on the door to the guest room. "Young man, I want to speak with you!"

"Later," Keyes mumbled.

"No, not later. Right now! Open this door!"

Keyes let Shivers in and met him with a scowl. "*Open*

this door right now! What do I look like, the Beaver? *Gee, Dad, I was only trying to get some sleep.*"

"That's enough, Mr. Keyes. You said you were going to be gone for one hour last night—one hour! The housekeeper says you got in at six."

"A situation came up. I couldn't help it."

"So you just run off and forget all about my daughter," Reed Shivers said.

"There was a squad car at each end of the block."

"All alone, the night before the big parade!"

"I said I couldn't help it," Keyes said.

Kara Lynn walked in wearing a shapeless pink robe and fuzzy bedroom slippers. Her hair was pinned up and her eyes were sleepy. Without make-up she looked about fourteen years old.

"Hi, guys," she said. "What's all the racket?"

Right away she saw that Brian had slept in his street clothes. She stared at the sticky brown stain on his clothes, somehow knowing what it was. She also noticed that he still wore his shoulder holster. The Browning semi-automatic lay on a nightstand next to the bed. It was the first time she had ever seen it. It seemed unwieldy, and out of place in a bedroom.

"The Cuban's dead," Keyes said flatly.

Reed Shivers rubbed his chin sheepishly. It occurred to him that he had underestimated Keyes or, worse, misread him entirely.

"Bernal kidnapped García last night and I had to shoot him," Keyes said.

Kara Lynn gave him a long hug, with her eyes closed. Keyes stood there stiffly, not knowing how to respond in front of her father. Reed Shivers looked away and made a disapproving cluck.

Keyes said, "I expect there'll be some police coming by a little later to ask me some questions."

Reed Shivers folded his arms and said, "Actually this is extremely good news. It means all those damn Nachos are dead. According to the papers, this Cuban fellow was the last one." He tugged his daughter safely back to arm's reach. "Pumpkin, don't you see? The parade's going to be wonderful—there's no more threat. We won't be needing Mr. Keyes anymore."

Kara Lynn looked up at Brian questioningly.

"Let's play if safe, Mr. Shivers. I've got my doubts about that helicopter crash. Sergeant García and I agree that everything should stay the same for tonight. Nothing changes."

"But it was on TV. All these maniacs are dead."

"And what if they're not?" Kara Lynn said. "Daddy, I'd feel better if we stuck to the plan. Just for tonight."

"All right, cupcake, if you'll sleep easier. But as of tomorrow morning, no more bodyguard." Reed Shivers marched down the hall, still wondering about that hug.

Brian Keyes closed the door quietly and locked it. He took Kara Lynn's hand and led her to the bed. They lay down and held one another; he, hugging a little tighter. Keyes realized that he had crossed a cold threshold and could never return to what he was, what he had trained to be—a professional bystander, an expertly detached voyeur who was skilled at reconstructing violence after the fact, but never present and never participatory. For reporters, the safety net was the ability to walk away, polish it off, forget about it. It was as easy as turning off the television, because whatever was happening always happened to somebody else; reality was past tense and once removed, something to be observed but not experienced. Two years ago, at such a newsworthy moment, Keyes himself would have been racing south with the wolf pack, jogging through the hammock to reach the jetty first, his notebook flipped open, his eyes sponging up each detail, counting up the bullet holes in the corpse, by now gray and bloodless. And two years ago he might have gotten sick at the sight and gone off to vomit in the woods, where the other reporters couldn't see him. Later he would have stood back and studied the death scene, but could only have guessed at what might have happened, or why.

"We don't have to talk about it," Kara Lynn said. She stirred against him. "Let's just lie here for a little while."

"I had no choice. He shot García."

"This was the same man we saw outside the country club. You're certain?"

Keyes nodded.

He said, "Maybe I ought to say a prayer or something. Isn't that what you're supposed to do when you kill somebody?"

"Only in spaghetti westerns." She slid her arms around his waist. "Try to get some rest. You did the right thing."

"I know," he said dully. "The only thing I feel guilty about is not feeling guilty. The sonofabitch deserved to die."

The words came out soulless. Kara Lynn shuddered. Sometimes he frightened her, just a little.

"Hey, Sundance, you want to see my gown?"

"Sure."

She bounced up from the bed. "Stay right here, don't move," she said. "I'll model it for you."

"I'd like that," Keyes said. "I really would."

At noon Al García awoke. He gazed around the hospital room and felt warmed by its pale yellow walls and the slivered shadows from the venetian blinds. He was too drugged to pay much attention to the burning in his arm or the huge knot on the base of his neck or the burbling sound from inside his chest. Instead the detective was washed by a mood of elemental triumph: he was alive and Jesús Bernal was dead. Deader than a goddamn cockroach. Al García relished the role of survivor, even if he owed his life not to his own faltering reflexes, but to Brian Keyes. The kid had turned out to be rock steady, and strong as a bear to haul him out of the ocean the way he had.

Groggily García greeted his wife, who offered spousely sympathy but peppered him with questions that he pretended not to hear. Afterward, an orthopedic surgeon stopped in to report that although García's left arm had been saved, it was too early to know if the muscles and bones would mend properly; the shoulder basically was being held together by steel pins and catgut. García worriedly asked if any shotgun pellets had nicked the spine, and the doctor said no, though the initial fall on his neck had caused some temporary numbness. García wiggled the toes on both feet and seemed satisfied that he would walk again.

He was drifting off to sleep when the chief of police showed up. García winked at him.

"The doctors say you're going to make it," the chief whispered.

"Piece-a-cake," García murmured.

"Look, I know this is a bad time, but the media's gone absolutely batshit over this shooting. We're trying to put together a short release. Is there anything you can tell me about what happened out there?"

"Found the body?"

"Yes," the chief replied. "Shot four times with a nine-millimeter. The last one really did the trick, blew his brains halfway to Bimini."

"Fucker blasted me with a sawed-off."

"I know," the chief said. "The question is, who blasted him?"

"Tomorrow," García said, closing his eyes.

"Al, please."

"Tomorrow, the whole story." Or as much of it as was absolutely necessary.

"Okay, but I've got to say *something* to the press this afternoon. They're tearing around like a pack of frigging hyenas."

"Tell 'em you don't know nuthin'. Tell 'em I haven't regained consciousness."

"That might work," the chief mused.

"Sure it'll work. One more thing . . ." García paused to adjust the plastic tube in his nose. "Tell the nurses I want a TV."

"Sounds reasonable."

"A color TV for tonight."

"Sure, Al."

"Don't want to miss the parade."

THIRTY

In the mid-1800's Miami was known as Fort Dallas. It was a mucky, rutted, steaming, snake-infested settlement of two hundred souls, perennially under attack from crafty Seminoles or decimated by epidemics of malaria. This was a time long before Fisher, Flagler, and the other land grabbers arrived to suck their fortunes out of North America's most famous swamp. It was a time when the local obsession was survival, not square footage, when the sun was not a commodity but a blistering curse.

No one knew what Fort Dallas might eventually become, not that knowing would have altered its future. The dream was always there, sustenance against the cruel hardships. Then, as now, the smell of opportunity was too strong to ignore, attracting a procession of grafters, con artists, Confederate deserters, geeks, bush-wackers, rustlers, gypsies, and slave traders. Their inventiveness and tenacity and utter contempt for the wilderness around them would set the tone for the development of South Florida. They preserved only what was free and immutable—the sunshine and the sea—and marked the rest for destruction, because how else could you sell it? In its natural state, the soggy frontier south of Lake Okeechobee simply was not marketable. Still, the transformation of the face of the land began slowly, not so much because of the Indians or the terrain as because of the lagging technology of plunder. Finally came the railroads and the dredge and the bulldozer, and the end of Fort Dallas.

For thirty years, beginning around the turn of the century, South Florida grew at an astonishing pace. Rabid opportunists seized as much land as they could, swapped it, platted it, sold it. Where there was no land they dredged it from the bottom of Biscayne Bay, manufactured an island, named it after a flower or a daughter or themselves, and peddled it as a natural oasis. All this was done with great efficiency and enthusiasm, but with no vision whatsoever.

Those wheeler-dealers who didn't blow their brains out after the Hurricane of '26 or hang themselves after the real-estate bust were eventually rewarded with untold wealth. Today they were venerated for their perseverance and toughness of spirit, and some even had public parks named after them. These characters are regarded as the true pioneers of South Florida.

It is their descendants, the heirs to paradise (and to the banks and the land), who put on the annual Orange Bowl Parade.

The pageant began a half-century ago as an honest parade, Main Street entertainment for little children and tourists. But with the ascension of television the event grew and changed character. Gradually it became an elaborate instrument of self-promotion, deliberately staged to show the rest of the United States (suffering through winter) a sunny, scenic, and sexy sanctuary. The idea was to make everybody drop their snow shovels and hop the next jumbo jet for Florida. To this end, the Orange Bowl Parade was as meticulously orchestrated as a nuclear strike. Those who would appear on camera were carefully selected: high-school bands from Bumfuck, Iowa, awe shining from their sunburned faces as they bugled down Biscayne Boulevard; a sprinkling of Caribbean blacks and South American Hispanics, evidence of Miami's exotic but closely supervised cultural mix; the most innocuous of TV celebrities, delighted to shill for the tourist board in exchange for comped rooms at the Fontainebleau.

From the Chamber of Commerce point of view, the most essential ingredient was subliminal sex. You cannot sell sun-drenched beaches without showing tanned female cleavage; Middle America hungered for it. Thus the pageant always featured droves of women in brief but not-quite-nasty bathing suits. The favored choice of models was the pneumatic blond teenager, suggestively hugging a neoprene palm tree or riding a stuffed alligator and smiling so fixedly that any idiot could see her makeup had been put on with a trowel.

Every year the Orange Bowl Committee chose a sunny new theme, but seldom did it touch on Florida's rapacious history. Swamp wars and slave raids and massacres of Indian children did not strike the Orange Bowl fathers as suitable topics for a parade; a parade intended purely as a primetime postcard.

As noted, this year's slogan was "Tropical Tranquillity."

At six P.M. the floats and clowns and high-school bands collected in the parking lots across from the Dupont Plaza Hotel. Dusky clouds rolled in from the north, smothering the vermilion sunset and dropping temperatures. The wind came in chilly gusts; some of the girls in bathing suits sneaked back to the dressing rooms to tape Band-Aids over their nipples, so they wouldn't be embarrassed if it got cold.

Before the parade could begin, a huge balloon replica of some comic-strip character with teeth like Erik Estrada's broke from its tether and drifted toward the high-voltage power lines. A policeman with a rifle shot it down, the first casualty of the evening.

Traditionally, the order of march began with a police honor guard and ended, a mile or so later, with the queen's float. This year the regimen would be different. Al García had insisted that a troop of cops be positioned within shouting distance of Kara Lynn Shivers, but the Orange Bowl Committee absolutely refused, fearing Major Image Problems if TV cameras were to show uniformed police in the same frame as the queen. Brian Keyes had suggested a compromise, which was accepted: a colorful contingent of Shriners on motorcycles was inserted between the queen's float and the City of Miami (Marching) SWAT Team.

The Shriners would be led, of course, by Burt and James, packing handguns in their baggy trousers. Of the forty men behind them, only twenty would actually belong to the Evanston Shrine; the rest would be motorcycle cops secretly conscripted by Al García. This part of the plan had never been revealed to the Orange Bowl Committee or to the Chamber of Commerce. However, to anyone paying close attention, it was obvious from the pained expressions on these unusually young and muscular-looking Shriners that something was screwy. The way they wore the fez hats, for one thing: straight up, instead of cocked ten degrees, jocular-Shriner style.

There was even more firepower: thirty undercover officers armed with machine pistols (and a mug shot of Viceroy Wilson burned into their memories) would move through the crowd, flanking Kara Lynn's float. From above, eight police sharpshooters with night-scopes would watch from various downtown buildings along Biscayne Boulevard and Flagler Street, the parade routes.

The queen's float shimmered gold and royal blue, by virtue of seventy-thousand polyethylene flower petals stapled to a bed of plywood, plaster, and chickenwire. The motif was "Mermaid Magic," featuring Kara Lynn in a clinging burnt-orange gown, her hair in tendrils under the Orange Bowl tiara, her cheeks glistening as if kissed by the sea. There had been a brief debate about whether or not she should wear a rubber fish tail, and though her father endorsed the idea ("More camera time, sweetcakes"), she declined firmly.

Kara Lynn's throne was a simulated coral reef built on the front end of the float. From this perch she would smile and wave to the throngs while a hidden stereo broadcasted actual underwater recordings of migrating sperm whales. Meanwhile the four runner-up contestants, dressed in matching tuna-blue mermaid gowns, would pretend to cavort in an imaginary lagoon behind Kara Lynn's reef. In rehearsal, with all the blond beauty queens making swimming motions with their arms, someone remarked that it looked like a Swedish version of the Supremes.

The queen's float had been constructed around a Datsun pickup truck, which would power it along Biscayne Boulevard. The truck's cab had been camouflaged as a friendly octopus in the mermaid lagoon; the driver of the float and Brian Keyes would be sitting inside. The windshield of the pickup had been removed to permit a sudden exit, just in case.

Despite these extraordinary precautions and the preponderance of high-powered guns, the pre-parade atmosphere was anything but tense. Even the Orange Bowl committeemen seemed loose and confident.

The sight of so many policemen, or the knowledge of their presence, was reassurance enough for those to whom the parade meant everything. These, of course, were the same buoyant optimists who believed that the violent events of the weekend had conclusively ended Miami's drama.

The parade was due to begin at 7:30 P.M. sharp, but it was delayed several minutes because of a problem with one of the floats. Acting on a confidential tip, U.S. customs agents had impounded the colorful entry sponsored by the city of Bogotá, Colombia, and were busily hammering sharp steel tubes through the sides of the float in search of a particular white flaky powder. Failing in that, they brought in four excitable police dogs to sniff every crevice for drugs. Though no contraband was found, one of the German shepherds peed all over the Colombian coffee princess and the float immediately was withdrawn. It was the only one in the whole pageant made with real carnations.

At 7:47 P.M., the West Stowe, Ohio, High School Marching Band and Honor Guard stepped onto Biscayne Boulevard, struck up a unique rendition of Jim Morrison's "Light My Fire," and the King Orange Jamboree Parade was under way. The skies were cloudy but the wind had steadied and there was no trace of rain. Standing five-deep along both sides of the boulevard was an enormous crowd of 200,000, most of whom had paid at least twelve bucks to park their expensive late-model cars in one of the most dangerous urban neighborhoods in the western hemisphere.

At precisely 8:01, the kliegs lighted up in the blue NBC booth, washing co-hosts Jane Pauley and Michael Landon in an unremitting white glare.

A teleprompter mounted on brackets above the cameras began to scroll. His cheeks burnished and his New Testament curls showing spangles of sun-induced blondness, Michael Landon spoke first to America, sticking faithfully to the script:

Hello everybody and welcome to Miami, Florida. What a night for a parade! [Cut to three-second shot of majorette with baton.] It's a mild sixty-seven degrees here in South Florida, with a tangy sea breeze reminding us that beautiful Biscayne Bay and the Atlantic Ocean are just over my shoulder. Down below, on Biscayne Boulevard, the King Orange Jamboree is in full swing. [Cut for four-second shot of swaying palm trees and Cooley Motors float.] The theme of this year's pageant is Tropical Tranquillity, and for the past week I've been enjoying just that, as you can see from my sunburn [sheepish smile]. Now I'd like to introduce my co-host for tonight's Orange Bowl pageant, the lovely and talented Jane Pauley. [Cut to close-up Pauley, then two-shot.]

Pauley: Thanks, Michael. We have had a great stay down here, though it looks like you spent a bit more time at the beach than I did. [Landon medium smile.] There's a lot of excitement in this town, and not just over the parade. As you know, tomorrow night the University of Nebraska Cornhuskers and the Fighting Irish of Notre Dame square off for the national college football championship in the Orange Bowl. NBC will carry that game live, and it looks like the weather's going to be perfect. Michael, who're you rooting for? [Cut to Landon close-up.]

Landon: I like Nebraska, Jane.

Pauley: Well, I think I'm going with Notre Dame.

Landon: Ah, still an Indiana girl.

Pauley [laughing]: You betcha. [Cut from two-camera to close-up.] On a serious note [turning to camera], if you've been following the news recently you probably know that this South Florida community has been struggling with a tragic and frightening crisis for the past month. A terrorist group calling itself the Nights of December has taken credit for a series of bombings, kidnappings, and other crimes in the Miami area. At least ten persons, many of them tourists, are known to have been killed. Now, as you may have heard, several alleged members of this terrorist group are believed to have died in a helicopter accident over the weekend. And last night, the last known member of this extremist cell was shot to death after abducting a Dade County police officer. It has been a trying time for the citizens down here, and in spite of all this difficulty they still managed to make us feel warm and welcome. [Cut to Landon, nodding appreciatively.] And, Michael, I know you'll agree as we watch some of these amazing floats go by: It's shaping up as another spectacular Orange Bowl extravaganza! [Cut to shot over Landon shoulder as he enjoys parade.]

Landon [big smile]: Is it ever! And look at some of these bathing beauties! I may never go back to Malibu.

The parade slowly headed north up the boulevard, past the massive gray public library and Bayfront Park, wino mecca of the eastern seaboard.

The cab of the pickup truck was oppressively stuffy under heavy layers of plaster and plastic. To keep from suffocating, Keyes held his face close to the open windshield, which also functioned as the smiling mouth of the friendly octopus. The driver of the float noticed the gun beneath Keyes's jacket, but said nothing and appeared unconcerned.

From inside the float, Keyes found it difficult to see much of anything past the prancing rear-ends of the four blue mermaids. Occasionally, when they parted, he caught a glimpse of Kara Lynn's bare shoulders on the front of the float. As for peripheral vision, he had none; the faces of the spectators were invisible to him.

To offset the racket from the Shriners' Harley Davidsons, the sperm-whale music had been cranked up to maximum volume. Keyes ranked the whales in the same melodic category as Yoko Ono and high-speed dental drills. It took every ounce of concentration to follow the chatter on the portable police radio that linked him to the command center. Each new block brought the same report: everything calm, so far.

When Kara Lynn's float reached the main grandstands, it came to a stop so that she and the other Orange Bowl finalists could wave at the VIPs and pose for the still photographers. Brian Keyes tensed as soon as he felt the Datsun brake; it was during this pause, scheduled for precisely three minutes and twenty seconds, that Keyes expected Skip Wiley to make his move, while the TV cameras settled on Kara Lynn. Forewarned, the police snipers focused their infrared scopes while the plainclothesmen slid through the cheering crowd to take preassigned positions along the curb. On cue, Burt and James led the Shriner cavalcade into an intricate figure-eight that effectively encircled the queen's float with skull-buzzing motorcycles.

But nothing happened.

Kara Lynn dutifully waved at everyone who vaguely looked important, flash bulbs popped, and the parade crawled on. The floats crossed the median at NE Fifth Street and headed south back down the boulevard, past the heart of the city's infant skyline. At Flagler Street the procession turned west, and away from the bright television lights. Instantly everyone relaxed and the floats picked up speed for the final leg. Kara Lynn quit waving; her arms were killing her. It was all she could do to smile.

At North Miami Avenue, one of the undercover cops calmly called over the radio for assistance. Some ex-Nicáraguan National Guardsmen who were picketing the U.S. immigration office now threatened to crash the parade if they did not immediately receive their green cards. A consignment of six officers responded and easily quelled the disturbance.

A block later, one of the motorcycle cops disguised as a Shriner reported sighting a heavyset black male resembling Daniel "Viceroy" Wilson, watching the parade from the steps of the county courthouse.

As the queen's float passed the building, Keyes leaned

out of the octopus's mouth to see a squad of officers swarm up the marble steps like indigo ants. The search proved fruitless, however; three large black men were briefly detained, questioned, and released. They were, in order of size, a Boca Raton stockbroker, a city councilman from Cleveland, and a seven-foot Rastafarian marijuana wholesaler. None bore the slightest resemblance to Viceroy Wilson, and the motorcycle cop's radio alert was dismissed as a false alarm.

Al García refused to take any painkillers while he watched the parade from his hospital room in Homestead. He wanted to be fully cognizant, and he wanted his vision clear. Two young nurses asked if they could sit and watch with him, and García was delighted to have company. One of the nurses remarked that Michael Landon was the second-handsomest man on television, next to Rick Springfield, the singer.

As the floats rolled by, García impatiently drummed the plaster cast that was glued to his left side. He worried that if trouble broke out, the TV cameras wouldn't show it; that's the way it worked at baseball games, when fans ran onto the field. Primetime was too precious to waste on misfits.

Finally the queen's float came into view, emitting a tremulous screech that García took for brake trouble, when actually it was just the whale music. One of the nurses remarked on how gorgeous Kara Lynn looked, but García wasn't paying attention. He put on his glasses and squinted at the dopey octopus's smile until he spotted Keyes, his schoolboy face bobbing in and out of the shadow. Pain and all, García had to chuckle. Poor Brian looked wretched.

At 8:55, the last marching band clanged into view playing something by Neil Diamond. The NBC cameras cut back to Jane Pauley and Michael Landon in the blue booth:

Pauley: Another thrilling Orange Bowl spectacle! I don't know how they do it, year after year. [Cut to Landon.]

Landon: It's amazing, isn't it, Jane? I'd just like to thank NBC and the Orange Bowl organizers for inviting us to spend New Year's Eve in beautiful South Florida. One of the local weathermen just handed me a list of temperatures around the country and, before we sign off, I'd like to share some of these [holds up temp list]. New York, twenty-one . . .

Pauley [VO]: Brrrrr.

Landon: Wichita, nine below; Knoxville, thirty-nine; Chicago, three degrees and snow! Indianapolis—Jane, are you ready? [Cut to Pauley.]

Pauley: Oh boy, let's have it.

Landon: Six degrees!

Pauley [pinning on a Go Irish! button]: Home sweet home. Well, I promised everyone I'd bring back some fresh oranges, but I'm just sorry there's no way to package this magnificent Miami sunshine. Thanks for joining us . . . good night, everybody.

Landon [two-shot, both waving, major smiles]: 'Night, everybody. Happy New Year!

García reached for the remote control and turned the channel. A show about humorous TV bloopers came on and García asked the nurses for a shot of Demerol. He lay thinking about the killing of Jesús Bernal and the peaceful parade, and contemplated the possibility that the madness was really over. He felt immense relief.

Ten minutes later the phone rang, sounding five miles away. It was the chief of police.

"Hey, Al, how you feeling?"

"Pretty damn good, boss."

"We did it, huh?"

García didn't want to quibble. "Yeah," he said.

"Did you see the pageant?"

"Yeah, it was just great."

"Looks like the Nachos are history, buddy."

"Looks that way," García said, thinking: This is the same bozo who thought *I* wrote the *Fuego* letters. But this time he just might be right. It looks like Wiley took the deep-six after all.

"What do you say we shitcan the task force?" the chief said.

"Sure." There was no good argument against it. The parade was over, the girl was safe.

"First thing tomorrow I'll do up a release."

"Fine, boss."

"And, Al, on my honor: you're getting all the credit on this one. All the credit you deserve."

For what? García wondered as he hung up. It wasn't like I shot down the goddamn chopper myself.

After the parade, Brian Keyes drove back to the Shivers house and started packing. Reed Shivers and his wife got home thirty minutes later.

"See, all that panic for nothing," Shivers said smugly.

"I get paid to panic," Keyes said, stuffing his clothes into a canvas athletic bag. He felt drained and empty.

The end wasn't supposed to have been this easy, but Wiley's moment had come and gone—if the bastard really had been alive, Keyes thought, he would have shown up. With bells on.

"Where's Kara Lynn?" Keyes asked.

"She went to a wrap party with the other girls," Mrs. Shivers said.

"A wrap party."

"A little tradition in beauty pageants," Mrs. Shivers explained. "Girls only."

"You'd best be off," Reed Shivers said. He was trying to light his pipe, sucking on the stem like a starving carp. "There was a lady from the Eileen Ford agency in the stands—she picked up on Kara Lynn right away. I'm expecting a call anytime."

"Wonderful," Keyes said. "Book a room at the Plaza."

The Shiverses walked him to the door.

"Is your friend going to be all right?" Mrs. Shivers asked. "The Cuban policeman."

"I think so. He's a tough guy."

"You're a brave young man yourself," she said. Her tone of voice made it plain that she was addressing the hired help. "Thank you for all you've done for Kara Lynn."

"Yes," Reed Shivers said grudgingly. He extended his golden-brown hand; a Yale man's polite but superior hand-shake. "Drive carefully now," he said.

"Good night, Mr. and Mrs. Shivers."

They nodded blankly and shut the front door.

Keyes was standing at the trunk of the MG, squirming out of the shoulder holster, when a brown Buick pulled into the driveway and Kara Lynn got out.

She had changed into blue jeans and a papery white sleeveless blouse; she carried her Orange Bowl gown on a plastic hanger.

"Where you going, Marlowe?"

"Back to the other side of town."

A female voice from the Buick shouted: "Kara, is that him?"

Kara Lynn smiled bashfully and waved her friends to leave. The Buick honked twice as it sped off.

"We had a little wine," she said. "I told 'em about you."

Keyes laughed. "The private eye in the octopus."

Kara Lynn laid the gown across the hood of the sports car and glanced up at the house, checking for her parents at the window. Then she put her arms around Keyes and said, "Let's go somewhere and make love."

Keyes kissed her softly. "Your folks are waiting inside. Somebody from a model agency is supposed to call."

"Who cares?"

"Your old man. Besides, I'm worn out."

"Hey, don't look so blue. We made it." Playfully she took his hands and placed them on her buttocks. "The mother lode is safe," she said, kissing him hard. "Good work, kiddo."

"I'll call you tomorrow."

A yellow porch light came on over the front door.

"Daddy waits," said Kara Lynn, frowning.

Keyes climbed into the MG and started the engine. Kara Lynn scooped up her gown and pecked him on the cheek. "Did I mention," she said in a breathy

Marilyn voice, "that I wasn't wearing any panties tonight?"

"I know," Keyes said. "It wasn't all bad, the view from the octopus."

On the way back to his apartment, he stopped at the office to check for burglaries and collect his mail, which consisted of a dozen bills, two large checks from the Miami *Sun* and a *National Geographic* with an albino something on the cover. Lost somewhere in the debris on Keyes's desk was a checkbook, and he decided to locate it, just in case he ever needed to buy groceries again. Afterward he tried to clean the aquarium, which had been consumed by an advancing greenish slime that threatened to overtake its borders.

These chores were undertaken mainly to stuff his mind with distractions and delay the inevitable. It was nearly one A.M. when Keyes finished, and he lay down on the battered sofa and fell asleep. Before long he felt the coarse grip of the Browning semiautomatic in his right hand. He looked down and saw that his hand was covered with lustrous black mosquitoes, which were swelling up and bursting one by one, little blood balloons. A bony-looking puppet appeared and began to dance, and the Browning went off. The bullets traveled slowly, leaving orange contrails. One after another they puffed into the limestone around the puppet's feet. Just as the puppet's likeness changed from Jesús Bernal to Ernesto Cabal, one of the bullets smashed its head into a thousand wooden splinters. The slivers flew in all directions, twanging the puppet strings which led to the sky. In the dream Brian Keyes saw himself racing toward the broken puppet and snatching the strings with blood-splashed hands. Then he was airborne over the ocean, clinging for life. In a wispy cloud high above, a familiar man with long blond hair and gypsy eyes twitched the puppet strings and muttered about the usurious price of coffins.

THIRTY-ONE

Port-au-Prince, Haiti. *December 28th—By the time this is published, I might be dead or in jail, or hiding in some bleak rathole of a country where I'd never get to read it anyway. Which would be a shame.*

But I suppose I've got it coming.

For many years I've written a daily column for this newspaper, a column that achieved an unforeseen but gratifying popularity. I admit that the reportage was not always faultless, but I never strayed too far from the truth. Besides, you folks knew what you were getting.

I probably could have continued to grind out fifteen inches of daily outrage, insult, poignancy, and sarcasm until I got old and my brain turned to porridge. See, I had a nifty deal going here at the paper. The brass liked me, and to keep me contented paid a salary nearly commensurate with my talents. This is what happens when you sell the merchandise: they make it worth your while.

About six weeks ago something changed. Whether it was my job attitude, spiritual diet, or moral equilibrium, I can't say. Things got out of hand, I suppose. The simple and convenient view is that I went berserk, which is possible though unlikely. In my business you learn that sanity, not insanity, is the greater riddle—and that there's nothing so menacing as a sane person suddenly alerted to his own fate.

One thing is true. Over time I came to see the destiny of Florida in a singularly horrid vision, and I took steps to change that destiny. Extreme steps. I assembled a few choice acquaintances and we made some moves, as they say.

In my ardor I might have committed a few unforgivable felonies, but my mission was to save the place and to inspire those who cared, and to that noble end I suppose I'd break almost any law. Which they say I did.

For once it was a fair fight, both sides battling with tantamount weapons: publicity versus counterpublicity. Their ammunition was fantasy and whitewash, and ours was the meanest of truths, random crime, and terror. What better way to destroy bogus mail-order illusions!

The odious reality is that we live on a peninsula stolen from the Indians, plundered by carpetbaggers, and immorally occupied by Yankee immigrants who arrive at the rate of one thousand per day, Okies in BMWs.

Most of us born here were always taught to worship growth, or tolerate it unquestioningly. Growth meant prosperity, which was defined in terms of swimming pools and waterfront lots and putting one's kids through college. So when the first frostbitten lemmings arrived with their checkbooks, all the locals raced out and got real-estate licenses; everybody wanted in on the ground floor. Greed was so thick you had to scrape it off your shoes.

The only thing that ever stood between the developers and autocracy was the cursed wilderness. Where there was water, we drained it. Where there were trees, we sawed them down. The scrub we simply burned. The bulldozer was God's machine, so we fed it. Malignantly, progress gnawed its way inland from both coasts, stampeding nature.

Today the Florida most of you know—and created, in fact—is a suburban tundra purged of all primeval wonder save for the sacred solar orb. For all you care this could be Scottsdale, Arizona, with beaches.

Let me fill you in on what's been going on the last few years: the Glades have begun to dry up and die; the fresh water supply is being poisoned with unpotable toxic scum; up near Orlando they actually tried to straighten a bloody river; in Miami the beachfront hotels are pumping raw sewage into the Gulf Stream; statewide there is a murder every seven hours; the panther is nearly extinct; grotesque three-headed nuclear trout are being caught in Biscayne Bay; and Dade County's gone totally Republican.

This is terrible, you say, but what can we do?

Well, for starters, you can get out.

And since you won't, I will.

It's been pure agony to watch the violent taking of my homeland, and impossible not to act in resistance. Perhaps, in resisting, certain events happened that should not have, and for these I'm sorry. Unfortunately, extremism seldom lends itself to discipline.

At any rate, my pals and I certainly got your attention, didn't we?

By the time this is published—if it's published—I certainly won't be where I am now, so I don't mind revealing the location: a palm-shaded porch of an old hotel on a mountainside overlooking the sad city of Port-au-Prince. Above my head is a wooden paddle fan that hasn't turned since the days of Papa Doc. It's humid here, but no worse than SW Eighth Street in July, and I'm just fine. I'm sitting on a wicker chaise, sipping a polyester-colored rum drink and listening to last year's NBA All-Star game on French radio. Upstairs in my hotel room are three counterfeit passports and $4,000 U.S. cash. I've got a good idea of where I've got to go and what I've got to do.

Evidently this will be my last column, but whatever you do, please don't phone up and cancel your subscription to the paper. The Sun is run by mostly decent and semi-talented journalists who deserve your attention. Besides, if you quit reading it now, you'll miss the best part.

Historically, the function of deranged radicals is to put in motion what only others can finish; to illuminate by excess; to stir the conscience and fade away in exile. To this end, the Nights of December leaves a worthy legacy.

Welcome to the Revolution.

For the first time in nearly half a century, the front page of the Miami *Sun* on New Year's Day did not lead with a story or photograph of the Orange Bowl Parade. Instead, the paper was dominated by three uncommon pieces of journalism.

The farewell column of Skip Wiley appeared in a

vertical slot along the left-hand gutter, beneath Wiley's signature photo. Stripped across the top of the newspaper, under the masthead, was a surprisingly self-critical article about why the *Sun* had failed to connect Wiley to *Las Noches de Diciembre* even after his involvement became known to a certain high-ranking editor. This piece was written, and written well, by Cab Mulcahy himself. Therein shocked Miami readers learned that Wiley's cryptic "where I've got to go, and what I've got to do" referred to the planned, but unconsummated, kidnapping of the Orange Bowl queen during the previous night's parade.

The other key element of the front page was a dramatic but incomplete account of the killing of fugitive terrorist Jesús Bernal on a limestone spit in North Key Largo. This story carried no byline because it was produced by several reporters, one of whom had confirmed the fact that private investigator Brian Keyes had fired the fatal shots from a nine-millimeter Browning handgun, which he was duly licensed to carry. Keyes's presence at the remote jetty was unexplained, although the newspaper noted that he had been hired recently as part of a covert Orange Bowl security force. The only other witness to the Bernal shooting, Metro-Dade Police Sergeant Alberto García, was recovering from surgery and unavailable for comment.

When Brian Keyes woke up in the dinginess of his office, Jenna sat at the desk, reading the morning paper.

"When are you gonna learn to lock the door?" she asked. She handed him the front page. "Take a look. The puddy tat's out of the bag."

Keyes sat up and spread the newspaper across his knees. He tried to read, but his eyes refused to focus.

"I figured you'd be decked out in black," he said groggily.

"I don't believe he's dead," Jenna said. "I will not believe it, not till I see the body." Case closed. She forced a smile. "Hey, Bri, seems you're a big hero for killing that Cuban kidnapper."

"Yeah, I look like a big hero, don't I?"

He glanced at Wiley's column. "December 28—the day before the helicopter crash. When's the last time you heard from him?"

"Same day. I got a telegram from Haiti."

"What did he say?" Keyes asked.

"He said to spray the lawn for chinch bugs."

"That all?"

She pursed her lips. "He also said if anything happens, he wants to be buried in that pine coffin he got from the swap meet. Buried with all his old newspaper clippings, of course."

"Very touching."

"I think he stole the idea from the Indian," Jenna said. "Seminole warriors are always buried with their weapons."

Keyes stumbled downstairs to a vending machine and bought three cups of coffee. Jenna took one look and said she didn't want any, so Keyes drank them all.

It put him in a perfect mood for Skip Wiley's farewell column, which Keyes found mawkish and disorganized and only slightly revelatory. He was more interested in Cab Mulcahy's companion story. In it, the managing editor explained that Wiley's key role in the Nights of December had not been exposed because of a threat that many more tourists and innocent persons would be murdered. For several days the information about Wiley was withheld while an investigator hired by the *Sun* searched for him; in retrospect, Mulcahy had written, this decision was ill-advised and probably unethical.

"Poor Cab," Keyes said, not to Jenna but himself. He felt hurt and embarrassed for his friend.

Jenna came around from behind the desk and sat on the tattered sofa next to Keyes. "Skip really got carried away," she said, stopping just short of remorse.

"He carried all of us away," Keyes said, "everyone who cared about him. You, me, Mulcahy, the whole damn newspaper. He carried all of us right into the toilet."

"Brian, don't be this way."

Jenna wasn't wearing any makeup; she looked like she hadn't slept in two days. "It was a good cause," she said defensively. "Just poor administration."

"What makes you think he's not dead?"

"Intuition."

"Oh really." Keyes eyed her with annoyance, as he would a stray cat.

He said, "I can't imagine Skip passing up that parade. National television, half the country tuned in. It was too good to resist—if he's not dead, he's in a coma somewhere."

"He's not dead," Jenna said.

"We'll see."

Jenna had never heard him so snide.

"What's with you?" she asked.

"Aw, nothing. Blew a guy's head off last night and I'm still a little bushed. Wanna go for a Danish?"

Jenna looked shaky. "Oh Brian," she said.

A plaintively rendered *oh Brian* usually would do the trick; a guaranteed melt-down. This time Keyes felt nothing but a penetrating dullness; not lust or jealousy, rage or bitterness.

"He was supposed to meet me at Wolfie's this morning, but he never came," she admitted. "I'm kind of worried." Her eyes were red. Keyes knew she was about to turn on the waterworks.

"He can't be dead," she said, choking out the words.

Keyes said, "I'm sorry, Jenna, but you did the worst possible thing: you encouraged the bastard."

"I suppose," she said, starting to sob. "But some of it sounded so harmless."

"Skip was about as harmless as a 190-pound scorpion."

"For instance, dropping those snakes on the ocean liner," she said. "Somehow it didn't seem so terrible when he was arranging it. The way he told it, it was supposed to be kind of funny."

"With goddamn rattlesnakes, Jenna?"

"He didn't tell me *that* part. Honest." She reached out and put her arms around him. "Hold me," she whispered. Normally another foolproof heartbreaker. Keyes took her hand and patted it avuncularly. He didn't know where it had gone—all his feeling for her—just that it wasn't there now.

"It wasn't all Skip's fault," Jenna cried. "This was building up for years, poisoning him from the inside. He felt a *duty*, Brian, a duty to be the sentinel of outrage. Who else would speak for the land? For the wild creatures?"

"Save your Sierra Club lecture for the first-graders, okay?"

"Skip is not a bad man, he has a vision of right and wrong. He's a principled person who took things too far, and maybe he paid for his mistakes. But he deserves credit for his courage, and for all his misery he deserves compassion, too."

"What he deserved," Keyes said, "was twenty-five-to-life at Raiford." Ten innocent people were dead and here was Jenna doing Portia from the *Merchant of Venice*. He let go of her hand and stood up, not wishing to test his fortitude by sitting too close for too long. He said, "You'd better go."

"I took the bus," Jenna sniffled. "Can you give me a lift?"

"No, I can't."

"But I really don't want to be alone, Brian. I just want to lie in a hot bath and think sunny thoughts, a hot bath with kelp crystals. Maybe you could come by tonight and keep me company?"

In the tub Jenna would be unstoppable. "Thanks anyway," Keyes said, "but I'm going to the football game."

He gave her ten bucks for a cab.

She looked at the money, then at Brian. Her little-girl-lost look, a pale version at that.

"If he's dead," she said softly, "what'll we do?"

"I'll varnish the coffin," Keyes said, "you spray for chinch bugs."

THIRTY-TWO

The annual Orange Bowl Football Classic began at exactly eight P.M. on January 1, when the Fighting Irish of Notre Dame kicked off to the University of Nebraska Cornhuskers before a stadium crowd of 73,411 and an estimated worldwide television audience of forty-one million people. The A. C. Neilsen Company, which rates TV shows based on sample American homes, later calculated that the Notre Dame-Nebraska football game attained a blockbuster rating of 23.5, giving it a 38 share of all households watching television that Tuesday night. These ratings were all the more remarkable considering that, for obvious reasons, the second half of the Orange Bowl game was never played.

Midway through the first quarter the rains came; stinging needles that sent a groan through the crowd and brought out a sea of umbrellas.

Brian Keyes huddled sullenly in the rain and wished he'd stayed home. He had decided to attend the game only because he couldn't reach Kara Lynn, and because he'd gotten a free ticket (the Chamber of Commerce, showing its gratitude). Unfortunately, his seat was in the midst of the University of Nebraska card section, where raucous fans held up squares of bright poster-board to spell out witty messages like "Mash the Irish!" in giant letters. No sooner had Keyes settled in when some of the rooters had handed him two red cards and asked if he wouldn't mind being their semicolon. Keyes was worse than miserable.

On the field Nebraska was humiliating Notre Dame; no real surprise, since the no-neck Cornhuskers out-weighed their opponents by an average of thirty-two pounds apiece. Many of the fans, already sopped and now bored, wondered whose brilliant idea the four-point spread was. By half-time the score was 21–3.

The second-string running back for Notre Dame was a young man named David Lee, who stood six-feet-four and weighed a shade under two hundred pounds and was about as Irish as Sonny Liston. Though nominally listed on the team roster as a senior, David Lee was actually several dozen credits short of sophomore status—this, despite majoring in physical education and minoring in physical therapy. David Lee's grade-point average had recently skied to 1.9, slightly enhancing his chances of graduating from college before the age of fifty—provided, of course, he was not first drafted by a professional football team.

Which now seemed unlikely. During the first half of the Orange Bowl game, David Lee attempted to run with the football three times. The first effort resulted in a five-yard loss, the second a fumble. The third time he actually gained twelve yards and a first down. Unfortu-nately the only two pro football scouts in the stadium missed David Lee's big run because they spent the entire second quarter stuck in line at the men's room, fighting over the urinals with some Klansmen from Perrine.

David Lee's fortunes changed at halftime. As the two teams filed off the field and entered the tunnels leading to the lockers, a muscular Orange Bowl security guard pulled the young halfback aside and asked to speak with him privately. The guard informed David Lee that there was an emergency phone call from his parents in Bedford-Stuy, and escorted him to a stale-smelling broom closet below the stands in the southwest corner of the stadium. Once inside the room, which had no telephone, the security guard locked the door and said:

"Do you know who I am?"

"No, sir," David Lee replied politely, as even mediocre Notre Dame athletes were taught to do.

"I'm Viceroy Wilson." And Wilson it was, not at all dead.

"Naw!" Lee grinned. "C'm on, man!" He studied the security guard's furrowed face and saw in it something familiar, even famous. "Shit, it's really you!" Lee said. "I can't believe it—*the* Viceroy Wilson. Man, how come you wound up with a shitty job like this?"

The young man had obviously not been reading anything but the sports pages in Miami.

"Having a rough time tonight?" Wilson asked.

"You got that right," David Lee said. "Those honky farmboys are built like garbage trucks."

"Field looks pretty slippery, too. Hard to make your cuts."

"Damn right. Hey, what about my momma and daddy?"

"Oh, I lied about that. Lemme see your helmet, bro."

Lee handed it to him. "Fits you pretty good."

"Yeah," Viceroy Wilson said, squeezing it down over his ears. "Lemme buy it from you."

"Sheeiiit!" David Lee laughed. "You really sumthin."

"I'm serious, man." Viceroy Wilson pulled out a wad of cash. "A thousand bucks," he said, "for the whole uniform, 'cept for the cleats. I got my own fuckin' cleats."

The money was Skip Wiley's idea; Viceroy was just as amenable to punching the young man's lights out and stripping him clean.

David Lee fondled the crisp new bills and peered at the visage inside the gold Notre Dame helmet. He wondered if the Carrera sunglasses were some kind of gag.

"Is it a deal or not?" Wilson asked.

"Look, the coach is gonna freak. How about after the game?"

"This *is* after the game. Believe me, son, the game is over." Viceroy Wilson nonchalantly handed the college halfback another one thousand dollars.

"Two grand for a football uniform!"

"That's right, bro."

"You want the jock strap, too?"

"Fuck no!"

When he finally made it back to the Notre Dame locker room, David Lee stood naked except for his spikes and athletic supporter. After apologizing for interrupting the team prayer, he soberly told the coach he had been robbed and molested by a gang of crazed Mariel refugees, and asked if he could sit out the rest of the game.

The Orange Bowl Football Classic is as famous for its prodigal half-time production as for its superior brand of collegiate football. The half-time show is unfailingly more extravagant and fanciful than the Orange Bowl parade of the previous evening because the Half-time Celebration Committee adopts its own theme, hires its own professional director, recruits its own fresh-faced talent, and performs for its own television crew. The effect is that of a wearisome Vegas floor show played out across ten acres of Prescription Athletic Turf by four hundred professional "young people" who all look like they just got scholarships at Brigham Young. In recent years the TV people realized that lipsynching by the New Christy Minstrels and clog-dancing by giant stuffed mice in tuxedos were not enough to prevent millions of football viewers from going to the toilet and missing all the important car commercials, so the half-time producers introduced fireworks and even lasers into the Orange Bowl show. This proved to be a big hit and new-car sales went up accordingly. Each year more and more spectacular effects were worked into the script, and themes were modernized with the 18-to-34-year-old consumer in mind (though a few minor Disney characters were tossed in for the children). In the minds of the Orange Bowl organizers, the ideal half-time production was conceptually "hip," visually thrilling, morally inoffensive, and unremittingly middle-class.

The emcee of the Orange Bowl half-time show was a television personality named John Davidson, selected chiefly because of his dimples, which could be seen from as far away as the stadium's upper deck. Standing in an ice-blue spotlight on the fifty-yard line, John Davidson opened the festivities with a tepid medley of famous show tunes. Soon he was enveloped by a throng of prancing, dancing, capering, miming, rain-soaked Broadway characters in full costume: bewhiskered cats, Yiddish fiddlers, gorgeous chorus girls, two Little Orphan Annies, three Elephant Men, a Hamlet, a King of Siam, and even a tap-dancing Willy Loman. The theme of the twenty-two-minute extravaganza was "The World's a Stage," an ambitious sequel to previous Orange Bowl half-time galas such as "The World's a Song," "The World's a Parade," and more recently, "The World's a Great Big Planet."

The heart of the production was the reenactment of six legendary stage scenes, each compressed to eighty-five seconds and supplemented when necessary with tasteful bilingual narration. The final vignette was a soliloquy from *Hamlet*, which did not play well in the downpour; fans in the upper levels of the Orange Bowl could not clearly see Poor Yorick's skull and assumed they were applauding Señor Wences.

Afterward all the performers gathered arm-in-arm under a vast neon marquee and, to no one's surprise, sang "Give My Regards to Broadway." Then the flood-lights in the stadium dimmed and the slate rainclouds overhead formed an Elysian backdrop for the emotional climax, a holographic tribute to the late Ethel Merman.

The audience had scarcely recovered from this bog-gling spectacle of electronic magic—scenes from *Gypsy* projected in three dimensions at a height of thirty stories—when the lights winked on and John Davidson strode to midfield.

"Ladies and gentlemen," he said, with a smile bright enough to bleach rock, "if I may direct your attention to the east zone, it's my great pleasure to introduce this year's Orange Bowl queen, the beautiful Kara Lynn Shivers!"

In the stands, Brian Keyes went cold. In his obsession with the parade he had forgotten about the game, and the traditional half-time introduction of the queen and her court. It was a brief ceremony—a few of the prize-winning floats circling once in front of the stands before exiting the east end zone. As Kara Lynn's father had griped, it was hardly worth getting your hair done for, eleven crummy minutes of airtime.

But eleven minutes was plenty long enough. An eternity, Keyes thought. A horrible certainty possessed him and he jumped to his feet. Where were the cops—where were the goddamn cops?

The mermaid float entered first, still trumpeting sperm-whale music; then came floats from Cooley Motors, the Nordic Steamship Lines, and the Palm Beach Lawn Polo Society. The procession was supposed to end with a modest contingent of motorcycle Shriners from Illinois, who had been awarded a half-time slot following the untimely cancellation of the entry from Bogotá.

However, something foreign trailed the betasseled Shriners into the stadium: a strange unnamed float. Curious fans who thumbed through their Official Orange Bowl Souvenir Programs found no mention of this peculiar diorama. In their reserved box seats along the forty-yard line, members of the Orange Bowl Committee trained binoculars on the interloper and exchanged fretful whispers. Since the NBC cameras already had discovered the mystery float, intervention was out of the question, image-wise; besides, there was no reason to suspect anything but a harmless fraternity prank.

Though its craftsmanship was amateurish (forgivable, considering its humble warehouse origins), the float actually made a quaint impression. It was an Everglades tableau, almost childlike in simplicity. At one end stood an authentic thatched chickee, the traditional Seminole shelter; nearby lay a dugout canoe, half-carved from a bald cypress; steam rose from a black kettle hung over a mock fire. Grazing in a thicket, presumably unseen, was a stuffed white-tailed deer; a similarly preserved raccoon peered down from the lineated trunk of a synthetic palm. The centerpiece was a genuine Indian, very much alive and dressed in the nineteenth-century garb of trading-post Seminoles: a round, brimless straw hat, baggy pants, gingham shirt, a knotted red kerchief, and a tan cowskin vest. Somewhat anachronistically, the nineteenth-century Indian was perched at the helm of a modern airboat, gliding through the River of Grass. A long unpolished dagger was looped in the Seminole's snakeskin belt and a toy Winchester rifle lay across his lap. His smooth youthful face seemed the portrait of civility.

Brian Keyes sprang for the aisle the moment he saw the Indian. Frantically he tried to make his way down from the stands, but the Nebraska card-flashers (*Irish Suck!*) were embroiled in a heated cross-stadium skirmish with the Notre Dame card section (*Huskers Die!*). Keyes pushed and shoved and elbowed his way along the row but it was slow going, too slow, and some of the well-fed Cornhusker faithful decided to teach this rude young fellow some manners. They simply refused to move. Not for a semicolon, they said; set your butt down.

As the floats trundled past the stands, wind-whipped rains lashed the riders and sent the ersatz Broadway actors scurrying off the field for cover. Kara Lynn was drenched and miserable, but she continued to wave valiantly and smile. Through a pair of field glasses (and from the dry safety of a VIP box) Reed Shivers assayed his daughter's bedraggled visage and noted that her makeup was running badly, inky rivulets marring impeccable cheeks—she looked like something from a Warhol movie. Reed Shivers anxiously wondered if it was time to buy the lady from the Eileen Ford Agency another drink.

Reed Shivers and almost everyone else in the Orange Bowl did not yet realize that the Nights of December were alive and well. Nor did they know with what ease Skip Wiley's troops had carried out the assault on the *Nordic Princess*, the ditching of the stolen Huey, and the staging of their own deaths: the gang had simply performed flawlessly (minus Jesús Bernal, who'd vanished before Wiley had revealed the scheme's final refinement, and who'd gone to his death haplessly believing that the helicopter crash was an accident).

Tommy Tigertail had played a heroic role as captain of the clandestine rescue boat, a twenty-one-foot Mako powered by a two-hundred-horsepower Evinrude. Posing as a mackerel fisherman, he had plowed rough seas for an hour, staying close to the ocean liner but attracting no notice. His night vision had proved crucial when they had all bailed out—the pilot, Skip Wiley, and Viceroy Wilson. The ocean had been a turbid and treacherous soup, littered with sinking or half-sunk chopper wreckage, but within minutes the Indian had found all his comrades and pulled them safely into the speedboat.

The daring helicopter pilot had been rewarded with twenty thousand dollars of bingo skim, a phony passport, and a first-class plane ticket to Barbados. The Nights of December had dried off, checked into a Coconut Grove hotel, and gone back to work.

The news of Jesús Bernal's violent fate had darkened Skip Wiley's mood, but he'd refused to let it drag him down. Bernal's passing had not similarly moved Viceroy Wilson, who merely remarked how inconsiderate it was for Hay-Zoos to have ripped off his private shotgun, and how supremely stupid to have used it on a cop. Tommy Tigertail had had absolutely nothing to say about the neurotic Cuban's death; he had understood Jesús even less than Jesús had understood him.

In truth, Bernal's death had changed nothing. *Las Noches* had gone ahead with the mission, working with a vigor and *esprit* that had warmed Wiley's heart. At the vortex of the plan was a rejuvenated, rock-hard, and recently drug-free Viceroy Wilson, much more than a shadow of his former self.

Viceroy had had no trouble choosing Notre Dame's uniform over the apple-red jersey of the University of Nebraska.

The reasons were simple. First, Nebraska's agribusiness hegemony represented a vile anathema to Wilson, whose radical sympathies were more logically drawn to the Irish Republican Army, and thus Notre Dame.

Second, and most important, Notre Dame was the only one of the teams with a number thirty-one on its roster.

In reconstructing Viceroy Wilson's movements about the stadium that night, it was determined that several fans saw him emerge from the broom closet at 9:40 P.M. Ten minutes later he was observed, in uniform, ordering a jumbo orange juice at the concession stand in Section W.

Four minutes after that, he was seen eating a raisin bagel in a box seat at the Notre Dame twenty-yard line. When the rightful occupant returned from the souvenir shop and requested that Viceroy move elsewhere, Wilson inconsiderately mutilated the man's shamrock umbrella and popped him in the face. No one in the stands called the police; it seemed more properly a matter for the NCAA.

An eight-minute period elapsed during which no one reported seeing number thirty-one—then half the households of America did, courtesy of NBC.

While the other football players clustered in the southwest tunnel, Viceroy Wilson broke onto the field in a casual but self-assured trot. Many Notre Dame fans applauded, thinking the half-time show was finally over but wondering why the rest of the green-and-gold did not follow. They wondered, too, why a second-rate fumbler like David Lee would be given the honor of leading the Fighting Irish into battle.

They were stunned by what happened next.

Number thirty-one ran a perfect beeline down the center of the football field, each great stride splashing in the soggy turf. For Miami Dolphin fanatics, it was an unmistakable if ghostly reprise—the familiar numeral on the jersey; the right shoulder, drooping ever so slightly, as if bracing for a high tackle; the thick arms pumping like watchgears, the black hands locked in fists; and of course that triangular wedge of muscle from the shoulders to the hips. All that was missing was a football.

By the time Viceroy Wilson crossed the fifty-yard line, he was in full gait and no $3.50-an-hour security guard on the face of the earth could have caught him. Viceroy's mad dash seemed to freeze the authorities, who did not wish to shoot, maim, or otherwise embarrass any Notre Dame player. Maybe the kid was psyching himself for the game, or maybe just showing off for South Bend. After all, there were TV cameras everywhere.

In the midst of Viceroy Wilson's virtuoso run, two other disturbances erupted in the stadium.

First, the Seminole float rumbled and began to shudder at the tail of the procession—it appeared as if it was about to blow apart. The Shriners slowed their motorcycles and wheeled around, believing that the dim-witted Indian had accidentally started up the airboat.

At the same instant John Davidson was accosted at midfield by a bald, barefoot, russet-bearded man who was dressed as the King of Siam. It was, of course, Skip Wiley.

Unintelligible bits of their argument went out over the stadium sound system and then a struggle began. The two men tumbled out of the spotlight.

Seconds later the King of Siam appeared alone, holding Davidson's cordless microphone.

The crowd seemed greatly confused about whether

this was part of the official program; half of them clapped and half murmured.

Skip Wiley beamed up at the stands and said, "Please allow me to introduce myself, I'm a man of wealth and taste."

Brian Keyes had extricated himself from the card-flashers and was bounding down the stadium, four steps at a time, when he heard it.

Skip Wiley shouted to the heavens: "Been around for long, long years. Stolen many a man's soul and faith."

Swell, Keyes said to himself, he's doing the Stones.

From the crest of the queen's float, Kara Lynn Shivers stopped waving at the crippled Cub Scouts in Section Q and turned to see what was going on. She did not recall "Sympathy for the Devil" being listed in the Orange Bowl music program. Nor did she recognize the bald performer in the gold Oriental waistcoat.

"Pleased to meet you," Wiley sang, "hope you guess my name...."

In the NBC trailer the assistant producer barked into his mike: "Keep two cameras on that asshole!" Which was the prevailing sentiment among his forty-one million viewers.

Skip Wiley's performance was queer enough to draw almost everyone's attention away from Viceroy Wilson—everyone except the Shriners. Reacting swiftly, Burt and James led the motorcycle squadron across the east zone to intercept the hulking ex-fullback. It was the ultimate test of Viceroy's reborn skill, zigging and juking through the stolid heart of the Evanston Shrine; stiff-arming fenders where necessary; using his All-Pro shoulder to knock the cyclists off balance; an elbow to the fez, a fist to the throat (in the old days, fifteen yards and loss of down). With each collision Viceroy Wilson gave a contented growl. *Thirty-one Z-right*. This was the only part he'd ever missed, the purity of contact. Galvanized by adrenaline, he rejoiced in the shining justice of his run—the abused black hero outwitting, outflanking, outmuscling the whitest of the white establishment, impotent against his inevitable assault on precious honky womanhood. In Wilson's wake the bruised Shriners squirmed in the slop, pinned beneath their spangled Harleys; defeated, Viceroy mused, by their own gaudy materialism. And all this played out with splendid irony in the theater of his past heroics.

With the pursuers in chaos, all that stood between Viceroy Wilson and the Orange Bowl queen was the United States Marine Corps Honor Guard, whose members had no intention of breaking formation or soiling their dress blues. Wilson threaded them effortlessly and bounded onto the mermaid float.

"Oh shit," said Kara Lynn Shivers.

"Come on, girl," Viceroy Wilson said, catching his wind.

"Where we going?" Kara Lynn asked.

"Into history."

The tuna-blue mermaids shrieked as Wilson slung the queen over his shoulder and sprinted back upfield.

At that second the Seminole airboat shot off the Everglades float, splintering plywood, disemboweling the stuffed deer, leveling the chickee; the aviation engine expelling a suffocating contrail of rain and kerosene fumes over the stands. The airboat's aluminium hull pancaked on the slick football turf and hydroplaned; it was perfect, the Indian thought, gaining speed—you couldn't ask for a better surface.

Brian Keyes had finally reached the ground level and was vaulting the fence when he found the cops he'd been looking for. Five of Miami's finest. Dogs, nightsticks, the works. Keyes protested at the top of his lungs but they pinned him to the fence anyway, and there, stuck like a moth, he watched the whole terrible scene unfold— the airboat wheeling circles; Viceroy running with Kara Lynn slung over his shoulder; Skip crooning at the microphone.

On the field Burt and James had righted their bikes and resumed the chase. The key element now was speed, not agility: dodging a Harley Davidson was one thing, outrunning it was impossible. Viceroy Wilson had no illusion about this: he was counting heavily on the Indian.

Tommy Tigertail was a wizard with the airboat. He cut the field in half and slid the howling craft between Wilson and the frowning white riders in purple hats. The Indian spun the boat on a dime, throwing a sheet of rain and loose sod into the teeth of the Shriners. James lost control and went down in a deep skid, chewing a trench from the Notre Dame forty-yard line to the Nebraska thirty-five. He did not get up. Burt alertly veered from the airboat's backwash and, to avoid the flying muck, crouched behind his customized Plexiglas windshield.

The airboat bounded up alongside Viceroy Wilson and coasted to a stop. Wilson heaved Kara Lynn Shivers onto the deck as if she were a sandbag. By now the stadium crowd had figured out that this was not part of the show and started to scream witlessly. The Orange Bowl chairman was on his feet, yelling for the cops, while Sparky Harper's Chamber of Commerce successor frantically tried to sabotage the cables on one of NBC's portable Minicams. Meanwhile some of the real Notre Dame football players ambled onto the field to watch the commotion; Tommy Tigertail feared that they might soon get chivalrous notions.

"Hurry," he said to Viceroy Wilson.

Wilson had one foot in the airboat when Burt's Harley buzzed him like a fat chrome bee. Viceroy looked down to discover that his right leg—his bad leg—was stuck fast in a Shriner death hug. With his other leg Wilson kicked and bucked like a buted-up racehorse. The motorcycle fell from under Viceroy's attacker but somehow Burt kept his balance and his grip, and wound up on his feet. Wilson thought: This guy would have made a helluva nose tackle.

"Let the girl go!" Burt commanded.

"Get in," Tommy Tigertail said to Wilson.

"I can't shake loose!"

The pain in Viceroy's knee—famously mangled, prematurely arthritic, now barely held together with pins and screws—was insufferable, worse than anything he remembered from the old days.

"Hurry!" said the Indian. He jiggled the stick and the airboat jerked into gear. They were on a drier patch of the field so the boat moved forward in balky fits. Tommy was aching to throttle up to top speed; through the cutting rain he had spotted a phalanx of helmeted police advancing from the north sidelines. In the bow Kara Lynn sat up, shivering in the deluge.

"Let her go!" Burt bellowed, tugging and twisting Wilson's leg until number thirty-one clung to the hull by only the tips of his fingers. A deep-bone pain began to rake Viceroy's mind and seep his resolve. He suddenly felt old and tired, and realized he'd spent all his stamina on that glorious run.

The Indian decided it was time to go—the police were trotting now, yellow-fanged K-9 dogs at their heels. Tommy hopped off the driver's platform, grabbed Viceroy Wilson by the wrists, and yanked with all his strength. Burt lost his grip and fell backward, the purple fez tumbling off. Wilson landed in the boat with a grunt.

Kara Lynn tried to scrabble out, but the airboat was already moving too fast. She huddled with her legs to her chest, hands pressed to her ears; the thundering yowl of the engine was a new source of pain.

She saw the sturdy Shriner running alongside the airboat, his sequined vest flapping. He kept shouting for Tommy to stop.

He had a small brown pistol in one hand.

Viceroy Wilson rose to the prow, breadloaf arms swaying at his sides, keeping steady but favoring his right leg. He tore off the Notre Dame helmet and hurled it vainly at the dogged Shriner.

Viceroy's bare mahogany head glistened in the rain; the stadium lights twinkled in the ebony panes of his sunglasses. He scowled imperiously at Burt and raised his right fist in a salute that was at least traditional, if not trite.

"Down!" the Indian shouted. The airboat was hurtling straight for one of the goalposts—Tommy would have to make an amazing turn. "Viceroy, get down!"

Kara Lynn saw a rosy flash at the muzzle of Burt's pistol, but heard no shot.

When she turned, Viceroy Wilson was gone.

With a grimace Tommy Tigertail spun the airboat in a perilous fishtailing arc. It slid sideways against the padded goalpost and bounced off. The Marching Cornhusker majorettes dropped their batons and broke rank, leaving Tommy a clear path to escape. With Kara Lynn crouched fearfully in the bow, the airboat skimmed out of the stadium through the east gate. A getaway tractor-trailer rig had been parked on Seventh Street but the Indian knew he wouldn't need it; the swales were ankle-deep in rainwater and the airboat glided on mirrors all the way to the Miami River.

Viceroy Wilson lay dead in the east end zone. From the Goodyear blimp it appeared that he was splayed directly over the F in "Fighting Irish," which had been painted in tall gold letters across the turf.

A babbling congress of cops, orange blazers, drunken fans, and battered Shriners had surrounded the Super Bowl hero. Brian Keyes was there, too, kneeling down and speaking urgently into Viceroy Wilson's ear, but Viceroy Wilson was answering no questions. He lay face up, his lips curled in a poster-perfect radical snarl. His right hand was so obdurately clenched into a fist that two veteran morticians would later be unable to pry it open. Centered between the three and the one of the kelly-green football jersey was a single bullet hole, which was the object of much squeamish finger pointing.

"I'm telling ya," the Notre Dame coach was saying, "he's *not* one of ours."

Outside the Orange Bowl, on Fourteenth Avenue, the King of Siam flagged a taxi.

THIRTY-THREE

Keyes made it from the stadium to Jenna's house in twenty minutes.

"Hey, there," she said, opening the screen door. She was wearing a baggy sweatshirt with nothing underneath.

Keyes went into the living room. The coffin was padlocked.

"Open it," he said.

"But I don't have a key," Jenna said. "What's the matter—he's alive, isn't he?"

"Surprise, surprise,"

"I told you!" she exclaimed.

"Put on some goddamn clothes."

She nodded and went to the bedroom.

"Do you have a hammer?" Keyes called.

"In the garage."

He found a sledge and carried it back to the living room. Jenna cleared the vase and magazines off the macabre coffee table. She was wearing tan hiking shorts and a navy long-sleeved pullover. She had also put on a bra and some running shoes.

"Look out," Keyes said. He pounded the padlock three times before the hasp snapped.

Inside the cheap coffin, Skip Wiley's detritus looked

as muddled and random as before—yellowed news-paper clippings, old notebooks, mildewed paperbacks, library files purloined from the *Sun*'s morgue. Keyes sifted through everything in search of a single fresh clue. The best he could do was a sales receipt from a Fort Lauderdale marine dealer.

"Skip bought a boat last week," Keyes said. "Twenty-one-foot Mako. Eighteen-five, cash. Any idea why?"

"Nuh-uh."

"When's the last time he was here?"

"I'm not sure," Jenna replied.

Keyes grabbed her by the arms and shook hard. He frightened her, which was what he wanted. He wanted her off balance.

Jenna didn't know how to react, she'd never seen Brian this way. His eyes were dry and contemptuous, and his voice was that of an intruder.

"When was Skip here?" he repeated.

"A week ago, I think. No, last Friday."

"What did he do?"

"He spent half the day reading the paper," Jenna said. "That much I remember."

"Really?"

"Okay, let me think." She took a deep theatrical breath and put her hands in her pockets. "Okay, he was clipping some stuff from the newspaper—that, I remember. And he was playing his music. Steppenwolf, real loud . . . I made him turn it down. Then we grilled some burgers with mushrooms, and the Indian man came over and they left. That's what I remember."

"He didn't say a word about the Nights of December?"

"No."

"And you didn't ask?"

"No," Jenna said. "I knew better. He was really wired, Brian. He was in no mood for questions."

"You're useless, you know that?"

"Brian!"

"Where's the garbage?"

"Out on the curb." Jenna started sniffling; it sounded possibly authentic.

Keyes walked to the street and hauled the ten-gallon bag back into the house. He used a car key to gash it open.

"What're you doing now?" Jenna asked.

"Looking for Wheaties boxtops. Didn't you hear?— there's a big sweepstake."

He kicked through guava rinds, putrid cottage cheese, eggshells, tea bags, melon husks, coffee grounds, yogurt cartons, chicken bones and root-beer cans. The newspapers were at the very bottom, soggy and rancid-smelling. Keyes used the toe of his shoe to search for the front page from Friday, December 28. When he found it, he motioned Jenna over. She made a face as she tiptoed through the rank mush.

"This is the one he was clipping?" Keyes asked.

"Right."

Keyes got on his knees and went through the news-paper, page by sodden page. Jenna backed away and sat on the floor. Pouting would be a waste of energy; Brian scarcely even noticed she was in the room.

He found Skip Wiley's scissor holes in the real-estate section. A long article had been clipped from the bottom of the first page, and a large display advertisement had been cut out of Page F-17.

Keyes held up the shredded newsprint for Jenna to

see; she shrugged and shook her head. "Stay here," he said. "I need to use your phone."

Three minutes later he was back. He took her by the hand and said, "Let's go, we're running out of time." Keyes had called a librarian at the *Sun*. Now he knew what Wiley had clipped out. He knew everything.

"What about this mess?" Jenna complained.

"This is nothing," Keyes said, yanking her out the front door. "This is a picnic."

They arrived at the Virginia Key marina within minutes of one another, Skip Wiley by car, the Indian by airboat. The Indian's round straw hat had blown off during the ride and his wet black hair was windswept behind his ears. Wiley had changed to a flannel shirt, painter's trousers, and a blue Atlanta Braves baseball cap.

The Mako outboard had been gassed up and tied to a piling. The marina was dark and, once Tommy stopped the airboat, silent. He carefully lifted Kara Lynn into the outboard; she was limp as a rag and her eyes were closed. Her blond hair hung in a stringy mop across half of her face.

"I gave her something to drink," the Indian said, hopping out. "She'll sleep for a time."

"Perfect," Wiley said. "Look, Tom, I'm damn sorry about Viceroy."

"It was my fault."

"Like hell. All he had to do was duck down, but the big black jackass decides to pull a Huey Newton. He really disappointed me, him and his Black Power bullshit—it wasn't the time or place for it, but the sonofabitch couldn't resist. A regular moonchild of the sixties."

Tommy Tigertail's eyes dulled with grief. "I'll miss him," he said.

"Me too, pal."

"I found these in the airboat." Tommy held up Viceroy Wilson's cherished sunglasses.

"Here," Wiley said. He fitted the glitzy Carreras onto the Indian's downcast face. "Hey, right out of *GQ*!"

"Where's that?" Tommy asked. With the glasses he looked like a Tijuana hit-man.

A pair of pelicans waddled up the dock to see if the two men were generous anglers. The Indian smiled at the goofy-looking birds and said, "Sorry, guys, no fish."

A red pickup truck with oversized tires pulled into the lot. The driver turned the headlights off and sat with the engine running.

Wiley worriedly glanced over his shoulder.

"It's all right," Tommy said. "That's my ride."

"Where you off to?"

"I've got a skiff waiting at Flamingo, down in the back country. There's an old chickee up the Shark River, nobody knows about it. The last few weeks I've had it stocked with supplies—plenty to last me forever." Tommy Tigertail had stored enough for two men. Now there would be only one.

"You've been so damn generous," Wiley said. "I wish you could stay and watch the fun."

"If I remained here," Tommy said, "I'd bring nothing but pain to my people. The police would never leave them alone. It's better to go far away, where I can't be found."

"I'm really sorry," Wiley said.

"Why?" The Indian wore a look of utter serenity. In a voice that carried a note of private triumph he said, "Don't you see? This way I will not die in prison." That much he owed his ancestors.

"If you ever get down to Haiti," Wiley said, "look me up in the phone book. Under E for Exile."

"Stay out of trouble," Tommy Tigertail advised. "Stay free."

Wiley scratched his neck and grinned. "We pulled some outstanding shit, didn't we?"

"Yes," Tommy said. "Outstanding." He shook Wiley's hand and gave him the red kerchief from around his neck. "Good-bye, Skip."

"'Bye, Tom."

The Indian walked briskly to the pickup truck. An ancient Seminole with thin gray hair and a walnut face sat behind the wheel.

"Let's go, Uncle Billie," Tommy said.

They could see Skip Wiley toiling at the console of the sleek boat, warming the big engine. He was singing in a stentorian cannon that crashed out over the carping gulls and the slap of the waves.

Rode a tank, held a general's rank, when the blitzkrieg raged and the bodies stank . . .

"Who is the strange one with the beard?" the old Seminole wanted to know.

"With any luck," Tommy Tigertail said affectionately, "the last white man I'll ever see."

When they reached the toll booth to the Rickenbacker Causeway, Jenna sat up and asked, "Where we going?"

"For a boat ride," Brian Keyes replied.

"I thought we were going to the police. Don't you think that's a better idea?"

"The goddamn marines would be a better idea, if I had that kind of time."

Keyes knew exactly what the cops were doing—setting up a vast and worthless perimeter around the Orange Bowl. The city was howling with sirens; every squad car in Dade County was in motion. There were no helicopters up because of the bad weather—and without choppers, Keyes knew, the cops could forget about catching the Indian.

Jenna shifted apprehensively. She said, "I think you ought to drop me off here. This whole thing is between you and Skip."

Keyes drove faster down the causeway. Years ago—a lifetime ago—he and Jenna used to park there at night and make love under the trees, and afterward marvel at how the skyscrapers glittered off the bay. Since then, the causeway had become extremely popular with ski-mask rapists and icepick murderers, and not many unarmed couples went there to neck anymore.

Jenna said, "Why don't you let me out?"

"Not here, it's way too dangerous," he said. "I'm curious—why'd you stop by the office today?"

"Just lonely," Jenna said. "And I was worried sick about Skip . . . I thought you might know something."

Keyes glanced at her and said, "Your little chore was to keep me company, right?"

"That's the dumbest thing I ever heard."

"You were in on the whole thing."

"I hate you like this," Jenna said angrily. "So damn smug, you think you've got it all figured out. Well, you don't . . . there's one thing you never figured out: why I left you for Skip."

"That's true," Keyes said, remembering how nasty she could get. She sat ramrod straight in the seat, chin out, a portrait of defiance.

"The choice was easy, Brian. You're a totally passive person, an incurable knothole peeper, a spy."

Keyes thought: This is going to be a beaut.

Jenna said, "You're a follower and a chaser and chronicler of other human lives, but you will not fucking *participate*. I wanted somebody who would. Skip isn't afraid to dance on the big stage. He's the sort of person you love to watch but would hate to be, because he takes chances. He's a leader, and leaders don't just get followed—they get chased. That's not your style, Brian, getting chased. The thing about Skip, he makes things happen."

"So did Juan Corona. You two would make a swell couple."

Keyes found himself strangely unperturbed by Jenna's emasculatory harangue; maybe there was hope for him yet. He hit the brakes and the MG skidded off the road into some gravel. He backed up to the gate of the Virginia Key marina.

"I believe that's your car," he said to Jenna.

"Where?"

He pointed. "Next to the boat ramp. The white Mercury."

"My car's in the shop," Jenna snapped.

"Really? Shall we go check the license tag?"

Jenna turned away.

"Skip borrowed it," she said almost inaudibly.

Keyes saw her hand move to the door handle. He reached across the seat and slapped the lock down.

"Not yet," he warned her. "You're not going anywhere."

"Hey, what is this?"

"It's called deep trouble, and you're in the middle, Miss Granola Bar."

"All I ever knew were bits and pieces, that's all," she insisted. "Skip didn't tell me everything. He was always dropping little hints but I was scared to ask for more. I didn't know about the new boat and I sure don't know where he is right now. Honest, Brian, I thought the stunt with the ocean liner was it; his big plan. I didn't know anything about tonight, I swear. I wasn't even sure he was still alive."

Her eyes couldn't get more liquid, her voice more beseeching. A metamorphosis in thirty seconds.

Keyes said, "You promised he wasn't going to hurt Kara Lynn."

"Maybe he's not," Jenna said ingenuously. "Maybe he's already let her go."

"Yeah, and maybe I'm the Prince of Wales."

Keyes drove past the Miami Marine Stadium and turned down a winding two-lane macadam. The shrimper's dock was at the dead end of the road, on a teardrop-shaped lagoon.

The shrimper's name was Joey and he owned three small trawlers that harvested Biscayne Bay by night. He worked out of a plywood shack lighted by bare bulbs and guarded by a pair of friendly mutts.

Joey was dipping shrimp when Keyes drove up.

"I don't know if you remember me," Keyes said. "I

interviewed you a few years back for a newspaper story."

"Sure," said Joey, peering past the end of his cigar. "You were askin' about pollution, some damn thing."

"Right. Look, I need a boat. It's sort of an emergency."

Joey glanced over at Jenna sitting in the car.

"Damn fine emergency," he said. "But you don't need a boat, you need a water bed."

"Please," Keyes said. "We need a ride to Osprey Island."

"You and the girl?"

"That's right. It's worth a hundred bucks."

Joey hung the net on a nail over the shrimp tank. "That island's private property, son."

"I know."

"It's black as a bear's asshole and fulla bugs. Why the hell you wanna go over there on a night like this?"

"Like I said, it's an emergency," Keyes said. "Life and death."

"Naturally," Joey muttered. He took the hundred dollars and struggled into his oilskin raingear. "There's more weather on the way," he said. "Go fetch your ladyfriend. We'll take the *Tina Marie*."

Osprey Island was a paddle-shaped outcrop in east Biscayne Bay, about five miles south of the Cape Florida lighthouse. There were no sandy beaches, for the island was mostly hard coral and oolite rock—a long-dead reef, thrust barely above sea level. The shores were collared with thick red mangrove; farther inland, young buttonwoods, gumbo-limbo, sea grape, and mahogany.

An old man who had lived there for thirty years had planted a row of royal palms and a stand of pines, and these rose majestically from the elevated plot that had been his homestead, before he fell ill and moved back to the mainland. All that remained of the house was a concrete slab and four cypress pilings and a carpet of broken pink stucco; a bare fifty-foot flagpole stood as a salt-eaten legacy to the old man's patriotism and also to his indelible fear that someday the Russians would invade Florida, starting with Osprey Island.

Like almost everything else in South Florida, the islet was dishonestly named. There were no white-hooded ospreys, or fish eagles, living on Osprey Island because the nesting trees were not of sufficient height or maturity. A few of the regal birds lived on Sand Key or Elliott, farther south, and occasionally they could be seen diving the channel and marl flats around the island bearing their name. But if it had been left up to the Calusa Indians, who had first settled the place, the island probably would have been called Mosquito or Crab, because these were the predominant life forms infesting its fifty-three acres.

There was no dock—Hurricane Betsy had washed it away in 1965—but a shallow mooring big enough for one boat had been blasted out of the dead coral on the lee side. With some difficulty of navigation, and considerable paint loss to the outboard's hull, Skip Wiley managed to locate the anchorage in pitch dark. He waded ashore with Kara Lynn deadweight in his arms. The trail to the campsite was fresh and Wiley had no trouble following it, although the sharp branches snagged his clothes and scratched his scalp. Every few steps came a new lashing insult and he bellowed appropriate curses to the firmament.

At the campsite, not far from the old cabin rubble, Wiley placed Kara Lynn on a bed of pine needles and covered her with a thin woolen blanket. Both of them were soaked from the crossing.

Wiley swatted no-see-'ems in the darkness for three hours until he heard the hum of a passing motorboat. Finally! he groused. The Marine Patrol on its nightly route. Wiley had been waiting for the bastard to go by; now it was safe.

When the police boat was gone he built a small fire from dry tinder he had stored under a sheet of industrial plastic. The wind was due east and unbelievably strong, scattering sparks from the campfire like swarms of tipsy fireflies. Wiley was grateful that the woods were wet.

He was fixing a mug of instant bouillon when Kara Lynn woke up, surprising him.

"Hello, there," Skip Wiley said, thinking it was a good thing he'd tied her wrists and ankles—she looked like a strong girl.

"I know this is a dumb question—" Kara Lynn began.

"Osprey Island," Wiley said.

"Where's that?"

"Out in the bay. Care for some soup?"

Wiley helped her sit up and pulled the blanket around to cover her back and shoulders, which were bare in the parade gown. He held the cup while she drank.

"I know who you are," Kara Lynn said. "I read the big story in the paper today—was it today?"

Wiley looked at his wristwatch. It was half-past three in the morning. "Yesterday," he said. "So what did you think?"

"About the story?"

"No, the column."

"You've done better," Kara Lynn said.

"What do you mean?"

"Can I have another sip? Thanks." She drank a little more and said: "You're sharper when you don't write in the first person."

Wiley plucked at his beard.

"Now, don't get mad," Kara Lynn said. "It's just that some of the transitions seemed contrived, like you were reaching."

"It was a damn tough piece to write," Wiley said thoughtfully.

"I'm sure it was."

"I mean, I couldn't see another way to do it. The first-person approach seemed inescapable."

"Maybe you're right," Kara Lynn said. "I just don't think it was as effective as the hurricane column."

Wiley brightened. "You liked that one?"

"A real scorcher," Kara Lynn said. "We talked about it in class."

"No kidding!" Skip Wiley was delighted. Then his smile ebbed and he sat in silence for several minutes. The girl was not what he expected, and he felt a troubling ambivalence about what was to come. He wished the Seminole sleeping drink had lasted longer; now that Kara Lynn was awake, he sensed a formidable undercurrent. She was a composed and resourceful person—he'd have to watch himself.

"What's the matter?" Kara Lynn asked.

"Why aren't you crying or something?" Wiley grumbled.

Kara Lynn looked around the campsite. "What would be the point?"

Wiley spread more tinder on the fire and held his hands over the flame. The warmth was comforting. He thought: Actually, there's nothing to stop me from leaving now. The job is done.

"Do you know Brian Keyes?"

"Sure," Wiley said, "we worked together."

"Was he a good reporter?"

"Brian's a good man," Wiley said, "but I'm not so sure if he was a good reporter. He wasn't really suited for the business."

"Apparently neither were you."

"No comparison," he scoffed. "Absolutely no comparison."

"Oh, I'm not sure," Kara Lynn said. "I think you're two sides to the same coin, you and Brian."

"And I think you read too much *Cosmo*." Wiley wondered why she was so damned interested in Keyes.

"What about Jenna?" Kara Lynn asked. "You serious about her?"

"What is this, the Merv show?" Wiley ground his teeth. "Look," he said, "I'd love to sit and chat but it's time to be on my way."

"You're going to leave me out here in the rain? With no food or water?"

"You won't need any," he said. "'Fraid I'm going to have to douse the fire, too."

"A real gentleman," Kara Lynn said acerbically. She was already testing the rope on her wrist.

Wiley was about to pour some tea on the flames when he straightened up and cocked his head. "Did you hear something?" he asked.

"No," Kara Lynn lied.

"It's a goddamn boat."

"It's the wind, that's all."

Wiley set down the kettle, took off his baseball cap, and went crashing off, his bare bright egg of a head vanishing into the hardwoods. Thinking he had fled, Kara Lynn squirmed to the campfire and turned herself around. She held her wrists over the bluest flame, until she smelled flesh. With a cry she pulled away; the rope held fast.

When she looked up, he was standing there. He folded his arms and said, "See what you did, you hurt yourself." He carried her back to the bed of pine needles and examined the burns. "Christ, I didn't even bring a Band-Aid," he said.

"I'm all right," said Kara Lynn. Her eyes teared from the pain. "What about that noise?"

"It was nothing," Wiley said, "just a shrimper trolling offshore." He tore a strip of orange silk from the hem of her gown. He soaked it in salt water and wound it around the burn. Then he cut another length of rope and retied her wrists, tighter than before.

The rain started again. It came in slashing horizontal sheets. Wiley covered his eyes and said, "Shit, I can't run the boat in this mess."

"Why don't you wait till it lets up?" Kara Lynn suggested.

Her composure was aggravating. Wiley glared down at her and said, "Hey, Pollyanna, you're awfully calm for a kidnap victim. You overdosed on Midol or what?"

Kara Lynn's ocelot eyes stared back in a way that made him shiver slightly. She wasn't afraid. *She was not afraid*. What a great kid, Wiley thought. What a damn shame.

They huddled under a sheet of opaque plastic, the raindrops popping at their heads. Wiley tied Tommy's red kerchief around the dome of his head to blot the rain from his eyes.

"Tell me about Osprey Island," Kara Lynn said, as if they were rocking on a front porch waiting for the ice-cream truck.

"A special place," he said, melancholic. "A gem of nature. There's a freshwater spring down the trail, can you believe it? Miles off the mainland and the aquifer still bubbles up. You can see coons, opossums, wood rats drinking there, but mostly birds. Wood storks, blue herons. There's a bald eagle on the island, a young male. Wingspan is ten feet if it's an inch, just a glorious bird. He stays up in the tallest pines, fishes only at dawn and dusk. He's up there now, in the trees." Wiley's ancient-looking eyes went to the pine stand. "It's too windy to fly, so I'm sure he's up there now."

"I've never seen a wild eagle," Kara Lynn remarked. "I was born down here and I've never seen one."

"That's too bad," Skip Wiley said sincerely. His head was bowed. Tiny bubbles of water hung in his rusty beard. It didn't make it any easier that she was born here, he thought.

"It'll be gone soon, this place," he said. "A year from now a sixteen-story monster will stand right where we're sitting." He got to his knees and fumbled in the pocket of his trousers. He pulled out some damp gray newspaper clippings, folded into a square. "Let me give you the full picture," he said, unfolding them, starting to read. Kara Lynn looked over his shoulder.

"*Welcome to the Osprey Club . . . Fine living, for the discriminating Floridian.* Makes you want to puke."

"Pretty tacky," Kara Lynn agreed.

"A hundred and two units from two-fifty all the way up to a million-six. Friendly financing available. Vaulted ceilings, marble archways, sunken living rooms, Roman tubs, atrium patios with real cedar trellises, boy oh boy." Wiley looked up from the newspaper advertisement and gazed out at the woodsy shadows.

"Can't someone try to block it?" Kara Lynn suggested. "The Audubon people. Or maybe the National Park Service."

"Too late," Wiley said. "See, it's a private island. After old man Bradshaw died, his scumball kids put it up for sale. Puerco Development picks it up for three mil and wham, next thing you know it's re-zoned for multifamily high-rise."

"Didn't you do a column on this?" she asked.

"I sure did." One of Wiley's many pending lawsuits: a gratuitous and unprovable reference to Mafia connections.

"Back to the blandishments," he said, "there'll be four air-conditioned racketball courts, a spa, a bike trail, a tennis complex, a piazza, two fountains, and even a waterfall. Think about that: they're going to bury the natural spring and build a fiberglass waterfall! Progress, my darling. It says here they're also planting something called a *lush greenbelt*, which is basically a place for rich people to let their poodles take a shit."

Kara Lynn said: "How will people get out here?"

"Ferry," Wiley answered. "See here: *Take a quaint ferry to your very own island where the Mediterranean meets Miami*! See, Kara Lynn, the bastards can't sell Florida anymore, they've got to sell the bloody Riviera."

"It sounds a bit overdone," she said.

"Twenty-four hundred square feet of overdone," Wiley said, "with a view."

"But no ospreys," said Kara Lynn, sensing the downward spiral of his emotions.

"And no eagle," Wiley said glumly.

He acted as if he were ready to leave, and Kara Lynn knew that if he did, it would be over.

"Why did you pick me?" she asked.

Wiley turned to look at her. "Because you're perfect," he said. "Or at least you represent perfection. Beauty. Chastity. Innocence. All tanned and blond, the golden American dream. That's all they really promise with their damn parade and their unctuous tourist advertising. Come see Miami, come see the girls! But it's a cheap tease, darling. Florida's nothing but an adman's wet dream."

"That's enough," Kara Lynn said, reddening.

"I take it you don't think of yourself as a precious piece of ass."

"Not really, no."

"Me, neither," Wiley said, "but we are definitely in the minority. And that's why we're out here now—an object lesson for all those bootlicking shills and hustlers."

Wiley crawled out from under the plastic tent and rose to his full height, declaring, "The only way to reach the greedy blind pagans is to strike at their meager principles." He pointed toward the treetops. "To the creators of the Osprey Club, that precious eagle up there is not life, it has no real value. Same goes for the wood rats and the herons. Weighed against the depreciated net worth of a sixteen-story condominium after sellout, the natural inhabitants of this island do not represent life—they have no fucking value. You with me?"

Kara Lynn nodded. She still couldn't see the big bird.

"Now," Wiley said, "if you're the CEO of Puerco Development, what has worth to you, besides money? What is a life? Among all creatures, what is the one that cannot legally be extinguished for the sake of progress?" Wiley arched his eyebrows and pointed a dripping finger at Kara Lynn's nose. "You," he said. "You are, presumably, inviolate."

For the first time in the conversation, it occurred to Kara Lynn that this fellow might truly be insane.

Wiley blinked at her. "I'll be right back," he said.

This time she didn't move. Wet and cold, she had come to cherish the meager protection of the plastic shelter. Wiley returned carrying a short wooden stake. An orange plastic streamer was attached to the blunt end.

"Survey markers," Kara Lynn said.

"Very good. So you know what it means—construction is imminent."

"How imminent?" she asked.

"Like tomorrow."

"Tomorrow's the groundbreaking?"

"Naw, that was Christmas Eve. Purely ceremonial," Wiley said. "Tomorrow is much more significant. Tomorrow's the day they start terrain modification."

"What's that?"

"Just what it says."

Kara Lynn was puzzled. "I don't see any bulldozers."

"No, those would be used later, for contour clearing."

"Then what do they use for this 'terrain modification'?" she asked.

"Dynamite," Skip Wiley replied. "At dawn."

Osprey Island

Kara Lynn thought she might have heard him wrong, thought it might have been a trick of the wind.

"Did you say dynamite?" she asked.

"Eight hundred pounds," Skip Wiley said, "split into three payloads. One at the northwest tip, another at the southeast cove. The third cache, the big one, is right over there, no more than twenty yards. Can you see it? That galvanized box beneath those trees."

From where she sat Kara Lynn saw nothing but shadows.

"I . . . I don't . . ." She was choking on fear, unable to speak. Hold on, she told herself.

"They do it by remote control," Wiley explained, "from a barge. We passed it on the way out, anchored three miles off the island. You were asleep."

"Oh . . ." The plan was more terrible than she had imagined; all the stalling had been futile, a wasted strategy.

"They have to do it at dawn," Wiley went on, "some kind of Army Corps rule. Can't bring boats any closer to the island because the blast'll blow the windows out."

He ambled to the campfire and stood with his back to her for several moments. His naked cantaloupe head twitched back and forth, as if he were talking to himself. Abruptly he turned around and said, "The reason for the dynamite is the coral. See—" He kicked at the ground with his shoe. "Harder than cement. They need to go down twenty-four inches before pouring the foundation for the condo. Can't make a dent with shovels, not in this stuff . . . so that's why the dynamite. Flip of a switch and—poof—turn this place into the Bonneville flats. Eight hundred pounds is a lot of firecracker."

Kara Lynn steadied himself just enough to utter the most inane question of her entire life: "What about me?"

Wiley spread his arms. "No life forms will survive," he said in a clinical tone. "Not even the gnats."

"Please don't do this," Kara Lynn said.

"It's not me, Barbie Doll, it's progress. Your beef is with Puerco Development."

"Don't leave me here," she said, just shy of a beg.

"Darling, how could I save you and not save that magnificent eagle? Or the helpless rabbits and the homely opossums, or even the lowly fiddler crabs? It's impossible to rescue them, so I can't very well rescue you. It wouldn't be fair. It would be like . . . playing God. This way is best, Kara Lynn. This way—for the first time in nineteen pampered years—you are truly part of the natural order. You now inhabit this beautiful little island, and the value of your life is the same as all creatures here. If they should survive past dawn, so shall you. If not . . . well, maybe the good people of Florida will finally appreciate the magnitude of their sins. If Osprey Island is leveled in the name of progress, I predict a cataclysmic backlash, once the truth is known.

The truth being that they blew up the one species they really care about—a future customer."

Kara Lynn was running low on poise. "The symbolism is intriguing," she said, "but your logic is ridiculous."

"Just listen," Wiley said. From a breast pocket he took another clipping and read: " 'Officials in South Florida estimate that adverse publicity surrounding December's tourist murders has cost the resort area as much as ten million dollars in family and convention trade.' " Wiley waved the clip and gloated. "Not too shabby, eh?"

"I'm impressed," Kara Lynn said archly. "A month's worth of killing and all you've got to show for it is one dinky paragraph in *Newsweek*."

"It's the lead Periscope item!" Wiley said, defensively.

"Terrific," Kara Lynn said. "Look, why don't you let me go? You can do better than this."

"I think not."

"I can swim away," she declared.

"Not all tied up, you can't," Wiley said. "Besides, the water's lousy with blacktip sharks. Did you know they spawn at night in the shallows? Aggressive little bastards, too. A bite here, a bite there, a little blood and pretty soon the big boys pick up the scent. Bull sharks and hammerheads big enough to eat a goddamn Datsun."

"That'll do," said Kara Lynn.

Something rustled at the edge of the clearing. A branch cracking in the storm, she thought. Skip Wiley cocked his head and peered toward the sound, but the hard rain painted everything gray and hunched and formless. The only identifiable noises were raindrops slapping leaves, and the hiss of embers as the campfire died in the downpour.

Wiley was not satisfied. Like an ungainly baseball pitcher, he wound up and hurled the survey stake end-over-end into the trees.

The missile was answered by an odd strangled peep.

Wiley chuckled. "Just as I thought," he said, "a wood stork."

Just then the thicket ruptured with an explosion so enormous that Kara Lynn was certain that Wiley had accidentally detonated the dynamite.

When she opened her eyes, he was sitting down, slack-jawed and pale. The red kerchief was askew, drooped over one eye. Both legs stuck straight out, doll-like, in front of him. He seemed transfixed by something close at hand—a radiant splotch of crimson and a yellow knob of bone, where his right knee used to be. Absently he fingered the frayed hole in his trousers.

Kara Lynn felt a surge of nausea. She gulped a breath.

Brian Keyes moved quickly out of the trees.

His brown hair was plastered to his forehead; rain streamed down his cheeks. His face was blank. He was walking deliberately, a little hurried, as if his flight were boarding.

He strode up to Skip Wiley, placed a foot on his chest, and kicked him flat on his back. A regular one-man cavalry! Kara Lynn was elated, washed with relief. She didn't notice the Browning in Brian's right hand until he shoved the barrel into Wiley's mouth.

"Hello, Skip," Keyes said. "How about telling me where you anchored the boat?"

Wiley's wolfish eyes crinkled with amusement. He

grunted an indecipherable greeting. Keyes slowly with-
drew the gun, but kept it inches from Wiley's nose.

"Holy Christ!" Wiley boomed, sitting up. "And I
thought you were dangerous with a typewriter."

"You're losing blood," Keyes said.

"No thanks to you."

"Where's the boat?"

"Not so fast."

Keyes fired again, the gun so close to Wiley's face
that the charge knocked him back down. Wiley clutched
at his ears and rolled away, over the sharp corrugated
coral. The bullet had thwacked harmlessly into the
stucco rubble of the old cabin.

Kara Lynn cried out involuntarily—she was afraid
she'd have to watch a killing. Keyes came over, untied
her, and gave a gentle hug. "You okay?"

She nodded. "I want to get out of here. They're going
to dynamite this place—"

"I know." He had to find Wiley's boat.

Joey the shrimper had been generous enough to
provide a tin of smoked amberjack and a jug of water
before letting them off, but he had not been generous
enough to wait around. Muttering about the obscene
cost of fuel, he had aimed the *Tina Marie* away from
the island, leaving his passengers to find their own way
back to the mainland.

Keyes stood over Wiley and ordered him to sit up.

"You're in an ugly mood," Wiley said nervously. His
ears rang. He felt like he was talking down a tunnel.

Keyes took off his shirt and tied it around Wiley's
mutilated leg. "We haven't got much time," he said.

Wiley studied Brian intently; the gun made him a
stranger. The violent eruption was unnerving enough, but

what sobered Wiley even more was the look of chilling and absolute indifference. This was not the same polite young man who'd sat next to him in the newsroom; Wiley feared a loss of leverage. Against this Brian Keyes, in this place, Wiley's weapons were greatly limited. Right away he ruled out charm, wit, and oratory.

"How'd you find me?"

"Never mind," Keyes said.

"Jenna told you, right?"

"No." So she had known. Of course she knew. "Give me the keys to the Mako," Keyes said.

Grudgingly Wiley handed them over.

He pointed at Kara Lynn. "It's the girl, isn't it? You fell for her! That's why you're in Charlie Bronson mode—defending the fair maiden. Just your luck, Brian. Seems like I'm always screwing up your love life."

Keyes didn't know how much longer he could hold up. He wanted to go now, while he still had the strength, while he was still propelled by whatever it was that let him pull the trigger one more time.

"Kara Lynn, would you like to know a secret about Mr. Keyes?"

She said nothing, knowing that it wasn't finished yet. Not as long as Wiley could speak.

"Don't you want to hear a war story?" Wiley asked.

"Shut up," Keyes said.

"You want the boat? Then you've got to listen. *Politely.*"

Keyes grabbed Wiley's wrist and looked at the watch. It was half-past five; they'd be cutting it close.

"A few years back, a little girl was kidnapped and murdered," Wiley said, turning to Kara Lynn, his audience. "After the body was found, Brian was supposed to go interview the parents."

"The Davenports," Keyes said.

"Hey, let me tell it!" Wiley said indignantly.

The rain had slackened to a sibilant drizzle. Keyes tore a piece of plastic from Kara Lynn's makeshift poncho and sat down on it. He felt oppressively lethargic, bone-tired.

"Brian came back with a great piece," Wiley said. "Mother, weeping hysterically; father, blind with rage. *Tomorrow would be Callie Davenport's fourth birthday. Her room is full of bright presents, each tenderly wrapped. There's a Snoopy doll from Uncle Dennis, a Dr. Seuss from Grandpa. Callie won't be there on her birthday, so the packages may sit there for a long time. Maybe forever. Her parents simply can't bear to go in her bedroom.*"

Keyes sagged. He couldn't believe that Wiley remembered the story, word for word. It was amazing.

"A real tearjerker," Wiley pronounced. "That morning half of Miami was weeping into their Rice Krispies." He seemed oblivious of pain, of the thickening puddle of blood under his leg.

"Kara Lynn," he said, "in my business, the coin of the realm is a good quote—it's the only thing that brings a newspaper story to life. One decent quote is the difference between dog food and caviar, and Brian's story about Callie Davenport was chocked with lyrical quotes. *'All I want,' sobbed the little girl's father, 'is ten minutes with the guy who did this. Ten minutes and a clawhammer.' A neighbor drove Callie's mother to the morgue to identify her daughter. 'I wanted to lie down* beside her,' Mrs. Davenport said. 'I wanted to put my arms around my baby and wake her up . . .' "

Keyes said, "That's enough."

"Don't be so modest," Wiley chided. "It's the only thing you ever wrote that made me jealous."

"I made it all up," Keyes said, taking Kara Lynn's hand. He was hoping she'd squeeze back, and she did.

Wiley looked perturbed, as if Brian had spoiled the big punch line.

"I drove out to the house," Keyes said in a monotone. "I was expecting a crowd. Neighbors, relatives, you know. But there was only one car in the driveway, they were all alone . . . I knocked on the door. Mrs. Davenport answered and I could see in her eyes she'd been through hell. Behind her, I saw how they'd put all of Callie's pictures out in the living room—on the piano, the sofas, the TV console, everywhere . . . you never saw so many baby pictures. Mr. Davenport sat on the floor with an old photo album across his lap . . . he was crying his heart out . . .

"In a nice voice Mrs. Davenport asked me what I wanted. At first I couldn't say a damn thing and then I told her I was an insurance adjustor and I was looking for the Smiths' house and I must have got the wrong address. Then I drove back to my apartment and made up the whole story, all those swell quotes. That's what the *Sun* printed."

"The ultimate impiety," Wiley intoned, "the rape of truth."

"He's right," Keyes said. "But I just couldn't bring myself to do it, to go in that house and intrude on those people's grief. So I invented the whole damn story."

"I think it took guts to walk away," Kara Lynn said.

"Oh please." Wiley grimaced. "It was an act of profound cowardice. No self-respecting journalist turns his back on pain and suffering. It was an egregious and shameful thing, Pollyanna, your boyfriend's no hero."

Kara Lynn stared at Wiley and said, "You're pathetic." She said it in such a mordant and disdainful way that Wiley flinched. Obviously he'd misjudged her, and Keyes too. He had saved the Callie Davenport story all these years, anticipating the moment he might need it. Yet it had not produced the desired effect, not at all. He felt a little confused.

Keyes said to Kara Lynn, "I had to quit the paper. I'd stepped over the line and there was no going back."

"At least I hawk the truth," Wiley cut in. "That's what this campaign is all about—dramatizing the true consequence of folly." He struggled wobbly to his feet. He gained balance by clutching a sea-grape limb and shifting all weight to his left side. The other leg hung like a dead and blackening trunk.

"Brian, I don't know if you'll ever understand, but try. All that wretched grief the Davenports spent on their little girl is exactly what I feel when I think what's happened to this place. It's the same sense of loss, the same fury and primal lust for vengeance. The difference is, I can't turn my back the way you did. My particular villain is not some tattooed sex pervert, but an entire generation of blow-dried rapists with phones in their Volvos and five-million-dollar lines of credit and secretaries who give head. These are the kind of deviants who dreamed up the Osprey Club, idiots who couldn't tell an osprey from a fucking parakeet."

Kara Lynn was amazed at Wiley's indefatigable fervor. Brian Keyes was not stirred; he'd heard it all before. Overhead the skies were clearing as the last of the rain clouds scudded west. On the horizon shone a tinge of magenta, the first promise of dawn. Time was running out and there was one last chore.

"Skip—"

"Brian, Kara Lynn, can you imagine the Asshole Quotient on this island one year from now? You'll need the goddamn Census Bureau just to count up all the gold chains—"

Keyes slipped the Browning into his belt. "Where's the boat, Skip?"

"I changed my mind," he said peevishly. "You'll have to find it yourself. If you don't, we all go boom together. That's a much better story, don't you think? *Condo Island Blast Claims Three.*"

"Try four," Keyes said.

Wiley fingered his beard. His needle-sharp eyes went from Keyes to Kara Lynn and back. "What are you talking about?"

"She's here, Skip."

"Jenna?"

Keyes pointed to the hardwoods.

"Jenna's on the island?"

"I thought we'd play some bridge," said Keyes.

"Why'd you bring her!" Wiley demanded angrily.

"So we'd be even."

Wiley said, "Brian, I had no idea you were such a mean-spirited sonofabitch." He looked profoundly disappointed.

"Wait here," Keyes said. Quickly he went into the woods.

"Did you know about this?" Wiley asked Kara Lynn.

"What're you so upset about?" she said. "It'll make a better story, right?"

Mulling options, Wiley nibbled his lower lip.

Keyes returned, leading Jenna by the hand. At the sight of her, Wiley's face drained.

"Oh boy," he said in a shrunken voice.

"I'm sorry, Skip," Jenna said. She acted embarrassed, mortified, like a teenager who'd just wrecked her father's brand-new car.

"She's a little shy," Keyes explained. "She didn't want you to know she was here."

"I ruined everything," Jenna said. She gasped when she saw Wiley's mangled knee but made no move to dress the wound. Florence Nightingale Jenna was not.

Wiley looked at his watch. It said 6:07. Dawn came at 6:27 sharp.

"Skip's through talking," Keyes said to Jenna. "He's said everything he could possibly say. Now all four of us are going to get aboard the boat and get the hell off this island before it blows up."

Wiley kneaded the calf of his right leg. "I can't believe you actually shot me," he said.

"I thought it might shut you up."

"Just what the hell were you aiming for?"

"What's the difference?" Keyes said.

Kara Lynn had climbed the old homestead plot. The elevation was scarcely ten feet, but it was high enough to afford a view of the surrounding waters, now calm. A distant wisp of brown diesel smoke attracted her attention.

"I think I see the barge," she said.

Keyes said, "What's it going to be, Skip?"

Wiley gazed at Jenna; Keyes figured it was about

time for a big sloppy hug. They both looked ten years older than before, yet still not quite like a couple.

"There's a mooring at the north end, on the lee side, opposite the way you came," Wiley said tiredly. "That's where the Mako's anchored up. You'd best get going."

"We're *all* going," Keyes said.

"Not me," Wiley said. "You can't make me, podner." He was right. The gun didn't count for anything now.

"Hey, there's an eagle," Jenna said.

The bird was airborne, elegantly soaring toward the pines. It carried a silvery fish in its talons.

"Just look at that," Wiley marveled, his eyes brightening beneath the Seminole bandanna. He took off his baseball cap in salute.

"It's a gorgeous bird," Kara Lynn agreed, tugging on Brian's arm. Time to go, she was saying, step on it.

"Skip, come with us," Keyes urged.

"Or what? You gonna shoot me again?"

"Of course not."

Wiley said, "Forget about me, pal. I'm beginning to like it here." He held out his arms and Jenna went to him. Wiley kissed her on the forehead. He touched her hair and said, "I don't suppose you want to keep a one-legged lunatic company?"

Jenna's eyes, as usual, gave the answer. Keyes saw it and looked away. He'd seen it before.

"Aw, I don't blame you," Wiley said to her, "the bugs out here are just awful." He patted her on the butt and let go.

To Keyes he whispered, "Help her pick out a new coffee table, okay?"

"Skip, please—"

"No! Go now, and hurry. These radio-controlled devices are extremely precise."

Keyes led the two women across the clearing. Jenna trudged ahead woodenly, but Keyes and Kara Lynn paused at the crest of the homesteader's hill. They looked back and saw Wiley in the clearing, leaning against the rusty flagpole. His arms were folded, and on his face was a broad and euphoric and incomprehensible grin.

"Hey, Brian," he shouted, "I didn't finish my story."

Keyes almost laughed. "Not now, you asshole!" The guy was unbelievable.

"But I never told you—they called."

"Who?"

"The Davenports. They phoned the day your piece ran, but you were already gone."

Keyes groaned—the bastard always wanted the last word.

Anxiously he shouted back, "What did they want?"

"They wanted to say thanks," Wiley hollered. "I couldn't believe it! They actually wanted to say thanks for butting out."

Keyes waved one last time at his old friend.

Lost forever, his odyssey now measured in minutes, Skip Wiley swung a ropy brown arm in reply. He was still waving his cap when Brian Keyes, Jenna, and Kara Lynn Shivers disappeared into the buttonwood.

They found the trail and, ten minutes later, the mooring where the outboard was anchored. The tide was up so they had to wade, skating their feet across the mud and turtle grass. Jenna lost her footing and slipped down, without a word, into the shallows. Keyes grabbed her under one arm, Kara Lynn got the other. Together they hoisted her into the boat.

The engine was stone cold.

With trembling fingers Keyes turned the key again and again. The motor whined and coughed but wouldn't start.

"You flooded it," Kara Lynn said. "Let it sit for thirty seconds."

Keyes looked at her curiously but did what he was told. The next time he turned the key, the Evinrude roared to life.

"Dad's got a ski boat," Kara Lynn explained. "Happens all the time."

Keyes jammed down the throttle and the Mako chewed its way off the flat, churning marl and grass, planing slowly. Finally it found deeper water, flattened out and gained speed. Already the rim of purple winter sky was turning yellow gold.

"How much time?" Jenna asked numbly.

"Three, four minutes," Keyes guessed.

They had to circle Osprey Island to reach the marked channel that would take them to safety.

"Brian!" Jenna blurted, pointing.

Keyes jerked back on the stick until the engine quit. The boat coasted in glassy silence, a quarter-mile off the islet. They all stared toward the stand of high pines.

"Oh no," Kara Lynn said.

Keyes was incredulous.

Jenna said, "Boy, he never gives up."

Skip Wiley was in the trees.

He was dragging himself up the tallest pine, branch by branch, the painstaking, web-crawling gait of a spider. How with a smashed leg Wiley had climbed so high was astonishing. It was not a feat of gymnastics so much as a show of reckless nerve. He hung in the tree like a broken scarecrow; ragged, elongated, his limbs bent at odd angles. From a distance his skull shone three-toned—the russet beard; the jutting tanned face; the alabaster pate. In one hand was Tommy Tigertail's red bandanna—Wiley was waving it back and forth and shrieking at the top of his considerable lungs; plangent gibberish.

"Brian, he wants us to come get him!"

"No," Keyes said, "that's not it."

It was sadder than that.

The object of Wiley's expedition was perched at the top of the forty-foot pine. With its keen and faultless eyes it peered down at this demented, blood-crusted creature and wondered what in the world to do. As Skip Wiley advanced, he brayed, flailed his bright kerchief, shattered branches—but the great predator merely blinked and clung to its precious fish.

"He's trying to save the eagle," Brian Keyes said. "He's trying to make the eagle fly."

"God, he is," said Kara Lynn.

"Fly," Jenna murmured excitedly. "Fly away, bird!"

"Oh please," Kara Lynn said.

That is how they left him—Skip Wiley ascending, insectine, possessed of an unknowable will and strength; the eagle studying him warily, shuddering its brown-gold wings, weighing a decision.

Brian Keyes turned the ignition and the boat shot forward in a widening arc. The Mako was very fast, and Osprey Island receded quickly in the slick curling seam of the speedboat's wake. Within minutes they were far away, safe, but none of them dared to look back.

Off the bow, at the horizon, the sun seeped into a violet sky.

Somewhere out on Biscayne Bay, a flat red barge emitted three long whoops of warning, the most dolorous sound that Brian Keyes had ever heard. He clung to the wheel and waited.

"Fly!" he whispered. "Please fly away."

CARL HIAASEN

Double Whammy

£6.99

'Sharp humour, energetic action, and a supporting cast of
well-drawn weirdos make this one of the most
imaginative, zippy and fun to read capers in years'
The Times

Dennis Gault, tycoon and fishing fanatic, was only the first
of private eye R. J. Decker's problems. Hired by Gault
to investigate cheating on the Florida bass-fishing circuit,
Decker found himself surrounded by murder, obsession and
plethora of characters from beyond the fringe, to whom
catching bass was more fun than sex. Pretty soon, Decker's
own neck is on the line as he discovers that fishing in
Florida doesn't involve killing just bass . . .

'I went for *Double Whammy* hook, line and sinker, and
I think you will too'
Washington Post

'An outrageously entertaining high-protein experience'
Christopher Wordsworth, *Observer*

CARL HIAASEN

Skin Tight

£6.99

'A wonderful indictment of the American obsession with beauty and success . . . probably the funniest book of its kind that you will come across all year'
Financial Times

Somebody wants Mick Stranahan dead. He knows because he's just had to spear an intruder with a stuffed marlin's head. And that wasn't the first time. There was the plastic surgeon with extremely shaky hands . . . the personal-injury lawyer with the beaming billboard face . . . the vanity-crazed star of TV's *In Your Face* . . . and the high-stepping hitman with the moonscape skin. Not to mention the barracuda.

The whole thing is downright harrowing. It's Hiaasen at his best. And life without him would be a pale imitation.

'The action flames, the wit's tinder-dry. For snappy prose alone, not to say neat plot, it's a classic thriller'
Mail on Sunday

'Hiaasen brings classic farce to the modern thriller. There is little humour darker than his, and little funnier'
Evening Standard